QUEEN OF REALMS

BOOK THREE OF THE FIRST WITCH SERIES

EMBER EAST

QUEEN OF REALMS

BOOK THREE IN THE FIRST WITCH SERIES

EMBER EAST

EXCERPT

My eyes locked onto my own reflection and to my horror, I watched as my mirror self smiled wickedly, a vicious sneer contorting my features. "Look into the dark, little Queen," she whispered, her voice a sinister murmur. "Look into the twisted chaos of your heart."

My reflection continued to change, becoming increasingly terrifying as the shadows within me swelled. My eyes blazed with an inner fire, the inky black of my palms beginning to creep up my arms. Flames danced along my skin, enveloping me until I was nothing but a living spark.

"Let it in," the woman purred seductively. "Let the darkness embrace you. It's what you truly are."

I couldn't tear my gaze away from the mirror, unable to break free as the flames soared higher and the void yawned wider, threatening to engulf everything in its path.

But I would not be consumed. The fire answered to me.

The flames continued to dance around me, responding to my will. The shadows, once a source of fear, now swirled around me like a protective shroud, empowering me rather than devouring me. I was not a victim of the darkness; I was its master, a queen of realms and shadows.

Cover Design by Muhammad Kaleem

Visit the author's website at www.embereastbooks.com

ISBN: 979-8-9892775-6-8 (paperback)

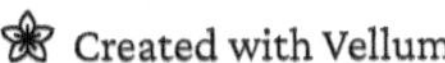 Created with Vellum

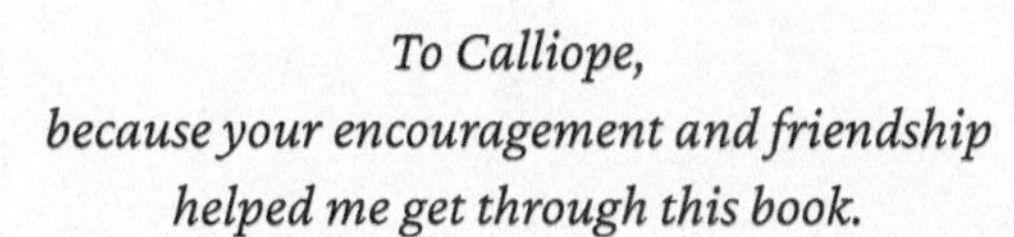

To Calliope,
because your encouragement and friendship
helped me get through this book.

And to my readers,
without you, I'm just screaming
into the void. Thank you for
reading my words.

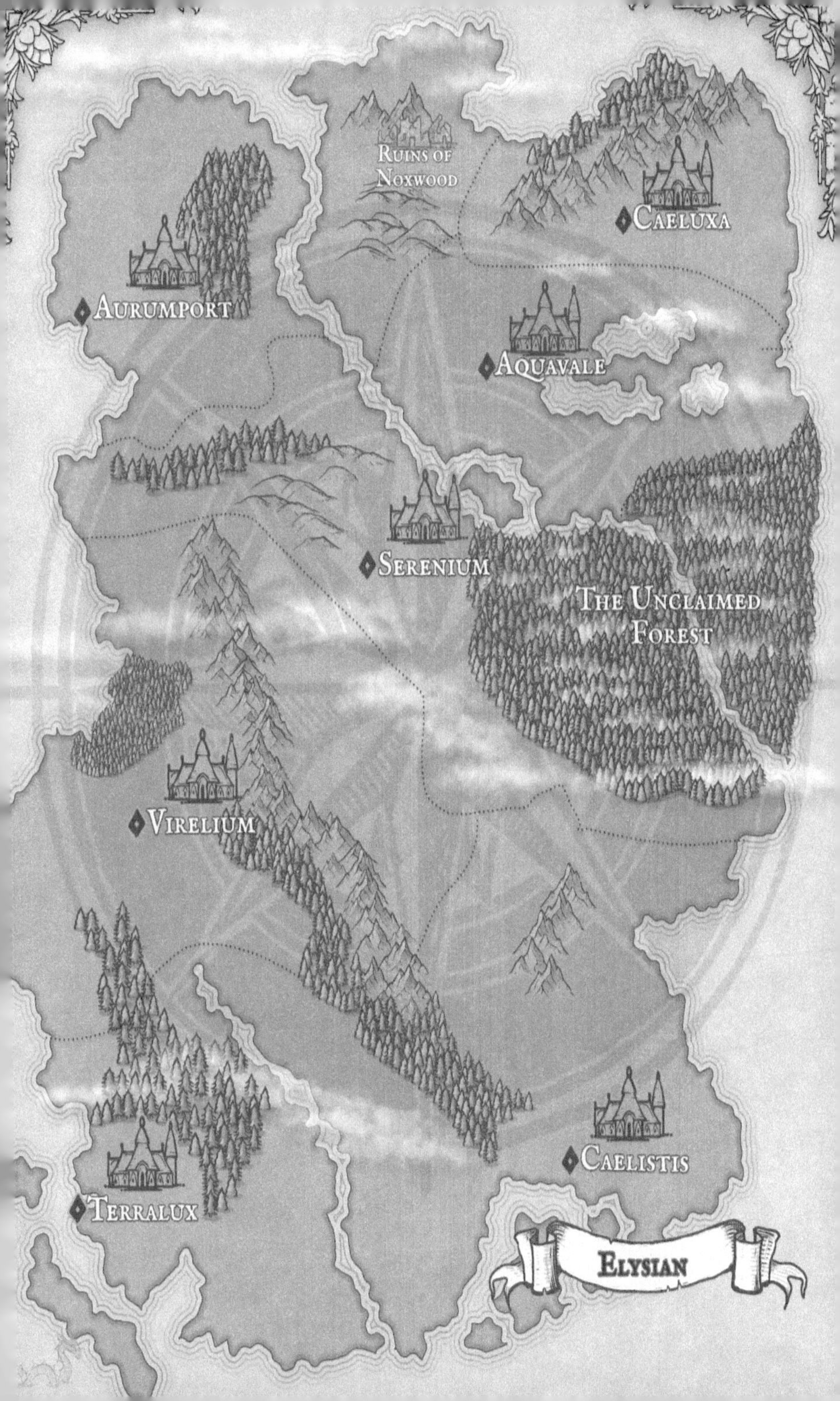

RUINS OF NOXWOOD
CAELUXA
AURUMPORT
AQUAVALE
SERENIUM
THE UNCLAIMED FOREST
VIRELIUM
CAELISTIS
TERRALUX
ELYSIAN

TRIGGER WARNINGS

Alcohol
  Anxiety
  Assault
  Blood
  Bones
  Child harm
  Death
  Demons
  Fire
  Gore
  Murder
  Occult
  Poisoning
  PTSD
  Sexual assault
  Sexually explicit scenes
  Torture
  War

PLAYLIST

Gasoline by Halsey *Chapter One*

Bitter and Sick by One Two *Chapter Nine*

As The World Caves In by Sarah Cothran *Chapter Fifty*

Control by Halsey *Chapter Fifty-One*

Darkness Falls by Unsecret x Cece and the Dark Hearts *End of Book*

Goddess by Xana

Castle by Halsey

Hold Me Down by Halsey

Worship by Amber Run

I Found by Amber Run

Wicked Game by Ursine Vulpine

Deeper (Female) by SATV Music

You Should See Me In A Crown by Billie Eilish

Gods and Monsters by Lana Del Rey

Play With Fire by Sam Tinnesz

Ashes by Stellar

Cravin' by Kendyle Paige and Stileto

PART
ONE

ONE

I was immobilized, bound to a metal table so frigid it felt like the ninth ring of hell. The cold sank deep into my bones, a chill that seemed to want to freeze me from the inside out. Metal restraints gnawed into my wrists and ankles, cutting into my skin, drawing thin lines of blood that trickled in small rivulets down my limbs. I felt like an offering on an altar of cruelty, my body the unwilling sacrifice.

The room felt like it was shrinking, its walls moving inward in a suffocating creep. A vile odor—thick and cloying—emanated from the very fabric of the room, making the air heavy with the stench of decay and mildew. It was as if the walls were sweating out the cumulative evil that had saturated them over the years. The smell invaded my nose, filled my lungs, and seeped into my pores.

Above me loomed Malachar, casting an intimidating shadow over my prone body. He was like an eclipse, his presence blotting out what scant light flickered from the guttering torches. His eyes, however, were darker still—bottomless voids that seemed to leach light from the air around them, empty of compassion, empathy, or humanity. Those eyes were portals to nothingness, eyes that threatened to consume all glimmers of light and hope, emanating endless despair.

He leaned down toward me, invading the scant inches of personal space that remained mine. His fingers, cold and intrusive, began to graze my skin in a macabre caress. Each touch made my flesh crawl and my soul cower. The very air between us seemed to curdle at his nearness. My muscles tightened involuntarily, every sinew in my body craving to contract, to recoil from his vile touch, but the restraints made it impossible. I was a captive audience to my own defilement, my insides churning with a loathing so intense it bordered on physical sickness.

"I've been waiting for this," he said, his voice a poisonous syrup that coated my ears and dripped into the pit of my stomach, making fear curl and twist around my insides like a living thing. With a deliberation that was a torment of its own, his hand moved to his belt. It returned holding a knife so malicious in design that it looked like a twisted artist's rendition of pain incarnate. Its blade gleamed with an unholy light, reflecting the dim illumination in the room in such a way that each facet seemed to promise a unique form of agony.

As the knife met my flesh, every fiber in my body screamed. Malachar began his sadistic artwork, carving patterns into my skin with the same care a master sculptor would chisel into marble, except each stroke of his blade was a hot ribbon of torment, branding me as though declaring ownership of my soul. The pain was a white-hot fire, but it was also something darker—each cut was a channel through which his twisted darkness flowed, flooding into me, an unholy union of his essence with mine. My soul darkened with each fresh cut.

I tried to scream, to release even a fraction of the horror that was filling me, overloading my senses. But the sound that emerged was a strangled sob, a meager, pitiful thing that seemed only to heighten his delight. He threw his head back and laughed, a sound devoid of any warmth, a laugh that was a desolate echo in a chamber already so full of nightmares.

Caught in this tableau of depravity, I realized how totally helpless I had become. I was imprisoned not just by metal shackles but by a web of terror from which there seemed no escape. Even as my physical boundaries were being violated, I felt the deeper invasion, as if the very core of my soul was under siege, threatened to be defiled and conquered by an evil I could neither understand nor combat.

My eyes snapped open as if I was forcibly yanked from the shroud of nightmares by some primal instinct to survive. A scream tore its way out of my throat, echoing in the confined space of my bedroom. For a disorienting second, the dream world and reality blurred, their borders melding in a haze of confusion. But when my eyes adjusted to the dim light filtering through the curtains, I was no longer in that chamber of horrors but back in my own bedroom in the mortal realm.

But my heart wasn't so easily pacified. It pounded wildly against the walls of my chest as if trying to physically escape the residual fear coursing through my veins. Adrenaline flooded my system, stretching seconds into elongated moments where every detail seemed both hyper-real and surreal. The textures of the bedsheets beneath me,

the muffled sounds of the night outside, even the air itself
—all felt strangely distorted.

Kaelan had jolted awake beside me. "Vale, what
happened? Are you alright?" His voice carried a note of
frantic concern and his eyes scoured my face as if he could
somehow read the story of my nightmare in my expression.

Trying to respond, I found my vocal cords had betrayed
me. Instead, I drew in a ragged breath, the air rushing into
my lungs as if filling an empty vessel. A tremor took hold of
my body, so violent it felt like I was coming apart at the
seams. My skin was slick with a cold sweat—as if my body
couldn't decide whether it was burning up with fever or
freezing with dread.

I lunged for the bathroom and my legs wobbled
beneath me, threatening to buckle with every step. As I
reached the sink, my stomach spasmed in revolt, ejecting
its contents in a visceral purge that left me doubled over,
gasping for breath.

Kaelan arrived a moment later, stepping into the bathroom as I pulled away from the sink. His strong hands
found my trembling back, tracing slow circles in a calming
rhythm. My hair clung wetly to my forehead. With shaking
hands, I gathered the long silver strands and pulled them
back from my face, tying them back. It was a futile gesture
of control but one I needed desperately.

"Was it Malachar or Haldir this time?" Kaelan's voice
was soft, barely above a whisper, but it rippled with barely
suppressed rage.

"Malachar," I managed to stammer, the word barely
more than a hoarse breath yet laden with an avalanche of
meaning.

"That monster got off too easy when he died," Kaelan

seethed, his grip on my back tightening momentarily as if imagining his hands around Malachar's throat.

Our eyes meet in the bathroom mirror, locked in a silent communion of shared nightmares and unspoken fears. "I wish I could kill him again," I confessed in a whisper, my voice laden with bitterness and regret.

He pulled me into an embrace that felt like a fortress against the dark. "It's over," he murmured into my ear, his breath warm against my cold skin. "He's gone, Vale, and he can't hurt you anymore."

His words were a balm, but they didn't entirely erase the gnawing sense of foreboding that had taken root in the deepest corners of my soul. Malachar may have been a nightmare of the past, but Haldir was a looming shadow on the horizon, an embodiment of fears yet to materialize. And I knew, with chilling certainty, that when he struck, the cost would not be mine to bear alone.

"It's not over," I whispered, my words a blend of prophecy and dread as I leaned further into Kaelan's arms. "It's only just beginning."

"We'll face it together," Kaelan vowed, pulling back just enough to cup my face in his hands. His voice was tinged with a conviction I longed to share but couldn't fully embrace.

For now, though, in this quiet moment in the aftermath of terror, it was enough. And so, we stood there, clinging to each other as if we could somehow banish the memories and the nightmares by the sheer force of our will.

But deep down, we both knew the past wasn't so easily forgotten. And neither were our enemies.

The first light of dawn punctured the darkness, its rays seeping through the gaps in the forest canopy like golden fingers of hope caressing a war-torn land. I stood among the wolves at the heart of their camp. My heart was a collision of emotions—worry, defiance, and an unyielding determination that clawed at my insides.

For the past two nights in a row, we'd been locked in a violent dance with the Academy, a relentless force hell-bent on capturing both me and Wren. They sought to criminalize the entire pack, to slap the label of 'outlaw' upon us as though it were some kind of indelible stain. But these wolves were no mere beasts to be tamed. Each growl, each calculated swipe of their claws, had been an exercise in disciplined aggression—aimed to wound but not kill. The Academy had egregiously underestimated their tenacity, assuming that sheer brute force could break the will of Wren's devoted followers.

As I watched the last vestiges of the Academy's forces retreat, their figures dissolving into the shadows of the surrounding forest, a decision solidified within me. This relentless game of cat and mouse couldn't continue indefinitely. The wolves were reaching their limits, and their spirits were wearing thin. The Academy's unyielding pursuit had to be countered. The wolves needed sanctuary —a haven safe from the Academy's influence. An idea had been festering in the corners of my mind and the events of the last two nights had only fortified my resolve.

My thoughts were interrupted as Kaelan approached. We had been separated in the battle, and a surge of relief washed over me at the sight of him unscathed. His eyes scanned mine, vigilant for any trace of harm, and I mustered a faint smile, nodding my head.

I cast my gaze over the throng of Otherworlders clustered around us. Their faces bore the toll of physical and emotional fatigue, a collection of visible scars and invisible burdens. Yet, here we stood, staunchly holding the line. We would do it again. We had no other choice.

Living on this razor's edge was a continuous stress, akin to treading water in a stormy sea, where every desperate gasp for air was met with another overwhelming wave. Yet, drowning was not an option. There were too many lives depending on our resilience, on our ability to keep fighting against the odds.

And so, we would. We would keep fighting, not just because it's our duty, but because deep within the battered chambers of our hearts, a fragile flicker of hope still burned. It was a small, vulnerable flame, constantly at risk of being snuffed out by the harsh winds of reality. But it was there, and we would guard it jealously. We nurtured it with each tiny victory, each life saved, each battle won, however costly.

As the initial rush of adrenaline gradually retreated, exhaustion descended on me. Kaelan draped an arm gently around my shoulders, pulling me close. I leaned into his embrace, savoring this sanctuary within the chaos swirling around us.

"You need to rest," he whispered, his voice laced with a concern that tugged at my heart. "You haven't been sleeping well lately."

I nodded in agreement, though the thought of sleep was a far-off dream, a luxury that seemed impossible right then. Rest was a fortress that seemed increasingly harder to breach, its walls fortified by the looming uncertainties of our relentless struggle.

"I'm just glad you're safe," I told him, my arms encircling him as if I could shield him from the rest of the world.

Though our nightly skirmishes with the Academy had been draining, they hadn't yet morphed into the existential threat I had initially feared. But I couldn't deny that this was unsustainable. Their strategy became more apparent with each encounter—exhaust us, bleed us dry of resources, and then pounce when our defenses were at their weakest. It felt like we were tightrope walkers on a fraying line, each step potentially disastrous.

Turning my gaze back toward Kaelan, I felt a subtle shift in the atmosphere as I murmured, "I need to find Wren."

"Of course, my Queen," Kaelan replied. His tone was playful, a gentle jab aimed to lighten the atmosphere. I reacted with an exaggerated roll of my eyes and a teasing shove, pushing him away lightly.

The title 'Queen' reverberated through my mind, each echo leaving behind a sliver of unease. To call it a heavy mantle would be an understatement; it was more like an ever-growing mountain of responsibilities, teetering on the brink of collapse. These past several months had been a whirlwind of challenges and unforeseen obstacles, a ceaseless tempest that had offered little in the way of respite or stability. Nevertheless, this crown—metaphorical or otherwise—was a weight I had chosen to bear, a solemn duty I was willing to shoulder for the sake of those who regarded me as their last bastion of hope and security.

As we navigated the camp's pathways, Nyxen rushed up to meet us, his form a blur of midnight shades. Throughout the recent battles, his contributions had been invaluable; he'd served as a shadowy lure, drawing the Academy forces away from our werewolf allies and deftly dodging their lethal blades. I bent to pass my hand through his intangible, mist-like form.

"Good job, Nyx," I said to him. Elated, the shadowy fox emitted a chirp of joy, a sound that broke through the heaviness of the atmosphere. He then scampered off toward the group of children hesitantly stepping out from the packhouse. As I watched Nyxen's playful antics bring tentative smiles to their young, traumatized faces, a knot of emotion tightened in my chest.

Our search for Wren proved swift, as he had already shifted back into his human form. Despite a few visible scrapes and bruises, he appeared relatively unscathed. A surge of relief washed over me as I rushed forward to embrace him tightly. "Thank the Gods you're okay," I murmured, my voice laced with gratitude. I pulled back slightly and looked up at his towering form, "We can't keep going like this every night."

Our discussion was momentarily interrupted by the

approach of Venna, Wren's beta, her concerned gaze locked onto him. Wren took a moment to assure her of his well-being before addressing us all. "Follow me," he said, his tone carrying a sense of urgency, "It's time we discuss our options."

We followed him, eager to hear his plans for ensuring the safety of the pack and putting an end to the ongoing threat from the Academy. Wren's new quarters were solemn as we gathered around a substantial oak table in the center of the room. The dim light filtering in through the room's windows cast long shadows across the polished surface.

With a determined tone, I voiced what had lingered in the air for far too long. "Wren, it's time. We can't keep enduring these attacks. The only viable solution is to consider my proposition seriously — to move the pack permanently to Terralux in the Fae realm. The Academy won't be able to reach us there, and we can finally have peace."

Wren hesitated, his gaze faltering for a moment before he lowered his head in reluctant agreement. It was a difficult choice for him, one that weighed heavily on his shoulders.

Venna, ever loyal and fiercely protective of our current home, couldn't hold back her concerns. "Are we really going to abandon everything we've built here? Our home, our territory?"

Wren met her gaze, his expression pained but resolute. "Venna, this is a decision I never wanted to make, but we can't keep fighting off the Academy like this. They're relentless, and they won't stop until we're weakened and vulnerable. Our only path to lasting peace is to remove ourselves from their reach completely. The Fae realm offers us that sanctuary."

I offered a sympathetic nod to Wren. "You're making the right choice for the pack, Wren, even if it means leaving behind the place they've called home for so long."

Kaelan, always the strategist, interjected with a sense of urgency. "We need to start planning immediately, Wren. If the Academy attacks again tomorrow night, we must be ready."

Wren's brow furrowed with concern as he considered the logistics of such a move. "Moving everyone in a single day is going to be next to impossible."

Venna chimed in, echoing his apprehension. "It's a massive undertaking, Wren. Are we sure we can pull it off?"

I shared a meaningful look with Kaelan, who had an idea forming. "Perhaps," he began, "a smaller group of us could stay behind and buy time for the others to make the move. They could hold off the Academy for as long as possible."

Kaelan's proposal seemed to spark a glimmer of hope in Wren's eyes. "That might work," he conceded, his voice tinged with a hint of relief. "If we can ensure the safety of most of our pack, it's a risk we should consider."

"I'll go inform the squad leaders and start getting the families ready to move. We need to begin preparing immediately," Venna said, finally relenting.

I turned my attention to the vital task of contacting Aerion in Terralux. I called Nyxen and he emerged from a shadowed corner of the room, looking up at me expectantly with bright yellow eyes. "Nyxen, go find Aerion and tell him that the werewolves are coming and to prepare rooms and accommodations. Tell him they are coming tonight."

Over the past few months, our bond had deepened and

the shadowkin had learned how to communicate, entering my mind as needed, and now he could do so with others as well. It made for a particularly convenient message system.

With an affectionate brush of his consciousness against mine, Nyxen melted into the shadows, disappearing as a dark blur of movement. Wren sighed heavily. "We have our work cut out for us, Vale."

The room seemed to constrict around us, filled with an air of weariness and the weight of unspoken fears. Wren's eyes were clouded with the immensity of the responsibilities that weighed him down like stones in deep water. I could sense his struggle, the herculean effort it was taking for him to keep his pack safe.

My heart ached for him, and on impulse, I reached out, laying my hand delicately on the solid muscle of his arm. "Take it one step at a time," I said softly, my eyes searching his for a sign that my words were getting through. "Delegate responsibilities; organize your leaders into shifts to oversee the move. And don't forget to be as discrete as possible. The less the Academy knows, the better."

He nodded, though his eyes still had that far-off glint, a tell-tale sign that his mind was racing ahead, already sorting through the intricacies of the tasks that loomed before him.

"I'll coordinate with Venna," Kaelan announced, "We have a monumental task ahead of us, shifting all those individuals to Terralux." He offered me a fleeting smile before exiting the room, his steps carrying him into the world outside, a world teeming with uncertainty.

It was Wren who broke the ensuing silence. "How are you holding up, Vale?" His words were tinged with concern, his eyes scanning my face, searching for clues to my inner turmoil.

Part of me wanted to downplay my feelings, to cast aside my fears and anxieties, so he could focus entirely on the monumental tasks ahead. But as my gaze met his, the layers of our years of friendship unfurled before me. I couldn't bring myself to lie to him.

"Honestly, I'm grappling with demons," I began, my voice no louder than a fragile whisper. "Whenever I close my eyes, whenever I try to find a sliver of peace, the faces of Malachar, Haldir, and even Zephyrian haunt me. Voices whisper in my head, convincing me I'll never escape them. I'm struggling, Wren, and I don't know how to put myself back together."

Wren's eyes darkened momentarily. With deliberate movements, he closed the distance between us and enveloped me in a warm embrace, becoming a sanctuary as I let silent tears flow. His friendship was a constant in a world that had grown increasingly chaotic, and for that, I would forever be grateful.

"You can't go through this alone, Vale," Wren implored softly, his voice filled with a heart-wrenching mix of concern and love. "We all see you in pain, even if you try to mask it. You need time to rest, to heal."

His words struck a chord, and though it pained me, I knew he was speaking the truth. "How can I, Wren? Ever since this all began, it's been one thing after another. Now, I have a kingdom to oversee. How can I do that when I'm falling apart at the seams?"

His hands framed my face as he pulled back slightly, ensuring our eyes locked. "Vale, you are the strongest, most resilient person I have ever known. Your determination and dedication to the safety and protection of others is inspiring. I know you will find the strength to overcome this, and I'll be there to support you every step of the way."

My eyes met his, seeing the unflinching sincerity there. I nodded, allowing a faint semblance of a smile to tug at the corners of my mouth. "Thank you," I murmured, finally allowing myself the luxury of believing that maybe, just maybe, everything would eventually be alright.

THREE

As Kaelan and I materialized in my bedroom, the rays of the early morning sun filtered through the curtains, casting a warm, gentle glow on the room. Yet, despite the tranquil scene, a sense of unease gnawed at me. I could feel it deep within, instinctually tugging at the back of my mind.

"Be careful, daughter. Something is amiss," murmured Rowena, the First Witch, her voice echoing in my thoughts. Her words sent a chill curling low in my stomach and I knew not to dismiss her warning lightly.

Turning to Kaelan, I furrowed my brow. "Kaelan, something's wrong," I said, my voice barely above a whisper, not wanting to alert anyone who might be lurking.

He nodded, his keen eyes scanning the room for any signs of intrusion or danger. He moved around the room silently, checking all the corners. Then, he moved through the rest of the apartment. After a thorough inspection, he shook his head. "I don't see anything out of place."

The tugging sensation within my mind persisted, growing more insistent. The same instinctual pull had guided me through countless precarious situations—a form of precognition that I had learned to trust implicitly. "It's my witch's intuition," I explained to Kaelan. "It's like a sixth sense and it's never wrong."

Kaelan took my concerns seriously, his expression reflecting the gravity of the situation. "What should we do?"

Contemplating our options, I hesitated for a moment before deciding, "Let's check the library. It's possible that whatever is wrong began there."

Kaelan agreed and we turned toward the library door, which was anchored in my bedroom. My hand rested on the doorknob and I took a deep breath, steeling myself for what we might find. As the door swung open, we were confronted by raised voices.

Inside the library, Harker, the female vampire who had taken up residence there, and Elara, the library's guardian ghost, were engaged in a heated argument. Elara's ethereal form practically crackled with frustration as she shouted at Harker.

"You're never careful enough with the books!" Elara exclaimed.

Harker crossed her arms defiantly, her expression one of irritation. "That's not true, Elara. You're just looking for a reason to kick me out of here." It was then that Harker noticed us standing in the doorway. She looked slightly surprised, perhaps not expecting to see us back so soon. "I thought you guys were supposed to be at the werewolf camp all night?" she remarked.

I exchanged a quick glance with Kaelan before explaining, "It's morning now." Harker's brows furrowed as she considered this. My unease continued to grow, and I decided to address the situation directly. "Is there anything wrong in the library, Harker? Anything at all?"

Harker seemed momentarily bewildered by my question. "Wrong? No, nothing's wrong here except for Elara," she replied, her tone dismissive.

Elara bristled at the comment. "That's not fair, Harker! I'm just trying to protect these books from any harm."

As I stood there, my intuition pulled at me again, stronger this time. I felt a distinct tug at the back of my mind, urging me to take action. Kaelan stepped forward, his suggestion breaking the tension I felt. "Maybe we should go check the factory's perimeter to ensure nothing's wrong out there."

I nodded in agreement. "That's a good idea."

Harker, however, wasn't about to be left out. Her tone was resolute as she declared, "I'm coming with you."

Elara let out an exasperated sigh. "Well, it's not like you two care about my library anyway."

We swiftly left the library and the grumpy ghost behind. As we left my bedroom, I locked the magical door behind us with a quick incantation. There was no telling what—or who—was setting off my intuition, but it was better to be safe than sorry. Elara would continue to guard the library in our absence. We exited the apartment and descended the factory's creaky stairs to the outside. My boots crunched against the gravel as we began to walk around the perimeter of the old button factory, each of us scanning the surroundings intently.

At first, everything seemed in order, just the usual blend of old bricks, overgrown weeds, and rusting metal. But then Harker stopped abruptly. "What's that?" she pointed at something near the ground.

We moved closer and saw what had caught her attention: a large spill of salt scattered across the ground. Confusion crossed Kaelan's face, mirroring my own thoughts. "Why would there be salt spread out here?"

Harker, who had been studying the salt, finally spoke up. "I know what this is for. Witches use salt like this to help breach wards."

"Witches?" I asked, my voice betraying the rising anxiety within me. Up until recently, I'd been the only witch—the First Witch to return after the witch genocide. The only other witches I knew were dead. One of which was Rowena whose soul had merged with mine. She had warned me that the Seven were returning. I just didn't think I had so little time before they came for me.

"This is definitely witch magic, Vale," Harker confirmed, locking eyes with me. "I see drips of candle wax, too."

"It must be a member of the Seven, then," I said, piecing it together. "There's no one else it could be." My heart pounded in my chest. "What were they after with this attempt? Testing my wards? Or were they after the library?"

Kaelan, who had been silent, finally spoke up. "Maybe it's time to think about moving more than just the werewolves to the Fae realm. The witches would have a much harder time reaching us—or the library—from there."

He had a point. My wards had been one of my strongest lines of defense, but if witches were finding ways to test them, perhaps it was time to consider stronger, more drastic measures. A wave of concern washed over me. Whoever had scattered that salt had not only breached my sense of security but had also fired a warning shot that the landscape was changing. The Seven were closing in, and I had to prepare—not just for myself but for everyone I was responsible for.

Harker nodded, her eyes narrowing as if contemplating

a hundred different scenarios. "I'm going to check the library again, just to be sure nothing is amiss."

She turned and went back inside, leaving Kaelan and me standing in the dim morning light, the factory's aged bricks casting long shadows around us. We continued our search, eyes sharp, senses keen. But aside from the eerie patch of salt, we found nothing. There were no more clues, no signs of intrusion, nothing to justify the electric sense of urgency pulsing through my veins.

Kaelan broke the silence, his voice tinged with concern. "What's going through your mind?"

I sighed deeply, my breath forming a brief cloud in the chilly air as I ran my hands through my hair in frustration. "I'm thinking that time's up. These past few weeks, I've been idling, pretending like we have the luxury of time. But the Seven—they've been out there scheming, plotting, doing gods-know-what. I've been treating them like some nebulous, distant threat, and now they're literally on my doorstep. It's just...overwhelming."

Kaelan stepped closer, placing his hands gently on my shoulders. "Just breathe, Vale. Whatever comes our way, we'll deal with it."

"But that's just it," I retorted, my voice tinged with a weary bitterness. "We can't 'deal with it.' I have to. Once again, it's all on me. I'm this one-woman army against a looming, incomprehensible threat. I'm tired, Kaelan. I'm fractured in places I didn't even know could break and there are powers within me that I still don't fully understand."

His face softened as he pulled me closer, his dark eyes full of empathy. "I know. But you're not alone, even if it feels that way." Kaelan hesitated, then changed the subject, pulling back slightly. "Do you think the Seven were after the library tonight? Or could they have been targeting something else?"

I shook my head, a grim expression settling on my face. "I wish I knew. But not knowing is like fighting shadows. I can't strategize against a faceless enemy. I wish I knew more about the Seven, about their motives or their methods. Anything."

"Didn't Elara encounter the Seven at some point?" Kaelan's words sparked a realization in me. "Maybe she could provide some more information, help us put a face to these shadows."

I blinked, surprised at myself for not having considered that angle. "You're right. I hadn't thought of that."

"We should go back and talk to her," Kaelan suggested. "Maybe she knows something that could give us an edge, something that could help us understand what we're up against."

And just like that, a sliver of hope threaded its way into the tapestry of my anxious thoughts. Sometimes, the answers we sought were closer than we thought, buried in the experiences of those who had traversed those dark roads before us.

We went back inside and upstairs to my bedroom. Pushing open the ancient wooden door, we re-entered the library. The smell of old parchment and bound leather filled the air, a comfort that was only slightly marred by the electric undercurrent of tension. Harker was there, her nose deep in an old book. She glanced up as we entered.

"Find anything more?" she asked, her eyes already darting back to the text as if it might vanish.

"Nothing more than what we'd already found," I admitted, a tinge of disappointment shadowing my voice.

"So we're still groping in the dark," Harker sighed, closing her book with a thud.

"Perhaps not entirely," I offered cautiously. "Elara might actually have some insights that could help us understand what we're up against."

"Elara? What could she possibly know?" Harker asked incredulously.

"Elara, could you come down here for a moment?" I said, calling out to the library's guardian, who was currently floating near the top of a towering bookshelf, cradling a couple of ancient tomes in her translucent arms like children. She placed them down on a table carefully and floated over to me.

"The books are quite chatty today," she said, a dreamy smile etched across her face.

I chose to ignore the remark. Solitude had played its tricks on Elara over her two centuries of isolation, but her mind was an untapped well of information, one I desperately needed to draw from now. "Elara, could you help us with something? It's rather urgent."

A wavering look of hesitation crossed her spectral features, but finally, she spoke, her voice tinged with curiosity. "What do you need?"

Gathering a lungful of air, I laid it all out. "We need to know more about the Seven. There are signs that they—or someone influenced by them—are attempting to infiltrate this place. Your past encounters with them could give us vital clues to understanding their motivations and plans."

She drew back slightly, her form flickering like a candle in the wind. "I don't like to dwell on the past."

"Elara, please," I pleaded, the urgency in my voice impossible to mask. "The future of this library—and possibly much more—could hinge on what you know."

She hesitated, but ultimately, her concern for the library won out, her voice dropping to a near whisper as if the very walls could hear her. "The Seven were a selfish and guarded lot. I was mostly their errand girl, fetching trinkets and cleaning up after their messes. They rarely acknowledged my existence, except when they needed something."

"And what of their intentions? Did they ever discuss the purpose of the library?" I pressed.

Elara glanced around nervously, her gaze finally resting on me. "They spoke of you, Vale, as the First Witch—the one who would bring the witches back. But their actions were inconsistent with their words. They often talked about the future as if they, themselves, would be a part of it."

"What do you mean?" I pressed.

"They didn't realize I could hear them—that's the thing with servants, you see, often overlooked and ignored. They spoke of books sometimes, tomes of darker magic, which never made it to these shelves. Where they hid them, I do not know."

My heart raced. "Do you think they hid something here? Something still buried within these walls?"

Elara hesitated, her eyes darting to a shadowy corner of the room. "I've always suspected there was more to this library than what meets the eye. Members of the Seven would sometimes appear seemingly out of nowhere. One moment, they were absent, and the next, there they were—always near that corner."

My eyes followed hers, narrowing at the darkened space she indicated. "You think there's something hidden there?"

She shuddered, an eerie ripple passing through her

ghostly form. "I was blindfolded during the ritual that bound me to this library," Elara continued softly, her voice trembling as she recalled her suppressed memories. "They led me into an unfamiliar chamber somewhere within these walls. I have never been able to locate it, nor have I wanted to."

A chilling silence enveloped us as we absorbed Elara's revelation. Whatever mystery this library held, it was intricately woven into its arcane framework, perhaps tucked away in that obscure corner Elara alluded to. But if the Seven were as inscrutable as Elara suggested, then unraveling their intentions was more critical than ever. If there were secrets concealed within these walls, then they were secrets no longer just of the past but ticking time bombs waiting to shape—or shatter—our future.

"So, what we need," Kaelan said slowly, breaking the ensuing silence, "might be right here, hidden in plain sight."

"Or concealed in shadow," I added, staring at the corner as if expecting it to yield its secrets. "Either way, we're far from helpless. Thank you, Elara. You've given us a place to start, a thread to pull. And sometimes, that's all you need to unravel a mystery."

As we made our way to the shadowy corner, every step felt like descending into an abyss of endless possibilities. What would we find? Forbidden books? Hidden chambers? Or the echoes of intentions, dark and unfathomable, left behind by the Seven?

We both walked over to the shadowy corner, our eyes scanning the intricate carvings and faded wallpaper that adorned the walls. I ran my fingers over the surface, pressing and prodding, half-expecting some hidden compartment to reveal itself. Kaelan knelt, examining the wooden floorboards, but nothing seemed out of place. It was frustratingly normal—a corner like any other.

"This is a waste of time," I said, finally letting my arms drop to my sides in exasperation.

"You should really read more of the books in this library," Harker said, glancing up from her seat where she'd returned to her research.

"What's that supposed to mean?" I snapped, not appreciating her condescension at that moment.

"What I mean is, if you're looking for something hidden by magic, it would be logical to use magic to find it," Harker explained.

"Do you have something in mind?" I asked, my frustration simmering down.

Harker got up from her seat and approached one of the towering bookshelves. She scanned the titles and then carefully pulled down an aged leather-bound book.

"Be careful with that!" Elara practically shrieked, floating anxiously behind her.

Harker rolled her eyes but ignored the ghostly guardian, bringing the book back to us. "This is an old journal, mostly an old witch's ramblings. But among its myriad entries, it has a wealth of spells—many for finding things."

Flipping through the aged pages filled with ancient script and strange symbols, she paused at a particular entry. "Ah, here it is. This spell is specifically designed for locating concealed traps. With a little adjustment, it should suit our needs perfectly. However, it requires a potion to activate it."

"Then let's get to it," I said decisively. "I'll gather the supplies we need."

FOUR

The atmosphere in my tiny kitchen was thick with the scent of herbs and roots. Jars and vials cluttered the countertop, their contents half-spilled in a hurry to assemble everything we'd need for the potion.

"Let the mixture steep for ten minutes before adding the snakeskin," Harker read from the book.

I stepped back from the stove, where a small pot emitted a fragrant, steaming brew. I sighed, my shoulders slumping as I leaned against the counter.

It was a brief moment of respite, a lull in the chaos that had recently upended my life. But even in that quiet, the weight of what lay ahead pressed against me. We were not just brewing a potion; we were seeking a truth—one that could either empower us or break us completely.

Harker lowered the book, her eyes meeting mine in a contemplative gaze. "So, should I be expecting a move to the Fae realm in the near future?" Her words hung in the air, laden with an unspoken tension.

Caught off guard by the question, I took a moment to

gather my thoughts. "I'm beginning to think we'd all be safer in Terralux—including the library," I finally said, the words tasting like both an admission and a resolution on my tongue.

Harker's eyes twinkled, a hint of a smile creeping up at the corners of her mouth. "Well, if we're heading to another realm, I have requirements. My room better be spacious, and I demand an abundance of secret, shadow-laden corners."

We shared a soft chuckle, a fleeting moment of levity amid the reality of our circumstances. "I wouldn't dream of moving the library without you," I assured her.

The timer buzzed, signaling that the ten minutes had passed. Snapping on a pair of gloves, I cautiously dropped the snakeskin into the potion. It met the liquid with a loud sizzle, sending up a noxious plume of smoke that made my eyes water.

"Bleh," I said, recoiling from the sudden, foul stench that filled the room. Harker delicately sniffed the air and wrinkled her nose in shared distaste.

"What's next?" I asked, eager to move on from this less-than-pleasant experience.

Harker's eyes refocused on the book, her finger tracing the ancient script before she spoke. "You just need to say the incantation over it, and then it's done."

"Alright, seems straightforward enough," I replied, steadying myself for the final step and pulling on my magic.

"Essence of sight, lend your gaze so divine,
Reveal what is hidden, let what's lost now be mine."

· · ·

THE POTION HISSED AND BUBBLED, steam spiraling upwards like a miniature whirlwind. Then, with a final, subdued murmur, it calmed. I hastily grabbed a small glass vial and filled it with the newly transformed, if still putrid, goo.

"Okay, that should be enough. Let's go start the spell," I announced, capping the vial securely.

We returned to the library, where we found Elara floating near Kaelan, watching him closely as he leafed through a book. Kaelan's eyes flickered up as we entered and I saw a glint of relief cross his face. It seemed he found Elara's attention a bit unnerving.

"Hope we didn't miss any excitement," I said, capturing the room's attention as I held up the vial of potion.

Elara drifted closer, eyeing the vial. "Ooo, what have you got there?" she asked, her voice a silvery chime that briefly masked the undercurrent of old sorrow.

"Just a little concoction that might unveil the secrets of your elusive chamber," I told her. Her eyes, large and round like moonlit pools, shimmered with astonishment and something akin to childlike wonder before she fluttered away—probably off to cuddle more books.

Kaelan's gaze followed her, a gentle smile playing on his lips. "That ghost is unsettling sometimes," he remarked, but the slight affection in his tone was unmistakable.

I nodded in agreement. "She's been isolated here for centuries. Imagine the thirst for interaction, for connection." My words were heavy ones, a reminder of Elara's unseen loneliness.

Harker's voice cut through, pragmatic as ever. "Don't start pitying the ghost. She's content in her literary sanctuary."

Turning back to the task at hand, I collected the remaining ingredients, my movements methodical as I approached the shadow-clad corner of the library. Kneeling, I traced a large circle on the floor with a stick of chalk made from bone dust. Around this circle, I placed silver candles, their flames coming to life one by one thanks to my magic, casting a warm, golden glow that pushed back the creeping shadows.

"Why do all so many spells start with a circle of candles?" Harker mused, her voice a thread of curiosity amid the thickening tension of my ritual.

I rolled my eyes at her casual observation and settled into the circle's heart, a small silver bowl in hand. Methodically, I added in herbs, their scents mingling in the air, before pouring in our freshly brewed potion. With a snap of my fingers, the mixture ignited, a flame leaping eagerly from the bowl as if to grasp at the words escaping my lips.

"*Inveni me, inveni me, veni et inveni me,*" I intoned, the dead language feeling both foreign and familiar on my tongue.

The spell took effect instantaneously, the smoke billowing from the bowl rapidly. It twisted and twirled, a serpent in the air, winding its way toward the corner we had scrutinized so intently before. The smoke was like a divining rod for the arcane, each tendril reaching out to caress the walls, seeking out the seams of hidden enchantments.

All eyes were riveted as the smoke began to coalesce near the floor of the corner, condensing into a thicker, more purposeful shape. A rumble filled the room, low and resonant, as the ground itself seemed to respond to the spell's call. With a sound like grinding stone, a section of the floor began to shift, revealing a staircase that descended into the shadows below.

"It worked!" I couldn't hide the astonishment in my

voice. Success was never a guarantee with magic, and the ease of this discovery felt like an omen. As I stood, the candles flickered, their light casting a dancing silhouette against the walls. Magic never ceased to astonish, each spell a leap into the unknown, and this time, it had revealed a path directly into the heart of our mystery.

Turning towards the others, I found their gazes locked onto the revealed staircase, an ancient structure that whispered promises of long-kept secrets. "I'm going to investigate," I said, slightly nervous about descending the steps.

Kaelan's eyes, alight with concern, met mine. "I'm coming with you. We can't predict what's down there," he stated firmly.

Harker stepped forward, her face alight with the thrill of potential discovery. "We're all going. Missing out isn't in today's plans," she said with a spark of excitement.

One by one, we began our descent, the darkness enveloping us like an ancient shroud. In my palm, I summoned a small ball of fire, its glow casting elongated shadows on the stone steps beneath our feet. Each step echoed back at us, a haunting rhythm that accompanied the quickened beats of our hearts.

"I hate this already," grumbled Harker, her voice bouncing off the walls.

"You and me both," Kaelan muttered in agreement.

With every step downwards, the air grew colder, the breath from our lungs forming wispy clouds that floated and dissipated into the darkness. A creeping chill traced my spine, leaving its trail of goosebumps as if the very air were laced with frost.

"It's like stepping into the heart of winter," I muttered, my words shrouded in visible breath.

The oppressive darkness pressed against us from all sides, a tangible force intent on swallowing any sliver of light until the stairway finally yielded to a vast, circular chamber. Flickering magical lamps were mounted along the curved walls, throwing a haunting, dancing glow that reached across the room.

There, in the room's heart, stood an altar of obsidian, its edges and surface etched with runes that seemed to writhe in the torchlight. Upon the altar lay a grim collection of bones, a stark white against the dark stone—a macabre centerpiece that immediately knotted my stomach.

"Elara, this is the place of your death, isn't it?" My voice broke the silence, hoarse and barely above a whisper.

The spectral form of Elara materialized beside me, her ethereal face stricken. "Yes," she murmured, her voice full of pain.

A frigid realization washed over me—the library was her haven, but it was also her tomb.

While this grim realization set in, Harker was drawn like a moth to a flame to a shelf lined with ancient tomes, her fingers tracing the spines with reverence and urgency. She grabbed one and flipped through the pages rapidly, her hunger for knowledge evident in the set of her jaw. Moments later, she looked up, her eyes serious. "These are filled with dark magic, no doubt about it." The truth of The Seven unraveled further, an intricate web of deceit.

Yet, an incessant nagging at the back of my mind suggested there was more. "Keep looking," I urged the others. "There's something else here. I can feel it."

Kaelan's hands swept the walls, methodical and thorough, searching for something unseen.

Compelled by that insistent force, I approached the

altar. My hand hovered above the cold obsidian, hesitating before disturbing the undisturbed. The bone pile seemed to beckon me closer as I noticed intricate sigils and runes etched into the fragments of bone themselves.

"Kaelan, come look at these," I called out, my voice barely concealing the unease that gripped me. As Kaelan approached, the dim light from my flickering flame cast a ghostly pallor over his features. He loomed over the pile of bones, his hand outstretched, his fingertips brushing the relics of the past.

Suddenly, the stillness shattered. A shrill cry, laced with terror and anguish, sliced through the chamber. "Don't touch my bones!" Elara's voice, laced with dread, filled the room. She manifested in a whirl of ghostly energy before Kaelan, her face contorted with panic.

But her warning came too late. A sinister plume of smoke rose from the bones, coiling like a viper. Kaelan, as though yanked by an unseen thread, inhaled sharply, the smoke funneling into his mouth. His eyes, wide with shock, rolled back, the whites flashing briefly before he succumbed to the darkness that pulled him into its fold.

"Kaelan!" My voice, tinged with fear, echoed off the chamber walls as I caught his collapsing body. Gently, I lowered his limp form to the cold stone floor, his breaths shallow and erratic.

"What the hell was that?" Harker's voice trembled with confusion as she looked accusingly at Elara.

"The bones... they bore a curse, a shadow of darkness long forgotten... I remembered only as he neared them," Elara's form flickered, her spectral face etched with sorrow.

"What kind of curse, Elara?" I pressed, anxiety sharpening my voice as I cradled Kaelan's head in my lap.

Her voice was a mere whisper, "I do not know," before she vanished, retreating from her mortal remains.

"Great," Harker muttered with a heavy dose of sarcasm, "a cursed Kaelan is just what we needed."

Stirring from his unintended slumber, Kaelan's eyes fluttered open, his hand instinctively rising to his head. "What happened?" His voice was groggy, disoriented.

"You touched the cursed bones," Harker stated bluntly, her voice tinged with exasperation.

Kaelan's gaze found mine, and unexpectedly, a playful grin sprawled across his features. "Vale, you look good from this angle," he said, a mischievous glint in his eye.

"Seriously? A brush with dark magic, and he comes out flirting?" Harker's disbelief echoed my own, even as I suppressed a relieved smile.

Choosing to sidestep Harker's outburst, I clung to the sliver of hope that his light-heartedness provided. "Let's get you standing," I urged, rising and pulling him up alongside me.

As Kaelan regained his footing, his attention shifted, a puzzled frown forming. "What's happened to the altar?" he asked, his gaze locked behind me.

In our collective panic, none had noticed the altar's transformation. Where once there was only solid obsidian, now lay an opening that cradled a tome of considerable heft, its leather cover aged.

Without a moment's hesitation, Harker reached for the book, her movements swift, her resolve undeterred by the potential for further curses. "Don't!" I cried, wary of more traps. But her fingers wrapped around the tome, and to our collective relief, the room remained still—no trap sprung, no curse unleashed.

"What is it?" My voice was hushed, thick with anticipation, as I leaned in, trying to glimpse the pages that captivated her.

She didn't look up, her fingers deftly turning the fragile pages, a look of intense focus etched into her features. "I'm not entirely certain," she murmured, her tone one of deep concentration.

In an instant, her demeanor shifted; her eyes flew wide open, her breath hitched, and a small, surprised gasp escaped her lips. "What? What have you found?" The urgency in my voice matched the pounding of my heart.

She turned to me, her voice barely a whisper but laden with the weight of our discovery. "I...I think it's the grimoire of the original Seven, the witches created by the First Witch herself centuries past."

A silence enveloped us, so profound I could hear the thumping of my own pulse. The implications of possessing such a tome were staggering—it was a piece of history, a weapon of immense power, potentially disastrous in the wrong hands.

Harker carefully handed me the book, her expression one of reverence and awe. I accepted it gingerly, aware of the potency and danger it represented.

The pages were yellowed with age, delicate and thin, and they rustled softly as I flipped through them. The spells within were indeed dire, the kind that chilled the blood and twisted the gut—rites and conjurations that toyed with forces that mankind was meant to leave alone. But there was something else, something I hadn't expected.

"Harker," I said, my voice steady despite the turmoil within, "these are not the creations of the Seven. They are the original incantations of the First Witch herself."

A voice then echoed in my mind, one both ancient and

immeasurably powerful. *"Tread carefully, daughter. This book was hidden for a reason. Its contents are perilous."*

Inwardly, I confronted the voice of the First Witch. "Why would you have such dangerous knowledge?" I questioned, my mental voice fraught with conflict.

"Darkness sometimes holds the solutions light cannot provide. And to keep your adversaries' secrets close can be your greatest shield. But beware—the tome is cursed to spread madness should it ever leave these walls."

The gravity of her admission set heavily upon me. This was a gambit centuries in the making, a ploy that wove together threads of power, knowledge, and danger.

Harker broke the silence. "What's the plan, then?"

My resolve solidified; this was a crossroads, and I chose the path of daring. "We study the book. We learn how to defeat the dark magic by using the dark magic. In the meantime, I move the library into the Fae realm. The witches will have a much harder time getting to it there."

"You want to go up against the most powerful witches of their time with their own spell book? Are you insane?" Harker asked incredulously.

I shrugged, trying to appear more confident than I felt. "Sometimes you have to embrace a little insanity in order to stay ahead of the game."

Kaelan was silent, his eyes fixed on me. I knew he didn't like the idea, but I also knew that he would support me.

"We have to leave the book in the chamber. There is a curse on it if it's removed," I informed him.

"Well, then let's get it back where it belongs and get the hell out of here," Harker said. "It's cold and I've had enough secrets for one day."

We ascended the stairs, and the stone floor ground

closed behind us, once again sealing off the chamber and its dark secrets.

I glanced at Elara, her ghostly form floating by the wall, watching us. "I promise we will move the library, and you won't be alone anymore."

She smiled sadly, and I knew she didn't believe me.

Exhaustion tugged at my eyelids, a gentle but persistent reminder that my body craved rest after the night's battle and this morning's harrowing discoveries. But the luxury of sleep was a distant dream, with a myriad of tasks gnawing at my consciousness. The werewolves, restless and wary, had to start on the path to Terralux before the Academy could orchestrate another assault. Their safety bore down on me like a physical burden.

The library, too, demanded my attention—it needed anchoring within the protective embrace of my new palace's walls. I would need to do that before anything else.

Then there was the bookshop. The thought of its closure brought a pang to my heart, but it was a necessary end. Ava would understand; she always did. The conversation played out in my mind, each word heavy with the finality of an era gone by.

New witches, too, had to be found and created. The task loomed large like a mountain, casting its foreboding shadow over the landscape of my thoughts.

And the grimoire lay in the back of my mind. It was a mystery wrapped in darkness, its pages filled with knowledge that both fascinated and repelled me. The First Witch was frustratingly elusive, a mentor whose lessons came in riddles and cryptic warnings. I wished, not for the first time, that Rowena would be a little more forthcoming with information instead of allowing me to be blindsided time and time again, but she had made it clear she couldn't interfere with events as they played out.

I sighed, running a hand through my hair, feeling the strands catch between my fingers. I thought of each tangle as a metaphor for the complexity of my current predicament. I steeled myself for the road ahead. There was no turning back, no moment to catch my breath.

As Kaelan and I emerged from the library's musty confines, the cool air of my bedroom felt like a crisp splash of reality on my face. I blinked away the fatigue that threatened to cloud my vision.

Kaelan turned to me, his brow creased with concern. "Vale, you need to get some sleep," he said, his voice a gentle command that he knew I would defy.

I met his gaze, my eyes speaking volumes. "You should check in with Wren and see if you can start shifting groups to the portal to the Fae realm and then to Terralux beyond. We need to get as many of them there before nightfall."

Kaelan studied me for a moment, perhaps searching for the slightest sign of relent, but I had none to give. Eventually, he nodded before pulling me closer. His embrace came as a sudden warmth in the chill, his lips finding mine in a kiss that made my toes curl in my boots, making the ground beneath seem less solid.

"Okay, do what you need to do here," he murmured

against my lips, "but then promise me you'll try and get some rest soon."

The corners of my mouth twitched into a half-smile, half-grimace. "I can't make that promise right now, and you know it," I replied, the stubborn set of my jaw firm as ever.

With a shake of his head and an exasperated smile, Kaelan kissed me once more. "I love you," he said, then, with a quiet whoosh, the shadows descended, and he was gone to the werewolf camp.

I let out another heavy sigh, the quietest of concessions to the relentless pace I was keeping. I needed to remember to grab the cat. Harker had been caring for him these last few months, so I found him comfortably nestled on the bed she had been using. They must have gotten along. He let out a soft meow as I picked him up and gave him a cuddle.

Turning back to the library, I found Harker engrossed once again in her readings. I unceremoniously placed the cat down on the table in front of her. She glanced up from her reading and looked at the cat for a moment before returning to her reading. If she wanted to act like she hadn't come to care for the creature, then I wouldn't say anything.

I moved to the supply drawers and pulled out a stick of chalk. The old spell, the one I had used to anchor the door to my former apartment, floated up from the depths of my memory.

Approaching the door, I hesitated for the briefest of moments before making a small, deliberate cut along my forearm. As the blood welled to the surface, I dipped my finger into it and anointed the doorknob, feeling the energy in the room intensify, hungry for the magic I was about to unleash.

My voice was a whisper, blending with the charged air,

. . .

"By mystic forces, I now beseech,
To erase this door, its presence breach.
With whispered words and gestures fine,
Vanish it from the threads of time."

As I grasped the doorknob and turned it, the door swung open to reveal the reality of my success—a solid wall where an escape once was. Just like that, the connection to my old life was severed, now just a memory.

It was time to create anew. Crouching down, I began sketching the outline of a door on the wall, focusing on the new rooms awaiting in the palace of Terralux. The image of the palace's grandeur filled my mind's eye, providing the anchor for the magic I was invoking.

With the outline complete, I once again dipped my finger into the cut on my arm and allowed a few drops to drip around the lines. Then, I knocked three times on the etched door. The chalk line shimmered, ignited by the latent energy, and then, as if a curtain had been lifted, a door stood before me, its frame sturdy and inviting.

"Here goes nothing," I muttered to myself, grasping the handle and swinging the door open to reveal the tapestry-lined hallways of Terralux's palace. A sigh of relief escaped my lips—a whisper in the silence of the library. The cat leapt off the table and ran through the open door, eager to explore his new surroundings.

"Well, that's one problem fixed," I spoke to the emptiness, to Harker, to myself. With the door now a gateway to a new chapter, I could cross off one more task from the ever-growing list. But there was no time for rest, not yet. There was always one more spell to cast, one more problem to solve. And so, with a weary resolve, I stepped forward— through the threshold and into the heart of my next challenge.

CROSSING THE DOORWAY, I entered the palace of Terralux, my boots echoing faintly on the stone floor. The castle's grandeur was hidden beneath a cloak of disrepair and neglect but was slowly transforming. Servants scurried about, a murmur of soft whispers and shuffling feet, their forms blurred as they worked tirelessly to restore the castle to a semblance of its former glory. The dust of ages hung heavy in the air, and I could almost taste the staleness of long-undisturbed rooms.

The quarters I had chosen as my own had been cleared first, at my insistence. I had declined the opulent chambers that had been destined for those who ruled this place, those once occupied by Haldir. The thought of dwelling where he had once stayed was intolerable—I needed a clean slate, free from the tarnish of his evil.

From the gloom beneath an ornate table, Nyxen emerged. He had always been an insubstantial wisp of shadows, more a fleeting thought than a creature of flesh. Yet now, as I reached out, expecting my hand to pass through him, I was greeted by the warm brush of fur.

Surprise jolted through me, my eyes widening at the touch. "Nyxen, when did this happen?" I asked, my voice betraying my astonishment.

"*Right now,*" he responded, his tone playful and mischievous. It was an answer, and yet, not one at all.

"And have you always been able to become corporeal?" I asked, curiosity and bemusement weaving through my words.

"*No,*" came his short reply as he brushed up against my legs.

A chuckle escaped me, a soft sound that seemed out of place amidst the solemnity of the castle's halls. Nyxen was another mystery, one I had long stopped trying to unravel. I suspected our deepening connection had awakened this new facet of his being, a thought both intriguing and comforting.

"Nyx, can you go and find Aerion or Thalion? Let them know I'm here," I asked.

With a chirp that echoed like a cheerful bell, he acknowledged my request and darted down the hall, his tail a spectral banner trailing behind him.

Alone now, I entered my new rooms, shedding the weight of my leather jacket and casting it aside onto the plush couch in my sitting area. The room welcomed me with the embrace of a cheerfully crackling fire, its warm glow a counterpoint to the cool stone that surrounded me. I let out another weary sigh and sank down before the hearth.

My bones were heavy with weariness, and the fire's dance was hypnotic, offering both warmth and an unspoken promise of rest. For a moment, I allowed myself to simply be, the list of tasks and looming challenges momentarily pushed aside. The flickering flames played across my vision and I felt a fleeting peace amidst the storm of my duties.

The dance of the flames hypnotized me, their soft crackles and the warmth lulling me towards a much-needed rest. As my gaze locked on the flickering light, my thoughts spun with the list of daunting tasks that awaited my attention. Yet despite the weight of responsibility that pressed upon me, my eyelids began to droop, the room's comfort a siren song coaxing me towards sleep.

Without realizing it, I surrendered to my tiredness. Sleep took me swiftly, its grip tightening until I was plunged into the realm of dreams, or more aptly, nightmares. There, the vivid horror of Haldir loomed over me, his presence as oppressive as the cold metal table I found myself once again bound to. His fingers grazed my head, and with that contact, a searing pain lanced through my skull. His smile was a ghoulish contortion, a visual echo of the agony he inflicted. My screams echoed throughout the dark room.

The nightmare fractured with the sound of a loud knock, pulling me from the depths of terror. My heart raced as reality came rushing back, but before I could collect myself, the door swung open, and Aerion's imposing figure appeared.

His eyes found mine, and I saw the concern etched on his features. "Are you alright?" he asked, his voice tinged with worry. "You look like hell, princess."

I hastily pushed aside the vestiges of the dream, setting my face into a mask of composure. "I'm fine," I lied, my voice steadier than I felt.

Aerion's skepticism was clear; he knew me too well to be fooled. Yet he respected my walls, choosing not to climb them but instead offering his silent support. He sat beside me, his arm a gentle weight around my shoulders. I allowed myself a moment of weakness, leaning into his embrace.

"You know, Vale, you aren't the only one here who can take care of things," he reminded me softly, his voice a low rumble.

"That's what everyone keeps telling me," I murmured in response, the exhaustion threading through my words.

His chuckle was soft, knowing. "I know it can be hard to sit back and let others handle your problems, but the world won't fall apart if you take a moment to rest."

A sigh escaped me, half in resignation, half in longing. "I'll rest after we get the wolves moved," I bargained, clinging to my duties like a lifeline. "How is that going so far? Have any made it yet?"

Aerion's answer came smoothly, his voice soothing against the storm of my thoughts. "A few groups have made it so far, the women and children first. Wren and Venna have organized them rather swiftly," he replied.

The mental image of Wren and Venna corralling the werewolves—mothers herding their young—brought a fleeting sense of pride. Despite the chaos that nipped at our heels, there was a semblance of order, a structure within the storm. It was a small victory, a testament to the resilience and strength of those who had chosen to stand with us.

Their efficiency didn't surprise me; Wren with his keen strategic mind, Venna with her nurturing yet commanding nature—they were the perfect pair to handle such a delicate operation. Knowing that part of my burden was in their capable hands allowed a sliver of tension to slip away from my shoulders.

"Swiftly is good," I murmured, trying to let the good news sink in, to let it fortify my determination. "We need all the swiftness we can muster." My gaze drifted back to the flames, watching them devour log after log, relentless and insatiable—much like the path that lay ahead of us.

"How are things progressing here in Terralux?" I asked, concerned for the kingdom's efforts at rebuilding.

Aerion's brows knit together, a crease forming there as he relayed the latest complications. "They are progressing, but not without issues. We've heard whispers—rumors of an underground black market being run by the remnants of the Unseelie court."

The Unseelie court, a dark mirror to the realm's former glory, had been one of the pillars we had toppled in reclaiming this place from Haldir's grasp. Its members, once high and mighty, were now like rats fleeing a sinking ship, although some still skulked in the kingdom's deepening shadows.

"Another problem to add to the list," I said with a weary sigh. The tasks seemed to multiply like heads on a hydra— cut one down, and two more would sprout in its place.

Aerion's eyes met mine, and there was a depth of understanding there. "Yes, but one that can wait," he reassured me. His voice was firm, yet not without warmth. "For now, let's focus on something more immediate—food. You must be starving." He stood, his hand reaching for mine, an unspoken invitation to leave my troubles behind, if only for a meal.

His suggestion felt like a reprieve and I allowed him to draw me to my feet. As we exited the room, the stone beneath our boots felt less like the bones of a once-captive kingdom and more like the foundation of something new.

Walking down the corridor, a comfortable silence settled around us. The walls echoed with the rhythm of our steps, a soothing counterpoint to the thunder of thoughts in my head. Here, within these walls, transformation was taking place. The evidence of restoration surrounded us— fresh paint, repaired tapestries, and clean, polished floors. It was a rebirth, slow and painstaking.

"It's so different now," I mused out loud, admiring a

newly hung tapestry vibrant with colors that seemed to dance in the light.

"Yes," Aerion's voice carried a note of reflection, perhaps a hint of loss for what had once been. "Much has changed since Haldir's reign, but now... now I can begin to see the Terralux I knew as a child."

As we turned a corner, a group of children's laughter cut through the solemnity of our conversation. They were engaged in a game, their bright eyes full of life, untainted by the darker shades of the world. One of the little girls noticed Aerion and stopped, a reverent gasp slipping from her lips.

Aerion's smile was gentle, almost wistful, as he acknowledged the child's awe with a nod, a simple gesture that unleashed a cascade of giggles among the youngsters. They continued to watch us with wide, admiring eyes as we passed by.

The purity of their joy left a lingering sweetness in the air. It was a poignant reminder of why we fought, why we rebuilt. These children, with their innocence and laughter, were the embodiment of hope—a hope that Terralux would thrive, not as a bastion of shadowy courts and silent fears, but as a haven of light and warmth.

As we neared the kitchens, the aromas grew richer and more enticing—a tapestry of scents woven with the warm, yeasty promise of bread and the savory depths of roasted meat. My stomach, which had remained steadfast during the day's earlier trials, now betrayed me with a fierce growl, reminding me of the mundane mortal needs I often neglected.

The moment we stepped into the kitchen, the homely sounds of culinary life enveloped us. The metallic song of pots and pans mingled with the chorus of cooks calling out to one another. Cooks, draped in white aprons, moved with urgency around steaming pots and sizzling pans, their expressions set in a grim ballet of focus and fatigue.

I reached for an apple, its skin a flawless sheen under the flickering kitchen lights, and tore a chunk from a loaf of bread still warm from the oven. The crust crackled satisfyingly under my fingers, releasing a puff of steam. With a nod of gratitude to a cook who barely had a second to acknowledge me, we retreated, leaving the organized chaos behind for the quiet of the corridor. I made a mental note to learn the name of the head cook at least.

Biting into the apple, its crispness burst upon my tongue, a sweet-tart rush that was grounding in its simplicity. The bread, dense and soft, was equally comforting, its flavor a testament to the care of its maker. It was a small pocket of normalcy, an oasis of contentment in the desert of endless duties.

But tranquility in times of change is often fleeting. A servant, breathless and swift, found us to report the arrival of more werewolves seeking sanctuary within our walls. Aerion's eyes met mine, an apology within their depths.

"I need to go and help them settle in," he stated, leadership ever present in his voice.

I nodded, the last bite of apple feeling suddenly leaden in my mouth. "Of course," I replied.

Aerion's smile was a flicker of warmth in the cool hallway, his lips brushing mine in a kiss that spoke of reassurance. It was fleeting, too brief to savor, yet it lingered like a whisper long after he had turned to depart.

Watching his retreating back, a tangle of emotions threaded through me—admiration, longing, and an acute awareness of the solitude that leadership often entailed. Part of me yearned to call out, to ask him to stay, to extend the interlude and delay the unstoppable march of responsibility.

Yet I remained silent, my hand absentmindedly brushing the place his lips had been. The echo of his touch was a bittersweet reminder of the life we were fighting to protect and the sacrifices such a fight entailed. There would be time, I assured myself, for softer things—for warmth, for comfort, for love. But for now, there was work to be done. And I, Valerian of Terralux, would not shrink from it.

CHAPTER

SIX

I found Ava in the bustling main hall. The intricate tattoos that adorned her arms seemed to dance under the hall's lighting.

"Ava, I've been looking for you," I called out, my voice cutting through the din of the crowd of Otherworlders who had joined Wren's pack.

Her head turned. Those verdant eyes—the color of new leaves in spring—fixed on me brightly. Her lips curved in a smile, the kind that reached her eyes and softened the world around her. She was motherly in the best sense, and being around her was a comfort.

"Vale, it's so good to see you again," Ava greeted, stepping closer. "Did you need something?"

I nodded, feeling the weight of my news anchoring my feet to the stone floor. "Yes, there is something I need to talk to you about," I said, my fingers wrapping gently but firmly around her arm, guiding her toward the secluded shadows of an alcove. Privacy was a scarce luxury in the palace these days and what I had to share demanded it.

Once hidden from prying eyes, I released her, the

51

anxiety of what I was about to propose coiling in my stomach. I raked a hand through my hair, a telltale sign of my unease, and exhaled a weary sigh.

"Vale, what's wrong?" Ava's voice was laced with concern, a reflection of the furrow forming between her brows.

I met her gaze squarely, feeling the gravity of my own words before they even left my lips. "Okay, what I'm about to tell you can't be repeated except to a select few, and it's... big. I've learned that I can create more witches."

Her response was written across her face—an interplay of surprise and curiosity. "And what does that have to do with me?" she asked, her tone steady despite the shock.

"That's the tricky part," I continued, finding strength in her attentive stare. "I was hoping you'd accept my offer of becoming one."

A soft gasp escaped her, a mirror to the flutter in my own chest. "Me? A witch? That's possible?" There was a flicker of something like wonder in her eyes.

I nodded yet held back the torrent of information that threatened to spill forth. This was a delicate tapestry we were weaving, and each thread needed to be placed with care.

Ava fell silent, her gaze drifting to the floor as she contemplated the enormity of my offer. "This is big, but I can't deny I'm intrigued. Would who I am...change?" Her question hung between us, a delicate filament of concern.

"No, nothing like that. But Ava, I need more witches than just you. I need at least five more willing Otherworlders, half-Fae or half-demon, to join us. We need seven witches, including me, to form a coven." I watched her face, searching for signs of retreat. "I can't promise it's not without its dangers, but I can promise that you won't be alone."

She processed my words, her gaze intensifying, sharpening. Ava always had the look of someone who saw the world not just for what it was but for what it could be.

"This is a lot, Vale," she said after a lengthy pause, her voice a soft echo in the hushed alcove.

"I know, and I understand what I'm asking of you, but it's important, extremely important." The plea in my voice was naked, unadorned.

"Okay," Ava's voice was barely above a whisper, yet it carried the weight of decision. "I can do it for you, for everything you've done for us." She paused, her resolve building. "And I know of others, ones who have been moved by your actions. I'll ask around discreetly and see if any more would be willing to listen to what you have to say."

Relief washed over me, followed closely by the realization of the magnitude of our undertaking. I reached out, touching her arm in gratitude, her skin warm under my fingertips.

"Thank you, Ava," I said, the depth of my gratitude resonating through those three words. "You don't know what this means to me." The journey ahead would be treacherous, but having her by my side was a solace I hadn't realized I'd needed until now. I wouldn't be the only witch any longer, wouldn't have to shoulder the burden alone.

Her lips curled up in a knowing smile, the glint in her eyes speaking of a wisdom beyond her years. "Oh, I think I do," she replied. Her voice carried the weight of shared secrets and the understanding of the stakes at hand.

"If you can't find anyone else, please come and tell me

right away, okay?" The words tumbled out, lined with an edge of concern.

"Okay," she responded with a firm nod, the kind that sealed promises and fortified the walls of trust we were building. She understood the gravity, the delicate balance on which our plan was perched.

"And one more thing," I found myself hesitating, my voice dropping to a whisper as if the walls themselves might be listening. "Please be careful with who you ask."

Her expression hardened with determination, a warrior's resolve etching her features. "I understand. This is dangerous information. I'll keep it to myself until the time is right," she assured me, and I believed her. Her loyalty was as unshakeable as the earth itself.

"Thank you, Ava, really." I stepped forward, closing the distance between us, and pulled her into an embrace. It was an embrace of warriors, of sisters in arms, and she returned it with equal strength.

Her voice was soft but steady as she whispered into my ear, "I won't let you down, Vale."

Pulling back, I met her gaze. "I know you won't."

She looked at me, her eyes softening. "You should get some rest," she said, echoing the counsel of others.

A wry chuckle escaped me as I shook my head. "That's what everyone keeps telling me."

Her expression shifted to one of stern admonishment, but her warmth bled through, bathing the reprimand in affection. "Well, maybe you should start listening," she said, her eyes locked onto mine, a gentle but undeniable command.

THE WEIGHT of my eyelids became stones, pulling me down into the depths of an unbidden slumber as I collapsed onto my bed. I had only sought a brief reprieve, a momentary pause in the relentless tempo of my existence. But the fatigue had become an ocean and I sank into its depths, quickly swept away into the realm of dreams.

I found myself standing in a forest where the trees clawed at the skies, ancient and watching. A thick mist hung in the air, a gossamer veil that obscured my vision beyond a few steps in each direction. The world seemed muted here, the silence almost reverent, and with each breath, the fog rolled over my skin, leaving a trail of goose-bumps in its wake.

I started to walk, my steps uncertain in this uneven terrain of dreams. The forest floor was a puzzle, a shifting tapestry where one step could carry me leagues forward or merely inches. The laws of physics were whimsical here, bending and twisting in the whims of the subconscious.

Out of the corner of my eye, I spotted a form, a dark shape flitting between the shadows of the trees. I froze, my heart a hammer against my chest. "Nyxen?" When it came out, my voice seemed alien, echoing oddly in the still air.

There was a rustling and then he appeared, emerging from the fog with grace. "*Vale,*" his voice resonated within my mind, a solid presence in the shifting uncertainty of this place.

"Where are we, Nyx?" I asked him, peering into the fog as it curled around us, an ever-moving serpent.

"*Dreams,*" he replied, his stoic calm a sharp contrast to the chaos of my heart.

He began to lead and I followed, placing my trust in him. We navigated the unpredictable landscape, each step a gamble, each breath a question. My senses strained against the mist, seeking clarity and truth.

The shadows in the fog began to take form—ambiguous figures that danced just out of clear sight. Here, a group of seven, their outlines shimmering. There, three men, a trinity of fate. The shadow of a young girl stood out as well. And farther out, a demon, its horns and wings a macabre silhouette against the misty backdrop.

Each vision struck a chord of recognition within me, a feeling that these were more than just ghosts of sleep. They were omens, pieces of a puzzle that my muddled head couldn't put together.

And then, a solitary man, his image clearer than the rest. He stood alone, an island in the mist. A sense of importance clung to him, but before I could ponder further, my gaze fell upon a figure sprawled on the ground. I instantly recognized this as a portent of death.

My heart raced, the scenes flickering before me like pages of a book being turned by an unseen hand. Fear twisted in my gut, but alongside it, a thrum of purpose. These were not just dreams; they were messages, warnings, perhaps even a map of what lay ahead.

Compelled by an unseen force, I pressed on, Nyxen my steadfast guide through this maze of dreams and premonition. The forest's dense canopy and the mists began to recede, drifting earthward to form a ghostly carpet that caressed the ground while leaving the air above it crisp and clear.

Emerging from the woods' shelter, Nyxen and I found ourselves at the threshold of a graveyard, one that seemed as ancient as time itself. Tombstones, like jagged teeth, rose from the earth and obelisks pointed accusingly at the sky, each a testament to lives long since passed. The air held the scent of moss and stone, and the silence here was profound, interrupted only by the whisper of the mist as it settled.

Nyxen navigated the sea of graves with a purposeful stride, his tail flicking in the half-light as if keeping time with the beating of my heart. We weaved between the monuments to the dead, some grand, others humble, all united by their testament to mortality.

And there, in the heart of the graveyard, stood a tree, twisted and ancient, its bark etched with the passage of countless years. From one gnarled branch swung a noose, an eerie sentinel beside a small, unadorned grave marked by a single stone.

That's when I saw her—the specter of a young girl drifting around the tree in a silent, sorrowful orbit. Her eyes found mine, and in a breath, she was before me, her face inches from my own. "You should not be here," she whispered, her voice a chill wind that seemed to seep into my bones.

Fear sought to clamp around my heart, but Nyxen stepped forward. With a growl that rumbled through the stillness, he issued a command, *"Stand down, witch."*

The ghost heeded Nyxen and backed away slightly, her gaze still locked with mine. Nyxen settled down but kept a watchful eye on the ghost. Witch, he had called her.

"Who are you?" I asked her, my voice steady despite my thunderous heat.

She hovered there, a wisp of a thing, yet her eyes held the depth of the grave. "Elowen," she answered, "I am one of the Seven."

Her words echoed in my thoughts like a sinister refrain. As I stood in the spectral silence of the graveyard, facing the spirit, I couldn't help but wonder if I was staring into the face of an enemy. Was she one of the fabled witches bound by dark intent to end me?

"I'm not among the ones who wish you harm, Vale," her words floated through the air, startlingly clear, responding to the silent suspicions that knotted within me. She knew my name without me having spoken it, a knowledge that betrayed an unnerving intimacy with my thoughts.

"But being here, in the dream realm, even with a guide, in your state is extremely dangerous," her voice was a gentle chime, but it carried an urgency that knotted my stomach. "Your presence here is a beacon, and those with ill will can sense it from leagues away. You must retreat to your body before something sinister reaches you."

I couldn't leave, not now when there were answers hanging within reach. "But wait, I need to know more about the Seven, please," I pleaded.

The ghost, Elowen, cast a sorrowful glance over her shoulder, her form starting to wane like the last wisps of mist at dawn. "Seek out this place, seek me out in the waking world, but you must leave now!"

It was then that Nyxen's fur bristled and he sprang to his feet, alerted to an unseen danger. A shiver coursed through me as a black mass surged at the forest's edge. Elowen's face contorted with fear, her spectral hands reaching towards me. "Go, go back to your body now!"

I turned just in time to see the behemoth lurching out of the fog—a nightmare made flesh, a great and vile creature, bristling with fury. A behemoth with the head of a bear and a human's twisted posture. Its roar was thunderous as it barreled toward us, its eyes wild and feral.

Terror lent strength to my voice, a scream tearing from my throat as my magic burst forth in a torrent, unrestrained and volatile. But here, in the realm of dreams, my power was a tempest without direction, a dance of fire signifying nothing. The arcane flames sputtered and writhed through the graveyard with a life of their own, but the monster still charged forward.

"Your magic is too wild here! You must return to your body, Vale!" Elowen's voice cut through the chaos.

The monstrous being was now a breath away, its vicious claws aimed at my throat. But in that breathless moment, Nyxen was swifter, a blur of protective fury placing himself between the beast and me.

"Nyxen!" I screamed the moment the world shifted.

The collision of soul and body was abrupt as I was wrenched from the dream. My physical body, lying in the safety of my bed, jerked violently with the force of my return. A ragged gasp escaped my lips as my eyes snapped open to the dim familiarity of my rooms.

Sweat drenched my skin, and my heart hammered against my ribcage, the fear from the dream lingering like poison. I gasped for breath, my throat raw from screams unvoiced in the waking world, my hands still tingling with the fading echo of unleashed fire. The images from the nightmare clung to the edges of my consciousness, a grim reminder that, while I had escaped this time, the realm of dreams was no longer a safe haven for me.

The danger of the dream realm had passed, but the foreboding it heralded clung to me, a shadow not even the dawn could chase away.

SEVEN

My heart was still racing, the roar of the beast echoing in my ears as I sprang upright in my bed. "Nyxen!" I cried out, my voice a hoarse whisper, the terror of losing him wrenching my heart.

Almost instantly, he emerged from the shadows of my chamber, whole and unscathed. A sob of relief broke from my chest, raw and earnest. With trembling arms, I wrapped them around his newly corporeal form, anchoring myself to him. "I thought you'd been hurt," I managed to utter between gasps of relief, my grip on him tight as if I could keep him safe from harm through sheer will.

"I can't be hurt there," he reassured me, his voice a steady constant that soothed the lingering panic. His response sparked a flurry of questions.

"Where was 'there' exactly? Were we really in the dream realm? How is that even possible?" The questions tumbled out, one after the other, my mind grappling for purchase in the slippery confusion of reality and dreams.

"Dreamwalker," he stated plainly as if the word itself were a key to understanding.

"What does that mean?" I asked, feeling the weight of my own ignorance.

"*Seek answers in the books,*" he advised, and I knew he referred to the library.

Then, a knock at the door sliced through our conversation, a mundane sound that felt alien after the spectral experiences of the dream. "Come in," I called, somewhat reluctant to break the bubble of solitude that Nyxen and I shared.

The door opened and Kaelan stepped through, exhaustion clouding his features. "Hey," he greeted, a small smile on his face. "Aerion told me you were in here sleeping."

I nodded, attempting to compose myself, to push away the vestiges of the dream that clung to me like cobwebs. "Yes, I was just resting," I said, brushing away the last tear with the back of my hand.

"What's wrong, another nightmare?" he asked, concern darkening his gaze. The bed dipped under his weight, a simple reminder of reality that felt grounding. I met his brown eyes, the harrowing journey of my dream still swirling in my head, and I felt a moment's hesitation. How could I articulate the surreal adventure that had left my heart racing and my mind reeling? I took a deep breath, trying to steady the rapid drumbeat of my pulse.

"I had a dream," I started, pausing to collect my thoughts. "No, not just a dream. It was more vivid, more... real than any dream I've ever had."

Kaelan listened intently as I recounted the towering forest shrouded in mist, how time and space seemed distorted with every step I took. I described the chilling sensation of being watched and the veiled visions among the dense mists. My words were a bridge, bringing the ethereal images from my mind's eye into the dim light of my room.

I told him of Nyxen appearing in the dream realm as my protector and guide. The urgency in my voice peaked as I relayed the appearance of the ghost, Elowen, and her dire warnings. Kaelan's expression shifted through the telling from fascination to concern. He remained silent, absorbing every detail, understanding the gravity of what I had experienced.

"The ghost, she knew me, Kaelan. She spoke of danger, of being hunted," I said, my words a whisper now. The memory of the hulking beast charging through the mist sent an involuntary chill through me.

"I...I used my magic on the beast, but it was chaotic, uncontrollable. Nyxen saved me in the end," I finished finally, looking at my loyal familiar, who was curled up at the end of the bed, watching me with intelligent yellow eyes.

Kaelan reached out his hand and gently cradled my cheek. "You're safe now," he assured me, his voice soothing.

But his eyes held questions, the same ones that echoed in my mind. What did it all mean? Why was I able to traverse the dream realm? And what were the implications for the challenges that lay ahead?

"We'll figure it out," he said, answering the fears in my eyes. It was more than just comfort; it was a vow from someone who had never wavered.

The fear that had taken root in my heart in the dream had found its way into my voice as I admitted, "I'm afraid of what it all means." The shadows of the dream were spilling into reality, dark tendrils threatening to overwhelm me.

Kaelan's response came not just from a place of support but of conviction. "You have the strength and courage to face whatever comes," he said. His confidence in me was reassuring, an anchor amid my doubts, but not enough.

"How do you know that?" The question came from a place deep within where my insecurities lay hidden. His faith was a beacon, but I needed to find that light within myself, too.

"Because I know you. You're the strongest person I've ever met." His voice was laden with emotion and his words enveloped me like a protective shroud, shielding me from my fears.

His promise followed, as solid and tangible as if he had sworn an oath, "And I'll always be here to help you, to support you in any way you need." It was more than just a pledge; it was a testament to the bond we shared. Not the blood bond forged from magic, but the one we had made ourselves, forged from love.

I allowed myself to be pulled close, his embrace a fortress against the chaos of my thoughts. Kaelan was my sanctuary, a reminder of days when the weight of destiny had not yet fully rested on my shoulders.

"Thank you," came the whisper from my lips, a soft exhalation that carried with it all my gratitude and reliance on his strength. "We'll figure it out together," I echoed, the words sealing our mutual resolve.

His smile was a quiet rebellion against any doubt, and it took my breath away. "Always," he agreed, and it was a promise for all the days to come, through challenges and uncertainties.

Time seemed to slow as we sat together, the silence not empty but filled with unspoken oaths and shared understanding. Together, we had faced much, and together, we would continue to stand against whatever darkness loomed ahead.

The twilight beyond the window was a canvas of color, but it was a beauty edged with the night's encroaching shadows. The world outside was changing, just as we were.

Yet, the thought of my other allies severed the brief respite as I realized what time it was. "Kaelan, where's Wren? Did the wolves all make it here?" The question brought back the urgency of our situation, the reality of our companions who might be in need, the wolves whose fates were intertwined with our own.

"Yes, they did," Kaelan said in a somewhat tired voice. "Aerion helped show them to their rooms. It took a lot out of me, shifting all those groups of people, but I managed it." A sense of pride, rightfully earned, lingered in his tone.

"Wren and Venna," he continued, "they took charge of the situation like seasoned commanders. The way they coordinated everyone and their possessions was a sight to behold." For a moment, his fatigue was replaced by admiration. "Honestly, I was quite impressed. Those two were meant to lead."

Relief washed over me like a gentle wave. "I'm glad everyone is safe and sound. I can't believe everyone managed it so quickly." It was a testament to the unity and strength of our group, something that, in darker times, I feared we might lose.

The silence that followed was a comfortable one as I leaned into his arms. After a moment, Kaelan pulled back slightly. His hand found its way to his hair, running through the dark strands in a gesture that signaled a shift in his thoughts. "I hate to kill our quiet bubble here," he started, his voice reluctant to break the peace we'd found, "but I actually came to tell you something."

"What is it?" I asked, apprehensive of his serious tone. The quiet bubble he mentioned had been a fleeting sanctuary, and I braced myself for the needle that was about to burst it. Whatever it was that Kaelan needed to tell me, I knew it was significant enough to warrant interrupting our moment of calm.

"Thalion wants to speak with you when you're ready," Kaelan said. "He didn't elaborate, but there was a certain... urgency in his tone."

My eyebrows furrowed, concern etching lines into my forehead. "Do you have any idea what it's about?" My question was more of a reflex, a grasp for any thread of understanding before facing the unknown.

He shook his head, the dark locks tumbling back into place. "No specifics. But he insisted it couldn't wait," he replied, reaching up to stroke my face lightly, almost absently.

I sighed, knowing that whatever respite I'd hoped for was quickly evaporating. "Okay, I'll go see him. Thank you for telling me."

His smile was a small comfort in the midst of brewing storms. He threaded his fingers through mine then his smile faltered, guilt creeping into his expression. "With the exertion of the shift, I'm... well, I'm spent," he confessed. "Do you think you and Nyxen can manage to get there without me?"

"Of course," I assured him, squeezing his hand. "Rest. You've carried a heavy load today. We'll be fine."

"I'll find you later, alright?" he said, already standing to grant himself the rest his body demanded. We had separate rooms but he stayed here most nights.

"That would be perfect," I assured him. Our kiss was a brief connection, a promise to find comfort in each other again soon. With one final, lingering glance, he left, the door closing softly behind him.

Alone, the silence was a presence that filled the room. The dream replayed in my mind with unsettling clarity. The sensation of my spirit returning to my body was something I was sure I wouldn't forget. The impossibility of it all was both a puzzle and a lure, drawing me toward a mystery I was both intrigued and hesitant to unravel.

The magic I possessed was a living mystery, growing in tandem with my understanding and yet always steps ahead, dancing just beyond the reach of full comprehension. As much as the logical part of my mind craved explanations, I sensed that the key to unlocking these riddles lay not in books or spoken words, but within me.

Nyxen stirred at the end of the bed, and I watched as he stretched, his lithe body arching and flexing. Then he sat up, regarding me with his yellow eyes. *"When you're ready,"* he said in my mind in his clipped tone.

"Then let's not keep Thalion waiting," I said, taking a deep breath. "We've got a lot to do."

Shadow travel was a peculiar sensation, like slipping through the cracks of reality itself, and each time I undertook the journey with Nyxen, it left me with an electric thrum of energy pulsing through my veins. When the world solidified around us, we were in Virelium, Thalion's kingdom. The crisp winter air was filled with the scent of silverwood trees.

The majestic walls of Thalion's palace rose around us, steeped in the timeless elegance only the Fae could weave into their architecture. I found myself momentarily disoriented, not just by the shadow shift but by the sudden change of scenery.

"Nyx, would you take me to Thalion?" I asked, and he was off before I could finish my sentence. His ability to sense others' locations was another facet of our bond I had come to rely upon.

As we walked, the halls of the palace unfolded with opulent splendor. Our footfalls echoed off high ceilings adorned with intricate frescoes depicting the valor and history of the Fae.

Turning a corner, Nyxen led me to the ornate doors of Thalion's private chambers. I knocked briefly but didn't wait for an answer before I walked in.

Upon entering, a surge of nostalgia hit me. Thalion and Aerion were engrossed in a map sprawled across a large table. We hadn't been alone together, just the three of us, in weeks, and the sight brought back a torrent of memories and emotions.

The complexities of my relationships with Thalion and Aerion — and Kaelan — formed a knot that tightened with each encounter. We still hadn't fully navigated the logistics of sharing my time with three different men, and I had been spending a considerable amount of time with Kaelan since we had reconciled. The two Fae princes had graciously, and quietly, given us that time together.

As I stepped into the room, Thalion and Aerion looked up, and their expressions brightened. The seriousness of their strategy session gave way to smiles of genuine warmth and I couldn't help but return the gesture. I still felt a flutter of astonishment at the affection directed toward me by the two of them.

"Vale, I feel like I haven't seen you in a month," Thalion said, standing. He closed the distance between us with a few strides and enveloped me in an embrace that felt both protective and welcoming. As he drew back, his lips found mine in a kiss that was both a greeting and a claim, his hand cradling the back of my neck.

"It's almost been that long," I responded, my voice light despite the tightness that lingered in my chest from the absence. My hands rested against the solid wall of his chest, grounding myself in the moment.

But the moment stretched and deepened as Thalion drew me back into a deeper, more intense kiss. His fingers wove through my hair with a gentleness that contradicted the strength in his arms. A fire sparked to life in me at his touch. As his lips brushed down my neck, I felt the heat rising in my core. The longing was a physical ache, a craving that had grown through the distance and separation.

The cough from behind us was a sharp reminder of our audience. Thalion's response was a playful roll of his eyes. "Getting jealous, are you?" Thalion teased, his tone light and his arms still wrapped around me.

Aerion's glare had none of the chill of real anger. "We have things we needed to discuss if I remember correctly," he said, his tone as pointed as his look.

"Yes, Aerion, there are always things to discuss." Thalion's response was as light as air, carefree as if he hadn't a concern in the world. "But there isn't always a beautiful witch standing in my rooms these days. So I thought we could take advantage of the situation a bit."

I watched the interplay between them with a chuckle building in my throat. They were like two sides of a coin, one light, one serious, yet both invaluable. Aerion's next pointed look seemed to pierce Thalion's playful facade and with a theatrical sigh, Thalion relented, releasing his hold on me.

Their bickering was a familiar tune that had often been

a backdrop to our time together. I moved to the couch before the fire, the flames casting dancing shadows on the walls, and sank into its plush embrace. Thalion and Aerion took their seats beside it, both looking at me expectantly.

"So what's so important?" I prodded, my curiosity getting the better of me.

Thalion responded with a smirk, his mood still light. "Maybe nothing. Maybe I made it all up just to get you over here," he said, his eyes glinting with mischief.

That drew a laugh from me, a sound that felt more liberating than I expected in the seriousness of the palace. "Well, your evil plan worked," I shot back, smiling at him.

Thalion's grin widened, a flash of fangs that might have been menacing if I didn't know the tender heart that lay behind them.

"Thalion..." Aerion's voice was a soft reprimand, a nudge towards the matter at hand.

With a huff, Thalion's demeanor shifted ever so slightly. "Oh, alright, you big bully. Vale, we need to discuss you being crowned queen of Terralux," he said, his words falling like stones in the stillness.

My heart seemed to stumble over itself at his words. "Oh, that," was all I could muster, a weak attempt to mask the roiling sea of apprehension within me. The idea of ruling a kingdom was as daunting as it was surreal, yet another unexpected turn in the already winding path of my life.

"Yes, that," Aerion echoed, his eyes steady on mine.

"When were you planning on announcing it? Maybe this is something we can keep to ourselves a bit longer?" My words were hopeful, perhaps too much so. I wasn't ready; I wasn't sure if I ever would be.

Aerion's response was gentle but firm, "You should

probably take the crown sooner rather than later. It's already causing a bit of a stir. We have to figure out how to make the announcement and the transition smooth."

"Smooth, that sounds nice," I murmured, but the word sounded like a far-off dream. "How do we do that?"

"There will have to be an official ceremony. And, of course, the transition of power would go a lot smoother if you were married," Thalion said, tossing the words into the space between us like pebbles into a pond, oblivious to the ripples they created.

Married. The word echoed through my mind. It was a simple word, yet it was anything but simple. It was a solution, a tie, a binding—a potential turning point that was both an ending and a beginning. And it lay there between us, as intangible as the shadows flickering across the walls.

The path ahead was suddenly alight with possibilities and pitfalls alike, and I found myself standing at the precipice of a future I had never envisioned yet was hurtling toward with inevitable force.

EIGHT

"Married," I echoed, the word seeming to hang in the air like a spell, both alluring and alarming. My eyes bounced between Thalion and Aerion, trying to read the earnestness in their expressions. "To who, exactly?"

"To me," Thalion's voice resonated with a calm certainty just as Aerion said, "To us." It was synchronized, almost rehearsed, yet the weight of their words felt like it was compressing the air I was trying to breathe.

My heart didn't just skip a beat—it seemed to cease altogether before resuming with a frantic cadence. Their gazes were locked onto me, Thalion's with a warm invitation and Aerion's piercing with earnest intensity.

"Both of you?" The question squeaked from me before I could compose myself, a raw and unfiltered response to the staggering proposition before me.

"If you'll have us," Thalion said, his voice smooth as velvet, eyes glinting with hope and something more profound, more vulnerable. His statement was like a key turning in a lock, an opening to possibilities I hadn't allowed myself to consider.

The room seemed to tilt, the gravity of their proposition pulling everything towards a nexus of impossible decisions. "But...but..." I stammered, my mind racing to keep pace with the rapid unfolding of events.

"Marriage to Aerion would cement you in the hearts of the remainder of his court in Terralux, and marriage to me would align our two kingdoms." Thalion continued, his explanation so matter-of-fact it bordered on clinical. The notion of marriage for love was entangled with duty, power, and the pressure of the crowns they offered.

Aerion's next words were soothing, an attempt to cushion the blow of stark reality. "We're aware of the political complications, Vale. This isn't the most romantic of propositions, not under the current circumstances. But it's a solid alliance and an option for you."

"An option," I echoed, the word tasting of cold steel on my tongue, not the warm, sweet confection one might associate with matters of marriage. I latched onto the word, even as it felt inadequate to describe the merging of lives, of kingdoms. "Is that how you'd think of marriage to me?"

His clarification was swift, "What I mean is this is a matter of state, not one of the heart. You wouldn't need to choose between us." The reassurance, intended to soothe, instead sent a chill through me. A marriage of convenience was a common enough concept, but to hear it laid out so starkly was startling.

The offer was as practical as it was passionless, a strategic move on the chessboard of royal intrigue. Yet the implication that it required no choice was as perplexing as the proposal itself.

"Would you even want to marry me, then?" I asked, the

fear that had been nibbling at the edges of my heart now voiced aloud. "Do you even see me that way?"

Their shock was almost comical, the way they turned to each other with wide eyes before facing me again. "Vale," Thalion began, his voice softer now, infused with a warmth that reached out and wrapped around me, "there is nothing that would make me happier."

Aerion's nod was solemn, his eyes sincere. "We're not trying to trap you into a loveless union. I can see how our suggestion might seem like that, but that's not our intention at all." His admission was soothing, a note of truth in a conversation that had started to feel like a negotiation.

"No, it's just the most practical and politically convenient way to unite our courts," I murmured, the words tasting bitter as they fell from my lips. The realist within me acknowledged the truth in their words, even as my heart longed for a different kind of proposal.

"You've had enough political maneuvering and manipulation to last a lifetime," Thalion admitted, and the trace of guilt that shadowed his gaze hinted at deeper currents of thought. His gaze held mine with an intensity that suggested his next words were not just formalities. "We don't want you to feel that we're trapping you or pushing you into a decision," he continued, his voice carrying an undercurrent of something more, something unspoken that thrummed between us.

"We want you to have choices and time to think about them," Aerion added.

They were offering me a future—a complex, tangled, potentially beautiful partnership. Not just a crown, but a shared life with all its intricate weavings of power, affection, and the promise of unity.

The suggestion hovered before me, challenging and

potent, a path I had not foreseen even in my most imaginative moments. The notion that I could choose this, choose them, felt at once liberating and overwhelming—a shift in the way I had understood my future to unravel.

"I think I'd like that," I found myself saying, the words emerging with cautious optimism, "but I want time to think it over. I appreciate you being so straightforward about it. It's not exactly the most romantic way to propose marriage, but you're right, it does make sense," I admitted, my eyes flitting between Thalion and Aerion, seeking both their assurances and gauging their sincerity.

Thalion's reaction was immediate; a weary sigh escaped him as he cradled his head in his hands, a gesture of remorse or perhaps disappointment. "This isn't how I pictured this going," he confessed as he looked up at me, his voice tinged with a sadness that seemed to reach out and gently squeeze my heart. "You deserve more than how we handled this. When the time comes, and if you say yes, I promise I'll give you a better proposal."

The laugh that burst from me was unexpected, a release of tension as much as an appreciation of his earnestness. "I'll hold you to that," I assured him, a smile softening my features as I met his gaze.

Thalion's lips curled into a half-smile, a shadow of his usual confidence returning. "Well, that's a good start, I suppose," he said, a spark of hope flickering in his eyes.

Aerion, ever the stoic, matched Thalion's vulnerability with his own brand of resolve. "The same goes for me, Vale. We've had enough complications." His eyes held mine and there was a depth to them, a sincere wish to see me happy, a rare hint of feeling he rarely showed. "If you'll have me, I'd very much like to marry you, but we can wait until things have settled down. And if you choose Thalion or both of us, or neither... I'll learn to live with that." His words were an offering of freedom.

As I rose, so did he, an unspoken acknowledgment of the seriousness of our conversation. He stepped closer, his presence commanding yet comforting, and as his hand came up to caress my cheek, the intimacy of the gesture sent a current through me. "Thank you," I whispered, savoring the warmth of his touch.

His smile was my undoing, the kind of smile that could ease the deepest of sorrows.

But a shard of reality intruded, a question that gnawed at me. "And where does Kaelan fit into all this?" My voice was barely a whisper, yet it carried the weight of my concerns and fears.

Aerion's shrug was nonchalant, yet his response was anything but. "Marry him too. He'll be a prince consort, just like I will be. I wouldn't dream of taking him from you and I don't think he'd let me," he said, and the smile he wore was one of genuine amusement.

The idea was audacious, yet strangely fitting in the chaos of our lives. To think that I could have them all, that we could forge a future together without the chains of traditional choice, was astonishingly sweet. That I could consider such a path without having to relinquish a part of my heart for the sake of politics was more than liberating— it was revolutionary.

As Aerion's eyes danced with a mischievous glint, he leaned in, and his lips met mine in a kiss laden with promises and the taste of a shared future. His scent— honeysuckle and cloves—surrounded me, a sensory anchor in the whirlwind of emotions. My eyelids fluttered shut, giving in to the sensation, of a future filled with complex, yet potentially fulfilling, love.

He finally pulled back and whispered against my lips, "Think about it, Vale. There's no need to decide now. Just know that we want you. If you'll have us, we'll be waiting."

And in that moment, amidst the uncertainty, the allure of their offer shone with the possibility of joy, of a life less ordinary. It was a decision I didn't have to rush. They had given me the freedom to choose and in doing so, had offered me the most valuable gift of all—time.

Though my next words didn't reveal the full breadth of my thoughts, they were nonetheless sincere, a glimpse into a heart that still held onto hope. "I will," I whispered, a promise. "I'll think about it."

"THEY ASKED YOU TO WHAT?" Kaelan's voice didn't just echo in the confines of my rooms; it seemed to reverberate through my very bones.

My hands lifted instinctively, trying to hush the tide of his outrage as much as to steady my rising panic. "Calm down, Kaelan, people are sleeping," I hissed, my voice barely above a whisper.

The look he gave me was fierce, sharp, and accusing, as if he could somehow challenge the reality of my words through sheer force of will. I saw him rein in his emotions, his chest heaving with controlled breaths, every muscle in his body wound tight. The news had struck a chord, shaken the bedrock of his restraint, and here he was, a silent image of thunderous fury.

"I'm calm, Vale," he insisted, though his words were a contradiction to the energy that radiated from him. His voice had dropped to a growl, the kind of sound that made the air feel thinner, cooler. His fists were tight at his sides, his posture rigid, like he was prepared for a battle.

"Kaelan, please, can we sit and discuss this?" I pleaded, nodding toward the bed with its royal drapings.

He was a tempest in human form, pacing like a caged animal, his agitation manifesting in every step. "No," came his terse reply, each stride punctuating his refusal.

I maneuvered to sit on the edge of the bed, the mattress dipping slightly under my weight. "Well, I'm sitting," I stated, a clear indication of my refusal to engage in his stormy display, my arms folding defensively over my chest.

Finally, he halted, turning to me with a frown that could sour milk. After a moment's pause, where it seemed he might protest further, he sat beside me, though every line of his body screamed reluctance. Close, but not touching—like two islands sharing the same sea but divided by the currents between them.

"It was a serious discussion about the future," I began, choosing my words with the same care I might select weapons for a duel. "The proposal... we can dissect that later, or not at all." I drew a breath, holding his gaze, searching for a sign of understanding. "What concerns me now is your reaction to them wanting me to marry both of them."

Kaelan's response was a deep, pained groan. He covered his face with his hands, a gesture of defeat, and then let himself fall back against the pillows. "The audacity," he murmured, his words muffled by his palms before they fell away to reveal his troubled expression. "And after everything you've been through..." His voice was a whisper, burdened with an unspoken heaviness.

"What do you mean?" My voice was soft, coaxing. I shifted, leaning over him, watching the play of emotions across his features. His eyes remained closed, his expression etched with troubled thoughts.

He was silent for a long heartbeat, his chest rising and falling with a sigh. "You've been through so much," he murmured, and I could feel the resignation in his voice, "and the thought of them asking you to marry them... They should have waited."

"Waited for what?" My heart thudded with a mix of confusion and an inkling of fear. His eyes opened and met mine and I saw the vulnerability they usually hid. "Is this about us? Don't you want to marry me?" My voice broke, revealing the chasm of my insecurities.

Kaelan sat up swiftly, his movements sharp with sudden energy. His eyes blazed, a stark contrast to the weary man who had just lain beside me. "What are you talking about, Vale?" he asked, his voice thick with an emotion I couldn't quite identify.

I looked away, a part of me wanting to retreat from his gaze. The truth I'd been trying to skirt around pressed against the inside of my chest, an ache that had been silent until now. I'd meant to reassure him, to be the rock against the current for once, but instead, I'd laid bare my deepest apprehension, one that had taken root in the shadows of my heart the moment Thalion and Aerion had made their extraordinary, complex proposal.

The hunger in Kaelan's eyes held a gravity that stilled the room as he tilted my chin up so my eyes met his. "Vale, don't think for a second that I would ever stop wanting you. Nothing could change that. Your soul is joined with mine and it would have to be ripped out of me before I could ever stop loving you, craving you, aching for you."

The intensity in Kaelan's voice echoed through the room, through the air I breathed. I was rooted to the spot, struck silent as his confession unfurled, raw and vehement. My name on his lips was a whisper, but the meaning behind it thundered like a storm. The ache I had been carrying swelled within me, acknowledging his words and recognizing their profound truth.

"Kaelan," I managed, my whisper a fragile sound in the vastness of all that went unsaid, my heart throbbing with fear, love, and an intense relief that cascaded through me, pooling in the space where my heart beat a frantic rhythm.

"And I'm not afraid to admit that I want to spend the rest of my life with you, Vale, however long or short that may be," he continued, the strain of unguarded affection in his voice drawing my gaze to the blaze in his eyes. "I just wish they had waited for me to ask you first. After everything, the uncertainty and the waiting, I wanted to get there first."

His confession cut through the silence, each word etched into the space between us, an invisible script of longing and regret. I could feel the flutter of countless unsaid words in my chest, a flurry of responses caught in the web of my throat. "Oh," was all I managed, a feeble response to the immensity of his emotions laid before me.

"Vale," Kaelan murmured, his hands cupping my face as if he were holding something precious, something irreplaceable. The gentleness in his touch was a stark contrast against the fervor in his voice earlier. "You're it for me. And if you're willing, I'd like to spend the rest of my life with you. I want to marry you. Now, tomorrow, whenever you'll have me."

A laugh bubbled up within me, breaking through the tension, a release valve for the overwhelming sensation that threatened to capsize me. "That's not a proper proposal, though." The words were playful, but they carried the weight of my overflowing heart, threatening to break into a sob of joy.

His response was a smile so bright and genuine it felt as if it could banish the shadows from every corner of the world, a smile that spoke of futures and promises. "Marry me, Vale, and I'll make up for that with a thousand proper proposals."

"A thousand?" I asked, the absurdity a light note in the gravity of our conversation.

"Maybe a few less," he conceded, a playful twinkle in his eye as the corners of his mouth lifted further.

"A few hundred should suffice, I'd say," I suggested, grounding myself in the moment, in the man before me, and in the future we might share.

"Then a few hundred you'll have," Kaelan vowed, his demeanor shifting to a solemn pledge. He took a deep breath and let it out, a release of pent-up anxiety. "I'm sorry. For being an ass."

"Yes," slipped from my lips, but his confusion at my prompt reply was evident in the furrow of his brow.

"I'm an ass, I know," he repeated, misunderstanding.

"No," I clarified, laughing, my heart light. "You asked, and my answer is yes. Of course, I'll marry you."

His expression transformed into a joy so radiant it was almost blinding. "Really?" he exhaled, the word a breath, a hope, a prayer answered.

My nod was my vow, my smile a testament to the certainty that filled me. His lips met mine in a kiss that was a seal of our intentions, a gentle, yet fervent affirmation of the bond we shared. When we parted, it was only so he could express his gratitude, "Thank you," the words a mirror to my soul.

"I want this, Kaelan. I want you, I want a future with

you, and the thought of marrying you... It's overwhelming and terrifying and wonderful, all at once." My admission was honest, the words spilling forth with a sincerity that matched his own.

"Vale," he said, his voice a husky counterpoint to the silence that had fallen upon us. Yet, his gaze never faltered, his eyes steadfast. And then his lips were once again on mine, a kiss that was a testament to his joy. His gratitude, whispered against my skin, was met with the fullness of my own, a mirror to the thankfulness that swelled in my heart.

NINE

Kaelan's breath was a warm whisper against the sensitive skin of my neck, sending a trail of goose-bumps cascading down my spine as he murmured, "I love you." Those three words, soft and full of longing, were more than a mere statement; they were a sacred promise, a pledge of eternal devotion. "I've never known anything as certain as my love for you, Vale." His voice was the most sincere melody to my ears, the sound of unwavering conviction.

His hands were everywhere as he pulled me closer, lifting me effortlessly into his lap. His arms entangled me, solid and reassuring. The world beyond his embrace ceased to exist as he held me.

"You're all I'll ever need, little witch. You're my queen, my best friend, my everything." Each title he bestowed upon me was a gem, a crown of endearment placed upon my head. "Whatever you choose, whatever path you take, I'm yours." His voice was a reverent whisper. "I want you to have the life you deserve. A family, a future, and the freedom to choose. I want to share that with you."

The dam within me broke at his declaration, and my own words tumbled out, eager and unrestrained. "I love you, too, Kaelan. Forever. There is no life for me without you in it. You are my home, the one thing I am certain of. I know that you will always be with me no matter where I am or what I become." I said. The love I felt for him was a living thing, a force that demanded release, and with every word spoken, I felt as if I were shedding the layers of my soul for him to see.

I could no longer resist the intoxicating pull between us. My hands reached for him, grasping his face, pulling him towards me with a need that transcended desire. Our lips met in a kiss that was a dance of flames, a fusion of passion and adoration. I poured every ounce of my love into that kiss, hoping to bridge the gap between heart and expression, striving to convey the immensity of my devotion.

Kaelan's response was immediate, his arms tightening around me. His hands pressed me closer, his fingers splaying across my back. "I know," he whispered against my lips, a murmur that filled the spaces between heartbeats. "Your soul speaks to mine, Vale." It was an acknowledgment of the deep connection that thrummed between us, a bond that needed no words, no visible signs, to affirm its existence.

His lips found mine once more with a hunger that mirrored my own. His hand, firm and guiding, slid up my back, tracing the column of my spine with a featherlight touch. I wrapped my arms around his neck, holding him to me, my fingers threading through his hair and clutching at him with a desperation born from a place of love so deep it was almost terrifying. Our kiss deepened, a crescendo of longing that bound us together, heart and soul, in the silent vows we made with each touch, each breath, each heartbeat.

"Mine," Kaelan's voice was a velvet growl as his sharp teeth grazed the tender flesh of my neck, his lips barely brushing my skin, sending a quiver of anticipation through me. The sensation was enough to coax a sharp gasp from my lips, a reflexive intake of breath that was part declaration, part surrender.

"Yours," I said, the word an ardent echo of his claim, my hands urging him closer. He yielded to the silent command. The solidity of his body against mine was a testament to the word spoken between us, a physical manifestation of the bond we shared.

"I need you," I confessed with a breath, the whisper a blend of vulnerability and longing. Kaelan's eyes captured mine, twin infernos that blazed with an intensity that set my pulse racing, the depth of his desire mirrored in his gaze.

"Tell me what you want, Vale," he coaxed, his voice husky, a whisper that could have melted stone.

"I want you," the plea tumbled from me, raw and unrestrained, my entire being aflame with want, with the need to feel him, to be as close as two people could possibly be.

"Show me," he challenged, his smirk a playful edge to the smoldering heat in his eyes, a mixture of mischief and promise that spurred me into action.

"I'll show you," I promised, my voice steady despite the desire raging within. I moved from the warm cradle of his lap, maneuvering him onto his back with a firm but gentle insistence, my hands pinning his arms above his head. The look of surprised delight that danced in his eyes was exhilarating, his grin unapologetic and full of anticipation. "You're going to enjoy this, aren't you?" I asked, a teasing lilt to my words, my heart dancing with the certainty of his pleasure.

"Immensely," came his breathless admission, the chuckle that followed vibrating against my skin, a tantalizing hint of the pleasure we would find in each other's arms.

"Good," I responded. With deliberate slowness, I raised to my knees and began pulling off my clothes, allowing each piece of clothing to fall away from my skin, feeling his gaze upon me like a caress. His eyes followed every curve of my now bare body, an artist admiring his muse, hunger etched in every line of his face.

I straddled his waist, my hands deft as they pulled his shirt over his head. When freed, his hands were immediately on me, their paths over my skin, leaving trails of heat in their wake. His grip on my hips was possessive, drawing me closer, the strength in his touch a testament to his barely restrained passion.

I leaned forward, my lips finding his in a kiss that felt like the first and the last all at once. I savored him—the taste, the scent, the very essence of Kaelan that was uniquely his. The heat from his bare chest seared my palms, his heart's rhythm beckoning to me, promising more if I dared to dip deeper. My tongue traced his lips before delving inside, and he responded with a low moan.

Vale," he breathed, his voice a ragged edge against the night. "I want you, now."

"Patience, my demon prince," I whispered back, a gentle reprimand laced with promise, my hand venturing down, tracing the contours of his well-defined chest and abdomen before slipping into the waistband of his pants to encircle him. The feel of him, hard and ready, in my grasp was a power that sent an electric thrill through me.

With a deft squeeze, I felt his body respond, his hips bucking instinctively, seeking more of the exquisite friction my hand provided. His eyelids fluttered shut, his expression one of agonizing pleasure. "Oh, don't tease me," the words were barely more than a breath, a plea laced with desperation and desire.

"Patience," I whispered again, a smile playing on my lips as I applied gentle pressure, a promise of what would come before letting go, leaving a void he was desperate to fill.

His eyes snapped open, the irises darkening to stormy pools of desire. The sound that emerged from him was elemental, a growl of pure, unadulterated want. It was a sound that spoke to something primal within me, igniting a fire that promised to consume us both. I knew, at that moment, that we were both utterly lost to the passion that we stoked in each other.

"If you keep testing my self-control like this, I might just have to teach you a lesson, little witch," Kaelan warned, the tone of his voice roughened by the edge of his arousal. His words carried the weight of a threat, but the fire in his gaze, the unbridled desire that danced in his eyes, belied any true notion of reprimand.

"Is that a fact?" I teased, my voice a sultry whisper as I slid down the length of his powerful legs. My fingers hooked into the waistband of his pants, pulling them along in my descent. "You wouldn't dare follow through with that threat." The challenge was clear in my tone, an invitation for him to prove me wrong.

"We'll just have to see, won't we?" he retorted, his reply sliced through by a sharp inhale as I bent to press a fervent kiss to the sensitive skin on the inside of his thigh. His body was a map of sensitivity that I navigated with deliberate intent, marking my journey with the touch of my lips.

"Yes, we will," I confirmed, shifting my attention to his other thigh, mirroring the intimate act. The heat from his skin seared my lips and I could feel the powerful sinew of his muscles, rigid with the effort of maintaining control, a testament to the strain of his patience.

Lifting my gaze to his, I was met with a look so laden with primal need it was almost tangible, a mirror of the hunger that thrummed through my veins. "I'm not sure how much longer you can resist," I teased him.

"Don't stop," he urged, his hand descending to cradle my head, his fingers weaving through my hair with a gentle firmness.

I reached for him, my hand encircling the rigid length of him, giving a firm, yet gentle stroke that elicited a sharp inhale from his lips. I leaned in, my breath ghosting over him before I enveloped him with the warmth of my mouth.

"Vale," he choked out as my tongue danced over him, teasing the sensitive tip.

I hummed softly in my throat as I welcomed him deeper, the sound vibrating against his flesh. I was deliberate, setting an exquisitely slow rhythm, my hands on his thighs guiding the motion, anchoring myself as I drew him in further until he met the back of my throat.

"By the gods, Vale," he groaned, his hand flexing in my hair, his body taut with the effort to remain still. The sensation of my mouth, warm and enveloping, seemed to be his undoing. "The way you use your mouth..."

I felt him pulse and twitch with every motion and with gentle pressure, I swallowed around him, a move that seemed to wrack his body with a tremor of ecstasy. He bucked involuntarily, a silent plea for more of the sweet torment I was administering.

After a few moments, his grip on my hair tightened, and he tugged, urging me to look up at him. "Fuck," he swore, his voice strained, "as much as I'm enjoying this, I need to be inside you."

The confession struck me like lightning, leaving a trail of goosebumps in its wake. I slid away, guiding his length from the warmth of my lips. Kaelan's groan was a low sound of protest, his yearning for continued connection evident in the raw edge of his voice.

"As you wish," I said with a soft murmur and began a slow ascent along his body, each movement deliberate, letting the curves and valleys of my form graze against the taut canvas of his flesh. His strong arms encased me, the world flipping as he moved us, his body now a protective expanse above me. The muscles in his shoulder taunt as he leaned over me.

"Mine," he declared with primal certainty. His gaze swept over me with an unbridled hunger. I lay beneath him, fully exposed, my body and soul bared for his eyes to claim.

"Yes," came my response, a fervid whisper, echoing his sentiment as flames of desire licked at my insides, fanned by the depth of his claim. His mouth descended upon mine in a storm of passion, his lips an onslaught of need, pressing against mine with a desperate urgency that left me gasping.

"Mine," he uttered once more into our kiss, his teeth lightly catching my lower lip, an exquisite pressure that hinted at the fire of his emotions.

"Always," I whispered into the heated air between us, my heart pounding a thundering rhythm against my chest.

His hands were insistent as they journeyed lower, strong fingers wrapping around my thighs, urging them to yield under his touch.

Breaking our kiss, his gaze locked onto mine, the depth of his eyes like the night itself. "Show me," he commanded, the raw edge of his voice sending a thrill straight to my core. "I want to see you touch yourself."

A current of arousal surged through me, potent and direct. Without a second thought, my hand trailed down, my fingers finding the slick center of my desire. As I caressed myself, the warmth of his intense gaze amplified every sensation.

"Like this?" My question was a throaty tease, seeking his approval.

"Exactly like that," he answered, his voice velvet, as his own hand mirrored mine, stroking himself with a firm grip. The sight of him, so powerful and yet so enraptured, sent tremors of pleasure radiating through me.

As he watched, I was unable to restrain myself, my hand working faster, seeking the release I knew was within reach. The pleasure was a storm, gathering and threatening to overtake me. I gasped, the sound a mix of desire and desperation.

Kaelan growled, the sound a blend of frustration and restraint. The primal urge in his voice was evident, his self-control tested as he watched me with hungry eyes.

I writhed, my hips rising to meet my fingers, seeking the sweet release that hovered just beyond my reach. My eyes squeezed shut, my focus solely on the mounting pleasure, my breathing rapid and shallow.

"Perfect," he praised, his voice laced with desire as I continued to touch myself. "Show me how you make yourself come."

His encouragement was potent. The tension within me spiraled tighter, a coil ready to spring free. "I'm close," I managed to utter, the world narrowing to the point of exquisite pressure where my fingers danced.

"Keep going," he commanded, and my motions became more insistent, my fingers plunging inside me. The buildup of pleasure was swift and fierce. My body responded, my back arching, seeking more of that delicious friction.

"That's it, Vale," he encouraged, his breath hitching as his pace quickened in response.

"Open your eyes," he demanded, his tone edged with the effort of his restraint. "I want to see your face when you come."

My eyes snapped open to meet his and the world narrowed to the electricity that leapt between us.

I cried out his name as the dam broke, pleasure cascading over me in relentless waves, each one a pulsating echo of my cry. I was lost in the rapture, each wave an intense pleasure that seemed to echo in the depths of his own eyes.

"That's it," he echoed, his hand a blur as he rode the tide of my release with me, his gaze never leaving my face, drinking in every detail of the moment he had orchestrated.

As the last quivers of my climax ebbed away, he wasted no time in shifting the balance of our embrace. With a fluid motion, he pulled me up and flipped onto his back, positioning me astride him. His voice, heavy with desire, left no room for uncertainty. "Now, ride me," came the imperative, a gentle but firm command as his hands found my hips.

Guided by his touch, I felt the insistent pressure of him at my entrance. With a shared breath, I descended slowly, the sensation of enveloping him entirely drew a prolonged moan from me. He filled me completely, the intimate stretch a delicious blend of pleasure and a sweet ache that pulsed through my very core.

"Fuck," Kaelan's curse was a prayer to the carnal gods, his gaze locked onto where we joined, watching as he entered me. "Vale," he breathed, a raw exclamation that echoed through the thick air. The look in his eyes was untamed, a storm of desire swirling in their depths. This transcended the mere act of sex; this was reverent adoration, this was worship.

I began to move, rolling my hips, finding a slow, steady rhythm. The motion was languorous at first, an exploration of sensation and a savoring of the moment. His response was immediate, a hiss of pure approval escaping him as his hands gripped me, silently pleading for more.

"Faster, baby," he said between clenched teeth, his grip on my waist both a plea and a direction. I obliged, surrendering to the crescendo of sensation that demanded release.

"Gods, you're beautiful," he groaned, the words falling from his lips like a worshiper at an altar. His hands were everywhere, claiming me, a testament to his words—palms cupping my breasts, fingers trailing down to assert ownership of my curves, driving me closer to madness.

"Harder," slipped from my lips, a plea for him to take me, to own me in the most primal of ways. His growl was visceral, a sound of pure animalistic intent as he once again grabbed me and flipped me over, his body hovering over mine.

His arms became my cage, a delicious prison of muscle. "I want you to remember this," he said, his voice a rough whisper that caressed my ears and burrowed into my memory as he thrust into me. "I want you to feel me, inside and out, whenever you think of marrying me." His declaration was intense, his eyes searing into mine with an intensity that could set the world aflame.

"Kaelan," his name escaped as a gasp, an invocation that seemed to trigger a deeper force within him. His movements became more deliberate. Each thrust a claim, a statement of possession that edged me closer to a precipice I was all too willing to tumble over.

"I want to feel you come," his breath was a heated stroke against my skin, and his hand reached up to wrap around my throat. "Give me everything, Vale."

"I'm yours," I declared amidst the crescendo of my rising pleasure, a vow of my own as the world narrowed to the sensation of him moving within me, taking me to the precipice of another earth-shattering release.

In a moment of raw, unfiltered passion, his mouth found the tender skin of my neck. The sharp sensation of his teeth sinking in was a catalyst, sending me shattering over the edge.

My body bucked, my cries mingling with the rhythm of his name. "Kaelan," my voice broke on the wave of overwhelming bliss, the world blurring into a tapestry of white-hot intensity.

He kept up his relentless rhythm, an unyielding force that propelled us through the storm of my climax. Each powerful thrust was a testament to the depth of our connection, an echo of the passion that bound us, leaving me gasping, clinging to him as the pleasure threatened to sweep me away.

"Vale," Kaelan's voice broke through the heated silence, his tone a rasp of pure ecstasy. The transformative expression of bliss etched upon his features was unmistakable as he edged toward the pinnacle of pleasure. His body's movements lost their measured rhythm, giving way to an unrestrained urgency. "Fuck, I'm going to—"

"Do it," my own voice was a heated whisper, my breaths coming in short, rapid bursts. I arched beneath him, my legs wrapping around his waist, drawing him impossibly deeper, a silent encouragement for him to delve into the depths of his abandon.

A primal growl erupted from the depths of his throat as he plunged into me with a final, decisive motion, and I felt him shudder, his essence spilling into me in hot, pulsating waves. His grip on my hips was a fierce assertion of the passion that overwhelmed him, a pressure that was almost bruising.

"Gods," he moaned, a raw sound that filled the room, resonating with the aftermath of our shared intensity. His breaths came in ragged gasps, his body collapsing on top of me.

The comfort of his body against mine was a familiar thrill, a soothing balm that followed the storm of our passion. I wrapped my arms around him, my fingers tracing the muscles of his back, delighting in the contours I'd come to know so well.

With a gentle roll, he shifted and pulled me into his arms. His breath was hot against the crook of my neck, his nose nestling into the space as though it were made for him. "You're perfect, you know that, right?" His voice was soft, a whisper that spread warmth through my chest.

"And you're insatiable," I teased in response, the joy bubbling inside me manifesting as a bright smile across my lips. The truth of my words was light, a playful acknowledgment of our shared happiness.

His chuckle vibrated against me, a sound that hinted at contentment and a touch of amazement. His fingers drew aimless patterns on my skin, every touch was a word in the language only we spoke.

"Maybe," he conceded with a note of playful confession. "But only for you, little witch."

Turning to meet his eyes, I found myself lost in their depths. There, in the clear windows to his soul, I saw the unwavering truth of his words, the love that shone as brightly as the stars themselves. "I'll never get tired of this, of you," I confessed.

"Neither will I," he whispered back, a soft brush of his breath against my lips as he drew me closer still.

As his arms tightened around me, a serene contentment washed over me, as soothing as the calm after a storm. With my eyes closed, I savored the embrace, the shared warmth, the tranquil rhythm of his heartbeat against mine.

For now, in the quiet after our passion, nothing else mattered. The chaos of the world beyond the walls of our sanctuary was a distant, inconsequential murmur. All that was real, all that had substance, was the man whose heart beat in unison with mine, and the love that tethered us together.

And it was more than enough—it was everything.

TEN

The world was hushed, painted in the serene hues of early morning. As my eyes fluttered open, I found myself still nestled securely in Kaelan's embrace. His arms were a comforting fortress around me, his chest a steady pillow for my head.

"You're awake," his voice was a low, husky murmur, the sound of a man who had battled with slumber and found himself on the losing side.

"Yes," I replied, my voice just as scratchy with remnants of rest. "And so are you, it seems." The stillness of the room felt sacred, a sanctuary from the rest of the world. We stayed awake late into the night, exploring each other with our hands and mouths. Lost in each other and the moments we stole as we hid away from the rest of the world.

"I couldn't sleep, not while you were dreaming." His voice had a curious note, a thread of something unreadable woven through his words.

"Dreaming?" I asked, trying to rake through the scattered remnants of my sleep-clouded memory.

"Yes. You were... talking in your sleep." His fingers were

light on my arm, a touch meant to comfort, perhaps to reassure me.

"What did I say?" My pulse quickened. It was rare for me to speak during dreams, and when I did, it often meant that the dreams were significant, echoes of my subconscious, or perhaps premonitions.

He hesitated, the silence stretching out between us. "You were talking about a choice and about a path."

I bolted upright, my heart now a frantic drummer setting a staccato beat against my ribs. "I don't remember any of it," I said, my voice a thread of sound in the quiet room.

"Maybe it'll come back to you," Kaelan's hand lifted to brush a strand of hair away from my face, a tender gesture that belied the concern etching his brow.

"Did I say anything else? Anything specific?" I pressed, hoping for a clue, a key to unlock the meaning of the dreams that had evidently stirred my lips to speech.

"No, not really. But you kept repeating 'a choice' over and over again." His gaze held mine, searching, perhaps hoping to find answers in my eyes that my words had not provided.

I delved into the fog of my mind, trying to grasp the dream that was already dissolving like mist at sunrise. "At least I didn't have any nightmares and I didn't slip back into the dream realm somehow," I mused aloud, a faint attempt to lighten the shadow of unease that had settled over me.

"Vale," Kaelan's tone shifted, carrying a weight that instantly commanded my attention. "We should talk about the future, your future. It's clear now more than ever that you've got choices to make, paths to choose from, and you're obviously worried. Let me help you."

I felt the magnitude of his words settle on my shoulders like a cloak. He was right, and the thought of what lay before me was daunting. The paths of my life were not simply roads in a forest; they were akin to the branching ways of fate itself.

"I don't even know where to start," I confessed, the admission an exhale of truth. "There are so many things to consider."

"Well, I can't claim to have all the answers," Kaelan's thumb traced the tender skin of my neck, ghosting over the mark he left there that was both a token of passion and a symbol of his claim. "But I think I can help."

The certainty in his voice was soothing to my frayed nerves. Here, in the quiet of the pre-dawn hours, with the man I trusted more than any other, I allowed myself to believe that the answers I sought were within reach.

The caress of his thumb against the sensitive mark on my neck coaxed a smile onto my lips. In the soft light of early morning, his touch was both soothing and seductive, stirring a longing within me.

"I'm listening," I said, my voice a low purr. The seriousness of his approach to our future was endearing, especially given the usual fierceness that defined him.

"As your future husband, my first priority is your happiness, of course," Kaelan's voice was earnest and his words, weighted with the promise of a shared future, wrapped around me like a vow.

The word 'husband' sparked a ripple of delight that I couldn't entirely suppress. The smirk that found its way onto my lips was a testament to the surreal quality of it all. Marrying a demon—how had my life taken such an extraordinary turn?

"That's very noble of you, demon prince," I teased, the

term 'prince' emphasized with a playful hint of sarcasm.

Our moment, however, was abruptly ruptured by a knock on the door. I sent Kaelan a swift, questioning glance, my heartbeat quickening just a notch at the unexpected interruption.

"Who is it?" I asked, shifting upright.

"It's us," came Thalion's voice from the other side of the door.

"Come in," I called, pulling the blanket up to cover my chest.

The door swung open to reveal Aerion and Thalion. "Sorry to interrupt," Aerion announced, his voice carrying a knowing smirk that matched the twist of his lips as the two Fae males entered the room. His gaze, too clever by half, suggested he understood exactly what kind of scene he had intruded upon. "But we have some news."

"Oh? What is it?" I asked, sitting up straighter and pulling the blankets with me.

Kaelan, however, seemed unfazed by our lack of attire or the sudden appearance of the two Fae males. He stretched lazily, arms resting behind his head, the picture of contentment and ease. His arms settled behind his head, his muscles flexing subtly—a silent exhibition of relaxed confidence. The smug look on his face hinted at a secret.

Both Aerion and Thalion seemed momentarily distracted, their eyes drawn to Kaelan. The smirk that played on Kaelan's face was one of undisguised triumph, a silent, challenging communication between them that I wasn't fully privy to but could guess at.

Thalion's voice, usually so measured and calm, took on a thread of irritation as he finally broke the silence. "What are you smirking about?" he asked, his eyebrow raised at Kaelan's uncharacteristically boyish display.

Kaelan's response was immediate and unabashed, his smug satisfaction spreading across his face like the first break of dawn. "We had sex, a lot of it," he announced, his gaze fixed firmly on the two men who had walked into our private aftermath. "It was glorious. You should've seen her, she was magnificent. And those noises she makes..." He trailed off with a wistful sigh.

A warmth that had nothing to do with the blankets spread across my cheeks and I was grateful for the cover that hid most of my burning face. Despite the flush of embarrassment, there was an undeniable zing of triumph buzzing through me at his words. To be spoken of with such admiration, even if boastfully, sent a contradictory surge of embarrassment and pleasure through my veins.

"Kaelan!" I couldn't keep the scandalized hiss from escaping as I reached out to swat at his arm, my hand connecting with his skin in a reprimand that lacked any real force.

"What? They wanted to know. Besides, they can see the evidence on your neck." His gaze dropped to the mark he'd left there, his smirk widening into a grin that showcased an almost predatory satisfaction.

I groaned, feeling like I was grappling with a child gloating over a game well played, rather than a demon prince. "It's not a competition, Kaelan," I said.

"Clearly, because I'm winning." His voice held a triumphant tone as he continued. "Out of everyone here who asked you to marry them last night, I'm the only one you said yes to."

"It. Is. Not. A. Competition." I punctuated each word with another smack to his arm, no longer amused at his teasing.

But Kaelan wasn't bothered. Seizing my wrist, he

turned the reprimand into a tender gesture, his lips pressing a kiss into the palm of my darkened hand. His eyes, filled with mischief, met mine. "If you say so, little witch," he said, his voice rich with fondness, still grinning like a rogue claiming victory in a game only he was playing.

Aerion's eyes rolled skyward in a gesture that was equal parts amusement and disbelief, but the faint smile tugging at the corner of his mouth betrayed his true feelings. "I can't believe I'm about to say this," he began, a mock sigh prefacing his words as if he were about to divulge a great secret, "but I'm happy for you." The sincerity was there beneath the layers of teasing and camaraderie that defined our relationship. Thalion nodded in agreement, if a little reluctantly.

Their congratulations, though unexpected, sparked a warmth within me, and I couldn't help but smile. "Thank you," I replied, my gratitude genuine.

"As fun as this is," Thalion cut in, a hint of annoyance lacing his words. "We did actually have some news."

"Right, of course," I responded, a flicker of curiosity lighting up my thoughts. "What is it?"

"There is a child here," Aerion announced, his statement short and lacking detail, yet it struck a chord of urgency.

"A child?" I echoed, seeking the clarity that was not offered.

"A girl, no more than ten, appeared at the gates this morning," Thalion elaborated with a certain gravity. "She looked as though she had been through a great ordeal, she's war-torn and ragged. She's been asking for the First Witch."

Understanding dawned on me suddenly. "She wouldn't happen to be a witch?" I asked, the knowledge settling within me like a remembered truth I hadn't been conscious of knowing. The words came from some intuitive place within me.

"She claims to be," Aerion confirmed, his brow furrowing slightly. "Though if I were to judge, I wouldn't have taken her for one."

"And why is that?" I pressed, my instincts already aligning the pieces of a larger picture I had yet to see.

"Well, she had no magical abilities that I could sense," he admitted, his tone suggesting that this fact was a puzzle piece out of place. "She seems like a normal child. But she was very insistent on speaking with you."

"Okay, let me get dressed. Then we'll go to her." I said.

An idea formed in my mind and with a deliberate slowness, I stood and allowed the covers to slip from my grasp, descending like a whisper to pool at my feet. I stood there brazenly as all three pairs of eyes swept over me. My skin, flushed from their attention, was now exposed to the appreciative—and in Kaelan's case, possessive—gazes of the three men in the room.

I could feel their eyes on me as I walked toward the wardrobe, acutely aware of the power that my form held over them. Thalion and Aerion's gazes were heavy with unspoken words, a clear hunger etched in their expressions. Kaelan's stare, however, was tumultuous, a storm of desire and an unyielding claim that spoke volumes of his inner turmoil regarding the complexity of our relationships.

"Like what you see?" I called over my shoulder, my voice dripping with a playful seductiveness. The question was a playful taunt, delivered with a sultry wink that left them momentarily speechless. Their silent, enthralled nods were the answer I'd expected — and somewhere deep down, craved.

A small ripple of triumph washed through me, a secret

thrill in the power of my allure. It was fleeting but fierce and as I dressed, the fabric of my clothes felt like armor draping over skin still warm from their lingering looks.

The green dress I chose was one of understated elegance, its fabric whispering against my skin as I slid it over my head. The color, a rich shade reminiscent of the deep forest, complimented my complexion, adding a touch of royalty to my bearing. It was simple, yes, but the way it hugged my figure spoke of a quiet confidence, a strength that did not need the trappings of luxury to make its statement.

When I turned to face the trio, I caught their stares, heavy with desire. Their gazes traced the lines of the dress, the curve of my waist, the slope of my neck. "Ready when you are," I said, a playful challenge in my tone as I attempted to keep my expression neutral, to not betray the smug satisfaction I felt at their evident approval.

"Right," Aerion responded, a bit too hastily, his throat clearing as if to dislodge the image of my naked form from his mind.

We all filed out of the room after giving Kaelan time to dress, following Aerion's lead through the palace corridors toward the kitchens. Our footsteps echoed along the stone corridors, betraying our approach to the mystery waiting.

The kitchen was alive with the early hum of morning activity, but all motion seemed to cease as we entered. There she was, the child in question, a small cyclone contained in human form. Her hair was a riot of red curls, entangled with the debris of her travels. It was as if she carried the wildness of the woods with her, a little nymph lost in the civilization of stone and wood. She was devouring her food with the urgency of one who had known hunger too intimately. Her curls framed a face too young to wear such world-weariness.

"Here she is," Aerion declared, an unnecessary introduction to the feral scene before us.

She looked up, her eyes as blue as a clear sky, fixing on me with an intensity that belied her years. "There you are," she accused as though I'd been hiding from her on purpose, her voice carrying a rough edge of challenge and relief.

"I've been looking for you. The other witch told me to find you," she said with a dismissive wave of her hand before taking a large bite out of a chicken leg.

"You've been looking for me? What witch, exactly?" I asked. What witch could she possibly be talking about?

"Yes, I have. It wasn't easy, I can tell you that," she retorted, her youthful face scrunching up in a frown. "The First Witch, the other one—that's confusing, isn't it? How many firsts can there be? Anyway, she led me here, told me you'd help me."

Rowena had nudged this child towards me with her usual cryptic touch. "How do you know Rowena?" I asked, crouching down to her level, making my presence less daunting.

"Who's Rowena? Oh, is that her name?" the girl questioned, a dollop of chicken grease dripping down her chin. Impatiently, she shoved another piece of chicken into her mouth, speaking between bites.

"She came to me while I was dreaming, really rude too, cuz I was dreaming about a pie, great big blackberry one with the sugar on top. You got any of those?" The girl's gaze darted around the kitchen with the focused intensity of a predator seeking its prey — or, in her case, a particular pie.

"No, sorry," I replied, the corner of my mouth twitching

upwards despite the situation. "But Rowena came to you in a dream?"

"Yeah, she was all, 'The First Witch, you've gotta go, find her,' and stuff," the girl shrugged, as if such visitations were commonplace, as if being plucked from the world of dreams by a witch was nothing out of the ordinary.

Her words spun in the air, mingling with the scents of the kitchen, forming a question mark that lingered above us, invisible but insistently present. Rowena's hand in this was unmistakable and yet her motives were wrapped in layers of mystery, as they so often were. Here was a child, sent by a dream, carrying messages from a witch who knew the threads of fate better than anyone. What could it mean? And, more importantly, what was I to do about it?

As I watched her tear into another piece of bread, her cheeks puffing out like a chipmunk's, I knew that this small, unassuming girl had unknowingly stepped into a much larger world. And I, as the First Witch she sought, was now irrevocably a part of her story.

"What's your name, child?" I addressed her gently, leaning forward slightly to bridge the gap between us with an open and gentle demeanor. I wanted her to see me as an ally, someone she could trust.

"I'm not a child," she protested firmly, her face twisting into a scowl that seemed too severe for someone her age, wiping her hands on what remained of her tattered dress. "And my name is Aisling." Her tone was defiant, a clear declaration of self that demanded recognition beyond her apparent youth.

"Okay, Aisling," I responded, nodding with respect for her demand. My voice carried a tone of understanding and patience, an olive branch extending towards this fierce little being before me. "Why don't we get you cleaned up with a nice warm bath, and after that, we can sit down and talk more about why you're here? If it suits you, we can arrange some rooms for you close to mine."

Her posture relaxed slightly at the offer. "Yeah, okay," Aisling conceded with a casual shrug, the dirt of her travels seemingly of no concern to her until now. "A bath would be nice. I'm covered in... well, everything."

Her acceptance of the offer was as straightforward as her arrival had been mysterious. "I can see that," I observed, the edges of my lips curving into a small, amused smile at the sight of her — so wild, so remarkably undaunted by her surroundings or her company.

She stood up, her movements a blend of childlike grace and the weariness of a traveler far too experienced for her age. "Well, then, what are we waiting for?" She was suddenly all business, a miniature adult in the guise of a mud-splattered waif.

"Come on, child," Thalion said, stepping forward and holding out his hand to her. "I'll help you find a room."

Aisling's scowl returned momentarily, a flash of defiance. "Not a child," she corrected him firmly, but her small hand disappeared into his much larger one.

"Of course," Thalion conceded, a light chuckle escaping him. "Lead the way, not child."

"It's Aisling," she insisted.

"So you've said," Thalion agreed with a conspiratorial wink as they began to walk away.

"Right," she answered, and I detected a flicker of something new in her — a hint of bashfulness perhaps.

We watched them depart, the unlikely pair – the battle-hardened warrior and the small, muddy girl with fierce blue eyes. There was a moment of collective contemplation as we each absorbed the strangeness of the morning's turn.

"That was odd," Aerion finally voiced, breaking the silence, his brow furrowed in thought.

"Indeed," I echoed, my mind already turning with possibilities and concerns.

Kaelan, always direct, addressed the heart of the matter. "Do you think it's true? That the First Witch sent her to us?"

"I don't see any other explanation for it," I admitted, feeling the truth of my words deep in my bones. The likelihood of this being a mere coincidence was slim to none.

"Why would she do such a thing? Why not simply tell you about the girl before she got here?" Aerion mused.

"Because the future is a tricky thing," I thought aloud. "Rowena is probably trying to avoid altering events too directly. It's about balance — revealing too much can be as dangerous as knowing too little. But honestly, I'm not sure. That's the trouble with the future; it never unveils itself plainly."

"Yet, she has no doubt shown you yours," Kaelan pointed out, a subtle strain of concern lacing his voice. His observation was sharp, cutting to the heart of our shared worries. "And strapped you with another responsibility while doing so," he finished.

"She's given us another mystery to solve," I added.

We remained there for a moment longer, lost in our thoughts, until the practical matters of the day called us back from the realm of prophecy and what-ifs to the needs of the present. There would be time enough to ponder Rowena's motives. For now, we had a young girl to care for, a not-child named Aisling, who had come searching for the First Witch with nothing but a name and a message from a dream.

CHAPTER

ELEVEN

My thoughts churned, threatening to overwhelm me as we returned to my rooms. My mind was a landscape of uncertainties and tasks that seemed as insurmountable as the mountains. With each step, the list expanded: Aisling and the realization that I might no longer be the sole blood witch, the other witches I had yet to awaken, the elusive graveyard and the dream-walking Elowen, the hidden grimoire's secrets, and the perplexing entanglement of impending nuptials with three men, each unique in his love and expectations.

The heavy sigh escaped me before I could rein it in, a silent testament to the burden.

Aerion's touch was light on my shoulder, grounding, yet it did little to still the maelstrom within. "Are you alright, Vale?" His voice was steady, the undercurrent of concern evident.

"Yeah, just thinking. I have a lot on my mind." The understatement of the century, and yet what else could I say? Every moment seemed to unfurl more questions than answers.

"Is there anything we can do to help?" Aerion's question was genuine, an offer of support I longed to accept.

"Not unless you can read the future and figure out exactly what Rowena is up to," I said, attempting to mask my apprehension with humor. I desperately wanted it to be true—for one of us to have the answers that seemed just out of reach.

Aerion's smile was wry, a flicker of shared amusement. "Unfortunately, that's not one of my talents. If it were, perhaps I would've already known about this not-child and saved us the trouble."

His attempt to lighten the mood worked briefly. A chuckle bubbled up from somewhere deep inside, momentarily cutting through the dense fabric of my concerns. "It's not a talent of mine either, unfortunately."

"We will figure it out," he promised with an assuredness I desperately needed to believe.

Kaelan's sudden groan shattered the fragile veneer of calm. My head snapped toward him, my heart lurching as I saw him collapse to one knee. "Kaelan, what's wrong?" The distance between us closed in an instant, my hands reaching out, fear coiling in my gut.

"I don't know, I don't feel right," he gasped, his breathing labored, his face contorted in pain.

Aerion moved quickly to Kaelan's other side, placing a hand on his forehead. "He's burning up," he said, his voice laced with urgency.

But then the air shifted and the tension spiked. Aerion's touch seemed to ignite something feral within Kaelan. "Don't touch me, bastard!" Kaelan's words were a venomous lash, unexpected and shocking in their vitriol.

He stood suddenly, recoiling from Aerion's touch, his eyes alight with a fury I had never seen before. "Kaelan,"

My voice was a mix of alarm and confusion, my heart hammering against my ribs. This anger, this hostility, was alien coming from him.

"Back off, bitch, slither back to your Fae plaything," he snapped at me, his words like daggers, his gaze flitting between Aerion and me with raw hostility. My blood ran cold at the malice in his tone.

I stood, rooted in shock. "Kaelan, what the hell are you talking about?" The words spilled out, laced with a fear I couldn't contain. The man before me was a stranger. His familiar features twisted into a mask of rage and hatred that was unrecognizable. This wasn't him; the Kaelan I knew would never speak to me like this—would never look at me with such loathing.

Something was terribly wrong. This wasn't the man I knew, the man I had agreed to marry, the man I loved. This was someone else, something else. My mind raced, every sense on alert. We were in the heart of our stronghold, and yet I had never felt more uncertain, more threatened. What had taken hold of Kaelan?

It dawned on me with a sickening certainty that this was no mere fever. The curse we feared was manifesting, twisting his mind, turning him against those he loved. My mind raced for a solution, any spell or herb that might combat the darkness that had taken hold of him.

My mind whirled, a frantic rush of thoughts like birds startled into flight, but before I could reach out, before I could tether him with a word or a touch, he took off at a run. My heart lodged in my throat, panic clawing at its walls.

"No," the denial was a whisper torn from my lips, the starkness of his absence a void that yawned wide and deep.

"Vale," Aerion's voice cut through the fog of my shock,

his own unease unmistakable, "what in the seven realms is going on?"

My mind snapped into focus, my voice finding strength despite the chaos. "It's a lot to explain, but I'm pretty sure he's been cursed," I confessed, the horror of the situation unfurling like a dark flag within my mind.

"Nyxen," I called, desperation sharpening my call into a command. Like a wraith, my familiar, the embodiment of night itself, emerged. "Nyxen, can you follow Kaelan?"

"Yes," came the simple yet powerful affirmation. He dashed ahead and I followed without a second thought, the hem of my dress catching and tearing on the stonework as we flew through the castle. Aerion was a steady presence behind me, his determination a silent promise that I was not alone in this.

Our pursuit led us upward, winding through the castle's veins until we emerged atop a desolate tower. There stood Kaelan, a solitary figure against the sprawling canvas of the sky, his body taut with an anguish that was almost tangible.

"Kaelan," I called to him, my voice stretched tight with fear and hope.

There was no response, no sign he heard me. But I drew closer, compelled by a need as vital as the beat of my heart. My hand reached out, grazing his back with the gentlest of touches. The tremor that passed through him was a knife to my heart.

"Kaelan, it's me, it's Vale," I coaxed, trying to infuse my words with all the calm and love I could muster.

His response was a shattered whisper, a sound that threatened to break me. "I'm sorry, Vale."

Guilt and fear warred within me as I coaxed him to face me. When he did, the sorrow in his eyes, the tear that traced his cheek, was a reflection of the battle raging inside him.

His words were a hushed confession, each word a shard of glass. "I don't know what came over me. I felt more like a demon than I have in a long time."

"It's alright, it wasn't you," I soothed.

He shook his head, a silent plea for me to understand the depths of his turmoil. "But it was, Vale," he countered, a confession of his darkest fears. "That darkness, that rage, it was a part of me once..."

His admission was a weight, but I refused to let it pull us down. "Shh, don't worry about that now," I said with gentle urgency, taking his hand, feeling the tremor of his skin against mine. "We'll figure it out. We'll get through this together, I promise," I assured him, repeating the words he had said to me so often.

Kaelan's hand was scorching beneath my fingertips, feverishly warm but no longer radiating the searing heat that had flared just moments before. There was a subtle tremor in his grasp, a testament to the battle raging within.

"Vale," Aerion's voice was a gentle intrusion, a whisper that seemed almost invasive in the intimacy of our silent exchange. "We should get him inside, where it's safe."

My head moved in a nod, the gesture mechanical, my gaze still locked on Kaelan. His groan sliced through the air, a sound of pure agony that wrenched my heart. "Vale, I'm burning," the words sizzled with his pain, and the raw fear in his eyes was a mirror to my own dread.

"I know," the words were barely audible, even to my own ears. "Let's go downstairs; we'll find a way to make it better." I hoped the conviction in my tone was enough to mask the uncertainty that gnawed at me.

With each of our arms around Kaelan, lending him our

strength, we descended the stairs with painstaking slowness back to my rooms.

Once inside my rooms, the door thudded shut, a definitive sound that seemed to seal us away from the rest of the world. Aerion's eyes met mine, a storm of concern swirling in their depths. "Vale, what's going on?" he asked, seeking an understanding that I was still piecing together myself.

I recounted the events in the library quickly, the words tumbling out in a torrent of worry and speculation. "It has to be the curse," I stated firmly, the pieces of the puzzle locking into a terrifying picture. "There's no other explanation."

Aerion absorbed this, his expression turning grave. "We have to do something. He can't stay like this and who knows how much it will spread through him."

The cold clasp of dread was a vise around my heart. "I know," I echoed, a silent vow that I would not let this curse consume him.

Kaelan's voice, though frayed with pain, carried a thread of steely resolve. "I can handle it, Vale," he insisted.

I turned to him, my gaze soft yet fierce. "You shouldn't have to," I insisted, gripping his hand with a strength born of desperation. "I'll figure it out for you, Kaelan."

My gaze flicked to Aerion. "Take care of him, watch him. I'm going to the library to see what I can find on curses." There was no room for argument in my voice.

His nod was all the confirmation I needed. "Of course."

With gratitude a tight lump in my throat, I whispered, "Thank you." I turned away, leaving them with a lingering look that carried all the worry I felt.

I paused just outside the door, the stillness of the corridor a stark contrast to the tumult within me. "Rowena?" I called into the silence, invoking the name of the First Witch, a plea for guidance, for an answer, for any semblance of understanding.

The silence that followed was as empty as a crypt, filled only by a sorrowful breeze that whispered across my skin, a spectral touch that offered no answers.

"Well, fine, don't talk to me then," I muttered under my breath, frustration biting at each word. My feet carried me towards the library, each step a declaration of my intent to unravel this curse that dared to lay its shadow upon us. The ancient tomes held secrets and I was determined to coax them into the light.

The library door swung open with a vengeance, nearly rebounding on its hinges as I stormed in, my presence akin to a tempest threatening to spill books from their shelves. "I need a book," I declared, my voice a crack of thunder, my patience as frayed as the edges of the most well-thumbed volumes.

Before the echo of my command had faded, an imposing tome tumbled from a higher shelf, landing with a definitive thud on the floor. "That had better be the one I need," I warned the library itself, my gaze sharp enough to slice through the dimness as I stalked toward the fallen book.

From her nook, Harker looked up, her features alight with the soft glow of the lamp by her side. "What's wrong, Vale?" she asked, her eyes narrowing at the storm clouds gathered in my gaze.

"Kaelan is sick," I spoke tersely as I reached for the book, my fingers brushing its leather surface with the barest hint of dread. "Or rather, cursed. He's behaving irrationally and was just teetering on the roof's edge."

Her eyes widened, "Is he alright?"

"For now. But this curse needs breaking before he's lost to us," I said, my voice hardened by urgency. "Can you help me find a spell or something?"

"Of course," she responded, rising to her feet. Her gaze then dropped to the book cradled in my arms. "What's that?" she asked.

"This was waiting for me, dropped off by the library itself," I said. "Hopefully it's helpful."

"Well, let's see what's in it," she said, her curiosity piqued.

We settled at the table and as I turned to the title page, my hope faltered, plunging into an abyss. "This isn't about curses," I murmured, my voice a mere wisp of despair.

"What is it?" Harker leaned in, her eyes scanning the ancient script.

"It's a compendium on the history of demons," I said, the words leaving a bitter taste. "Why would this be of any use now?"

Her gaze met mine. "Perhaps the library knows more than we do. Could there be a link between the curse and the old tales of demons?" Harker mused, her analytical mind already sifting through possibilities. "If the library deems it pertinent, it might hold the key we're overlooking."

With a deep, steadying breath, I steeled myself. "Right," I conceded, my resolve hardening. We had been given a direction, albeit an obscure one, and I was determined to follow it through.

"We'll start at the beginning," Harker declared with the tenacity of a seasoned scholar. Her eyes sparkled with the challenge. "There's bound to be a thread we can follow, a clue to unravel his curse."

I couldn't help but feel a thread of skepticism weave

through me. "I hope you're right," I replied, though I was still uncertain.

We leaned into the book, our world narrowing to the aged, crackling pages that turned beneath our fingers. The words spoke of ancient times, of the first demons called forth into our realm by rituals arcane and forbidden. Their presence on Earth was a story of nightmare and shadow, one that seemed all too real as Kaelan battled his own darkness.

"There's a wealth of history here," Harker observed, her finger tracing lines of ink as if she could divine secrets from their very shape.

"Yes, but it's not very helpful," I admitted, the edges of my patience fraying. Frustration was a luxury I couldn't afford, yet it clawed at me, eager to take hold. "I can't figure out how to use any of this for our needs."

"Don't give up," Harker said, her eyes never leaving the book. "Keep looking. There has to be something."

Drawing a deep breath, I tried to quell the impatience gnawing at me and turned to another page. My heart skipped a beat as I was met with an illustration so familiar it sent a chill down my spine. "That's Kaelan," I whispered, my mind grappling with the implications. This book was ancient, its origins lost to time, and yet here he was.

Harker leaned in, her curiosity alight. "What does it say?"

With a trembling hand, I read aloud, "It claims that Kaelan—referred to here as a demon prince, progeny of Azazel—was called forth from Erebus by a blood-born witch wishing to learn the secrets of the future. It speaks of a ritual that bound him to her will."

"That's... incredible," Harker murmured, the words

tinged with awe and a hint of dread. "To think he has such a history...I had no idea."

"Nor did I," I confessed, the revelation sending my thoughts into a whirlwind.

"Is there more about him?" Her question pulled me back to the book in my hands.

Turning the brittle pages, I scanned the text, my eyes catching on a passage that recounted a tale of betrayal and retribution. "Here it says the witch's grasp faltered. Kaelan, despite his chains, broke free and in his wrath left only ruin in his wake."

Harker frowned, the puzzle pieces not aligning in her mind. "But what does this have to do with the curse that afflicts him now?"

I closed the book with a thud, a cloud of dust rising like a specter from between the pages. Running my fingers through my hair, a gesture of exasperation, I grappled with the disjointed pieces of this puzzle. "I'm at a loss. It feels like we're chasing echoes instead of answers. Maybe it's time we redirected our efforts to the study of curses themselves."

Harker nodded, her gaze meeting mine with renewed purpose. "Let's do that. The answer is here, somewhere. We just need to find it."

I agreed with Harker's suggestion with a nod, feeling the weight of our task pressing on my shoulders. "Let's get to work," I replied firmly, mustering the composure needed to face the enormous shelves filled with ancient tomes and scrolls.

Harker was already in motion, her hands deftly choosing books from the shelf, her movements as familiar with the library's collection as a seasoned navigator charting a well-trodden course. The thumps of books being laid out before us were like drumbeats to battle.

"So, the story of Kaelan as the trapped demon prince, huh? That's interesting," Harker said, almost to herself, the glimmer of academic interest not entirely overshadowed by the urgency of our quest.

"And terrifying," I echoed, letting the full weight of my thoughts into my voice. "To think that Kaelan was once under the control of a witch, that someone might wield such influence over him again..."

An idea struck me, a theory forming from the shadows of possibility. The thought struck me like a thunderclap. "Harker, what if this curse is related to that ancient story? What if it's designed to revive Kaelan's darker nature for someone to harness? What if the Seven knew this would happen and orchestrated it?"

Harker considered this, her scholar's caution tempering the fear that was beginning to take root. "It's possible," she admitted. "But we're speculating wildly without proof."

I knew she was right, but I couldn't shake the feeling. "Why else would the library guide us to that story? It feels like the Seven might be playing a game we're just now joining."

"If that's the case," Harker said, her eyes serious and focused, "we need to uncover their strategy and fast."

"Right," I said, my determination bolstering my next words. "I'll ask the library for books specifically about curses."

We settled into our research with a renewed sense of purpose, our fingers flipping through pages with urgency. It wasn't long before I found something—a potion that could potentially buy us some time. I grabbed a notebook from the stack Harker had collected. My pen flew across the paper, listing ingredients and chants.

"What have you found?" Harker asked, peering over.

"It's a temporary measure—a potion to slow the curse's onslaught," I explained. "It's not a cure, but it could give us the time we need."

"That's great, Vale," she said.

I sighed, the heaviness of the situation settling on me once again. "Yeah, but it's only going to stall things. It won't rid him of the curse. Time is slipping through our fingers and with every minute that passes the curse will become harder to break ."

"You're right, but let's not get ahead of ourselves," Harker counseled. "We have to take this one step at a time."

"Okay," I replied, trying to tamp down the rising panic. "One step at a time."

TWELVE

WREN

Wren stood at the edge of the training grounds, his gaze fixed on the scene unfolding before him. The werewolves, formidable and agile, were engaged in a vigorous training exercise with the Fae troops, their movements a fluid dance of strength and precision. Wren, usually the heart of such activities, now observed from a distance, his posture relaxed yet alert, as if his body was ready to spring into action at any moment.

Beside him, Venna stood watch, her eyes tracking every move with an intensity that spoke of her dedication. Wren knew he was fortunate to have her. As his beta, she embodied a blend of vigilance and tenderness that was rare to find. She was the firm hand that guided the pack with a careful balance of discipline and compassion. When she spoke, she carried the weight of her responsibility lightly.

"Everyone is settled into their rooms," Venna informed him, her voice carrying over the clashing sounds of the training ground. "Vale has designated the third-floor kitchens and dining hall as ours; the whole floor is ours."

Wren merely nodded, his attention never wavering from the training exercise. Her words washed over him, bringing a semblance of peace to the responsibility-laden existence he had led. His eyes remained locked on his wolves, the warriors he had nurtured and trained. He felt a swell of pride at seeing them integrating so well with the Fae.

The wolves were taken care of, their welfare secured within the palace's stone walls. A new normal was dawning, one where the nightmarish uncertainty of their past was slowly being replaced with the solid predictability of routine.

Yet, as the dust swirled in the air, kicked up by the pounding of boots and paws, Wren felt an undercurrent of restlessness. What role was he to play now in this period of calm? The need to fight, to protect, to survive had been his guiding star for so long that its sudden dimming left him unsure.

He needed to talk to Vale. As the notion took root, Wren felt a path carve itself out before him. With the security of his pack ensured, he could now afford to turn his attention to helping her, to shift his priorities to whatever she deemed necessary. This luxury of choice was new and unfamiliar, yet it invigorated him.

With a slight tilt of his head, still lost in contemplation, Wren decided. He would seek out Vale. There were still dangers that loomed on the horizon, shadows that threatened the peace they were all desperately trying to maintain. If he could aid in fortifying their defenses or unraveling the mysteries that Vale wrestled with, then that was where he would be needed most.

Venna's gaze flickered toward him, noting the subtle shift in his demeanor. She knew him well enough to understand that the gears were turning in his mind, plotting a new course.

"Venna, keep them sharp," Wren said finally, his voice carrying the undercurrents of a new purpose. "I need to speak with Vale. There's more to be done and I intend to be of use."

Venna nodded, understanding the unspoken depth of his words. She watched him for a moment as he started to turn away, his silhouette a testament to the strength and determination that had carried their pack through dark times.

"I'll be back," Wren announced, his voice unwavering yet infused with an unmistakable hint of anticipation that sparked something akin to excitement in Venna's observant eyes. "Keep them focused. They've earned a good meal." The edges of his mouth curled into a brief, comforting smile that offered reassurance, an unspoken promise of his return.

He then pivoted on his heel, a decisive motion that carried him away from Venna and the training grounds. As he walked, the Fae soldiers instinctively cleared a path for him. Their glances lingered, a mixture of respect and curiosity, but Wren hardly noticed. His mind was already swirling with the multitude of challenges that awaited him, the same challenges that occupied every waking moment of Vale's thoughts.

Entering the castle's majestic main hall, his boots met the stone floor with a rhythmic assurance. Each step took him closer to Vale, to the heart of another storm they would weather together. He ascended the grand staircase with a familiar ease, each step taken with a purpose. He was well aware that Vale would initially resist his offer of assistance. Her nature to shoulder burdens alone was as much a part of her as her own shadow. Yet he also knew she needed him, perhaps now more than ever.

Through their partial blood bond, he could sense exactly where Vale was. Approaching the library's door, he announced his arrival with a courteous knock and then pushed the door open. His gaze immediately sought Vale, finding her trapped in a fortress of books and scrolls, the very picture of distressed concentration as she frowned down at a notebook she was scribbling in.

"Wren, what are you doing here?" Vale's surprise was swiftly replaced by a warmth that only his arrival could bring. She rose to hug him, a movement that seemed as natural to them as breathing.

"I'm here for you," he said, returning her hug, "whatever you need, I'm on it." He pulled back slightly, his eyes scanning her face, reading the layers of fatigue and determination that resided there.

"What's wrong, now?" he asked softly, his concern deepening as he took in the weary resignation lining her face.

Vale sighed, the weight of her struggles momentarily visible as she stepped back and ran her black hands over her face. He would never forget the lengths she had gone to save him. The dark magic she had unleashed on her demon father had resulted in those very hands turning black, the inky residue creeping along her fingertips and down her palms.

"Where do I even start?" she lamented, collapsing back into her chair with a fatigue that seemed to seep into her bones. "Kaelan has been cursed, and I need to find a way to cure him without even knowing the full nature of the curse. I'm worried the Seven are ten steps ahead of us at every turn. What could they possibly be planning?"

Her voice trailed off for a moment, heavy with the burden of unanswerable questions. "The only lead I have is a ghost in a mysterious graveyard that could be anywhere. We found the grimoire of the First Witch herself, a book full of dark magic, and just when I could use her answers, she's silent. And there's more," she paused, her gaze lifting to meet his, "the First Witch sent a child here to me. There's a girl here now who is a witch, Wren. I'm not the only witch anymore, not by far."

Wren absorbed her words, the weight of their implications settling on his shoulders. Yet, instead of feeling burdened, he felt a clarifying sense of purpose. This was where he was needed. This was where he would stand, unwavering, as Vale's ally and protector, as he had always been.

"Slow down and take a breath, Vale. Let's take things one step at a time. What are you working on right now?" His voice was soothing and methodical as he offered her a lifeline in her storm.

"A potion," she exhaled, the words tumbling out with an urgency that betrayed her inner turmoil. "I'm trying to slow the effects of the curse that's afflicting Kaelan. It's not a cure, but it might buy me more time."

"Okay, perfect. Why don't you and Harker go to the kitchens and start on this potion," Wren directed with the calmness of a seasoned leader, "and I will check on this girl for you. After we get that settled, we will tackle the rest together. Got it?" He knew she needed someone right now who could break the process down for her. She always had trouble separating the big picture into smaller, more manageable pieces. He would gladly do this for her if it eased some of her burden.

"That would be incredible. Thank you, Wren," Vale

replied, the storm in her eyes calming as a glimmer of hope broke through the clouds.

"Of course," Wren reassured her with a nod, the silent strength in his stance reinforcing his words. "You've been shouldering so much alone. Let me help carry the burden."

"Thank you," she repeated, her gratitude evident even as she prepared to leave. "The girl was with Thalion when I last saw her."

"There's no need for thanks," he responded, his words tinged with a protective warmth. "It's what I'm here for."

He could see the tension in her body relax, and she stood, picking up the book and heading towards the door. Harker followed close behind, waving to him on her way out.

Turning from the now-empty library and entering the hall, Wren contemplated his next move. The girl—where could she be? The castle was vast, and he would be useless to Vale if he wandered like a lost pup.

Closing his eyes, he honed his senses, his innate wolfish instincts elevating his hearing beyond the ordinary. The ambient noise of the castle filtered through his consciousness until he detected the distinct timbre of Thalion's voice, filtering through the expanse of the hall.

He picked up his pace, following the sound until he stood outside the door to a set of rooms.

Wren raised his hand and gave a firm, authoritative knock on the heavy wooden door, which swung open after a moment. A Fae maid, her eyes wide, acknowledged Wren with a silent nod before stepping aside to grant him entry into the room warmed by a crackling fireplace.

As he stepped through the door, Thalion looked up from his relaxed posture on the plush couch, a look of mild interest crossing his features. "Wren, what brings you here?" he asked casually.

Scanning the spacious room, Wren's gaze landed on the small, fiery-haired child seated on the floor. She was a contrast of wildness and innocence, perched on the floor in front of a platter of food. Her large, inquisitive eyes locked with his, while behind her, a maid exhibited a mix of frustration and determination as she grappled with the challenge of the child's tangled locks.

"Vale sent me to check on the girl," Wren replied, his attention briefly returning to Thalion before settling back on the young redhead. "She's got enough to manage at the moment."

Acknowledging Wren's words with a nod, Thalion's lips curled up in a wry smile as he gestured towards the child. "She's a feral little thing," he remarked, a note of fondness betraying his jest. "Seems like she could consume the castle's food stores single-handedly."

A short snort of laughter escaped Wren as he approached the girl, his demeanor relaxed. He offered her a respectful nod. "I'm Wren," he introduced himself.

The girl regarded him with a discerning squint, stuffing a sizeable portion of cheese into her mouth with unabashed gusto. "Aisling," she replied, the word muffled by her mouthful.

"Nice to meet you," Wren responded, finding a chair nearby and making himself comfortable.

"Is it?" The skepticism in Aisling's voice was evident as she narrowed her eyes. "No one's nice without wanting something in return."

A flicker of amusement passed over Wren's face. "And what leads you to believe that?" he asked, genuinely intrigued by the young one's insight.

"People always want something," Aisling declared, a hard-earned wisdom beyond her years painting her words.

"I suppose you're not wrong," Wren conceded, watching her with amusement and curiosity. "But right now, my only desire is to ensure you're doing well."

Aisling fixed him with a probing stare. "Why?"

Wren leaned forward, elbows resting on his knees, reducing the distance between them. "Because you're under our roof," he explained, his voice a gentle rumble. "Here, we take care of our guests. And since Vale cares about you, that also makes you my responsibility. We protect our own, and now, that includes you."

"Responsibility," the word echoed in the room, spoken with a slight twist of Aisling's mouth as if the syllables were foreign and bitter on her tongue. Aisling's eyes scrutinized Wren with a child's unrestrained intensity as though trying to decipher a puzzle. "I don't like that word," she said, the distaste clear in her youthful tone.

"It's not a favorite of mine either," Wren conceded with a soft chuckle, acknowledging the weight that came with such a term. "But, you're stuck with it. Like it or not, you're stuck with me."

Her face puckered into a scowl, not quite in anger but in the stubborn resolve of a child, and she diverted her eyes, focusing intently on the platter before her as if it held great secrets. "You're weird," she mumbled defiantly, almost to herself, as she casually stuffed another morsel into her mouth. "I can tell. Sometimes I just know things and then they happen to be true, so I'm probably right."

"I've been called worse," Wren quipped, the smirk playing on his lips suggesting he took a certain pride in her assessment. "But you might be onto something there. I guess that makes you special."

"That's what the First Witch told me," Aisling said, her voice gaining a note of seriousness. "When she visited me in a dream, she said I was special."

"She did?" Wren said, probing a little, trying to figure out the mystery behind the girl.

Aisling nodded solemnly. "Yeah. She told me, 'Aisling, you are very special, and you're going to save many lives.' So I guess I have important things to do."

"It certainly sounds like it," Wren agreed, his voice steady and reassuring. "You should take it seriously."

Aisling bit into another chunk of food, speaking through her generous bite. "I'll think about all that important stuff... after I finish eating."

"And then what will you do?" Wren's voice was gentle.

The question seemed to catch Aisling off guard and she shrugged. "Don't know. The First Witch didn't give me directions for this part."

"Well, we can't have that," Wren said as he rose to his feet. "We'll just have to figure it out together," he declared, a protective promise laced within his words.

Aisling's gaze snapped upward, wide and shimmering with uncertainty and intrigue, a piece of bread pausing mid-journey to her mouth. "Don't worry," he assured with a light-hearted chuckle. "I won't make you do anything too terrible. But, if you're going to be staying here, there's a lot you should learn. How about you let the nice ladies finish getting you cleaned up and dressed and then I'll show you around?"

She nodded, a flicker of excitement passing over her features, momentarily displacing the wariness. "Alright," she agreed, a softness in her voice that hadn't been there before.

"Good," Wren said, his smile spreading. "Once you're ready, we'll be waiting just outside for you."

"Fine, bye," Aisling replied, her attention already swiveling back to her meal.

Wren exited the room with Thalion in tow, the latter's eyes reflecting a mix of bemusement and concern. "She's an odd little thing," Thalion remarked, glancing back at the door they had just closed.

"Yes, she is," Wren mused, his arms folding as he gazed at the door as if through it, he might untangle the web of Aisling's fate. His mind was already weaving plans, not just for the day but for the many that would follow.

"But, I've got a good feeling about her," Thalion's voice cut through Wren's contemplations, echoing lightly off the stone walls of the corridor. His eyes held a flicker of genuine intrigue, the kind that came from years of evaluating potential on the battlefield. "There's a resilience in her."

Wren gave a thoughtful nod, his gaze lingering on the closed door as if he could see through it. "So do I," Wren murmured, lost in thought. "It's hard to say where she'll fit in or how. Her place in the grand scheme of things... well, it's as if she's a wild card in Vale's deck. She could end up changing the game entirely."

The corner of Thalion's mouth quirked up and he clapped a hand on Wren's broad shoulder. "I need to return to my duties. Those new recruits won't spar themselves into shape," he said with a chuckle that spoke of anticipation more than drudgery.

"Remember, we're shaping warriors, not sending them to the healers," Wren called after him with a half-smile.

"Of course," Thalion replied with a salute that was equal parts formal and teasing. "But the last thing I want is to give Vale reason to think I've gone soft."

Watching Thalion's retreating form, Wren felt a brotherly fondness tempered with the sobering remembrance of the tasks ahead. As Thalion's footsteps receded, a new sound captured Wren's attention—a gentle, unassuming click. He watched as the door slowly creaked open.

She stood there, a stark contrast to the untamed child who had first entered the castle. Her red hair was subdued, its fiery tangles tamed into damp waves, and she was clothed in a dress that hinted at the young lady she might become. But it was the unchanged spark in her eyes that held Wren's attention—the unyielding spirit that seemed to challenge the world.

"I'm ready," Aisling declared with a certainty that belied her size.

"Good," Wren said. "I have a lot to show you and very little time to do it in."

"Okay, then." She stepped out her posture straight with a touch of defiance that seemed as much a part of her as her shadow. "Let's get this over with. I've never been patient," she said.

He couldn't help but grin, a response elicited by her fiery spirit. "Noted," he replied, the warmth in his smile reflecting his approval. She scrutinized him, her eyes sharp as flint, as if trying to read his thoughts, gauge his sincerity.

As they started down the hall, he was aware of her presence just behind him, her steps silent but assured. Casting a glance over his shoulder, Wren's smile softened. Yes, she would indeed keep him on his toes. But he found himself surprisingly grateful for it.

In the tilt of her head, the set of her jaw, there were echoes of Vale, indeed—the same determination, the same fire. The notion didn't unsettle Wren; instead, it grounded him. Vale had grown from a headstrong child into a force to be reckoned with. If Aisling were to walk a similar path, then he would be there to ensure it started with a firm footing.

And so, with curiosity and a burgeoning sense of guardianship, Wren led Aisling through the corridors, through the heart of a place that was to become a crucible of her destiny. And he, unbeknownst to even himself, had become the first to aid her on that journey.

THIRTEEN

The subtle clinks and clatters of the kitchen were the only sounds punctuating the otherwise heavy silence between Harker and me. We were sequestered in one of the palace's lesser-used kitchens, a place of solitude away from the chaos that too often engulfed the castle. Warmth radiated from the stovetop as I leaned forward to gently stir the pot, watching as the viscous liquid swirled into whirlpools before settling back into a simmer.

Before us on the worn counter lie the ingredients of salvation—or at least, a temporary reprieve. The kitchen was unusually still, the silence amplifying the scraping sound of Harker's knife against the cutting board as she methodically chopped the bloodroot.

"What are you going to do about the girl?" Harker's voice cut through the quiet, a sharp note of concern lacing her words.

I sighed, the weight of uncertainty pressing on my shoulders. I set the wooden spoon aside and stepped back from the stove, feeling the change in temperature as I moved away from the heat. "I don't know yet," I confessed, looking at the array of ingredients laid out on the counter as if they might hold an answer. "I can't see how she fits into the larger puzzle. If she's even a part of it at all."

The thought of the young girl, Aisling, brought a frown to my face. "Aerion said he sensed no magical ability in her." The skepticism in his voice had been clear, but it was the worry that lingered beneath the surface that gnawed at me.

My mind wandered to the sight of Aisling when she first arrived—wild-eyed, disheveled, a creature forged of survival and instincts. "I can't begin to imagine what she went through to reach us," I said, my words thick with concern. "By the state of her, she must have walked to and from the portal."

The portals—rips in the very fabric of the realms, bridges between worlds that weren't meant to be traversed so lightly, so haphazardly. The thought of that young, untrained girl taking such a perilous journey made my heart clench. How many horrors had she witnessed? What desperation drove her through that vortex of shadows and light?

Harker paused, the bloodroot idle under her blade. She watched me with eyes that had seen too much yet still managed to display a modicum of softness. We both knew the gravity of our situation, the implications of every newcomer, every anomaly that we couldn't account for. Yet, in this instance, my heart leaned towards protection, towards a desire to shield Aisling from further harm.

"Then there's the question of her safety," I continued, the leader within me wrestling with the caretaker. "If she's not a witch, she's still a child alone in a world that is far from gentle to our kind. We need to find a place for her."

Harker's hands found their rhythm again, the sound of her chopping bloodroot syncing with the careful cadence of her words. "I can teach her. If she's a witch, then who better to teach her, besides you, than me? I've consumed half the library by now. You've got your hands full and everyone else is occupied with keeping this castle from crumbling. Time is a luxury I have in abundance."

I felt a smile touch my lips, warmed by the sincerity of her offer. "You would do that?" I asked, genuinely touched.

She stopped her meticulous chopping and looked up, her eyes locking with mine. "I may be an old soul, but the memories of my youth have not faded—the fear, the uncertainty. The pain. The confusion. If I can offer the girl even a shred of guidance, then I will gladly do so."

I watched as she deposited the chopped bloodroot into the bubbling pot, and I resumed stirring. The earthy scent of the root melded with the other ingredients and I contemplated my next request, feeling the weight of it on my tongue. "There's something else I need to ask of you," I began, my voice betraying a hint of my unease.

"Of course. Whatever you need," she replied without hesitation.

"I need to create new witches soon. I can teach them what I know, but they'll need guidance. Your guidance. If the Seven come after me, this realm will need strong witches to protect it. I can't do it on my own, Harker." The words tumbled from my lips, and I let them hang in the air. It was a request that needed to be made, but one that I felt hesitant to voice. Asking this of her was no a small favor, no inconsequential task.

"Like I said, who better?" Harker responded with a soft chuckle. "I suppose I should prepare for a lively library."

Relief washed over me, loosening the tightness I hadn't

realized had taken hold. "I am so grateful, Harker. Thank you," I said.

"I should be the one thanking you," she responded with a wry smile. "Some company other than Elara's constant chatter will be a welcome change. Perhaps she'll find someone else to bother."

"Elara will always find time for her favorite sparring partner," I laughed, and with a light heart, I retrieved the dried foxglove from a ceramic bowl. I sprinkled it into the potion, stirring as the herb melded into the dark mixture.

The kitchen fell into a comfortable silence, save for the gentle bubbling of the potion and the occasional rustle of ingredients. The final ingredient, however, could not be plucked from any shelf or drawer.

Harker extended a small dagger to me, the blade glinting in the dim light of the kitchen. "Thank you," I said, taking the dagger with a nod. I pressed the sharp edge to my forearm, feeling the sting as a fine line of crimson welled up. Droplets of my blood fell into the brew, the surface swallowing them, turning from a foreboding black to a vibrant, pulsing scarlet—a living thing waiting to be harnessed.

I placed the blade on the stone counter, feeling the coolness of the surface seep into my skin for a moment before I picked up a cloth to wrap around my arm. With practiced motions, I tightened it, the pressure staunching the flow with an efficiency born of necessity.

"Well, that should do it," Harker noted, peering into the bubbling pot with a critical eye.

I sighed, a breath heavy with the weight of what this potion signified. "Let's hope it works," I murmured. The importance of our creation was not lost on either of us. "We need to save as much of it as we can. I don't know how often he'll need to take it."

Harker frowned, her hands stilling. "There's an issue," she said softly, a crease of concern marking her forehead.

I turned to her, my intuition already sensing the impending problem. "What is it?"

"We're running out of ingredients," she explained, her gaze now on the nearly empty jars and wilted herbs that lay scattered across the kitchen. "Some of these ingredients... they aren't easy to come by."

"Shit," I hissed.

Harker's expression turned apologetic. "We might scavenge some from the gardens," she suggested, "but some of these are harder to come by."

Another sigh, deep and frustrated, left me as I pressed my palm to my temple. The motion was reflexive, an attempt to ease the pressure building behind my eyes. "I'll figure something out," I murmured, the promise as much a plea to the universe as a declaration of intent.

"We'll figure something out," Harker corrected gently, reminding me that the burden was shared, that I was not alone.

A smile, weak but sincere, broke through my concern. I nodded in grateful acknowledgment. Together, we poured the scarlet liquid into glass vials, ensuring not a drop was wasted. The vials clinked softly as we placed them into my bag.

Once we finished, I hoisted the bag over my shoulder. "I should get these to Kaelan," I stated, feeling the pull of urgency.

"Alright," Harker replied, her tone steady as always. "Be careful, Vale. I'll scour the library. There must be something —anything—that could help with breaking curses."

"Thank you, Harker," I told her. "I don't know what I'd do without you."

"You'd probably burn the castle down," she teased, her eyes sparkling with mischief.

"Probably," I conceded, grinning at her.

With a wave of her hand, she ushered me away. "Go on, before Kaelan's gets worse."

Her words, though spoken with a hint of humor, quickened my step. I left the kitchen, the light-hearted banter fading behind me, replaced by the gravity of my mission. I moved through the palace corridors, the weight of the vials in the bag a constant reminder of the stakes at play.

I navigated the palace's winding corridors, the silence enveloping me like a cloak. The familiar stonework and flickering torches did little to soothe the growing worry within me. The vials in my bag seemed to carry the weight of the world, each step toward my rooms a reminder of the delicate balance upon which Kaelan's well-being rested. The ornate door to my rooms loomed ahead and I paused momentarily outside, gathering my composure with a deep, steadying breath.

I pushed open the door open and the tension in the air was immediate and thick enough to strangle the comfort from the room. Aerion stood like a statue carved from ice, his arms crossed, eyes fixed with unwavering intensity on Kaelan. Kaelan, in contrast, was a tempest unleashed, a wild, dark presence beside the bed. His hands were tense, fingers arched like claws, ready for a fight that seemed to rage within him.

"What's going on?" My voice broke the heavy silence as I addressed Aerion, my gaze flickering between the two men.

"He was calm until moments ago," Aerion responded,

his voice as controlled as his posture, "but something's triggered him again." His gaze never strayed from Kaelan as if he were a predator contemplating its next move.

I edged closer to Kaelan, my approach careful and measured. His eyes met mine, and the wildness in his—a feral, untamed gleam—sent ice curling low in my stomach. His mouth parted, those sharp fangs bared in a silent challenge, and a primal growl vibrated from his chest, sending waves of dread through me.

"Stay back," Aerion's voice was a quiet thunder, stepping a fraction towards me, an instinctive protective measure.

"No," came my determined whisper, drawing upon a strength I wasn't entirely sure I possessed. Aerion stilled, his body coiled, ready to act on my behalf, but his eyes remained watchful, analytical.

"Come here," I coaxed Kaelan, my voice a soft but forceful.

His response was unsettling. The dangerous grin that sliced across Kaelan's face was one of a hunter that had cornered its prey. His eyes roamed over me, lascivious and unashamed. "I can smell you," he hissed, his voice a serpentine caress, "I can smell how much you want me."

"Kaelan," I pleaded, my voice barely more than a fractured whisper, betraying the storm of emotions within me.

He prowled closer, each step deliberate, a predator closing in. Mere inches separated us now, his heat nearly searing, his breath a tantalizing caress against my skin.

"Give yourself to me," he purred, his voice a velvet threat, low and seductive.

I stepped back, the space between us a gulf I was desperate to maintain. "No," escaped me, a gasp of resistance.

His amusement at my defiance was clear, his eyes alight with the thrill of the hunt and his grin widened, his eyes shadowed with dark intent. "I could take you right now," he whispered, each word a taunting stroke. "I could pin you down, take what I want, and you would be powerless to stop me."

The words were like a strike, a threat that left me momentarily breathless. "You wouldn't," I managed to say, though it felt like speaking through a maelstrom.

His grin only broadened, a predator baring its teeth. "Oh, but I would," he assured me, the sight of his fangs a stark contrast to the velvety threat of his words.

I stood frozen, his presence overwhelming, the scent of danger and desire mingling in the charged air, leaving me speechless, my heart pounding a frantic rhythm against the cage of my ribs.

Kaelan's hand reached out, the air between us charged with dangerous energy, as his fingers lightly brushed the delicate skin at my throat. "I want to taste you," he whispered, his voice a velvet caress that belied the sharpness of his fangs just inches away. "I want to hear you scream my name as I drink from you, as I fuck you until you're begging for mercy."

I felt a tremor of involuntary desire as his words conjured images that were both frightening and enticing. My body's reaction was a betrayal, heat pooling within me, a raw and primal response to his commanding presence.

"That's what I thought," he taunted, a knowing smirk curling the edge of his mouth.

"Kaelan, please." The words left my lips in a breathy plea, my voice betraying the fear and need entangled in the depths of my soul.

"Vale," Aerion's voice cut sharply through the tension, a stark reminder of our reality.

I focused on Kaelan, demanding his attention with a stronger voice. "Kaelan, look at me," I insisted, my command slicing through the haze that seemed to cloud his eyes.

For a moment, his predatory gaze wavered, a flicker of confusion passing over his features as if my words reached something human within the beast. "This isn't you," I implored, trying to pierce the darkness that had overtaken him.

His response was a sneer, a mask of defiance over whatever struggle raged within. "Isn't it?" he challenged, but his eyes held a storm of emotions too complex to decipher.

"No," I responded with all the conviction I could muster. "You're not a monster, Kaelan."

In an instant, his hand shot out, grasping my throat with a brutal certainty, pinning me against the wall. His words were a twisted promise. "I don't think you know what I am, little witch. Maybe you need a reminder," he hissed, his fingers tightening.

His grip was iron, my breath a trapped bird within my chest. Panic began to claw at my senses, but before it could take hold, Aerion intervened. His hands were steel bands around Kaelan's wrists, the unmistakable sound of his formidable strength threatening to crush bone. Kaelan snarled viciously, a cornered beast, yet he didn't turn his fangs on Aerion.

"Enough!" My voice, though strained, carried the weight of command, breaking through the violent tableau.

For a heartbeat, Kaelan's eyes locked with mine again, the ferocity wavering, replaced by a glimpse of the man trapped inside the monster.

"This isn't you," I breathed out, the air I managed to draw in burning my throat.

In his gaze, I saw the conflict and after a moment, the clarity won. "I can't...I can't control it," he confessed in a ragged whisper, his grip faltering, his hands falling away even as Aerion's hold remained unyielding.

"I know," I assured him, my voice a fragile thread amidst the chaos of his breakdown.

He stumbled back from me, reaching for his head as Aerion let him go. My hands, gentle but trembling, lifted to his face, my touch a stark contrast to the violence of moments before. "It's alright," I said soothingly, my palms framing his jaw, my thumbs stroking the skin there. "It's alright. We're going to fix this, okay?" I promised, my words a lifeline thrown into the dark waters that threatened to drown him.

My hand delved into the bag, fingers searching until they closed around a vial. "Drink this," I directed, my voice steady despite the storm of emotions raging within me.

Kaelan's hand, now steady, took the vial. He tilted it to his lips, the contents disappearing as he swallowed them in one fluid motion. My eyes never left his face, searching for any sign of change, any glimpse of relief.

"How do you feel?" I asked, my question laced with silent prayers.

Kaelan paused, a visible struggle flickering across his features as he assessed the internal battle waging within him. "Better," he finally answered, the roughness of his voice smoothing out with each passing second. "I can feel the fog lifting."

"Good," I exhaled, relief washing through me. My gaze flitted to Aerion, seeking reassurance. His nod was subtle, but his expression remained carved with concern.

Turning my attention back to Kaelan, I suggested softly, "Let's get you some rest," guiding him toward the bed with a gentle but firm hand.

Aerion's voice was sharp, cutting through the momentary calm. "Vale, you need to be careful," he cautioned, his eyes dark slits of worry. "If he can't control it, he could hurt you."

"I know," I responded, my voice a soft whisper of acknowledgment. "The potion should work for a while, though."

"Hopefully," came Aerion's muttered reply, the single word heavy with doubt.

A spark of defiance ignited within me. "I'm not helpless, Aerion. I can defend myself if necessary."

"That's not the point," he shot back, frustration tinging his voice for the first time. "We don't know what this curse will do to him. What it might make him capable of."

"Then we'll just have to deal with that when the time comes," I stated, meeting his challenge with a resolute tone.

Kaelan interjected then, his voice laced with shadows. "Vale, he's right. You shouldn't be around me right now." His eyes bore into me, the dark depths swirling with conflict.

But I stood firm, my resolve as unwavering as the ancient stones of the castle. "I'm not going anywhere," I declared, leaving no room for argument.

Kaelan's eyes, stormy and conflicted, seemed to plead with me, but exhaustion was winning, dimming the intensity of his gaze.

Aerion broke the tense silence. "I'm going to go fill Thalion in," he stated, making his way to the door. "Let me know if anything changes."

I nodded, my eyes never leaving Kaelan.

The moment the door clicked shut, the space between us shifted and became more intimate and fragile. Kaelan's hand rose, fingers trembling as they brushed my cheek in a feather-light caress. "I'm so sorry, Vale," he murmured, his voice raw with emotion. "For all of this."

"I know," I reassured him, leaning into the comfort of his hand. "It's not your fault."

But his expression was tormented. "You shouldn't be near me. Not like this," he insisted, his tone heavy with an agony that went beyond physical pain.

But I wouldn't be sent away. I wrapped my arms around his neck; my embrace a physical manifestation of my spoken vow. "I'm not going anywhere," I repeated.

He rested his forehead against mine, and we stayed like that for a long moment, neither of us speaking.

When he drew back, his eyes held a new intensity, a spark of the leader and protector I knew him to be. "You can't do this, Vale," he said with heartfelt urgency. "You can't keep putting yourself at risk for me."

His words were a plea, a desperate wish to shield me from the darkness that enveloped him. But my decision had been made long before this moment, sealed with each trial we'd faced together. I was here, by his side, and that was where I intended to stay.

"You would do the same for me," I said, my voice unfaltering in its conviction. I saw the muscle in his jaw clench, a sign of his inner turmoil.

"That's different," he muttered, looking away, his words quick and sharp like the crack of a whip.

"How is it different?" I pressed, challenging him to explain the inexplicable.

He faltered, his words dissolving into a frustrated silence. "Because... I'm a demon, Vale. My existence is one of shadow and death. I am not..." He hesitated, the vulnerability in his eyes piercing me more acutely than any blade. "I am not worth the risk."

I could scarcely believe the shadow of doubt that had crept into his words. My heart clenched at the pain underlying his admission. "You can't truly believe that," I spoke, my voice quivering with the effort to stay calm.

"I do," he confessed in a whisper as if admitting a sin.

With a surge of enthusiasm, my words became an oath, an incantation to banish the lies he'd been told, the lies he'd told himself. "You're wrong. You are not defined by the worst things you've done. But by the best things," I said, the anger in me awakening not at him but at the injustice of his self-condemnation.

"Vale," he sighed, a sound that held a world of resignation.

I wouldn't let him dismiss my words. "No, listen to me," I commanded, drawing his full attention. "You are not a monster, Kaelan. You have never been worthless. And I'm going to prove it to you, even if it's the last thing I do."

I watched the battle play out in his eyes—a battle of shadows and light. I held his gaze, unwavering, until slowly, the hardness began to recede and something else took its place.

"I won't leave you," I whispered again, a soft promise amid the storm that was his life. "I can't just walk away from you, remember? We are bound by more than fate or curses."

His voice, a mere whisper, conceded, "I remember."

"Then trust me," I urged, my hands cradling his face, my thumbs tracing the sharp lines of his cheekbones.

"I trust you," he admitted, the wall he'd built around himself crumbling.

I leaned in, my lips finding his, and kissed him with a tenderness that belied the fierce beating of my heart. He kissed me back, his lips parting against mine with a hunger that was as much about need as it was about passion.

"Vale," his voice was a hushed echo against my lips, his fingers tracing a path of fire down my spine. He whispered my name like a caress, a plea, and I answered it without hesitation.

"It's okay," I reassured him, my lips brushing against his in a featherlight touch, inviting him to lose himself in our connection. "Just let go."

And he did. His lips met mine again, this time with a desperate hunger, as if he was searching for salvation within the kiss. As he kissed me, a deep and primal part of him seemed to unravel and I felt him let go of the control he fought so hard to maintain.

FOURTEEN

Kaelan's growl was a sound torn from the depths of primal desire, echoing through the charged air. His lips, which had teased and nipped at my own, traveled with an insatiable intent down the column of my neck. Each brush of his mouth against my skin felt like a brand, marking me with an intensity that pulsed through my veins. I felt his hand on my breast, his thumb brushing across my nipple. I shuddered, my back arching against him.

"Kaelan," I gasped, my breath coming in short, heavy pants. His name was a plea, a keening call that seemed to stoke the fire within him.

The warmth of his tongue painted my skin with a wet, sensual trail, lapping at the salt of my flesh, each stroke sending quivers through my body. Then, the sensation of his teeth, not quite gentle, not quite harsh, grazed the tender skin of my neck, threatening to pierce, to claim, sending tremors of anticipation racing through me.

His eyes, wild with an untamed hunger, locked onto mine, and in them, I saw the feral gleam of his nature. The

bite was a shockwave, a surge of pain that swiftly transformed into raw pleasure, sparking through my every
nerve. His lips sealed around the puncture with an enthusiasm that matched the thudding of my heart.

My legs faltered beneath me, but his arm, an unyielding
band of steel, was there, holding me against him. My hands
clutched at him, seeking an anchor as the room tilted and
swayed with the intoxicating mix of agony and ecstasy.

My senses were heightened to a realm of pure feeling,
each pull at my neck resonating down to the core of me,
throbbing in time with my heartbeat. The pleasure
bloomed and spread, a kindling heat that begged for attention, for fulfillment.

"Kaelan," my voice broke on a pant, each breath a
struggle as my body quaked with the overwhelming need
for him.

He pulled away, his eyes blazing as he looked at me. His
fangs dripped with my blood, and I could feel the wound on
my neck healing rapidly.

"More," the word escaped my lips, a sultry whisper, a
testament to the hunger that raged within me, a hunger
that matched his own in its ferocity and depth.

Kaelan's passion was all-consuming, a torrent of desire
that swept away any semblance of restraint. His mouth,
feverish and possessive, reclaimed mine with an urgency
that left no room for doubts or fears. It was a kiss that spoke
of dark nights and raw emotions, one that promised untold
pleasures laced with a hint of danger.

I returned the kiss eagerly, my tongue tangling with his,
tasting the coppery tang of my own blood. He pushed me
back against the wall he had pinned me to earlier and I
gasped as I recognized the same hunger in him now as he
had then. The cool stone of the wall was a stark contrast to

the heat of his body as he pinned me with a force that spoke of a barely restrained beast.

He grabbed my hands, lifting and holding them above my head, his fingers like bands of iron declaring his control. "Now you're mine to play with," he murmured, the words a velvet threat that danced down my neck, his lips barely grazing the shell of my ear. It was an oath, a promise of the possession to come, and it sent tremors of excitement through me.

"Yes," came my breathless consent, my body instinctively moving against his, seeking the friction that promised sweet release.

"Say it," he commanded, and his voice was the dark rumble of a storm on the horizon, potent and dominating.

"I'm yours to play with." The words he demanded spilled from my lips in a breathy plea, stripped of all pride and reduced to the base instinct to feel him, to be claimed by him.

"I'm going to take you hard and fast, and you're going to scream my name when you come," he vowed, his words painting a picture of primal intimacy, of unbridled possession.

"Yes," I moaned, my hips grinding against his. Each word I uttered in return felt like an incantation, a spell that wound tighter and tighter around us.

"Then beg," he growled, his grip on my wrists tightening.

"Fuck me, Kaelan," I begged, my voice shaking, my plea a raw sound that matched the naked hunger in his eyes. "Please."

His kiss was an intoxicating mix of ferocity and tenderness, a chaos of lips, teeth, and tongue that fueled the fire within me. When his hands were finally relinquished from their hold on my wrists, a sense of freedom mixed with a tinge of loss washed over me.

The force of his kiss broke only long enough for him to strip away my dress, revealing my skin to his gaze. His fingers traced a scorching path over me; each touch a spark that ignited fires within. When he reached my breasts, the feel of his hands—a mix of tenderness and demand—coaxed a whimper from my throat.

"So perfect," he murmured, his voice a whisper of awe laced with the edge of his dark craving. His lips followed the path blazed by his fingers, each kiss a brand, each nip a claiming, as he moved with a predator's grace down my body.

The cold air of the room caressed my skin where his hot touch had been, but it was quickly replaced by the warmth of his mouth. His attentions to my body were both worship and conquest, leaving me teetering on the brink of an abyss that promised a fall into blinding ecstasy.

As his hands ventured lower, tracing the contours of my figure, I felt the exquisite tension only his touch could bring. With a precision that betrayed his eagerness, his fingers danced across my skin, igniting fires along paths only he could see. When his fingers finally reached between my legs, the evidence of my desire for him made his breath hitch, his gaze turning dark.

The softest groan slipped from him, a sound that vibrated through the charged air between us, "Gods, Vale, you're so wet for me." His voice was laced with a raw hunger that mirrored the burgeoning need within me.

The moment his finger slipped inside me a gasp tore from my throat. It was as if he'd unlocked something primal within me, each movement of his finger urging me on.

"More," I begged, the word torn from my throat. My hands found him, seeking his flesh, driven by the primal need to feel the strength of his skin against mine.

He was all too willing to oblige. More fingers joined the first, and his movements coaxed my body to stretch and welcome him. The roughness in his touch was a counterpoint to the swirling tenderness I'd seen in his eyes moments before. His thumb found my clit and began a relentless campaign, drawing circles with a precision that bordered on wickedness.

"Please, Kaelan," I cried out, the edge of bliss so near, yet his growl cut through the fog of my desire, a stark reminder that this crescendo was his to command.

"Not yet," he said, lowering to his knees. His tongue joined his fingers, flicking out to taste me, and I grasped fistfuls of his hair in my hands, pulling him closer.

With each thrust of his fingers, he took me higher, his pace unyielding, driving me toward a precipice of ecstasy. His tongue, a relentless force, propelled me to the brink until his rough voice gave the last command: "That's it, Vale, come for me."

The world shattered into a million points of pleasure. My climax tore through me, a cataclysm of sensation that obliterated thought, my cries a testament to the potency of his touch.

As I trembled, waves of after-shocks coursing through me, Kaelan's praise was a caress, "Good girl." He removed his fingers and brought this up to his lips. His gaze held mine as he licked his fingers clean, holding me in place with the look in his eyes.

"You taste so fucking good," he said, his voice thick with desire. Then he stepped back, his movements swift as he shed his clothes, revealing himself to me in all his glory.

There he stood, every inch the warrior, the protector, the lover, ready to claim his consort.

Kaelan's hands were like vices, unyielding and firm, as he lifted me with an ease that belied the fury that was bubbling beneath his skin. I wrapped my legs around his waist, my aching core pressing against his considerable length.

His movements were not gentle. With a swift motion, my back met the wall, the cool surface a stark contrast to the heat of our bodies. The force of his movements pressed him even closer, and the rough texture of the wall against my skin only amplified the raw sensuality of the moment. His hips, unforgiving and demanding, ground against me, drawing a cry from my lips that was a blend of surprise and sheer ecstasy.

His breath was a hot whisper against the shell of my ear, the teasing question, "Are you ready for me, little witch?" reverberated through the very marrow of my bones, his voice a velvety threat.

"Yes," slipped from me, a vow wrapped in a moan as I moved against him, an implicit plea for him to end the exquisite torture of waiting.

"I don't think you are," his tone was a growl, a teasing admonition that was cut short as he claimed me in one swift, brutal thrust. The air was driven from my lungs as he filled me completely, the sweet stretch sending shocks of delight radiating throughout my body. I cried out, my nails raking across his back.

"Fuck," he cursed, a primal sound torn from his throat as his hands, unyielding on my hips, found their rhythm. The pace he set was punishing, a relentless onslaught that each time he withdrew felt like a loss and each entry was a victory. The sound of our bodies colliding filled the air, mixed with my moans and his growls.

"Scream for me, little witch. I want the whole castle to know that I'm between your legs," he instructed, each word punctuated with a powerful thrust, a litany of possession spoken through action. "That it's me," Thrust. "Filling you," Thrust. "Claiming you," Thrust. "Owning you."

His relentless drive pushed me to the precipice, and as I screamed his name, a declaration, a surrender, the world narrowed down to the feeling of him moving within me. The lines I drew upon his skin with my nails were a testament, an indelible mark of the raw moment. My orgasm crashed through me and he fucked me relentlessly, prolonging the ecstasy.

"That's it, Vale," his voice was a rough caress against the chaos. "Let them hear. Let there be no doubt." His hand left my hip to tangle in my hair. The pull, sharp and sudden, sent a thrill of pain that spiraled into pleasure, drawing a louder cry from me, the sound a raw edge of pure sensation.

"Who do you belong to, Vale?" he demanded, his pace a relentless force that pushed me ever closer to the edge once more.

"You," was all I could muster.

"Louder," he commanded, his hips slamming into me.

"You," I obeyed, my voice hoarse.

"Who do you belong to?!"

"Kaelan!" I screamed, his name echoing through the room. It was a shout, a chant, a surrender.

His response was primal, a growl that was a visceral response to my claim as he pounded into me.

I felt him, a surge within me. The pulsing warmth of him inside me triggered my own second shattering release, a pleasure so intense it bordered on pain, a blurring of senses that was both his gift and my undoing.

Exhaustion wrapped around us like a thick blanket as Kaelan held me up against the wall, our breaths coming out in heavy gasps. "Holy fuck," escaped my lips, a whispered testimony to the intensity that still thrummed through every nerve ending, making my voice waver with residual pleasure.

Kaelan's chuckle was a low sound that vibrated against my fevered skin. "You're not the only one," he confessed, his words a soft caress as his lips found the curve of my neck, his breath cooling the beads of sweat that clung to my skin. His tongue traced a path down my throat, the soothing sensation contrasted with the wildness of moments before.

He gently lowered me to the ground. His hands, so demanding before, now roamed over me with a gentleness that caused my heart to swell as much as my body had ached for him. I melted into his arms, my cheek against the steady beat of his heart, a rhythmic comfort that cradled my exhausted body. We lingered in the quiet, too sated for words. For a few timeless moments, we just existed.

His kiss was tender, a soft press of lips to my forehead. "You should get some rest, Vale," he whispered, concern laced in the tone of his voice, his words cutting through the tranquil haze that had begun to settle over me.

I wanted to protest, to stay locked in the timelessness of post-bliss clarity, but his observation was sharp. "I'm okay," came my quiet protest, even as my body betrayed my true state, sinking further into his embrace, craving the support, the stillness.

Kaelan's response was gentle but unyielding, the softness in his tone contrasting against the firmness of his words. "No," he insisted, "You're exhausted." It was a statement, not a discussion.

My attempt at resistance was feeble at best. "But—"

His interruption was swift, a soft command that wrapped around me. "Don't argue with me."

With a resigned sigh, I surrendered, my body no longer capable of holding back the tide of weariness that demanded submission. "Fine," I said, a whisper of surrender.

"That's my girl," he said with a note of pride, and his arms closed around me. He carried me to the bed, the gentle bob of each step lulling me further towards slumber, and laid us down with a careful grace.

As I closed my eyes, I felt his arms pull me close, a fortress of safety. His warmth seeped into me, a promise against the chill of the night. "Get some sleep," he whispered. "I'll be here when you wake up."

"Promise?" I murmured, the darkness of sleep already pulling me under.

"Always," he replied, and it was the last thing I knew before sleep claimed me fully, his vow the steady shore that I drifted towards, secure in the knowledge that when morning came, he would be there, just as he said.

PART
TWO

CHAPTER

FIFTEEN

The chamber was a shadow of its former glory, an expanse of emptiness where echoes of past grandeur seemed to linger like ghosts. Sunlight filtered through the tall windows, casting a solemn glow on the recently polished floors, where shadows played hide and seek. The room felt hollow, its heart—the laughter, the music, the life—swept away with the remnants of its former glory. The grand piano stood silent, a relic of melody and memories, while a modest arrangement of furniture appeared almost lost in the vastness.

I sat rigidly, my gaze fixed intently on Thalion, who reclined with an ease that was beginning to grate on my nerves. There was a smirk tugging at the corner of his mouth, a silent taunt that added fuel to the fire of my growing frustration.

My focus was razor-sharp, directed at him, willing my magic to respond, to act, to do anything other than lie dormant within me. I could feel the potential there, like a coiled spring, but no matter how I coaxed it, it refused to unfurl. It was like trying to summon a breeze in the dead calm of a stifling summer's day—impossible and utterly disheartening.

"You know, you could wipe that smug smirk off your face. It's definitely not helping," I snapped, my voice sharper than I intended. The room's acoustics carried the sound to the lofty ceiling, a testament to its design for grand events and music, not the tense silence of a magical standoff.

Thalion's eyes danced with unrestrained amusement and the smirk that I so pointedly mentioned only broadened. He leaned forward in his chair, elbows resting on his knees, fingers laced together.

"But, I find your concentration face quite endearing, princess," he teased, his voice smooth, soothing yet somehow infuriating.

I sighed, a soft sound of surrender, and leaned back in the chair, the wood creaking under my weight. I felt every inch the petulant student in the face of his teasing. "Endearing isn't exactly what I'm aiming for," I retorted, trying to match his light tone despite the tightness in my chest.

Thalion rose gracefully, closing the distance between us with measured steps. He came to a halt a few paces away, his presence as commanding as the room was large. "If I have learned anything in my long life, it is that sometimes frustration can be the catalyst for discovery. The tension you feel, the irritation—it's all part of the process."

Thalion extended a hand, palm up, an offering and a challenge all at once. "Come," he said, "let's redirect that fiery spirit of yours."

Hesitantly, I placed my hand in Thalion's, feeling the cool press of his skin against mine, a stark contrast to the warmth that had built up within me. His grip tightened just enough to draw me upright from my chair.

"Trust me," he said, his voice a gentle command that wove through the air. "Close your eyes."

The world disappeared as darkness bloomed behind my closed eyelids, and I was acutely aware of every sensation—the steady thrum of my heartbeat, the brush of Thalion's thumb over the back of my hand, the measured cadence of his breathing.

"Picture a sanctuary in your mind," he guided, his words painting a picture in the darkness. "Somewhere you can retreat to, a place that is wholly yours." I did as he suggested, my mind's eye drawing forth the familiar and comforting surroundings of the library, the place where knowledge and magic intertwined, where the scent of ancient parchment and leather was as much a part of me as the magic coursing through my veins.

I felt Thalion move to stand behind me. His voice was a whisper in my ear. "Good. Can you feel your power there? It's coiled, restless, seeking release."

In the silence of my mental library, a vibrant sphere of energy pulsated, a living thing that hungered. It glowed with the intensity of a star, a representation of the magic that lived within me—wild, unbridled, and seeking freedom.

"Imagine a door there, ready to open," Thalion coaxed, his fingers trailing along the slope of my back. "Then let it out."

A door appeared, ornate and ancient, creaking on its hinges as I willed it open. The energy surged forward, hungry for the connection, reaching through the darkness toward Thalion. I sent the magic surging forward, only to meet an abrupt wall of sheer ice. The shock of cold snapped through the connection. The chill seeped into my skin, a shock that reverberated through my soul. I gasped, my eyes fluttering open, and stumbled into Thalion's grasp.

"Too cold for you, princess?" he teased, his voice a playful taunt that only fueled my stubbornness.

Without a word, I shut my eyes once more, summoning the wellspring of my power. This time, when my magic met the ice, I didn't shrink away. I let the chill seep into my bones, welcomed it, allowed it to become a part of my being until I felt it no more than I would feel the air. I became one with the cold, my fear of it dissipating like frost in the morning sun.

The once solid barrier began to shift under my will. The ice became malleable, a liquid state that ebbed away with the persistence of my magic's warmth, dissolving until only water remained. I pressed on, now unimpeded, and felt the tentative brush of Thalion's mind against mine—a push-back of power, a ripple of resistance. His magic was a fortress, but I was the siege, relentless and indomitable. My will became ironclad. My resolve a shield against his defenses.

I felt a surge of triumph as his magic relented, the connection solidifying, our minds becoming one. I could sense his emotions, the calm, cool detachment, the thread of excitement, and the undercurrent of desire that pulsed through him. The sensation was heady, intoxicating, and I drank it in, reveling in the power I was just beginning to master.

I could feel him probing my thoughts, his presence like a whisper in the back of my mind. He was gentle and careful, but still, the intrusion made me recoil, and the connection shattered, my mind pulling away from his, leaving me feeling suddenly empty.

The room was still, charged with an energy that pulsed with the rhythm of our breathing. The intimate dance of our minds had been a kind of magic I'd never felt before. Thalion's mental touch had been a caress, soft as silk yet potent enough to stir the depths of my consciousness. I felt a vulnerability that was both frightening and exhilarating. A door to my soul cracked open under his gaze.

Thalion's voice, laced with approval, broke through the silence that followed. "Your shields are strong," he said, his tone warm with a hint of surprise.

His smile held a hint of mischief, a playful edge to the chiseled line of his jaw. "Your emotions were very distracting," I confessed, my voice a mere whisper in the vast chamber.

His grin, both charming and disarming, did little to ease the tension. "Yes, I should have warned you about that," he replied, the apologetic tilt to his head suggesting he hadn't considered the impact.

"It was overwhelming," I breathed out, remembering his raw desire echoing in the recesses of my mind, a ghostly sensation that prickled my skin.

His eyes held a spark, a flicker of something primal as he leaned in slightly. "You've got to learn not to let the emotions of others affect you so much when you enter their mind," he instructed. "It's dangerous. You can get lost in the chaos."

"How do I do that?" I asked, my voice a whisper of silk against the roughness of his.

"Practice," he simply said. "You need to be able to separate your emotions from those you're entering. To do that, you have to have a strong grasp of your own emotions. To know yourself."

I considered his words. It sounded simple enough, but I knew it would be anything but.

"Well, I think I've had enough for today, don't you?" Thalion said, his hand reaching out and brushing against my cheek. The gesture was casual, but the ghost of his desire still lingered in my mind.

"I wanted to practice some more," I protested, my words a feeble attempt to extend the moment.

"You need a break. We can continue tomorrow," he insisted, his hand falling away, the loss of contact leaving a void that hungered to be filled.

"Fine," I said, knowing better than to try to change his mind.

He chuckled, amusement dancing in his eyes. "You look cute when you pout," he teased.

Anger flared within me. "I do not pout," I shot back, the denial sharp and reflexive.

"Of course not," he agreed, his voice dripping with feigned earnestness. I couldn't help but roll my eyes in response and he chuckled again, stepping closer.

I felt the heat of his body even before his hand came to rest gently on my chin. He tilted my face up, forcing me to meet his violet eyes. "Do you know how hard it is to keep my hands off you, Vale?" His question was a husky whisper, a caress in itself.

Thalion's grip on me was both gentle and firm, a physical question hanging between us, his eyes searching mine for an answer he wasn't willing to voice just yet.

"Why are you holding back?" The question slipped from me, delicate yet heavy with implications, floating through the charged air that wrapped around us like a cloak.

"Because I've been trying to give you and Kaelan space

to figure things out," he replied, his thumb delicately tracing the contour of my bottom lip.

"We've... figured things out," I managed to reply, though my voice was a frail whisper, lost in the vastness of what lay unsaid.

"Have you? From what I can tell, he's being very possessive of you," Thalion observed, his gaze lingering pointedly on the marks on my throat, each one a silent testament to Kaelan's claim.

"Kaelan is..." My voice faltered, the complexity of our relationship defying a simple explanation.

"Possessive, territorial, a demon who has marked his mate," Thalion filled in the silence, his words sharp, cutting through my hesitation like a knife through the fog.

"You make him sound like a wild animal," I countered, my brow arching, a feeble attempt to deflect the truth in his assessment.

"When it comes to you, he is. And, if I'm being honest," he leaned in closer, his breath a warm whisper against my cheek, "I understand the feeling. But, unlike him, I have more control over my urges."

His self-assured declaration hung in the air between us, a challenge that sent a rush of heat coursing through my veins. "You have a high opinion of yourself, Thalion," I said.

"Don't tempt me, Vale," he murmured, his lips grazing the sensitive skin beneath my ear.

"Or what?" The words were out before I could catch them, laced with a provocation I wasn't entirely sure I was ready to face.

His hand shifted to the nape of my neck, his fingers deftly weaving through my hair and gently tugging my head back to expose more of my throat to his searching lips. His kiss was a promise, a soft pressure against my pulse.

"I'd be happy to show you," he promised, his voice a low rumble of restrained power.

"Do your worst," I replied, daring and desire making me momentarily reckless.

"Oh, sweetheart, you don't know what you're asking for," Thalion growled. His fingers, entwined in my hair, tugged gently, drawing my attention back to his dark gaze.

His lips crashed against mine with an urgency that left me breathless, the kiss a storm of raw passion. I was consumed by him, his presence overwhelming every sense. His free hand moved across my skin, mapping the contours of my body with a boldness that spoke of deep hunger. He reached up and grasped my breast, teasing my nipple through the fabric of my dress.

His touch sparked jolts of desire that coursed through my veins. His fingers teased, coaxed, and awakened every nerve, sending me into a whirlwind of need. I arched into him, desperate to feel the full weight of his body against mine, to be crushed under the strength of his passion.

As the kiss broke, we were left gasping, our foreheads pressed together, sharing the same air, the same thunderous storm of emotions.

His gaze held mine, a silent question burning in the depths of his eyes. "Tell me you aren't worried about what Kaelan will do when he finds out about this," he challenged, the intensity of his stare unwavering.

I faltered, my resolve waning. The mention of Kaelan was like the strike of a match, illuminating the shadowed corners of consequence I had chosen to ignore. My hesitation was my answer, and Thalion knew it.

His voice, now a seductive whisper, was a tender torment. "Tell me you aren't, and I'll rip your clothes off and take you right here. Over and over again until you beg me to stop. I'll make you forget the world outside this room. But you have to be sure."

The allure of his proposal ensnared me, the part of me that yearned to abandon whispering sweet justifications. Yet the thought of Kaelan's reaction, the potential hurt that lay in the wake of such actions, held me back. I was caught in the storm of my desires, the pull of my heart against the anchor of my fears.

His touch was gentle as he brushed his lips against mine again, a featherlight caress that belied the ferocity of his earlier kiss. "You can't," he murmured, a note of finality woven into his words. "And so, I can't. I couldn't send you back to him afterward knowing it would cause you grief."

"Thalion—"

He silenced me with a finger to my lips. "This situation is new for everyone. I just hope you two can get it figured out sooner rather than later because I miss you," his voice was a soft echo of longing.

"I've missed you too," I confessed, the admission a fragile thread between us.

"Go back to Kaelan, Vale. Figure this out," he urged, his words a gentle push toward resolution.

"Are you going to be okay?" I found myself asking, a worry for him stirring within me.

He smiled, a bittersweet curl of his lips. "Yes, princess. I'm a big boy. I can handle it. Just...don't make me wait too long."

SIXTEEN

WREN

Wren stood with his arms folded, a mix of sternness and encouragement etched into the lines of his face as he watched Aisling. The girl was a compact bundle of energy, her red curls bouncing with each exerted effort to strike the straw dummy. Her frustration was evident each time her fist connected with less force than she intended.

"Thumb on the outside," Wren reminded her again, his voice steady. Despite the repetition, there was no hint of annoyance. He understood the importance of these foundational lessons. Wren, ever the patient teacher, had taken it upon himself to teach her self-defense, a task he approached with the same seriousness as he did his duties as alpha.

Aisling paused, panting, and looked down at her hands as if they were separate entities that had betrayed her. She adjusted her grip, clearly trying to imprint the correct position into muscle memory. With a determined scowl, she took another swing, and this time, the satisfying thump of her fist against the dummy signified a direct hit.

"Remember, power comes from your shoulder, not just your arm," Wren instructed, stepping closer to demonstrate. "Rotate your torso as you punch. Yes, like that." He watched as Aisling mimicked his movements, her fist connecting with the straw dummy, a small grunt of effort escaping her.

Venna stood to the side, observing the exchange, a small smile playing on her lips. There was a gentleness to his strength, a controlled power that he conveyed in every lesson. There was pride in her eyes — pride for Wren's teaching ability and the progress of the young girl she too couldn't help but care for.

"That's enough for now," Wren said after a few more minutes, his tone leaving no room for argument. He could see the redness beginning to form on Aisling's knuckles, a testament to her determination and a sign she was pushing herself hard.

Aisling gave the dummy one last scowl as if it were a personal adversary before nodding and stepping away. "Alright," she agreed, though her voice carried a note of disappointment. She wanted to keep going, to throw more punches, to learn more, faster.

"Go rewrap your hands. We don't need you injuring yourself," Wren said, his tone softening. He watched her walk off towards Venna, who held out a pair of fresh wraps.

As Aisling left, Wren took a moment to survey the training grounds, his gaze lingering on each member of his pack as they trained. He had a new member to protect, a fiery young girl who needed guidance, just as Vale had once needed. He was molding Aisling, just as he had once helped mold Vale — not into weapons, but into individuals who could face the world's harsh realities.

He turned back to Venna, who approached him after

ensuring Aisling was set on her task. "She's got spirit," Venna commented, her eyes following Aisling.

Wren nodded, a small smile playing on his lips. "She does at that. And one day, she'll know how to use it."

Venna returned his smile, her eyes sparkling. Wren noticed, not for the first time, how pretty they were. "That she will. Though, I'm not sure if that's a good or a bad thing."

Wren chuckled, a deep rumbling sound. "Probably both. But for now, I'll settle for her being able to defend herself." Aisling, fierce and untamed, might just be the ember that set their world aflame—in the best and most daunting ways.

"And what about us? Who's going to defend us from her?" Venna joked, raising a brow at him.

Wren's eyes remained on the young girl, a blend of admiration and concern coloring his thoughts. "If she's anything like Vale, she'll turn that fire into something formidable," he said.

Aisling's return from wrapping her hands was marked by the scowl etched deeply across her brow, her lips pressed into a thin line that spoke volumes of her thoughts on discipline and structure. Venna's hand clapped onto Aisling's shoulder, a grounding presence as the girl tied the last knot on her wraps. "What's the plan, boss?" she asked, her voice brimming with impatience.

"Drills," Wren announced. "They're the foundation of everything we do here."

Aisling's protest was immediate, her disdain for monotony etched onto her face. "But—"

"No buts," Wren interjected, his tone brooking no argument. "You'll thank us later when you're standing your ground instead of picking yourself up off the dirt."

"Fine," she conceded, her voice a grudging whisper of defeat, eyes darting to the ground before meeting his once more.

Wren fought the urge to roll his eyes, choosing instead to simply nod. "Good. Go with Venna and start your drills. I expect you to give it your best."

As Venna took Aisling under her wing, leading her towards the waiting drills, Wren felt a tiny spark of pride. The path was laid bare before them, rocky and unforgiving, yet he saw in Aisling the same spark that had once ignited Vale's spirit—a spark that had the power to ignite the world.

WREN LEANED back against the cool stone wall, his arms folded across his broad chest, the soft murmur of Harker's voice blending with the rustle of pages in the vast and shadowy library. His keen eyes moved from the ancient text in Harker's hands to the young girl beside her. Aisling's restless energy was evident in the stillness, her foot tapping an impatient rhythm on the floor, her gaze darting around the room as if seeking an escape from the scholarly confines.

Beside the young girl, Harker was the epitome of patience, her voice a steady cadence as she read from the worn pages of a book that had seen the rise and fall of kingdoms. Her eyes, however, betrayed a hint of concern, a slight wrinkle forming between her brows as she noted Aisling's wandering attention.

Elara observed the scene with a silent curiosity. She hovered near a bookshelf, her form barely more than a wisp of mist, her attention fixed on Aisling with an intensity that spoke of her own intrigue. Wren watched her, too, his instincts as a protector never at rest, even with the benign presence of a ghost.

Aisling shifted in her seat, her fingers tracing the intricate carvings on the table's edge, her mind clearly anywhere but on the words Harker read. The history of witches seemed to hold little allure for the restless girl.

Harker closed the book with a gentle thud, her question cutting through the quiet with the sharpness of a well-forged blade. "None of this is getting through to you, is it?" Her voice was kind, but it held a note of exasperation that even Aisling could not miss.

Aisling's response was hesitant, her fingers fiddling with the edge of a page as she mustered a response. "Um, I remember the bit about the First Witch, but not much after that," she admitted sheepishly.

Harker leaned back in her chair, a sigh escaping her as she regarded Aisling with fondness and frustration. "Yes, well, that was the first thing I talked about thirty minutes ago," she pointed out, the corner of her mouth quirking up despite herself. Wren gave Harker a sympathetic smile. The challenges of teaching a wild-hearted girl were not lost on him.

Wren had kept quiet watch over the girl's struggle, but now the stillness was broken by his deep voice, resonating through the hushed air of the library. "There are other ways to learn," he said, his voice carrying the weight of his experience and the softness of his understanding of her restless spirit.

Harker regarded him with curiosity, her scholarly features softening into a thoughtful expression. "And what ways would those be?" she asked, a note of hope threading through her words.

"Practical learning," Wren replied, the corners of his mouth lifting ever so slightly with the promise of action. It was a method he knew well, one that spoke to the instincts rather than just the mind.

The girl's demeanor changed instantly, the promise of action igniting a fire in her eyes. "Oh, can I learn how to wield fire like Vale?" she asked, the words tumbling from her lips, a hopeful lilt in her voice.

"Absolutely not," Wren responded, the decisiveness in his tone reflecting the visions of chaos he foresaw if Aisling's raw energy were given such a dangerous outlet. He quickly tempered the disappointment with an alternative. "But we can start with the basics. If you are willing, that is," he added, turning to Harker with a look that sought her agreement.

Harker nodded, conceding to the shift in tactics. "I suppose we can take a break from the books for now," she said, her tone conveying a gentle resignation. "No one's tested her abilities yet; we don't even know for sure if she has any."

Aisling jumped at the opportunity, her voice lifting with enthusiasm. "You could test me," she offered, practically bouncing on the balls of her feet. "I can do lots of neat tricks. I'll show you."

Harker held up her hand, stilling the girl. "You can show us, but not here. Come on, we can go outside where there's plenty of space."

Aisling's reply was a murmur, her tone laden with relief and a dash of mischief. "And no books," she muttered, her grin wide and brimming with cheeky confidence.

Harker's expression shifted to fond annoyance and understanding. With a knowing glance at Wren, she led them out of the library, stepping into the corridor that would take them to the open expanse of the courtyard.

As they stepped out into the bright sunlight, the fresh breeze of the outdoors washing over them, Aisling let out a whoop of delight. She took a few steps away from the others, her gaze darting from Harker to Wren, her body poised with excitement, a bundle of energy waiting to be unleashed.

The empty courtyard stretched out before them. The fountain bubbled and flowed behind them. Wren stood back, arms crossed, as Harker faced Aisling, ready to gauge the girl's untrained abilities.

"Alright, Aisling," Harker said, her voice carrying a note of challenge, "show us what you can do."

With a confident smirk, Aisling stepped away, giving herself room. She lifted her hands, her brow creasing with focus. Wren watched, his gaze sharp, as the air around them stirred, a few stray leaves dancing in a sudden breeze. Above, clouds gathered and a light drizzle began to fall, droplets catching in Aisling's wild hair.

"There," she said, dropping her hands and turning to them with a triumphant grin. "I made it rain! The wind was new, though. I've never done that before."

Wren's lips twitched in a half-smile. "Impressive," he allowed, his tone even but approving.

Harker nodded, her arms folded now as well. "Basic elemental manipulation," she assessed. "A good sign for someone without any training."

Aisling's face lit up at the acknowledgment, her chest puffing out slightly in pride. "What else should I try?" she asked, looking between Harker and Wren.

Harker considered for a moment before responding. "The fact that you've managed even this indicates potential. If you can manipulate these, it stands to reason you can learn others," she explained, her tone matter-of-fact.

"What are the others?" Aisling's voice was full of curiosity, eager for the knowledge.

"There are four primary elements: fire, air, water, and earth. It's rare, but some witches can control all four, especially blood-born witches," Harker informed her, her voice clear and direct.

"I want to do all four!" Aisling declared, her voice tinged with excitement.

"Slow down," Wren interjected, his voice firm. "You need to walk before you can run."

Aisling's face fell slightly, but Harker was quick to encourage her. "Let's see which elements come naturally to you first. We already know you can stir the air and summon rain. Let's try earth next."

Aisling nodded, her earlier disappointment forgotten in the face of a new challenge. "Okay, what do I do?"

"Concentrate," Harker instructed. "Connect with the ground beneath you. Feel its energy."

Wren watched as Aisling closed her eyes, her feet planted firmly on the ground. The air grew still, the brief rain ceasing. For a moment, there was silence. Then, the smallest of vibrations began, a tremor that rippled through the courtyard, rustling leaves and making small pebbles dance on the flagstones.

Aisling opened her eyes, a look of awe on her face. "Did I do that?"

"You did," Wren confirmed, a note of respect in his voice.

Harker smiled warmly. "You're a natural, Aisling. With the right training, there's no telling how far you'll go."

Aisling bounced lightly on the balls of her feet, her grin

spreading across her face with uncontainable joy. The energy that radiated from her was almost tangible, a vibrant force that seemed to fill the space around her.

Wren couldn't help but return the girl's infectious smile, even if it was only with the slightest upturn of his lips. There was something about her energy that was comforting, reminiscent of the calm that follows a storm or the warmth of the sun breaking through clouds after a dreary day.

He exchanged a knowing look with Harker, a look that conveyed an unspoken understanding between them. This fiery young girl was going to grow up into something extraordinary. She was a witch with the potential to master the elements, to command the forces of nature, and, with their guidance, she would one day stand among the best of them.

As Harker continued to put Aisling through her paces with a series of tests, Wren hung back, content to observe. His role was that of a mentor and protector, a guiding hand rather than an intervening force. Yet, even in his role as an observer, Wren felt an affinity for Aisling that went beyond duty—a genuine fondness and a protective instinct that was growing stronger with each passing day.

Aisling was like a wild flame, her energy raw and untamed. Wren saw in her a fire that could either illuminate the darkest paths or, if unchecked, consume her. He silently hoped it would be the former, that she would learn to channel this incredible energy into something magnificent.

As the last rays of the sun faded, the sky turning to dusk, Wren turned to the girl. Her cheeks were flushed from the exertion, her wild curls sticking out in all directions. "We'll resume this tomorrow," he said, his deep voice steady and composed. Despite his even tone, there was an undercurrent of emotion, a sense of pride and anticipation for what the future held for her.

Harker nodded in agreement, a look of satisfaction and pride on her face. "She has quite the aptitude," she observed, watching Aisling with admiration.

"I can't wait to try more," Aisling piped up, her enthusiasm undiminished by the day's exertions.

"Tomorrow," Wren promised, allowing himself a small, genuine smile.

"Alright, fine," Aisling responded, her words a rapid, breathless agreement. "But can we get some food now? I'm starving."

"Of course," Harker replied, her hand resting gently on Aisling's shoulder. "Let's get you cleaned up and then we can have a nice dinner."

As Harker and Aisling started towards the keep, Wren lingered behind, his gaze fixed on the fading sunset. The sky was awash with gold and crimson, a beautiful end to the day. A sense of hope, unfamiliar yet welcome, began to stir in his chest—a hope for a future where Aisling would shine brightly, a beacon in their often dark world.

With the last of the daylight slipping away, Wren turned and followed them inside, the sound of Aisling's laughter echoing behind him, a small, content smile playing on his lips.

SEVENTEEN

I lingered in the corridor just outside Ava's door, taking a deep breath before knocking. The soft sound echoed in the empty hallway, and within moments, the door swung open.

Ava's face brightened upon seeing me, a warm smile spreading across her features. "Vale, I got your message. They're all here," she said with a hopeful tone as she stepped aside to let me in.

The room was cozy, filled with the soft glow of late afternoon light filtering through the curtains. My eyes scanned the small crowd that had gathered, a curious mix of anticipation and anxiety on their faces.

Ava introduced them one by one. Calliope was a curvy, brown-haired half-Fae with an easy smile. Sam and Harlow stood close together, the blonde half-demon woman and the black-haired half-Fae woman nodding politely in my direction. Griffin, the dark-haired half-demon man, had a guarded look, but his eyes held a certain resolve. Mikel, the short half-Fae with unruly brown hair, waved as he was introduced. Lastly, there was Archer, his light brown hair falling into his eyes as he gave a tentative smile.

"I'm sure Ava has explained why you're here since you've all agreed to come," I began, my voice steadier than I felt. "I need to create the next generation of witches and you're the ones who have answered that call."

Silence stretched between them, thick with unspoken questions and the weight of uncertainty. I scanned their faces, searching for any sign of doubt or fear.

"I can't promise that this is without its risks. The ritual itself is risky. If anyone has reservations, now is the time to voice them," I said, my voice firm. No one stirred, and I took that as a silent agreement to proceed.

A nervous energy buzzed through me. "Okay," I exhaled, raking a hand through my hair. "Let's drop the formalities. You are all looking at me like I'm some kind of strange animal."

They shifted, some with looks of embarrassment, others with curiosity. "I'm as new to this as you are. We're navigating uncharted waters, so I ask for your patience. Let me start from the beginning."

I told them my story, leaving no detail untouched, recounting every moment that had led me to them. From the revelation of my witch lineage to the blood magic that bound me to Kaelan, from the expansive library of ancient texts to the soul merge with the First Witch. I told them of demons and battles, of Wren's capture and my father's demise. I spoke of my torment under Haldir's hand, my escape from the spirit realm, and the support of the First Witch.

I laid bare my soul, my victories and traumas, wanting them to understand the gravity of the journey they were about to embark upon.

"Now, I stand against the Seven," I concluded, my voice firm. "They are the unknown I must confront. But together, we stand a chance against whatever is coming. Together, we can be a force that shapes the future."

The stillness in the chamber hung like a thick veil, and I could sense their apprehension, the unspoken questions that lingered on the tip of their tongues, heavy with the weight of uncertainty.

I drew in a deep breath, letting it fill my lungs and steel my nerves. "I know this is overwhelming. I won't think less of any of you for feeling afraid. This isn't a battle you sought out. It's your right to choose. But if you choose to stand with me, you're binding yourself to the fate I've set into motion."

Ava, her emerald eyes ablaze with unwavering spirit, stepped out from the collective uncertainty. Her stance was one of defiance, a bold declaration without uttering a word. "I'm with you, Vale. You've protected us time and time again. Wherever this path leads, whatever the sacrifices might be, I'm ready."

The echo of her conviction seemed to ripple through the room, stirring a silent strength in me. I swept my gaze over the group, lingering on each individual, silently imploring them to understand the importance of this moment.

It was Archer who broke the silence next, his voice a low thrum of solidarity. "You have my support," he affirmed, nodding solemnly in my direction.

"I stand with you," Griffin stated, unyielding and resolute.

Sam's voice, light but laced with determination, followed suit. "You can count on me." Beside her, Harlow paused, a flicker of uncertainty crossing her features as she glanced at Sam before stepping forward. With a nod, she silently conveyed her assent.

Mikel stepped forward, the smallest of them, but with a presence that radiated an unexpected strength. His brown eyes locked with mine, a flash of steel behind them, and his chin lifted. "I am with you, Vale. I will not abandon this world to the whims of tyrants," he declared in a quiet but determined voice.

All eyes turned to Calliope, who met my gaze with a serene smile. "I'm with you," she said softly.

As each of them pledged their allegiance, something within me fortified. They had each been touched by the tides of destiny and yet they chose to sail with me into the storm. It was a humbling moment, one that filled my chest with a warmth that pushed back the cold fingers of doubt.

"Thank you," I said, my voice swelling with gratitude and pride. "For your bravery, for your trust, for choosing to walk this path with me. Now, come with me."

Ava's nod was the push I needed, and I led them through the palace's silent corridors into the hallowed walls of the library. The room was bathed in the gentle hues of twilight, the stained glass casting kaleidoscopic patterns across the ancient tomes and marbled floors.

The library was silent, a sanctuary of ancient knowl- edge and untapped power that seemed to watch and wait with bated breath as the future of magic was ushered into its heart.

"Our knowledge, our power, it starts here," I said as their eyes took in the scene around them. "This is the foun- dation we build our future on."

Calliope was the first to break the stillness, her words suffused with wonder. "It's incredible," she whispered, her gaze sweeping over the vast expanse of leather-bound tomes and parchment scrolls that adorned the shelves like jewels.

Sam was next, her voice a hushed echo of Calliope's amazement. "So many books," she said, her eyes glittering with the thrill of discovery.

Griffin, whose practical nature shone through his doubt, asked with a raised eyebrow, "You're not seriously expecting us to go through all of these, are you?"

"No," came Harker's timely interjection, her voice slicing cleanly through the air from her position obscured by the tower of books she sat around. The heads turned in unison, their expressions conveying surprise and intrigue —a testament to Harker's presence, unnoticed until she chose to make it known. "That's where I come in."

"Harker has made significant headway in all these. Together, we've identified the texts that will best serve our needs and the order in which they should be tackled," I said. "She's your mentor when I'm otherwise occupied."

"You still haven't explained how we're even supposed to become witches," Harlow, ever direct, cut to the heart of the matter. "You mentioned a ritual?"

"Yes," I acknowledged with a nod, my eyes meeting hers directly. "The ritual is our goal, but we're not ready for that just yet. Harker and I need to get to know each of you. Also, the ritual calls for a specific phase of the moon. We'll be ready by then."

Restlessness began to simmer within the group, a natural reaction to the unknowns that loomed ahead. "Everything you need to know will be shared with you," I promised, my voice firm yet understanding of their impatience. "Patience is as much a part of this journey as the learning itself. Harker will initiate you into the fundamentals of witchcraft. You'll start with the very essence of magic, the core principles that I was never formally taught."

"And you? What will you be doing while we're buried in books and lessons?" Archer asked, arching an eyebrow.

"I'll be gathering the materials we need and securing a location for the ritual. Preparation is key and I won't let anything be left to chance." I told him patiently.

Harlow, who seemed to always be skeptical, crossed her arms, her stance demanding further clarification. "So, until then, what do we do?"

"You learn," I told them, my voice echoing with the conviction of a battle cry. "Absorb everything you can, as swiftly as you can. The Seven's arrival is a mystery; it could be days, weeks, or months. We don't have the luxury of time. But we must be prepared."

I AGAIN FOUND myself in the ethereal embrace of the vast, towering forest within the dream realm. Mist veiled the ancient trees like a shroud, and the air held an otherworldly chill that seeped through my cloak, even with the hood pulled up to shield me from the frigid surroundings. At my side, Nyxen stood watchful.

"Uh oh, how do we keep finding ourselves back here, Nyxen?" I mused aloud, my voice carrying in the stillness of the forest.

Nyxen's response came with a touch of cryptic simplic-ity. *"You, shifting in sleep."*

The revelation that I was somehow shifting in my sleep was both intriguing and disturbing. My previous visits had left my physical body in bed and I recalled the eerie sensa-tion of my soul re-entering my body upon waking. This experience added yet another layer of complexity to the mysteries of the dream realm.

Curiosity guiding my steps, I ventured further into the forest with Nyxen at my side. Each step I took seemed to propel us forward several feet, an unusual sensation that reinforced the dream-like quality of this realm.

"What do you suppose we'll find this time?" I mused, my voice carrying a sense of curiosity as I continued walking. Another step brought us to a small clearing, and my breath caught as I took in the sight before us—a murky lake, its surface still and reflective, with patches of mist skimming its top like ghostly apparitions. The eerie atmosphere of the place was undeniable and ice settled into the pit of my stomach.

Nyxen remained silent, his golden eyes scanning our eerie surroundings with a sense of wariness that mirrored my own unease. It was as if the very forest itself held secrets it was reluctant to reveal and we were intruders in this dark realm. The disconcerting feeling in the air validated my suspicion that we were intruding upon a place not meant for us.

"It feels like we're not supposed to be here," I whispered softly, my voice barely more than a breath of mist in the haunting stillness that surrounded us.

"*We're not,*" Nyxen replied, his response terse and filled with an edge of caution that made my skin prickle.

"Have you been here before?" I asked, my gaze shifting from the still, mist-shrouded surroundings to his narrowed, searching eyes.

"*No.*" His response was curt and left me with more questions than answers.

My eyes continued to roam the eerie landscape, seeking

any clue or sign of what had drawn us here, but the forest offered nothing but its haunting stillness.

A sudden movement from the lake seized my attention and my breath hitched in my throat as I watched in a mix of dread and fascination. Something was stirring beneath the water's murky surface, something large and undeniably menacing.

I watched in growing dread as a dark, shadowy form began to emerge. The head of a creature, obscured by the mist that clung to the water's edge, materialized before us. Two immense eyes, their pupils slitted like those of a predatory beast, fixed on me through the haze.

A woman, if one could call her that, emerged from the depths of the lake, her appearance more aquatic than human. Her skin was ghostly pale, almost translucent, and her features were sharp and otherworldly. Two small fins stood out from the sides of her neck. Rows of pointed teeth were revealed as she smiled at me, and her grotesquely wide mouth seemed to stretch unnaturally across her face. Long, dark hair clung to her like seaweed, adding to the macabre image.

The creature's gaze remained locked on mine, and an icy chill seeped into my veins. She opened her mouth, unleashing a scream so piercing, so agonizing, that it reverberated through the very earth beneath our feet. The sheer agony and intensity of the sound forced me to my knees, my hands instinctively covering my ears. Nyxen snarled, his hackles raised, but the creature paid him no heed.

Summoning every ounce of willpower, I struggled to my feet, my need to escape overpowering my fear. I staggered backward, taking one uncertain step after another. And then, in the blink of an eye, Nyxen and I were transported once again. A mere step had transported us away from the nightmarish siren, depositing us back among the misty trees.

"What the hell was that thing?" I said more to myself than to Nyxen as I scanned the forest we just left for any trace of the woman following.

"*We should go,*" Nyxen's voice broke through the lingering echoes of the siren's scream in my mind.

I needed no further encouragement. My heart raced, fear and panic coursing through me like a wildfire. The forest's secrets were best left undisturbed and I had no intention of lingering in this eerie, unfathomable realm any longer than necessary.

Turning away from the haunting lake and the siren's terrifying scream, I set my sights on a narrow path that wound its way through the towering trees, Nyxen faithfully at my side. Each step we took through the forest felt like a battle against the pervasive eerie feeling that clung to us like a shadow.

With each step, the atmosphere began to change, evolving into something even more chilling. The once still and mist-shrouded landscape began to shift and change, sometimes passing by in a dizzying blur. It was as if the very essence of the dream realm itself was in constant flux.

"I've really had enough of this place, Nyxen," I muttered, my frustration simmering just beneath the surface. "You're my guide here, right? So guide me back home."

Nyxen's response was a low growl, his yellow eyes filled with a sense of helplessness that mirrored my own. "*I can't do that.*"

"Why the hell not?" I retorted, incredulousness lacing my tone.

"*Your shifting, your dreams... They're a doorway to the*

realm, Vale." Nyxen explained, his voice tinged with an unusual seriousness. *"Your consciousness is anchoring your soul here. Only you can shift yourself back."*

Despite the implications of his words, I halted in my tracks, my mouth open as I stared at my foxlike shadow familiar. "Nyx, that is the most you've ever said to me."

"I know," he said, offering no more than a simple acknowledgment.

Despite the dire situation, I couldn't help but let out a nervous, fond laugh at the unexpected conversation with my usually stoic companion.

"Vale," a sudden whisper drifted through the mist, a soft, lilting voice that seemed to emanate from all directions at once.

My head whipped around, searching for the source of the disembodied voice. "Who's there?"

"Vale," the voice called again, this time closer, its haunting cadence more chilling than the frigid air.

The mist around me began to thicken, swirling ominously, and a creeping sense of fear clawed its way up my spine.

"Come," the voice beckoned, its tone filled with a strange urgency as if it held a solution to my predicament. I could feel a strange tug, a pull deep within me, compelling me to move forward.

"What do you want from me?" I shouted, my voice quivering.

"You're lost, Vale," the voice whispered, its words a haunting echo. "You're wandering in the darkness. Let me show you the way."

The pull grew stronger, and I could feel the encroaching darkness seeping into my thoughts, clouding my mind.

Despite my uncertainty, I took a hesitant step forward, the mist swirling around me like a sinister dance.

"Vale, no!" Nyxen's voice rang out, a warning that echoed in the recesses of my mind, fighting against the pull of the unknown.

The voice taunted me with a blend of amusement and malice. "Ugh, clever little witch, to bring a guide to protect you. But who will protect your guide should something befall them?"

Dread coursed through me as I realized the implications of those words. The mist began to swirl and thicken around Nyxen, closing in on him like a predatory beast. Panic surged within me and I lunged forward, reaching out to him, but the mist moved too quickly, closing around him and cutting him off from my sight.

"No, stop!" I screamed, my voice echoing through the oppressive fog.

There was a sound, something akin to a snarl, followed by an eerie silence. When the mist finally cleared, Nyxen was gone.

Terror gripped my heart, and I spun around, disoriented in the thickening mist. The path we had been following had vanished, leaving me in an unfamiliar, haunting landscape.

"Nyxen! Where are you?" I called out, my voice trembling with fear.

There was no response, only the haunting stillness of the mist-shrouded forest. I was alone.

EIGHTEEN

I began to run mindlessly, my steps fueled by desperation and fear, my senses straining to find any sign of Nyxen or a way out. The mist had become impenetrable and the vast forest seemed to stretch on infinitely.

"Nyxen!" I shouted again, my voice echoing through the eerie trees, desperate and pleading.

Still, there was nothing but the sound of my rapid breathing.

I continued running, my panic mounting with every passing moment, but the forest showed no sign of relenting.

"Why do you run, Queen? Why not rest with me? I'll help you find your way," the same enchanting voice whispered seductively as if it were right in my ear.

I spun around, frantically searching for the source of the voice, but the mist was dense, and I could see nothing but the swirling fog.

The voice continued to coax and entice, luring me toward it. "Come to me, Vale. Let me show you the way."

The words were hypnotic and I felt an irresistible pull toward the voice before I forcibly shook my head, dispelling the fog that had begun to cloud my mind. I had to break free from its grip, had to find Nyxen, and escape this nightmare.

Suddenly, the path I had been following reappeared before me as if summoned by my desperate need and I stumbled toward it, my steps becoming more confident as the mist began to thin and the trees became less dense.

"Come back, Vale," the voice called again, this time with a hint of desperation.

I ignored its pleas and pressed forward, determined to escape the forest. The mist was dissipating, and the way ahead was becoming clearer.

And then, just as I thought I had broken free, a figure materialized before me—a woman with dark hair and ghostly pale skin, her presence haunting.

The woman before me was a nightmarish apparition, her appearance a stark contrast to her soft, honeyed voice. Her ragged dress was little more than a patchwork of tattered cloth and her emaciated frame seemed to barely hold her upright. Her bare feet were covered in dirt, blood, and filth, her toenails cracked and bleeding. Her hands were equally gruesome, the fingers crooked and dirty, the nails broken and caked with grime. When she grinned, her teeth were a nightmare, broken, rotting, and yellowed with decay.

"Don't leave me," she implored in a breathy whisper, her eyes locked onto mine, her filthy hands inching closer, reaching out toward me.

My heart pounded in my chest and I took a hesitant step back, my hand instinctively moving toward the dagger strapped to my thigh.

"You don't need that, little Queen," she taunted, her sweet words turning vicious.

Before I could react, her bony hand shot out and clamped around my wrist, her grip like an iron vice. I struggled against her, but she was unnaturally strong, and her jagged nails dug into my skin, causing searing pain where they pierced my flesh.

"Let me go," I gasped, my desperation mounting as I tried to break free from her grasp.

She only smiled, her eyes glinting with an otherworldly light. Her grip remained unyielding, and her dirty, cracked nails dug deeper into my flesh. "But I can show you the way," she said, gesturing into the air before us. With a twisted power, she conjured a large, dark mirror that hovered ominously in front of me and my eyes were drawn to it.

In the mirror's reflection, I saw a version of the forest, but it was a nightmarish vision. The trees were twisted and gnarled. The ground was covered in rotting moss and decay. The woman's smile in the mirror was wicked and her grip on my wrist tightened even further.

My eyes locked onto my own reflection and to my horror, I watched as my mirror self smiled wickedly, a vicious sneer contorting my features.

"Look into the dark, little Queen," she whispered, her voice a sinister murmur. "Look into the twisted chaos of your heart."

My reflection continued to change, becoming increasingly terrifying as the shadows within me swelled. My eyes blazed with an inner fire, the inky black of my palms beginning to creep up my arms. Flames danced along my skin, enveloping me until I was nothing but a living spark.

"Let it in," the woman purred seductively. "Let the darkness embrace you. It's what you truly are."

I couldn't tear my gaze away from the mirror, unable to break free as the flames soared higher and the void yawned wider, threatening to engulf everything in its path.

But I would not be consumed. The fire answered to me.

The flames continued to dance around me, responding to my will. The shadows, once a source of fear, now swirled around me like a protective shroud, empowering me rather than devouring me. I was not a victim of the darkness; I was its master, a queen of realms and shadows.

"The darkness is mine to command," I declared defiantly.

The woman recoiled, hissing as she released her grip on my wrist. I staggered back, the mirror vanishing into a wisp of smoke. Her taunting words had no power over me now.

"You think you can deny your fate?" she spat, her voice laced with frustration. "You're a fool, little Queen."

"You know, I've met a lot of assholes like you who claim to know my fate, yet none of them have been right." I met her words with a fierce determination, flames flickering in my eyes and the palms of my hands as I stood my ground.

"Where's my familiar?" I demanded, breathing heavily, the rage within me all-consuming.

The woman responded with a cruel laugh, her dark eyes filled with mockery. "You think I fear your pitful fire? You have no idea what awaits you, witch. But soon, you will see. Soon, the darkness will devour you. And when it does, you'll welcome it."

Driven by a surge of anger, I lunged forward, my hand closing around the woman's throat, my fingers burning with searing heat.

"Where is he?!" I shouted, my voice ringing through the trees with fury.

The woman's eyes widened in surprise, but her mocking grin remained. "He's mine now, little Queen. He belongs to the dark, just as you will."

With those chilling words, the woman vanished, swallowed by the surrounding mist. My fiery determination remained undiminished. I would not allow her taunts and threats to defeat me. I had to find Nyxen, and I had to get out of this eerie forest.

The fire within me burned brighter, my resolve unwavering. I began to move, my footsteps sure, and the path through the forest started to reappear. The mist was thinning, and the oppressive atmosphere lightened. The trees, though still twisted and gnarled, seemed less malevolent.

I stopped in my tracks, my thoughts racing as I tried to form a plan. If Nyxen couldn't reach me, perhaps I could reach him. If I had shifted here, I could sense him through our bond and potentially shift to his location. It was a slim hope, but it was all I had to go on.

Consciously shifting was an uncharted territory for me. With a deep breath, I closed my eyes, focusing my mind. I needed to find Nyxen, to sense his presence through the depths of my mind. My mental shields were up, guarding against any unwanted intrusions as I delved into the darkness within.

Reaching out mentally, I sought that familiar glimmer of recognition that was Nyxen. It felt like an eternity as I searched through the shadows of my mind, the seconds ticking by with agonizing slowness. But then, just as doubt began to creep in, I found him—a faint, distant sensation like a rope that I could grasp.

With determination, I pulled at that connection, willing

it to grow stronger. It was a disorienting sensation as my body seemed to be pulled in a multitude of directions simultaneously. The world around me blurred and dissolved into darkness, the shadows enveloping me entirely.

The transition was abrupt, leaving me standing alone in an endless void of darkness. The silence in this place was deafening, pressing in on me from all sides, making every breath feel like a thunderous roar in my ears.

"Nyxen," I whispered into the abyss afraid to shatter the overwhelming silence.

There was a brief moment of stillness, during which I feared he might not answer. Then, his voice echoed back to me in my mind, a welcome sound, solid and clear. *"Vale."*

"Where are you? I'm lost. I can't see you," I replied urgently, my panic bubbling just beneath the surface.

"Shadows cannot exist without the light," Nyxen cryptically replied.

It made sense—he was a being made of shadow, and this place was dominated by darkness. Desperate to find him, I held up my palm, conjuring flames that danced along my blackened fingertips. The sudden light pierced the enveloping darkness, and Nyxen emerged from the shadows.

"Clever witch," Nyxen praised, his yellow eyes glowing with approval.

"We should get out of here," I said, the urgency in my voice unmistakable. "Wherever 'here' is, it's not a place I want to linger."

"I cannot follow you from this place," he said solemnly, his yellow eyes filled with a sorrow I had never seen before.

His words struck me like a dagger to the heart, and

panic surged within me. "What? What do you mean?" I stammered, my heart racing.

"I'm trapped, Vale," Nyxen confessed, his words like a death sentence. *"This place is like a cage, imprisoning me in the darkness."*

I felt a sinking feeling in the pit of my stomach and my mind raced as I searched for a solution. "Well, I can't leave you here. There has to be a way."

"There is a way for you, but not for me," Nyxen replied, his voice heavy with resignation.

I shook my head vehemently, refusing to accept his fate. "No, I'm not leaving without you," I declared firmly.

"Vale—" Nyxen began, but I cut him off.

"Nyxen, I'm not leaving you," I said obstinately. "Tell me how to help you."

"You're a stubborn creature," he chided softly.

"So are you. Tell me how to get you out of here," I demanded once more.

He hesitated before finally conceding, *"You must find a way."*

"How? How do I find a way?" I pressed urgently.

"I don't know. You must figure it out. You don't have much time."

"Nyxen-" I began, but he cut me off.

"You must wake up," his voice turned urgent.

"Not without you," I protested, clinging to the hope that there had to be a way.

"Vale, wake up. Now," his words were a command and I felt a powerful force pulling me away from the darkness that had ensnared me.

I blinked, and suddenly, everything shifted. My surroundings changed and I found myself sitting up in my own bed, gasping for breath. A sob escaped my throat as the realization dawned on me—I was back in the Fae realm, back in the palace with Kaelan by my side.

"Vale, you were having a nightmare," Kaelan's voice broke through the haze of my fear and confusion. Concern etched on his handsome features, he reached out to touch my trembling form.

I wiped the tears from my face, my heart still racing from the ordeal. "It wasn't a nightmare," I replied, my voice quivering. "It was real, and Nyxen, oh gods, Nyxen!" I called out into the night for my familiar, desperately hoping he would appear, but the room remained empty and the shadows clung to their silence.

"Vale, tell me what's wrong," Kaelan implored, his hands resting gently on my shoulders.

"Nyxen," I replied, my voice catching in my throat. "He's trapped."

Kaelan's brows furrowed in concern. "What do you mean?"

"We were in the dream realm," I began, my words spilling out in a frenzy. "And there was this... this creature. She took him. And now he's trapped." Panic surged through me, and I felt like I was drowning in fear.

"Slow down, Vale. Take a breath," Kaelan urged, his soothing words cutting through the chaos in my mind. He held me close, running a calming hand down my hair.

"I can't slow down!" I cried out. "He's trapped and I have to get him back. I can't leave him."

"You're not leaving him," Kaelan reassured me, his voice a comforting presence in the darkness.

"You don't understand," I insisted, shaking my head. "I don't know what is happening to him."

"Vale," Kaelan said, his voice calm and steady as he

tried to calm the storm within me. "Listen to me. We will find a way to get him back, okay?"

I nodded, sniffing and wiping away more tears. "Okay."

Kaelan pressed his forehead to mine, his hand continuing to stroke my hair. "I promise you, Vale. We will find a way."

I nodded again, taking a shaky breath. "Thank you."

He pulled me close, and I allowed myself to melt into his strong embrace, seeking solace in the warmth of his presence.

I didn't know how we would rescue Nyxen from the clutches of the dream realm, but I knew that Kaelan was right.

We would find a way. We had to.

NINETEEN

KAELAN

aelan rubbed at his face, the weight of exhaustion settling heavily on his shoulders. He had barely slept, haunted by the vivid memory of Vale's distressing nightmare. It was not the first time he had witnessed her dreams and the turmoil they brought, but this one had been different, more urgent, more ominous.

He had been woken by her cries in the night, the fear in her voice slicing through his dreams like a blade. Without hesitation, he had followed her to the library, knowing that whatever plagued her thoughts was a threat that required their immediate attention. Vale's distress was his primary concern, and he wouldn't let her face her fears alone.

He understood that Nyxen was more than just a companion to her; he was a vital part of her magic and her life.

In the dim light, Vale and Harker hunched over piles of old tomes and scrolls. The air was thick with the scent of old paper and dust, and the only sound was the rustling of pages as they searched for answers.

Kaelan worried for Vale. The lines of fatigue etched on

her face, her eyes bloodshot from lack of sleep, the thread of dread that drifted down through their bond. But her determination was resilient, and he admired her for it. She was a force to be reckoned with, a queen in every sense of the word, and she had no idea. Self-doubt plagued her at every turn.

As he watched, Vale and Harker exchanged hurried whispers, their fingers pointing to passages and illustrations in the books. They were desperately searching for clues, for any information that could lead them to Nyxen and the dream realm where he was trapped.

Kaelan couldn't begin to comprehend the magnitude of their search. The dream realm was a mysterious, unknown place, a plane of existence that few beings had access to. It was a world apart, a realm of shadows and secrets, and even he didn't have the power to reach it.

Still, he was determined to help Vale, to do everything in his power to rescue Nyxen and ease her mind. He knew the toll the ordeal was taking on her, and he wanted nothing more than to take her into his arms and shield her from the pain and worry. But he knew she wouldn't accept that, not until Nyxen was safe. So, he would remain by her side, helping her search and lending her his strength.

"I'm just not finding anything useful or relevant!" Vale cried, throwing up her hands in frustration.

"Let's keep going," Harker said, her tone gentle but firm. "There has to be something here."

"What about searching for books on the creatures that walk the dream realm?" Kaelan offered, joining them at the table.

Harker shot him a dark look, "We've already checked. We don't have any books specifically about creatures that reside in the dream realm."

"It might be helpful to check Thalion's library," Vale mused aloud.

"I can shift you there if you'd like to go search," Kaelan said, standing up and extending his arm to Vale.

"What if I try shifting there myself?" she asked. Vale had told him about that part of the dream, how she had shifted to find Nyxen. He wasn't surprised by the emergence of this new power and he would usually encourage her to try but the thought of her alone with Thalion turned his blood cold.

"We'll try that out some other time when you're not exhausted," he told her. "Shifting isn't an easy skill to learn."

She nodded and he was surprised. He hadn't thought she would give in that easily, she must be more exhausted than he realized. She placed her hand in his and he pulled her close as he always did, inhaling the familiar smell of her as the shadows swallowed them.

They stepped out of the shadows in front of Thalion's door. "I really need to ward this whole place so no one can shift in like in Terralux," Vale said absently while she knocked, the sound echoing through the quiet corridor. After a few tense minutes, the door creaked open to reveal Thalion. His face lit up with warmth when he laid eyes on Vale, but that light dimmed considerably as he took in Kaelan's presence, a fleeting shadow of disappointment crossing his features. Kaelan couldn't help but battle the twinge of jealousy within him.

"Thalion, Nyxen has been taken, and I need to find books in your library that might help," Vale blurted out, her words rushed and urgent. Thalion stood there for a moment, blinking as he processed the information.

"Taken? How?" Thalion's voice held genuine concern and his brow furrowed with worry.

"That doesn't matter right now," Vale said firmly, leaving no room for debate. "I just need to get into your library."

Thalion appeared torn for a moment, but ultimately, he nodded, his expression growing more serious. "Of course. Follow me; we'll need to wake up the librarian."

They followed Thalion through the darkened palace, making their way to a corridor near the library's entrance. There, Thalion knocked on a wooden door a short distance down the hall. A drowsy Fae male, unfamiliar to Kaelan, answered the summons.

"Bertrand, I'm sorry to disturb you at this hour, but we require your urgent assistance in the library. If you would please get dressed as quickly as possible and meet us there?" Thalion's request carried an undertone of command, leaving no room for debate.

"Right away, Your Majesty," Bertrand replied dutifully before promptly closing the door.

Returning to the imposing library doors, they waited impatiently. Thalion paced back and forth, his expression troubled, while Vale's impatience manifested in the rhythmic tapping of her foot and her body's tense posture.

Kaelan recognized Thalion's significance as an ally and resource, but his presence felt like an unwelcome intrusion, triggering Kaelan's territorial instincts. He understood the urgency of their mission, but part of him wished he could sweep Vale away to their chambers, shielding her from the world's harsh realities. But he knew that she would never allow such a thing, and so he was forced to accept the fact that she would continue to put herself in danger, no matter how much it terrified him.

When Bertrand arrived, the group entered the library, and Vale turned to the Fae male, her determination evident. "I need to see any books you have on creatures that lurk within the dream realm. After that, I need any books about the dream realm at all."

Still looking slightly perplexed, Bertrand quickly set about collecting a stack of books. One by one, he piled them onto a desk, not wasting any time as they began their search. Hours passed with the group poring over the volumes, but they couldn't find any mention of the woman Vale had encountered in the dream realm. It seemed as though she remained a mysterious entity, unrecorded in the Fae library's vast collection.

Then, as Vale flipped through a small, unassuming cloth-bound journal, her eyes widened with relief. "I've found something!" she exclaimed, unable to contain her excitement. Her voice echoed through the library's quiet halls as she continued to flip through the journal's pages, finally landing on a small, hand-drawn illustration.

"What is it?" Kaelan asked, curious as he leaned over her shoulder to get a better look.

"It's a picture of the woman I met," Vale explained, her voice filled with awe and realization. "And there's a folk story about her. She's called the Dreamcarver."

"The Dreamcarver," Kaelan repeated, his brow furrowing. "I've never heard of her."

Vale continued to read from the journal, sharing the newfound information. "It says here that she's an ancient being and that she resides in the dream realm. It also mentions her ability to control the dreams of others. There's not much else here, just some basic information and a bit about how she's believed to have been imprisoned in the dream realm long ago."

She skimmed over the passage again, "Wait, there's a small bit about how she trapped a witch in a place of nightmares and the witch escaped by using her powers. But there's nothing about how she did it."

"This is a start, though. We know more about who we're dealing with and that's a step closer to helping Nyxen," Thalion encouraged her, his gaze filled with understanding.

Vale's shoulders slumped, and she nodded, though her eyes shone with unshed tears. "It's not enough, though. I don't even know how to return to the dream realm."

"What did you do before, Vale?" Thalion asked, his voice gentle.

Vale hesitated, then admitted, "I just fell asleep and woke up in the dream realm. It's happened before."

"Perhaps it will happen again?" Kaelan suggested optimistically.

Vale glanced at him, her expression weary. "I'm not sure I can do this again. I feel so drained, so tired," she confessed, her voice cracking with emotion.

Thalion reached out, placing a comforting hand on her arm. "It's okay, Vale. You're exhausted. You should rest and try again later. You can use your old rooms and stay here."

Kaelan's jealousy flared at Thalion's suggestion, and he couldn't help but growl, "I'll take her to bed."

Thalion's eyes lingered on Kaelan for a moment as if assessing whether he was worth the trouble, then he spoke up again. "Vale, did you ever have that conversation with Kaelan like we discussed?" His words seemed to make Vale cringe and Kaelan's anger simmered.

"Conversation? What conversation? You were discussing me?" Kaelan demanded.

"Thalion, this is not the time," Vale warned, but her eyes were pleading.

Thalion raised an eyebrow and smirked. "Well, I think this is the perfect time. Otherwise, you may never actually get around to it."

Kaelan's anger flared and he interrupted before Vale could say anything more. "I don't understand. What are you talking about?"

Thalion's grin widened, his gaze hard as he decided to elaborate. "Oh, I'll explain it to him."

"No, Thalion," Vale interjected, attempting to defuse the situation.

"No, Thalion, please continue. What is it that you were discussing about me with her?" Kaelan said, his voice laced with danger, his eyes locking onto Thalion's.

Thalion, not one to back down from confrontation, didn't mince words. "You've got a problem with being a territorial demon prick. Biting her and leaving marks all over her neck, having her scream your name at all hours of the night, acting like she's yours. She's supposed to be viewed as a queen, not some demon plaything," he snapped, his eyes narrowing as he glared at Kaelan.

"She is mine," Kaelan seethed, his tone defiant. "I'm not going to apologize for being a territorial demon prick, as you say, when it comes to her. And I don't remember asking for your opinion on the matter."

Thalion didn't back down, his face inches from Kaelan's, their noses nearly touching as he retorted, "Well, it's not what Vale wants. She's made that perfectly clear. At least, she's made it clear to me," he added with a smug smirk.

"I don't remember Vale ever saying she doesn't want those things. In fact, I remember she couldn't stop begging me for more," Kaelan shot back, his lip curling up to reveal his elongated fangs.

Vale had had enough of their bickering. "Enough," she barked at both of them, her voice commanding attention. "This is ridiculous. And this is not the time to be arguing amongst ourselves. This is about Nyxen. He needs our help, and here you two are squabbling like children."

Kaelan, however, was not ready to let the matter drop. "No, Vale, I want to know what he's talking about and why you haven't brought it up with me before now."

"Kaelan, not now," Vale pleaded, the stress of the situation taking its toll on her.

"Is this about you wanting to be with them too? Is that what he's talking about?" Kaelan demanded, pointing an accusatory finger at Thalion.

Thalion didn't hesitate to confirm, "Yes, it is. And you're being a selfish ass, Kaelan. You can't keep her all to yourself; she's not your pet."

"You have no right to interfere," Kaelan growled, his jealousy and anger surging.

But Vale had had enough, and her voice cut through the escalating argument. "Stop!" she yelled, her frustration and anger resonating in the library's confines. "I'm not a fucking toy or an object to fight over. You can't own me. I belong to no one."

The room fell silent. Fury radiated from Vale, mixed with hurt and frustration, leaving Kaelan and Thalion speechless, their anger dissipating in the face of her raw emotion.

Vale's anger continued to smolder, her eyes still burning with fury as she spoke. "You have no idea what I'm going through right now. No idea. So don't stand there and argue about who I belong to. I don't belong to anyone. And if you can't respect that, then maybe you're not the men I thought you were."

Kaelan was stunned into silence by the venom in her voice, the conviction in her words. He felt a wave of shame wash over him, realizing how selfish and thoughtless he had been, and how deeply he had wounded her.

"Vale, I'm sorry," Kaelan whispered, his voice laden with remorse. "I never meant to make you feel like a possession or that you didn't have a choice."

"And I'm sorry, too, Vale. I should have spoken to you directly instead of starting a fight with Kaelan," Thalion said, looking abashed.

Vale nodded, her shoulders sagging with weariness as the anger drained from her. "I'm so tired. I can't deal with this right now. Can we just talk about it another time, when Nyxen is safe?"

"Of course, Vale. We can discuss it later. And I'll support whatever decision you make," Thalion assured her.

"Kaelan, maybe you should go back to Terralux for the night. I'll stay here. You need to take your potion soon, anyway," Vale said, her voice soft as she avoided looking at Kaelan. The request stung and he couldn't believe she was asking him to leave.

"I'll stay and look through the books again," Thalion offered, trying to be helpful and mend the rift.

Kaelan felt a sharp stab of hurt and betrayal, but he knew that now was not the time to argue. He fought the urge to pull her into his arms and carry her back home with him. He could see the exhaustion etched on her face, but he didn't want to add to her burdens, so he simply nodded and watched her walk away from him.

As he stood in the doorway of the library, watching her retreating form, he felt the familiar ache in his chest. It was a pain he was all too accustomed to, a pain that had been his constant companion since the day he had lost her.

It was a pain he knew would only intensify as he was forced to watch her walk away from him, over and over again.

TWENTY

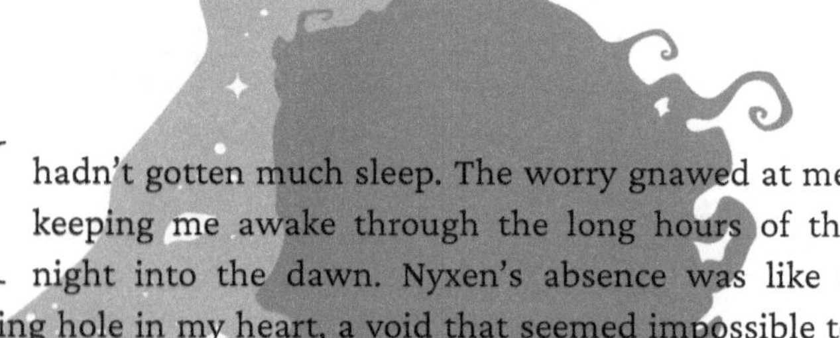

I hadn't gotten much sleep. The worry gnawed at me, keeping me awake through the long hours of the night into the dawn. Nyxen's absence was like a gaping hole in my heart, a void that seemed impossible to fill. I realized I had taken his presence for granted, always assuming he would be by my side. I had never stopped to consider how it would feel if he were ever gone and now I felt empty, like a part of my soul was missing.

The First Witch's silence only added to my frustration. I longed for her guidance, for her wisdom, but she remained silent, leaving me to navigate this crisis on my own. I had no one to turn to but myself, and the weight of responsibility pressed down on me like a heavy burden.

I tossed and turned in the large four-poster bed, unable to find comfort. Thoughts of Nyxen and our predicament swirled in my mind. I found myself on my back, staring up at the ornate ceiling of the room. Once again, I was faced with multiple monumental tasks, each demanding my attention. It seemed like there was an endless list of things to worry about and I couldn't help but wonder if this was what being a queen was always like. Would it ever slow down, or would this be my life from now on?

With a frustrated sigh, I swung my legs over the side of the bed and sat up. I ran my hands through my hair, responsibility weighing me down like an anchor. There were so many things that needed my attention and the list only seemed to grow longer by the day. Maybe it was time to consider getting an assistant. I had heard that queens often had people to help them manage their affairs and perhaps it was time I did the same.

A soft knock on the door interrupted my troubled thoughts. "Who is it?" I called out, my voice tinged with weariness.

"It's me, Vale," Aerion's voice came from the other side of the door.

"Come in," I replied, grateful for the distraction from my restless thoughts.

Aerion opened the door and entered the room, his handsome face etched with concern. His presence was a welcome sight as he walked over and sat beside me on the bed. "Now, how did I know you would be up at this hour?" he asked with a teasing hint of reprimand in his voice.

"I can't sleep," I confessed, my voice heavy with the weight of worry. "Not without Nyxen here. His absence feels like a physical pain."

Aerion's expression softened and he placed his arm around my shoulders, pulling me gently against his chest. "Thalion told me what happened. You'll get him back, princess. I know you will," he reassured me.

I allowed myself to relax into his warmth and comfort, if only for a moment. "I'm afraid, Aerion," I admitted softly. "I'm more afraid than I have been in a while."

"I know," he murmured, pressing a tender kiss to the

top of my head. "I wish I could shoulder this burden for you."

"Me too," I sighed, closing my eyes and leaning into his touch.

We sat like that for a moment, our bodies pressed close, finding solace in each other's presence. Finally, Aerion broke the silence, his voice gentle and soothing. "Why don't you try to sleep a little longer and then we can find the others and start researching this Dreamcarver?"

"I'm not sure I'll be able to sleep," I admitted, even as the fatigue weighed heavily on me.

"Try. I'll be right here," he assured me, his voice a soothing lullaby. He gently guided us down onto the pillows and I allowed my head to rest against the softness.

I let my eyes drift closed, listening to the steady rhythm of Aerion's breathing. His presence was comforting and I felt the tension slowly easing from my body. I wasn't sure if it was his calming energy or the exhaustion finally catching up with me, but I found myself slipping into a peaceful sleep, lulled by the sound of his heartbeat. This time, there were no dreams or nightmares to plague me as I finally allowed myself to rest.

I woke up hours later, my head feeling heavy and my mind muddled with sleep. The room was shrouded in darkness, the curtain drawn against the sunlight, and for a brief moment, I couldn't remember where I was. Then it all came rushing back, the fear and the worry, the ache of Nyxen's absence. Aerion wasn't there either. The solitude weighed on me like a crushing boulder, threatening to drown me in its depths. I allowed myself a brief moment to feel the weight of it, to let it overwhelm my senses and darken my soul just a bit more.

But I couldn't afford to wallow in self-pity, not now. Nyxen was in danger, and I had to find a way to save him. I couldn't let my despair hold me back. With a determined sigh, I pushed the loneliness and hopelessness away, burying them deep within.

I dressed quickly, my movements automatic and sluggish from sleep. It was only after I had finished dressing that I noticed the folded note sitting on the side table. My heart fluttered as I recognized Aerion's handwriting.

Vale,
You looked so peaceful sleeping
I didn't want to wake you.
Meet us in the library.
Aerion

A SMALL SMILE tugged at the corners of my lips as I read the note. I appreciated Aerion's thoughtfulness. I tucked the note into my pocket and headed out of the room.

The castle was quiet as I made my way to the library. The hour was still early and most of the servants were off doing morning chores. The walk to the library felt like a silent procession, the silence enveloping my mood like a dark cloak.

The silence was broken the moment I opened the heavy wooden door to the library. The room was filled with the presence of everyone I held dear, all huddled over stacks of books, searching for any shred of information that could help me. I couldn't believe they were all here, gathered together for my sake.

The collective gaze of my friends shifted to me as I walked in, and I couldn't hide the shock in my voice as I spoke. "When did you all get here?"

Kaelan, Thalion, and Aerion were sitting together, an unexpected sight that left me momentarily speechless. Wren and Venna were standing over a pile of books, their faces etched with determination, while Harker was pulling more volumes off the shelves with the help of Ava and Calliope.

"We've been here for a few hours now," Wren replied, stepping over to hug me tightly, his warmth comforting.

"You've been working on finding a way to free Nyxen?" I asked, unable to conceal the surprise and gratitude in my voice.

"Of course, Vale. You needed us, so why wouldn't we be here?" Wren responded, pulling away to meet my eyes.

"Thank you," I whispered, my voice filled with gratitude and emotion. I felt a profound sense of relief at the sight of my friends gathered here.

"Don't thank me, thank Aerion. He's the one who gathered us all together," Wren replied.

My gaze shifted to the brown-haired Fae male seated at the table and he appeared almost bashful under the attention.

"Aerion, I..." I began, but he interrupted me gently.

"Vale, it's okay. You don't need to say anything," he said, his eyes warm and understanding.

"Okay, then. Did you guys find anything yet?" I asked, shifting my attention to the others.

"We've found plenty, actually," Harker said, plopping a stack of books onto a table. "Wren and Venna have been scouring witches' journals for any traces of other witches who've walked the dream realm."

"And your three boy toys over there," she said, gesturing to Thalion, Aerion, and Kaelan, "when they're not squabbling, have been looking up stories about this Dream-carver character you encountered."

"While Ava, Calliope, and I have been searching for anything and everything about the dream realm itself," she finished.

"Wow, you guys really came together," I said, feeling a surge of gratitude.

"That's not all," Ava spoke up. "Wren mentioned how some witches could control their dreams. They could do more than just walk the dream realm; they could shape it."

"Shape them?" I asked, intrigued.

"Yes, control them completely. It was a lost skill that was said to be passed down from the First Witch. Only a handful of witches ever mastered it, it seems," Harker added.

"The First Witch," I murmured, my thoughts drifting back to the first dream where the mysterious figure of the First Witch had appeared to me. I still didn't understand why she wouldn't help me now.

"Wait, what's this?" Venna's voice broke through the focused silence of the room, and we all turned our attention to her.

"What did you find?" I asked, my anticipation growing as I hoped for any lead that could help us.

"It's a reference to a spell, though I'm not sure what kind. But it mentions a dream catcher," Venna explained, her brow furrowing in concentration. "Some witches used them to catch their dreams."

"What good will that do?" Kaelan questioned, curious.

Venna's eyes gleamed with a hint of excitement as she responded, "It could be useful if you wanted to trap a dream creature, like this Dreamcarver."

"So, we have a way of trapping her? That's definitely a good start," I replied, feeling a glimmer of hope amid our dire situation.

"Yes, we're not out of the woods yet, but it's something," Thalion added, his tone serious and determined.

"Okay, well, keep searching for anything you can find. I'll get to work on this dream catcher," I said, feeling a renewed sense of purpose.

As the others returned to their respective tasks, the library hummed with activity. I began gathering the required ingredients for the dream catcher, but my thoughts kept returning to the First Witch. She held answers, I was certain of it and I couldn't shake the feeling that there was a reason for her reluctance to help.

"Kaelan, can you help me?" I finally spoke up, breaking the library's silence.

"Of course, what can I do?" he replied, his gaze fixed on me.

"There's one ingredient on this list that we don't have and I'll need your help to obtain it," I explained.

"What is it?" Kaelan asked, his expression now one of curiosity.

"A crow's feather," I replied, a small smile playing on my lips.

We stood in the courtyard, gazing up at the towering spires of the castle against the backdrop of the winter sun.

The cold air nipped at our cheeks, but there was a sense of excitement in the crispness of the morning.

"There!" I exclaimed, extending my arm and pointing upward to draw Kaelan's attention to a crow perched on the pinnacle of one of the castle's turrets. It seemed poised to take flight any moment.

Kaelan let out a resigned sigh and shook his head, his immense leathery wings folded neatly against his back, a stark contrast to the wintry surroundings. "I can't believe you're making me do this," he grumbled, though his eyes sparkled with playful protest.

I couldn't help but chuckle at his reluctance. "Oh, hush and go get the birdie," I urged, my tone teasing and light.

"Fine, but you owe me," he replied, a grin forming on his lips.

A mischievous glint danced in my eyes as I replied, "I'm sure we can work out some sort of arrangement."

With a chuckle and a powerful leap, Kaelan took to the sky, his wings unfurling with grace as he soared upwards. He moved with incredible speed, closing the distance between himself and the crow in the blink of an eye. In a flash, he was hovering above the crow, his massive form casting a shadow over it. Before the bird could react, Kaelan swooped down and snatched it from its perch. He returned to the ground, holding the squawking and flapping crow gently in his hand.

"That was amazing," I remarked in awe as I took the crow from him and carefully placed it inside a small cage that I had brought with me.

"What are you going to do with it?" Kaelan asked, his gaze never leaving me as he watched my every move.

"I need to pluck one of its feathers," I explained, taking

a closer look at the crow in the cage to ensure it was unharmed.

"Why are you keeping it?" Kaelan asked, his expression wary as he eyed the caged bird.

I reassured him, "I'll release it once I'm done. It won't be harmed."

Kaelan grudgingly conceded though he crossed his arms in a show of reluctance. "Fine, but make it quick."

With nimble fingers, I swiftly plucked one of the crow's feathers, careful not to harm the bird. I also took a few extra feathers and tucked them away safely into my pocket.

"There, all done," I declared, opening the cage fully so the crow could exit at its own pace. The bird eyed Kaelan warily for a moment before tentatively stepping out.

I couldn't help but tease him. "See, now, was that so hard?"

Kaelan shook his head, a fond smile tugging at his lips. "No, but we could have gotten the feather from a dead crow instead."

I laughed, taking a step closer to him. "And miss the chance to see you fly? No way."

He closed the distance between us, his large frame towering over me as he gently cupped my face in his warm hands. My heart quickened at his touch and I couldn't help but be drawn into his intense gaze.

"Such an enchanting little witch," he whispered, his voice a velvety caress.

A playful grin curved on my lips, my earlier worries temporarily forgotten. "And you're such a helpful demon," I quipped, our banter a delightful distraction.

"Anything for you," he murmured, his words a promise that resonated deep within me. In a heartbeat, his lips met mine, and our kiss was a slow, sweet dance of desire. I couldn't get enough. His hands traveled down my body, fingers curling around my hips and pulling me closer to him. My own hands found their way up his neck, fingers tangling in his dark hair as I pulled him nearer, not wanting this moment to end.

"If you keep kissing me like that," he murmured, his voice low and husky, "we're not going to make it back inside."

I couldn't help but tease, my voice a sultry whisper. "Would that be such a bad thing?" I punctuated my words with a playful nip at his bottom lip, eliciting a throaty groan from him. He responded by tugging at my hips, his intentions unmistakable.

"Not at all," he admitted, his breath hot against my throat as he leaned down to place a trail of heated kisses along my neck, a stark contrast to the chilly air of the courtyard.

However, the serenity of the moment was interrupted by his next question, one that I knew was bound to surface sooner or later. He sighed and pulled back slightly, his intense gaze locked onto mine. "Vale, what was Thalion talking about last night?"

I hesitated, my mind racing as I searched for the right words. The tranquility that had enveloped us was shattered and I took a step back, running my hands through my hair in a gesture of frustration, trying to gather my thoughts.

"It's complicated," I finally admitted, avoiding his penetrating gaze.

Kaelan's voice grew sharper, tinged with a hint of accusation. "Is it?"

I swallowed hard, trying to find the courage to explain. "Thalion mentioned that you might be... a bit too possessive of me. Both he and Aerion have been giving us space to work things out and well, they're growing impatient."

Kaelan's demeanor shifted, and he growled softly, his eyes flashing dangerously. "Waiting for what?"

I hesitated, my anxiety mounting. "Kaelan, you know what. Look, I told you what I wanted, and I know it's selfish of me, but you agreed to it. You need to come to terms with how things are."

He sighed, a deep and frustrated sound, and turned away from me. "I know, Vale, I know. It's just... I don't like it. I don't like having to share you, especially with them."

Determined to bridge the gap between us, I closed the distance and wrapped my arms around his waist, resting my head against his back. "Kaelan, I can't choose between the three of you. That's not how this works. If we're going to have a future together, you all have to accept that."

He turned to face me, pulling me into a tight embrace. "I know, Vale, and I'm trying. For you, I'm trying."

TWENTY-ONE

Back in the library, I set to work on crafting the dream catcher enchantment while Kaelan headed back to join Thalion and Aerion in their research. As I meticulously wove the intricate spell, my focus was entirely on the task at hand, trying to shut out the worries and doubts that had plagued me since Nyxen's disappearance.

But I wasn't alone for long. Harker approached, carrying a notebook with her, and sat down beside me. She leaned closer, her eyes sparkling with enthusiasm. "I'm loving Thalion's library, why haven't you brought me here sooner? Anyway, I've found some interesting things about the dream realm," she said, her voice filled with growing excitement. "It directly mirrors our realm, whichever realm you may be in while you dream. Which makes it unique in that it's practically all three of our realms at once while also being its own realm!"

I paused in my work, intrigued by her words but also finding it hard to wrap my head around the concept. "That sounds ridiculously complicated," I admitted, a hint of bewilderment in my tone.

Harker's enthusiasm only grew as she continued to explain. "It is, but that's not the best part. Anything can happen in the dream realm and it doesn't affect the waking world. The possibilities are endless, Vale!" Her smile was infectious, her fangs on full display.

"I'm not sure I could survive in a place where the laws of physics are completely out the window," I admitted, struggling to match Harker's enthusiasm. The idea of a realm where anything was possible was both intriguing and terrifying.

Harker nodded, her excitement undeterred. "Yes, that does make it more complicated."

Her words only added to the growing list of worries and challenges I had to face. Learning to shift to the dream realm was going to be a daunting task and I couldn't afford to make any mistakes.

As Harker continued to talk, I suddenly had a realization and my mind began to spin with possibilities. If the dream realm mirrored the physical realms, then the forest where I had first encountered the Dreamcarver was real. And if I could find that forest, I might be able to easily shift to the dream realm from there, possibly leading us to the Dreamcarver herself.

"Vale, did you hear me?" Harker snapped her fingers in front of my face, pulling me out of my thoughts.

I blinked and refocused on her. "I'm sorry, what?"

"You spaced out on me. What were you thinking about?" Harker asked, curiosity evident in her expression.

I hesitated, not yet ready to share my thoughts with her. "Oh, sorry. I just had a thought."

Harker didn't press the matter, merely giving me an inquisitive look before turning her attention elsewhere.

Leaving Harker behind, I made my way to where Aerion, Thalion, and Kaelan were sitting, surrounded by old books and tense silence. They all looked up at me simultaneously, their faces lighting up with a shared delight at my arrival. The realization that they had been waiting for me gave me a small thrill, which I quickly pushed aside.

Placing the dream catcher I had been crafting in front of them, I leaned in and addressed Aerion and Thalion. "I've been thinking about the forest I was in. If I can figure out where it is, I can figure out where the Dreamcarver is. So let's get to work figuring out where this forest could be."

"That is an excellent plan," Thalion declared, his approval clear in his voice.

"We should start by researching forests that fit the description," Aerion suggested.

"Is there a map of Elysian somewhere around here?" I asked, eager to get started.

"There's one in my study," Thalion replied, prompting me and Aerion to follow him.

Before I left, I exchanged a meaningful look with Kaelan. "I'll keep looking here, go," he urged me, smiling slightly. I knew it was his way of saying this was him trying to learn to share.

Thalion's study was a treasure trove of knowledge, with the massive oak desk covered in stacks of books and a beautifully detailed map of Elysian adorning one wall. Thalion pointed to the map.

"This is the most accurate map I have," he said, his fingers tracing the intricacies of the landscape.

The map revealed numerous forests, any one of which

could potentially hold the answers we sought. Overwhelmed by the possibilities, I turned to Thalion for guidance.

"How will we narrow down which one?" I asked, feeling uncertain about where to start.

"If you could describe it in more detail, we might be able to eliminate some options," Thalion suggested.

I racked my brain, trying to recall the specific details of the forest from my dream. "I don't know, it was like any other forest. The trees were tall, dark, and ancient. The ground was covered in a layer of moss, and it had an eerie feel to it. The forest seemed vast, extending for leagues."

Aerion chimed in with his insight. "The only forest vast enough to match that description would be the Unclaimed Forest."

"The Unclaimed Forest?" I echoed, turning to him for more information.

"Yes, the Unclaimed Forest. No one owns the land, hence the name. It's notorious for being inhabited by dark creatures, so it wouldn't be surprising if it were the forest you were searching for."

"But it could still be another forest," Thalion cautioned. "There are other forests in Elysian with ancient trees and moss. We'll need to narrow it down further."

"Well, that should at least limit our options," I acknowledged, feeling a sense of progress.

Aerion, however, voiced his concerns. "What do we do once we figure out which forest it is? Vale, it's incredibly dangerous. You're not just trying to traverse realms, but you'll also have to face the Dreamcarver once we find her."

I met Thalion's and Aerion's concerned gazes with determination. "I have no other choice," I asserted, my resolve unwavering.

"She has a point, Thalion," Aerion interjected, his voice calm and measured.

Thalion sighed, clearly torn between his protective instincts and the necessity of our mission. "But that's a risk we should not take. What if the Dreamcarver captures you like she's captured Nyxen?"

"Then I'll fight her," I declared defiantly.

Thalion shook his head, clearly exasperated. "That's not what I mean, Vale."

I snapped, feeling the weight of my emotions bearing down on me. "I'm not sending anyone else into the dream realm."

Thalion sighed, clearly wrestling with his own worries. "That wasn't what I was going to say."

"Then what were you going to say?" I asked, raising an eyebrow.

"I was going to suggest that we send one person with you as backup in case you need help," he proposed.

I paused to consider his suggestion. While it made sense to have someone accompany me for safety, I wasn't sure if I could manage it. It had its merits, but I had reservations. "I have no idea if I could shift myself there, let alone someone else with me."

"You can't do it on your own, Vale," Thalion's voice carried a tinge of frustration, and his eyes pleaded with me.

"I can and I will," I insisted stubbornly, my resolve unyielding. Thalion huffed in frustration and threw up his hands, walking away from me.

Aerion, who had been observing the exchange, approached me and offered a softer perspective. "You're not going to get him to change his mind."

"He's the one who is wrong. He's underestimating me," I retorted, my frustration bubbling to the surface.

"No, he's worried about you. We all are. You shouldn't do this alone," Aerion reasoned.

"I can't put anyone else in danger," I insisted firmly.

Aerion leaned in closer, his eyes locking with mine. "We are already in danger, Vale. Just like you."

I understood his point, but the weight of responsibility still pressed heavily on my shoulders. "I know that," I snapped, my emotions roiling within me as the gravity of our mission weighed on me.

Thalion's determination and worry for me had reached a breaking point, and he acted on his emotions. He swiftly closed the distance between us, backing me up against the wall, his intense gaze locked onto mine. Our faces were mere inches apart and the tension in the room grew thick.

"You are ridiculously stubborn, do you know that?" he whispered, his warm breath caressing my lips and his arm effectively caging me in.

I couldn't help but tease him, even in this intense moment. "So are you," I breathed, my heart pounding in my chest.

"Thalion, maybe now isn't the time," Aerion interjected, attempting to defuse the situation.

Thalion, however, remained undeterred, his focus solely on me. "Maybe you're right, maybe not. All I know is I can't lose you," he confessed, his eyes searching mine for a response.

"You won't," I whispered, my fingers gently brushing his cheek.

He sighed, his forehead resting against mine, his hand tenderly holding my jaw. "So it's to be a battle of wills, is it?" he mused, his warm breath brushing against my lips.

"Yes," I whispered, my resolve unyielding as I closed my eyes, knowing I couldn't waver.

Thalion leaned in, kissing me softly and with tenderness. My heart wavered for a moment, but I held firm, conveying to him that I wouldn't back down easily.

I spoke with conviction as our lips parted, "This doesn't change anything."

Thalion, however, had a different perspective. "Oh, I'd say it changes a few things."

"Not those things. You're going to have to let me go," I said, my thumb gently brushing his lower lip.

His determination wavered for a moment, but he ultimately took a step back. "Not happening," he insisted, though his tone held a hint of resignation.

"Thalion," Aerion interjected again.

"This isn't over," Thalion warned, his eyes locked onto mine.

I met his gaze steadily. "We'll see about that."

Thalion appeared as though he wanted to say more, but he shook his head and exited the room. Aerion glanced at me with concern before following after Thalion. I knew they were both worried about me, but this was my battle and it was one I had to face alone.

I RETURNED TO THE LIBRARY, my heart still racing from the encounter with Thalion, and resumed weaving the enchantment into the dream catcher. This type of magic was entirely new to me and there were no guarantees that it would work, but I couldn't afford to sit around doing nothing.

As I meticulously wove the final thread through the center of the dream catcher, a surge of magic coursed through me. A smile crept across my face as I stood up, holding the completed dream catcher in my hand. It had worked—I had successfully crafted my first enchanted item.

Wren approached me, his eyes fixed on the dream catcher. "Impressive," he remarked.

"It certainly seems that way," I replied, my voice tinged with excitement and uncertainty. "But there's only one way to find out if it works."

"How are you going to test it?" he asked me curiously.

I sighed, realizing that I didn't have a concrete plan. "I don't have any way to test it for sure. I'll just have to trust that it does what it should."

Wren raised an eyebrow, concern etching his features. "That does seem a bit risky."

A wry smile tugged at my lips as I retorted, "This whole situation is risky. What's one more risk?"

Wren chuckled, his laughter momentarily lightening the mood. But then his expression grew serious as he began sharing the information they had discovered.

"We've found some information on witches who were able to walk through the dream realm," he began, his voice brimming with intrigue. "It's incredible—the things they were capable of. These witches could enter the dream realm and communicate with anyone they chose through their dreams. They could even pull that person into the dream realm with them, astrally."

"And physically?" I asked, hoping for a positive answer.

Wren's expression darkened as he replied, "We haven't found any evidence to suggest that they could physically travel through the realms."

"Shit," I muttered, that could potentially be a setback.

"But there's more," Wren continued. "Once in the

dream realm, these witches could accomplish nearly anything. Their magical abilities were heightened and they could effortlessly navigate the dream realm by simply thinking of their destination and stepping into it. They could fly, shapeshift—the possibilities were endless."

"That's exactly what Harker said," I pointed out, intrigued by the information.

"That's because she's smart," Wren replied. "There's still a lot we don't know about the dream realm, but these witches seemed to be the only ones who truly understood its power."

I sighed, feeling a twinge of regret. "It's a shame those witches aren't here now," I remarked, my frustration growing at the thought of all the knowledge that had been lost when the witches were wiped out.

Wren offered me a reassuring smile. "We've got something better anyway, Vale. We've got you."

"Thank you, Wren," I replied with a small smile.

"I aim to please," he said, a mischievous glint in his eyes.

Wren made his way back to Venna and they exchanged warm looks as he rejoined her. Lost in thought, I contemplated the possibilities presented by the knowledge of these ancient witches. If they could achieve such feats, then there was a chance I could, too. It sounded simple enough and Harker was right—there seemed to be no limitations in the dream realm, whether physical or magical. But I was still new to this and doubts crept in. Could I truly defeat the Dreamcarver at her own game? It had to be possible; I had no other choice.

I shook off my uncertainties and made my way over to where Kaelan, Thalion, and Aerion were seated. I sunk into the chair in front of them with a sigh. "What have you three found out about the Dreamcarver?"

"It's mostly old folk tales, to be honest," Thalion began.

"But some of those legends might actually hold some truth. According to the stories, she was once an Other-worlder cursed by a witch who trapped her in the dream realm," Kalean added.

My mind raced as I made a connection. "That explains why she specifically targeted me. She must have a deep-seated hatred for witches."

Aerion chimed in with another perspective. "She may be using this as an opportunity for revenge."

I raised a finger to my lips, considering Aerion's point. "It doesn't quite add up, though. If she despised witches so intensely, why didn't she simply come for me while I was asleep and vulnerable?"

"We can't be certain that she hasn't tried. Your mental shields have grown formidable and you may be uncon-sciously protecting yourself," he suggested.

His words gave me pause. It was unsettling to think that the Dreamcarver might have been lurking in the shad-ows, attempting to infiltrate my dreams. I couldn't afford to let my guard down.

"What else do the stories say about her?" I asked, my interest growing.

"Most of them are quite vague, but there's one that's rather descriptive," Thalion replied, catching my attention.

"Let me see it," I said, wanting to absorb every detail.

Thalion handed me the story, and my eyes quickly scanned the words. The tale spoke of the Dreamcarver capturing people within their dreams, imprisoning them to keep herself from being alone. It aligned with what I had experienced in the dream realm.

"This story could be accurate. We already know she has the ability to trap someone in the dream realm; now, we just need to figure out how to break Nyxen free or defeat her," I concluded, passing the story back to Thalion.

"The story doesn't offer any clues on how to break the spell," Thalion pointed out, his tone tinged with concern.

"That's just one more puzzle to solve," I replied, sighing and leaning back in my chair.

"I think, with everything we've found, we have a solid foundation to accomplish this," Aerion interjected with a hint of optimism.

"You're right," I agreed. "But first, I need to figure out how to get into that place."

"If anyone can do it, it's you," Thalion, with his carefree smile, chimed in.

"Thanks for the vote of confidence," I replied, returning his smile. I left them to their research and turned to Harker, who seemed equally excited about her findings.

"Any luck?" she asked, her eyes gleaming with anticipation.

"We're making progress. How about you?" I asked.

"Actually, yes. I've found a way you might be able to locate Nyxen," she replied, her tone brimming with excitement.

"Really? How?" I asked, a glimmer of hope emerging.

"You try scrying for Nyxen," she explained.

"Scrying?" I questioned, unfamiliar with the concept.

"It's a method of locating someone using a crystal, map, or reflective surface. It's quite simple once you know the spell. I've got everything we need for it, but we should wait until later tonight when you'll have better focus," Harker elaborated.

"I'm ready now," I insisted, impatient and determined to find my familiar.

Harker hesitated, then offered a gentle reminder. "You're tired. We can do this after you've rested."

But I was adamant. "No, let's do it now," I told her.

"Fine, if you insist," Harker said.

TWENTY-TWO

Harker led me to a quiet corner of the room, where we had ample space to work. She laid out Thalion's large map of Elysian in front of me, taking care to ensure it was flat and steady. From the supply drawers, she retrieved a clear, perfectly cut crystal hanging from a string.

"Take the crystal and think of Nyxen. Let it guide you to him," Harker instructed, her voice steady and reassuring.

I obediently gripped the crystal, allowing it to dangle and swing freely above the map. With my eyes closed, I focused all my energy and thoughts on Nyxen, straining to connect with that deep bond between us. As the crystal began to move, it emitted a gentle warmth in my hand. I sensed a slight tugging sensation guiding me toward a specific location on the map.

I crystal came to a halt, hovering over the map. My eyes snapped open and I let the crystal drop into my other hand, stunned by the revelation.

"It's the Unclaimed Forest," I breathed, my voice barely audible.

Harker nodded in agreement. "It seems so."

"She's got Nyxen locked away somewhere in there," I stated, pointing to the specific area on the map where the crystal had hovered.

Harker's determination shone through as she responded, "Then we know exactly where to start searching."

"I hope so," I said nodding, though uncertainty still lingered in my mind.

"We've done all we can for today," Harker said with a hint of maternal concern. "You need to rest and eat. When's the last time you had a meal?"

I hadn't realized how consumed I'd been by our research and efforts, neglecting basic needs like food. Exhaustion and hunger had indeed begun to take their toll.

"I'll take her to get something," Aerion volunteered from across the room, his voice filled with genuine care.

Harker acknowledged his offer with a nod. "See that you do," she instructed, her concern for my well-being evident in her eyes.

Aerion's warm hand held mine as he led me through the grand halls of the palace, our footsteps echoing in the silence. The tantalizing aroma of freshly prepared food wafted through the air, causing my stomach to emit an audible rumble. Aerion chuckled softly.

As we entered the bustling kitchen, he handed me a plate piled high with various dishes, each one more enticing than the last. I wasted no time and sat down at a nearby table. My hunger had taken control. With each bite, I barely paused, my ravenous appetite devouring the meal. Aerion, sitting across from me, observed my voracious eating habits with an amused glint in his eyes.

"Are you trying to impress me with your table manners?" he teased, his voice lighthearted.

I swallowed a mouthful of food and smirked at him. "I was starving. Excuse me for not having perfect table etiquette."

"You're excused," he replied with a charming smile, his eyes never leaving mine.

After savoring every morsel on my plate, I leaned back in my chair, a pleasant fullness settling in my stomach.

"Thank you," I expressed my gratitude, gazing at Aerion sincerely.

His brow furrowed as he asked, "For what?"

"For taking care of me. For bringing everyone together today. And for being there last night."

"Vale," he whispered, his voice gentle.

"I mean it," I continued. "Without you, I don't know what I'd do."

Aerion's gaze held mine, his piercing grey eyes full of emotion. "You'd survive," he stated, his tone solemn.

I studied his face intently, and my eyes locked onto his gaze, which had captivated me on countless occasions. "Do you really think so little of your importance to me?" I asked, my voice carrying a hint of seriousness. These were words I needed him to understand.

Aerion paused for a moment before responding. "I meant that you are stronger than you know," he explained. "You would survive because you would refuse to let the crushing weight of despair overtake you."

I shook my head slightly. "You give me too much credit."

"You're not giving yourself enough credit," he said earnestly. "Vale, you are a fighter—a survivor. And a damn stubborn one at that," he added with a slight smirk.

Our playful banter continued as I retorted, "So are you."

Aerion chuckled softly and admitted, "True, but nowhere near as bad as you."

"You're being stubborn now," I playfully pointed out.

He returned the smile and conceded, "Yes, but so are you."

Our laughter filled the air, lightening the mood as we exited the bustling kitchen. Together, we made our way back to Thalion's library, the weight of our responsibilities momentarily set aside.

However, halfway there, Aerion halted our steps, a serious expression crossing his face. "You should really go back to your rooms, Vale. You've barely slept."

"Aerion, I can't sleep now," I argued. "Not until we've come up with a solid plan."

"You've already located Nyxen, which was the goal for the day," he pointed out. "Now is the time for rest."

"But..."

"Vale, please," he pleaded, his voice gentle.

I let out a resigned sigh. "Fine."

He led me back to my rooms, opening the door and gesturing for me to enter. However, I stopped halfway through the doorway and turned to face him instead, closing the distance between us. I looked up at him through my lashes, a mischievous glint in my eyes.

"You know, I really don't think I'll be able to sleep," I said softly, my fingers tracing the chiseled lines of his chest.

Aerion's eyes darkened as he spoke, his hands hanging at his sides. "Do you really want to do this now, princess?"

I slid my arms over his chest, my lips brushing his collarbone. "I don't know what you mean," I replied innocently, placing a tender kiss along his neck.

A low growl rumbled in his chest, making heat pool low

in my stomach. "Don't tempt me," he warned, his voice husky.

I lifted my face, letting my lips brush against his ear as I whispered, "It's too late for that."

A shiver coursed through him and his control snapped. Without hesitation, he grabbed my wrists, pulling me inside the room and kicking the door behind us. Pinning me against the door, he breathed heavily as his face hovered just inches from mine.

"Is this what you wanted?" he asked, his voice filled with desire. "I know Thalion is still giving you space to work things out with Kaelan, but I am no such gentleman. So tell me, princess," he said the word in a seductive purr. "Is this really what you want?"

I could feel the intensity of his desire in every touch, sending electric pulses of pleasure throughout my body. His voice, rough and husky, and his firm grip on my hips left no doubt about his longing.

"Yes," I breathed, surrendering to the undeniable pull between us.

That single word was all it took. Aerion's lips crashed onto mine. His kiss was possessive, claiming me entirely. Our mouths moved in a frenzy, tongues dancing together, teasing and tasting each other.

His strong hands explored my body, setting my skin ablaze as they moved over my curves. He pushed up the hem of my shirt, exposing my bare skin to the cool air. A soft sigh escaped my lips as he cupped my breasts, his thumbs brushing over my sensitive nipples, sending delicious shocks of pleasure through me.

His lips traced a path down my neck, nipping and sucking at my skin enough to bruise. My breath hitched as his fingers ventured lower, skimming the waistband of my pants.

"Touch me," I gasped, my desire for him reaching a fevered pitch.

He smiled against my skin, his lips hot and teasing. Without hesitation, his hand slipped beneath my pants, making me gasp in delight. His fingers found my wetness, stroking and caressing me in ways that left me a trembling mess.

With strength born of desire, he lifted me into his arms, carrying me to the bed and gently laying me down. His fingers deftly worked to remove my pants and I gasped in surprise as he grabbed my ankles, pulling me toward the edge of the bed. Kneeling down, he placed my legs over his shoulders.

A hot, wet trail of kisses traveled up the inside of my thigh, making my body tingle. His warm breath sent shivers of pleasure coursing through me as he got closer to his destination. My breath grew ragged as his mouth finally claimed me, his tongue exploring.

Pleasure washed over me in waves, and my hips moved against his mouth as he continued his impassioned assault.

"More," I moaned, my voice filled with desperation.

He smiled against my skin, his tongue and lips moving in a slow, sensuous rhythm. My body writhed beneath his touch, desire building to a fevered pitch.

And just when I thought I couldn't take any more, his fingers joined, slipping inside me and finding that sweet, sensitive spot that had me seeing stars. My moans grew louder as he expertly brought me closer and closer to the edge of ecstasy.

I cried out his name as pleasure overwhelmed me, my legs locking around his head to keep him right where I needed him. His tongue and fingers continued their exquisite dance, driving me to the pinnacle of pleasure until I shattered, my world exploding into a kaleidoscope of sensation.

I held him there, unwilling to let go of the euphoria that coursed through me, and he obliged, keeping his mouth and fingers moving slowly and sensually as my body trembled with aftershocks.

But my heart plummeted as I looked up and saw Kaelan standing in the doorway, his hand still gripping the doorknob, his knuckles white.

Panic and guilt coursed through me like a tidal wave. How long had he been there? I couldn't fathom the thoughts racing through his mind at that moment as he looked at me with my legs wrapped around Aerion's head.

"Kaelan," I whispered, my voice trembling as I searched for words.

"Vale," he finally responded, his tone flat and neutral.

Aerion rose from his knees, his gaze locked on Kaelan defiantly. "Can I help you with something, prince?" he challenged, his posture unapologetic.

Kaelan's eyes briefly flickered toward Aerion before returning to me. "I came to see if you wanted to go home. It seems you're in capable hands," he said tersely, his voice strained.

"Kaelan," I said again, my words feeling inadequate to bridge the chasm that had suddenly opened between us.

"We'll talk later," he stated before turning on his heel and exiting the room, his footsteps echoing down the corridor.

I quickly sat up, pulling my pants back into place, and glanced at Aerion for any semblance of an explanation. Had he known Kaelan was standing there?

"Aerion, why didn't you stop?" I questioned him.

He met my gaze with an unapologetic grin, his confidence unwavering. "I told you, princess, I'm not a gentleman."

I shot him a half-hearted glare before rushing after Kaelan, my heart pounding in my chest.

"Kaelan," I called out as he stormed down the hall.

"Not right now," he snapped without looking back.

"Wait," I pleaded, catching up to him and grabbing his arm.

He abruptly halted, his face now a mask of hardened resolve as he faced me. "What do you want from me, Vale?" His voice was laced with frustration and hurt, the emotional turmoil evident in his stormy eyes.

My heart ached as I desperately tried to salvage the situation, to bridge the growing chasm between us. I swallowed hard, struggling to find the right words.

"To talk," I managed to say, my voice trembling with regret.

His response was curt, his tone devoid of its usual warmth. "Fine. Let's talk," he said, his words sharp.

"I'm sorry you saw that. It wasn't... I didn't mean to..." I began, my voice trailing off as guilt gnawed at me.

"Hurt me?" Kaelan finished my sentence, his voice rising with anger and hurt.

"Kaelan," I attempted again, reaching out to touch his arm gently. He reacted with surprising force, shaking my hand off with a low growl. His eyes, once filled with depth and warmth, now held nothing but darkness, an unsettling change that sent a chill through me.

"Kaelan, how long has it been since you've had your potion?" I asked, my concern for him overriding my own turmoil.

His response shattered any pretense of control. "It's not the curse. It's me, losing control," he bit out as his hand found my throat. His thumb pushed my chin upward, forcing me to meet his gaze.

"Is this how it's going to be, Vale?" he growled, his voice low and filled with accusation. "You go have your fill of one of us and then you go take your fill of the next? Or are we to have you all at once?" His words were like a dagger through my heart, his anger and bitterness cutting deep. "Will that satisfy your appetite?"

I gasped as his grip tightened and then he lightly shoved me away, turning around and storming away, his form swallowed by the shadows of the corridor.

"Kaelan!" I cried out, reaching out for him, but he was gone.

I stood there in the dimly lit hallway. My arms crossed tightly over my chest as if trying to hold myself together. A sick feeling settled in the pit of my stomach and self-disgust coursed through me for having hurt Kaelan.

Yet, there was also a spark of anger within me. He had no right to speak to me like that, to accuse me of using him or the others for mere physical satisfaction. It was unfair, untrue, and he knew it.

But the most painful aspect was the look on his face—the anger, the sense of betrayal, the raw pain. I had caused him harm and deep emotional wounds and it was all my fault.

I had hurt him.

I was the one responsible for his pain.

The weight of that realization threatened to crush me, and I was left standing there in the darkness, grappling with the devastating consequences of my actions.

TWENTY-THREE

WREN

On the next moonlit night, Wren and Vale ventured through the maze of back alleys in Terralux, the city hidden in shadows. The sliver of the moon offered little illumination, shrouding their movements in secrecy. Both were hooded and cloaked, their attire chosen to blend into the darkness and to guard against the night's chill. They were heavily armed, prepared for whatever challenges lay ahead.

"Are you sure this is the way they said?" Vale asked, her voice a quiet murmur, her eyes darting around nervously within the depths of her hood.

"Yes, now keep up," Wren replied, his own expression hidden beneath the concealing folds of his hood. His sharp eyes scanned their surroundings, alert and watchful.

They pressed on, moving swiftly and stealthily through the city's winding streets. After a few minutes, they reached the dimly lit docks, their destination marked by a sewer grate nestled between two weathered brick buildings.

Wren knelt down and scrutinized the grate, his brow

furrowing as he assessed its condition. "This is the place," he confirmed, his voice a hushed murmur.

"Great," Vale muttered under her breath, her reluctance evident as she no doubt contemplated the prospect of crawling through the city's sewers.

"Let's go," Wren urged, his strength effortlessly lifting the heavy grate from its resting place.

Without hesitation, they descended the ladder, entering a dimly lit tunnel where the air was tainted with the unmistakable stench of waste. Vale extended her hand, conjuring a ball of flame that illuminated their surroundings and startled a few rats into a hasty retreat.

"Always a neat trick," Wren commented with a faint smile as Vale responded with a smirk.

"Follow me," Wren instructed, taking the lead. They proceeded cautiously, their senses on high alert, but their only companions were the scurrying rats. As they delved deeper into the sewer system, the air grew progressively fouler and the pungent odor became nearly unbearable.

The journey through the tunnels felt endless, a seemingly perpetual descent into the heart of the earth. The air grew cooler and damper with each step, echoing with the subtle, eerie sounds of the underground—a distant dripping of water, the faint rustle of some unseen creature, and their footsteps echoing off the close walls. The darkness was broken only by the flickering light of the flames in Vale's hand, casting long, dancing shadows that played tricks on Wren's eyes.

The path twisted and turned, each corner leading to another identical stretch of tunnel, creating a sense of disorienting sameness. Just as exhaustion and doubt began to creep in, they finally reached the fork in the path they had been so eagerly anticipating.

Remembering their instructions, Wren led the way as they turned left at the fork, feeling a subtle shift in the environment around them.

The tunnel gradually began to widen, its walls slowly receding and the ceiling rising, as if the earth itself was opening up to welcome them. Wren felt a change in the air, too; it became lighter, less oppressive, as if heralding the approach of their destination.

Finally, the tunnel opened up dramatically into a vast, cavernous chamber. It was a spectacle of nature's architecture, grander than any man-made cathedral. Stalactites hung from the high ceiling like ancient chandeliers, and stalagmites rose from the ground to meet them, creating a surreal landscape of natural pillars. The walls of the chamber were lined with intricate patterns of minerals that glinted in the torchlight, casting a kaleidoscope of colors across the expansive space.

The room was shrouded in dim light, the flickering torches mounted on the damp stone walls casting elongated shadows that danced eerily across the space. Vendors occupied the perimeter, each hawking a variety of illicit goods and services, their faces concealed by hoods and cloaks, mirroring Wren and Vale's secrecy.

Wren and Vale navigated their way through the crowd, cautiously avoiding the sellers peddling various wares and services. They passed stalls offering weapons specifically designed to be laced with deadly poisons, elixirs that could alter a person's appearance, and charms capable of manipulating one's thoughts and desires. It was clear that the Fae in this underground market didn't possess the kind of magic Vale wielded.

As Wren and Vale meandered through the bustling marketplace, Wren noticed Vale's pace slowing. He turned to see her standing before a stall, her attention captured by an array of knives displayed on a wooden table. She was examining one particular knife, her fingers tracing the intricate carvings on the handle. A slight frown creased her brow as she scrutinized the craftsmanship, absorbed in her contemplation.

Realizing that Vale had become momentarily sidetracked, Wren retraced his steps back to her. He leaned in close, ensuring that only she could hear him amidst the cacophony of market noises. "I didn't bring you here to shop," he murmured, his voice low but not without a hint of amusement.

Vale glanced up from the knife, meeting Wren's gaze. "I'm just looking," she replied, her voice firm yet light. She turned her attention back to the knife in her hand, admiring its balance and the feel of it. "I lost one of mine recently and I need a replacement. This one is really nice."

Wren observed the knife for a moment, considering its quality. "Come on, I'll have a blacksmith make you a much better one," he suggested, reaching out to gently pull her away from the stall.

Vale hesitated for a second, still holding the knife, her eyes lingering on its design. Then, with a soft huff of resignation, she placed the knife back on the table. "Fine," she agreed, allowing Wren to guide her away from the stall.

As they continued moving through the maze of tents and stalls, they passed a large tent with women clad in dresses that left little to the imagination. One of the women reached out to Wren, her hand resting on his shoulder.

"Why don't you come in with me for a tumble, it's been a while since I had a visitor as big as you are," she purred, a suggestive smile playing on her lips. Wren promptly shrugged off her hand and continued walking, his expression unfazed. Vale, however, couldn't resist smirking and waggling her eyebrows at him, though she wisely refrained from commenting.

"Do you see him yet?" Wren asked Vale, scanning the faces of the vendors around them as they continued to walk through the crowded marketplace.

"No, there are too many people in this damn crowd," she replied, obviously frustrated. Wren knew that large crowds had always made Vale uncomfortable.

"Stay close," he cautioned, keeping an eye on her to ensure they didn't get separated in the throng of bodies.

"I will," she assured him, following his lead as they pressed on in their search.

Finally, they spotted their intended target—a stocky, rotund Fae with a balding head and a substantial beard. He projected an overly friendly and jovial demeanor while interacting with a customer, but Wren saw through the facade. There was a calculated manner in which he engaged with his patrons, revealing a shrewd intelligence beneath the surface.

They waited patiently as the merchant concluded his business before approaching him. The man cast a fleeting glance at Vale as they drew nearer, dismissing her with a curt remark. "This ain't the whorehouse, take that one back that way."

Wren's voice took on a low growl as he retorted, "She's not for sale. We're here for you."

"What can I do for you?" he asked, regarding them suspiciously.

"We're here for certain ingredients we have heard you can procure. If you have them or can get them, we'll place a repeating order," Vale said, taking a step forward. She made sure to keep most of her face hidden beneath her hood, fully aware that revealing her identity as the future queen could lead to complications they could ill afford.

"Oh?" the merchant's demeanor instantly changed. She had clearly caught his interest. "What might those ingredients be?" he asked with a raised eyebrow, leaning in slightly to hear Vale better.

Vale lowered her voice, cautious not to draw any unwanted attention to their transaction. "The ones we are interested in are a bit...unorthodox. I assume you can keep our conversation discrete?"

"Of course," the man assured her, matching her tone. "Please, follow me."

Wren followed closely behind Vale as the merchant led them behind a partition that provided a semblance of privacy amidst the bustling marketplace.

Once they were somewhat shielded from prying eyes, the merchant turned his attention back to them. "So, what ingredients did you need?" he asked, eyeing them carefully.

"I have a list here," she replied, handing him a short list of ingredients.

The merchant raised an eyebrow, taking the list and looking it over. "And what are you intending to use these for, if you don't mind me asking?" he asked, curiosity getting the better of him.

"I do mind you asking, thank you," Vale replied curtly, her tone making it clear she had no intention of divulging further information.

"Fair enough, fair enough," the merchant conceded, raising his hands in a gesture of surrender. "I have what you need now, except for the opals. In the future, you can pick up the order here once a week."

"That will do," Vale agreed.

The merchant, still eyeing Vale with a lingering sense of

curiosity, continued his line of inquiry. "I'm curious, though," he began, his gaze assessing her, "Are you the same customer that placed a similar order a couple of weeks back? I've had an unusually high demand for those ingredients recently."

"Perhaps," Vale replied vaguely, her tone conveying her unwillingness to elaborate.

"With the demand being so high, it'll cost you, though," the merchant warned her.

"How much?" she asked patiently.

The Fae merchant paused briefly, assessing Vale with a calculating look before finally quoting a price. "For the opals, it'll be... one hundred twenty," he said with a sly grin. "And eighty weekly for the rest of it."

Two hundred gold coins in total. Among these people, it was practically a king's ransom.

Vale reached into her cloak, producing a bag of coins, and dropped it onto the table in front of the merchant. "That's half now, half later."

"Pleasure doing business with you," the Fae merchant replied, his hand darting out to snatch the bag of coins from the table.

"Likewise," Vale replied coolly. She turned around, her cloak billowing behind her, and Wren followed suit. But the Fae male wasn't quite ready to let them go. "Wait, what's your name, miss? I like to know the names of my best customers," he called after them.

Vale glanced over her shoulder, her hood concealing most of her features but revealing a glimpse of the side of her face. "Adeline," she answered cryptically.

"Good to meet you, Adeline," he said with a friendly smile. "Name's Dagda. See you next week."

"We'll be back," she confirmed, her tone inscrutable. "Just remember, discretion is key."

"Always," Dagda assured her, his expression conveying the gravity of his commitment.

With that, they turned and exited the tent, melting back into the crowded marketplace, leaving behind the clandestine meeting with the shadow market merchant. No one around them had any inkling that their future Queen had just engaged in this covert transaction.

"Let's get out of here," Wren muttered, and Vale nodded in agreement.

They hastened their way back through the sewer system, making their exit to the surface without detection. They had successfully completed their mission without arousing suspicion.

As they began walking through the dimly lit streets toward the palace, Wren's sharp senses picked up on a presence trailing them. He began to notice a shadow moving behind them, and he strained to hear the telltale sound of footsteps.

"Someone's following us," Wren murmured, keeping his voice low enough for Vale to barely hear.

Vale's response was equally hushed, "Yes, I know."

Wren contemplated their options. "Are we going to confront him or try to lose him?"

"Losing him sounds like more trouble than it's worth," Vale replied, her eyes darting about as she kept an eye on their pursuer.

"If you say so," Wren shrugged.

Wren and Vale quickly turned down a narrow side alley, their footsteps echoing softly against the cobblestones. Sure enough, the shadowy figure behind them followed, drawing closer this time. As they turned to confront him, they realized they weren't alone – two more menacing figures emerged from the shadows on either side, and Wren's keen ears detected the faint sound of two more assailants descending from the rooftops behind them. They were surrounded and the thugs seemed to think they had the upper hand.

"What's this?" the leader of the group sneered, his malicious grin revealing a mouthful of rotten teeth. "A whore and her customer thinking they can play in the shadows?"

"I think they might need an escort," another one chimed in with a sinister chuckle.

"We can pay you double whatever he's paying," a third thug offered, nodding toward Wren.

"Or we can just take it," a fourth growled, brandishing a dagger.

"How about you all go fuck yourselves," Vale responded with ice in her voice, her hand resting on one of the knives concealed beneath her cloak.

"I bet I can get her to change her mind," one of them leered, casting a lustful glance in Vale's direction.

Vale's patience wore thin. "Last warning, go now, or you won't live to regret it," she warned, her tone deadly.

Their arrogant laughter persisted and the leader drew his dagger, making his intentions clear.

"We're taking you with us," the first thug sneered again.

Wren locked eyes with Vale and she gave him a knowing look. It had been a while since they had a bit of fun, and these miscreants had just volunteered to be their playthings.

With lightning speed, Vale drew twin knives and Wren swiftly transformed into his true form—a massive russet-colored wolf. There was no need to keep his true nature a secret from these five; they wouldn't live long enough to tell anyone.

The transformation was swift and almost effortless, his body elongating and covered in thick fur. His senses heightened as he took in the scent of fear and adrenaline that emanated from the thugs. Moonlight glinted off his sharp, ivory fangs and his golden eyes gleamed with an unsettling intelligence.

"It's a fucking werewolf!" one of the thugs stammered out in shock.

Without further hesitation, the two of them sprang into action. Wren lunged at the three thugs in front of them, his wolf form a blur of fur and fangs. His first target attempted to block with his dagger, but Wren's jaws clamped down on the weapon, shattering it and sinking his teeth into the thug's forearm. The other two thugs scrambled back in panic, trying to draw their weapons, but Wren was faster.

In one fluid motion, he twisted his body and lunged at the nearest thug, his powerful jaws snapping shut around the fae's throat. With a quick shake of his head, Wren ended the thug's futile struggles, his lifeblood spilling onto the cobblestones.

Meanwhile, Vale had swiftly turned and charged toward the other two thugs, her knives glinting menacingly in the dim light. She moved with a grace and agility that seemed almost unnatural, effortlessly sidestepping their clumsy attempts to grab her.

One of the thugs made the mistake of lunging at Vale with a reckless swing of his club. She deftly parried the attack, disarming him with a swift flick of her wrist. With calculated precision, she incapacitated him with a swift kick to the chest, sending him crashing into the alley wall.

The remaining thug hesitated for a moment, his confidence waning as he witnessed his comrades falling one by one. He turned and tried to make a run for it, but Vale was faster. She took one step forward and flicked out her wrist, her knife finding its mark as it buried itself in the thug's back. His eyes widened in shock as he staggered backward, collapsing to the ground with a gurgling gasp.

They hadn't sustained much more than a few scratches and scrapes during the confrontation, which had been more of a sport than a true battle. With a satisfied grin, Vale turned to Wren, her knives disappearing as she did. "Well, that was fun," she quipped, her adrenaline still pumping.

Wren returned her grin with a playful snarl before transforming back into his human form. He looked around at the dead bodies littering the alley. They should get out of there before anyone found them.

"Come on, let's get back," he said, taking Vale's hand in his, their blood still running hot.

As they walked back towards the palace, Wren couldn't help but steal glances at Vale's flushed face. He knew she was dealing with a complicated situation involving Kaelan, Aerion, and Thalion. She had confided in him about the tangled web she found herself in, and he felt a deep empathy for her.

"Hey, what are you thinking about?" Wren asked.

"I was just thinking about the last time we hunted down a demon back home," she replied with a wistful smile.

"You mean when I got my ass handed to me and you saved us both?" Wren chuckled, recalling the incident.

"That's the one," she said, smirking and winking at him.

He knew she was deflecting, avoiding any deep conversations about her current predicament. Nevertheless, he decided to press on. "How are you dealing with everything right now?"

"Right now," Vale sighed, her expression weary. "Right now, I can't think about much besides getting Nyxen back. I have no idea how to navigate this situation I'm in, Wren. But right now, that has to wait."

Wren nodded, understanding that her mind was consumed with the urgency of rescuing her familiar. "What will you do after we find him?" he asked, probing gently.

"I guess I'll have to stop avoiding the situation, won't I?" she replied, offering him a weary grin.

"Maybe it won't be as bad as you're thinking," Wren suggested, trying to offer her a glimmer of hope.

"That's optimistic," she responded, raising an eyebrow, "But I'll take it."

They walked in comfortable silence for a while longer, the tension from their recent encounter gradually dissipating. Wren found himself wondering where Vale's thoughts had wandered.

"How's Aisling doing?" she asked, breaking the silence.

Wren's smile grew fond as he thought of the young girl. "She's doing well," he replied. "She's been working with Harker to practice her control and I've started teaching her how to use knives. She hasn't stopped eating since she got here, though. Elara hates her, always yelling about how Aisling's dirty hands ruin the books."

"Elara should have been more careful when she wished for company," Vale chuckled, shaking her head.

Wren and Vale continued their walk through the shadowy streets of Terralux, the cool night air sweeping around them.

"And how is Venna?" Vale asked after a moment of silence.

Wren furrowed his brow, genuinely puzzled. "Venna? I guess she's fine. Why do you ask?" He had no inkling of why Vale would be interested in Venna's well-being.

"Come on, Wren, you have to at least suspect," Vale prodded, her words carrying a hint of something unspoken.

"What are you talking about?" Wren asked, still not understanding where Vale was going with this.

"You can't tell me that Venna doesn't at least want to get in your bed," Vale stated matter-of-factly, her eyes locking onto Wren's.

Wren's laughter burst forth involuntarily at Vale's audacious comment. "You've lost it, Vale," he said, shaking his head in disbelief.

"No, I haven't, Wren," Vale replied, her tone suggesting she knew something he didn't. She was alluding to a deeper truth.

"What are you trying to imply?" Wren asked, his amusement giving way to curiosity.

"The way she looks at you," Vale continued, her words laced with mischief. "You have to see it."

Wren's expression shifted from amusement to mild exasperation. "The way she looks at me? She's my beta," he pointed out, his tone slightly defensive.

Vale, undeterred, pressed on. "So? That doesn't mean she doesn't have feelings for you."

"Even if that were true, it doesn't matter," Wren stated firmly, his tone leaving no room for debate.

"Why not?" Vale asked, clearly not willing to drop the subject.

"Because I can't get involved with my beta," Wren explained, hoping to put an end to the conversation.

"You can't deny the way she feels about you. I see the way you two interact," Vale persisted.

"What, do you have nothing better to do than to spy on us?" Wren teased, trying to lighten the mood and steer the conversation in a different direction.

"You're not getting out of this that easily," Vale countered, grinning wickedly. She was determined to get to the bottom of this.

Wren sighed, realizing that Vale wasn't going to let the matter rest. "Look, I just can't be interested in her like that, no matter what I might feel about her," he admitted, shrugging. "She's my friend and second-in-command, and that's all I need her to be."

"I wouldn't be so quick to dismiss her like that if I were you," Vale conceded, finally relenting.

"I'm not dismissing her, but I just can't feel that way about her," Wren reiterated, hoping Vale would finally drop the subject.

"Okay, I'll drop it," Vale finally relented, her playful grin returning as they continued their walk.

As they hurried down the empty streets, a figure watched them from the shadows, unseen and unnoticed.

TWENTY-FOUR

The following day, I found myself back in the small, dimly lit kitchen, my hands deftly measuring out ingredients and carefully mixing them. The room was filled with the earthy scent of herbs and the gentle bubbling of a pot as I worked diligently on crafting the potion that had become an essential part of Kaelan's life.

After a restless night filled with turbulent dreams from which I had woken sobbing and running to the bathroom to retch, I had risen early to prepare the potion for Kaelan.

Finally, after adding my blood, the potion was ready, its crimson surface shimmering in the dim light. I carefully poured it into small vials, sealing them with a waxen cork. It should be enough to last him the next week, as long as his curse didn't progress further.

Kaelan and I hadn't spoken much since that night two days ago. I spent most of my time going back and forth between feeling guilty and angry. But I didn't know who I was more upset with, him or myself.

My emotions were a chaotic whirlwind, a tempest of uncertainty and longing that left me feeling adrift. I carefully placed the last vial in the small box, the delicate glass clinking softly against the others as I sealed it shut. It was a small gesture, but one that felt significant, given our recent encounter.

Thanks to our blood bond, I could sense Kaelan's presence before I even heard the soft shuffle of his footsteps. His entrance into the room was marked by a tension that made my heart skip a beat. His gaze was locked onto mine, unwavering and intense, as if he were searching for something within those depths.

"Is that a new batch of potion?" he asked, his voice a low, gravelly murmur.

I nodded, my voice momentarily failing me. "Yes, here," I managed to say, extending the small box of vials toward him. He accepted it without a word, his fingers brushing mine briefly.

The room fell into a heavy silence, and I could feel the weight of our unspoken thoughts pressing down on us. I knew I had to say something to break the silence that threatened to suffocate us.

"I should go to the library," I finally said, my voice sounding small in the stillness.

"Yeah," Kaelan agreed, his response barely more than a whisper. His voice held an unreadable quality and I couldn't quite discern the emotions that lay beneath the surface.

Turning away, I began to walk toward the door, my steps slow and deliberate. But before I could reach it, I felt his touch, a gentle pressure on my arm that brought me to a halt. I turned to look at him, our eyes locking in an unspoken connection that spoke volumes.

"Vale," Kaelan murmured, his voice low and husky, carrying with it a weight of regret and longing.

I swallowed hard, trying to steady the tremor that threatened to betray my composure. "What is it, Kaelan?" I asked, my voice soft but steady.

His gaze bore into mine, the intensity of his stare making it difficult to breathe. "I...I'm sorry. For the other night," he confessed, his voice filled with a raw pain that mirrored the turmoil within me.

"Me too," I whispered, my heart aching as I saw the torment in his eyes. I wanted to reach out, to offer comfort, but the gulf between us felt insurmountable.

For a moment, we stood there, suspended in a fragile moment of understanding, our emotions swirling around us like a maelstrom. Then, with a heavy sigh, he released my arm and I turned away.

I moved to step through the doorway, my mind filled with confusion and the weight of unresolved emotions. But before I could take another step, I heard a low, frustrated exclamation behind me.

"Fuck this." Suddenly, Kaelan's strong arm encircled my waist, pulling me back into the small, dimly lit kitchen as he slammed the door shut with a force that sent a tremor through the room.

"Kaelan?" I began to utter, my voice trailing off in bewilderment as I turned to face him. But any further words were stolen from my lips in an instant, replaced by the searing heat of his mouth descending upon mine.

A fierce, unexpected passion consumed us both as our lips crashed together. My knees grew weak, and I succumbed to the intensity of the kiss, my body molding to his as our tongues tangled in a heated dance. His arms tightened around me, drawing me impossibly closer as the kiss deepened.

In our hunger, pots and pans scattered to the floor,

making a loud clatter that went unnoticed in the heat of the moment. Kaelan swept them aside with a careless gesture, his urgency evident as he lifted me up and sat me down on the countertop.

My hands found their way into his unruly hair, fingers threading through the dark locks as I pulled him closer, our lips never parting. Our kisses grew increasingly frantic, a desperate need consuming us as our bodies pressed together, seeking solace in one another's warmth.

Finally, he broke away, his breath ragged and uneven, his eyes reflecting a potent blend of lust and longing.

"Vale, I can't do this anymore," he confessed, his voice a mere whisper, filled with torment and desire.

Confusion swirled within me at his words. "What do you mean?" I managed to ask, my heart pounding erratically.

"This," he said, his hand gesturing between us with frustration. "This distance, this separation. I can't bear it any longer. I need you like I need to breathe."

"Kaelan, we need to..." I began to speak, but he silenced me with another scorching kiss, his hand firmly gripping the back of my neck.

A low moan escaped my lips as his other hand trailed down my body, resting possessively on the curve of my hip. He pulled me even closer and I could feel his undeniable hardness pressing against me, igniting a fierce, throbbing heat between my legs.

His hands were relentless as they pushed the hem of my dress up and over my trembling thighs, spreading my legs apart roughly. His fingers trailed up my inner thigh, teasing me through the fabric of my underwear.

"Fuck, Vale, you're so wet," he groaned, his voice thick with a potent need that mirrored my own. With a deliberate pull, he hooked a finger around the edge of my underwear and forcefully pulled it aside, exposing my swollen, throbbing clit. A gasp escaped my lips as his thumb brushed over the sensitive flesh, causing my body to arch in response.

"We really should—" I attempted to voice my hesitation, but my words were abruptly cut off as he pressed forward, pushing a finger inside me roughly. My back arched further, and a sultry moan spilled from my lips as he expertly maneuvered his finger, finding that elusive sweet spot deep within me.

"We should what?" he growled, his voice laced with an insatiable lust that echoed through the room.

"We should...oh, fuck," I gasped, my attempts at coherent speech shattered as he continued to work his fingers inside me. Each thrust sent electrifying waves of pleasure coursing through my body, rendering me unable to think or speak.

His thumb pressed firmly against my clit, circling it in slow, tantalizing motions that sent sparks of ecstasy dancing through my senses. My fingers clenched onto his shoulders, a desperate grip that anchored me to reality as the sensations threatened to overwhelm my every thought and desire.

He persisted, relentless in his pursuit of my pleasure, thrusting his fingers in and out of me, each motion setting my body ablaze. My climax loomed, the pressure within me building with an unbearable intensity.

Just as I teetered on the precipice of release, he withdrew his hand abruptly, leaving me gasping for more. My eyes flew open and I gazed up at him with need and frustration, my body yearning for completion.

"Please, Kaelan," I whimpered, my voice a desperate plea for him to continue, to take me.

His response was an intense, unrelenting stare, a hunger that blazed in his eyes. Fingers nimble and skilled, he unbuckled his belt with a swift motion, freeing his throbbing, engorged cock. The sight of it, hard and ready, left me reeling, an aching hunger consuming me.

"You want this?" he rasped, his voice a low, seductive rumble.

"Yes," I panted, unable to contain my longing.

"Then you should get on your knees," he purred, a wicked grin tugging at the corners of his lips. I could hardly contain my eagerness as I slid off the countertop and knelt before him. His fingers found their way into my hair, firm yet gentle, guiding his throbbing cock toward my waiting mouth. I couldn't wait to taste him, to feel the weight of his desire on my tongue.

I parted my lips, my tongue flicking out to moisten them in anticipation, and he slid himself inside, the sensation sending a shiver down my spine. Closing my mouth around his hardness, I began to suck, the taste of him intoxicating and familiar. My tongue danced and swirled around the tip, eliciting a chorus of low groans of pleasure that escaped his parted lips.

With a growing intensity, he started to thrust himself deeper, his grip on my hair tightening as he pushed his length further into my throat. I relaxed my jaw, inviting him to slide even deeper, taking him entirely into my mouth and throat.

"Fuck, Vale," he growled, his voice strained, his head thrown back in ecstasy. His fingers dug into my hair, tugging gently as his hips began to buck, driving himself into my mouth with wild abandon.

I moaned, the feeling of being dominated by him fueling the fire between my legs. My free hand drifted down to my aching clit, fingers circling it slowly as I continued to pleasure him.

"Damnit," he muttered, withdrawing from my mouth. With a swift motion, he guided me up and over to the small kitchen table. He bent me over the table's surface, pushing my dress upward and tugging my underwear down in one swift motion.

He positioned himself at my entrance and pushed inside, eliciting a loud moan from my lips, the sound echoing off the kitchen's walls. His strong hands found purchase on my hips, and he began to thrust into me with a powerful rhythm, each movement driving me wild with need.

My fingers gripped the table's edges, knuckles turning white as he pounded himself into me. His cock stretched and filled me completely, pleasure and a hint of pain mingling together in an intoxicating mixture that threatened to overwhelm me.

My legs trembled, unable to withstand the electrifying waves of ecstasy that coursed through me. "Fuck, you feel so fucking good," he growled, his voice ragged with desire.

"Don't stop," I pleaded, gasping for breath. "Please, don't stop."

"Not a chance," he grunted, his fingers digging into my hips relentlessly. Each thrust pushed me closer to the edge and I clung to the table for dear life.

His rhythm grew erratic and his thrusts became more frantic as he chased his own release. Each movement sent tremors of pleasure coursing through me, and I could tell he was on the brink.

"Come for me, Vale," he demanded, his voice raw and

primal, pushing me closer to the edge.

I felt his cock swell inside me and a tidal wave of pleasure tore through my body. I cried out, my body convulsing in ecstasy as the climax washed over me, consuming every thought and sensation.

He gave one last powerful thrust and with a loud groan, he came, his cock pulsing inside me. His weight pressed me down onto the table as he collapsed onto me, both of us panting and gasping for breath.

We lay there, entangled in each other, our hearts racing, trying to catch our breaths amidst the tangled mess of desire and emotion that enveloped us.

"Kaelan," I began, and he raised his head to meet my gaze. "I think we should talk," I said, my voice soft yet determined.

"What about?" he asked, his eyes searching mine.

"Us," I replied, my heart heavy with the weight of our tangled emotions.

He sighed and rested his head back on my shoulder, a sign that he knew the conversation was long overdue.

"You're right," he admitted, his voice tinged with regret.

"We can't keep going on like this," I said.

"No, we can't," he agreed, his voice heavy with the weight of our shared turmoil.

"So, what do we do?" I asked.

"I don't know," he answered, his voice laced with sadness.

"We have to find a way," I insisted, my determination unwavering. "We can't keep hurting each other like this."

"I know," he murmured, his voice barely a whisper.

He pulled out of me and I stood with his help. He reached for my dress, pulling it back down, and straightened his own disheveled clothes.

"We should clean up the mess we made," he suggested, looking around at the scattered pots and pans strewn across the floor.

"Good idea," I agreed, nodding. We set about cleaning up the aftermath of our passionate encounter, working in silence as we restored order to the small kitchen. He began to pick up the items while I gathered the ingredients and cleaned the countertop. When we finished, he turned to me and spoke, "This situation, it's difficult for me when all my instincts are screaming at me to own you, to claim you. Demons don't share, we take, that's all we're good at."

He stopped, his body sagging as he leaned back against the kitchen counter, exhaustion etched into every line of his face. Rubbing his hands wearily over his eyes, he struggled to put his thoughts into words. "I'm worried I'm not enough for you, and that..." he trailed off, his sigh heavy with the weight of his insecurities. "That kills me, Vale."

His sudden movements caught me off guard as he closed the distance between us swiftly. With a gentleness that belied his earlier passion, he cradled my face between his hands, his touch tender yet possessive. His thumbs stroked my cheekbones gently as his eyes looked into mine with a deep sadness.

"You say I'm enough, but then I just don't understand why you'd need more," he confessed, his voice a whispered plea.

"You're more than enough, Kaelan," I replied, my voice filled with sincerity and affection. "At the end of the day, when I feel alone, I know you'll be there if I need you. You're there, always there. I know that I can fall apart with you because you'll be there to catch me. When we're together, it feels like home."

His eyes searched mine as if seeking confirmation, and I

continued, "But you have to know, just because I want them doesn't mean I want you any less. I want their love, their friendship, just as much as I want yours. I want to be seen, be loved, be longed for. I don't want to have to choose who owns my heart; I want to give it to all of you. I want to love and be loved as much as I can."

He sighed, the tension in his shoulders easing slightly and he rested his forehead against mine. In that silent moment, my heart ached for him. How could I ask him to understand when I barely understood myself?

"You deserve that, Vale," he finally whispered, his voice filled with acceptance. "You deserve everything I can give you and more. If this is what you need, then I can be satisfied knowing that you're being loved the way you should be."

"Thank you," I whispered, tears threatening to spill over as he held me against his chest, his arms a comforting embrace that chased away the shadows of doubt.

"But that doesn't mean I'm going to stop claiming you in any way that I can, little witch," he said, his voice taking on a playful edge as he leaned down and nipped at my neck, easing the tension between us.

I laughed softly, my heart lightening, and replied, "I wouldn't have it any other way, demon."

As we stood there with our arms around each other, the tension that had once hung in the air between us evaporated, leaving only a profound sense of peace. We had finally broken through the wall of fear and uncertainty that had held us back and the promise of what lay ahead was both exciting and terrifying.

The path ahead of us was uncertain, but for now, in this moment, we were exactly where we were meant to be: in each other's arms.

TWENTY-FIVE

The library's atmosphere was charged as Kaelan and I entered, our footsteps echoing in the silence. I could feel the weight of everyone's gaze on us, their collective hopes and worries etched on their faces.

I moved purposefully to one of the tables, my palms resting firmly on its surface, grounding myself as I prepared to address the room. Taking a deep breath, I began, my voice strong and determined, "Okay, let's go over the whole plan so everyone is up to speed."

All eyes were fixed on me as I continued, "We're after the Dreamcarver, who has Nyxen trapped somehow. Wren, Kaelan, Thalion, Aerion, and I will be going to the Unclaimed Forest in hopes that the proximity will help me shift to the dream realm. I'll be pulling Wren in with me, hopefully, while the others stand guard over us. Now that I know how the dream realm works, I can locate the Dream-carver and capture her with the dream catcher. Any questions?"

Ava, her expression filled with concern, spoke up hesitantly. "You're not physically shifting to the dream realm, are you?"

I shook my head quickly to reassure her. "No, we've found no evidence that I can do that. So I'll be astrally projecting myself in my sleep. I've made light sleeping potions that will help get that job done."

"The Unclaimed Forest is unclaimed for a reason. We have no idea who or what is in there, waiting," Thalion said, his worry etched on his face.

I couldn't resist a snarky retort. "Then it's a good thing I will have you big, strong males there to protect me," I replied, raising an eyebrow playfully.

Thalion's reaction was immediate, his brows shooting up. I knew that if it weren't for the others present, he would already have pinned me against the nearest wall.

Aerion wisely shifted the conversation, focusing on the practical aspect of our mission. "How many sleeping draughts do you have, Vale?" he asked.

"I had five," I began, "but we only need two. I can't even be sure I'll be able to pull Wren in, let alone more of you."

Kaelan crossed his arms over his chest, "One person protecting you in there isn't enough."

Thalion chimed in, his comment laced with sarcasm, "Well, it seems there are some things we can agree on."

"It'll have to be enough. I can't guarantee more, and I can't risk you all getting stuck in the dream realm. It's far too dangerous. Wren is coming and that's final," I said firmly.

The three exchanged glances, their eyes filled with worry and unease. They knew the risks and they also knew that they had no choice but to trust me.

"I will be fine. We will be fine," I stated confidently,

hoping to instill some reassurance in them, even as doubts swirled in my own mind.

Kaelan finally relented, his voice betraying his concern. "Very well. When do we leave?"

"Now, if everyone is ready, the sooner the better."

With a collective nod, we gathered our belongings and left the library. As we walked, a wave of anxiety washed over me. What if I failed? What if we got trapped in the dream realm and never made it back? I pushed the thoughts away and steeled my resolve. There was no time for doubt. We had to move forward.

EMERGING FROM THE SHADOWS, we stepped into the heart of the untamed forest. Towering trees, their branches reaching for the heavens, framed our entrance. The world above was veiled in a mosaic of leaves, each one adorned with a silvery sheen from the feeble sunlight that managed to pierce the dense canopy. Shafts of light danced gracefully among the trees, painting a mesmerizing tapestry of light and shadow upon the forest floor.

Amidst this natural cathedral, Thalion's voice broke the tranquil silence, his uncertainty evident in the furrowed lines of his brow. "Well, where do we go from here?" he asked, his gaze darting about, attempting to discern a path through the densely packed woods.

Closing my eyes, I sought the thread that bound me to Nyxen. It was hazy, the bond faint, but it was there, a faint whisper of emotion tugging at my chest like a spectral hand. "This way," I declared, my voice ringing with newfound confidence as I pointed in the direction of the subtle pull.

We navigated through the wild underbrush and the towering sentinels of the forest, guided by the faint but persistent tug that beckoned me forward. Time seemed to stretch as we ventured deeper into the woods, the verdant foliage closing in around us, swallowing the fading sunlight. The forest's embrace grew more intimate, the trees standing close together as if guarding the secrets hidden within their ancient boughs.

Hours passed before we reached the brink of an expansive clearing. It sprawled out before us, an open expanse amidst the densely packed woods, a patchwork of fading sunlight and shadow.

"We can set up the tent here; it'll be dark soon," I suggested.

The group nodded in agreement and set about their tasks, creating a temporary sanctuary in the heart of the wild.

"What should we expect to encounter?" Kaelan's voice cut through the somber atmosphere, his eyes scanning the surroundings, ever vigilant.

Aerion's shoulders shrugged, his expression full of uncertainty. "I honestly have no idea," he admitted, his voice a whisper in the forest's hushed air.

"We can only hope it's nothing we can't handle." Thalion said.

"I'm sure you three can handle the creepies that go bump in the night," Wren joked, offering a wry grin.

"Wren and I should be able to handle ourselves as well," I said, determined to see this through.

However, doubt lingered in Kaelan's eyes, his unspoken concern etched upon his features. "If you say so," he conceded.

"I do. Now, Wren and I are going to drink these sleeping

potions and get to it." I said, handing a potion to Wren, who held it cautiously as if it might bite him.

"We'll keep watch," Thalion said, stepping forward.

I nodded in gratitude and turned to Wren. "Shall we?"

He swallowed hard and nodded. "Let's do this."

With a deep breath, I uncorked the bottle and drank the bitter potion, ready to embrace the uncertainty that stood before us.

Wren and I entered the tent, which had been prepared with a makeshift pallet of blankets. I sat down and Wren laid down beside me, the worry evident in his voice as he asked, "You'll try and pull me in with you, right?"

I offered him a reassuring smile. "I'll do my best, Wren."

His concern still lingered as he pressed, "And if you can't?"

I tried to lighten the mood with a teasing tone, though my own anxiety gnawed at me. "Then I guess I'll continue on my own, and you get a nice nap."

But Wren's face was grave, his brow wrinkled in concern. "Not funny, Vale."

"Sorry, Wren," I replied, offering a more sincere apology. "I'm just nervous."

"I know," he sighed, and I could see the anxiety in his eyes. "I am, too. Just try and relax."

As we both lay down, I felt Wren's hand intertwine with mine. I took another deep breath, trying to steady my racing heart. Closing my eyes, I focused on the connection to my familiar, hoping that by tugging on the bond, I could shift us into the dream realm.

Slowly but surely, my consciousness began to fade, the world around me slipping away into darkness. At that moment, I clung to Wren's hand as the only anchor in the vast sea of uncertainty.

I STOOD within the depths of a vast forest and something felt amiss. I glanced at the wolf by my side and a nagging feeling tugged at the edges of my consciousness. Shouldn't there be a fox here instead? In my dreams of this place, it was always a fox. Wait...this was a dream, wasn't it? But it felt different, more real like there was something more to it that I couldn't quite grasp.

My attention shifted back to the wolf beside me. He whimpered and gazed at me with familiar green eyes. Eyes that seemed to belong to someone I knew. Wren. It was Wren, and he was here to help me with something important. What was it, though? My head felt foggy, just like in dreams. Dreams. No, this wasn't just a dream; we were in the dream realm. The realization hit me like a bolt of lightning, clearing the haze in my mind. We were here to find Nyxen. But why was Wren in the form of a wolf?

"Do you always appear as a wolf in your dreams, Wren?" I asked, my voice breaking the silence of the forest.

Wren cocked his head to the side and let out a low whine, shaking his head in response.

"Then why are you a wolf now?" I questioned, hoping for some clarity. Another whine and my frustration grew. "This is confusing. Come on, we have to find the Dreamcarver."

I closed my eyes and focused on Nyxen; he was close, close enough that I wouldn't need to shift to reach him.

"Let's go," I said, moving forward. Wren followed as we ventured deeper into the surreal forest. The towering trees reached for the sky, casting dappled shadows in the dim light. The air was filled with the scent of earth and dampness, and the leaves rustled softly in the breeze.

Wren abruptly stopped beside me, his nose in the air, sniffing intently.

"What is it?" I asked, my senses heightened by his sudden alertness.

Wren's ears perked forward, and his lips curled back, revealing his sharp canines. He growled, a low and menacing sound.

Turning in the direction of his intense gaze, I strained to listen, my own ears searching for any sound beyond the eerie silence.

"I don't hear anything," I whispered, trying not to disturb the unsettling stillness.

Wren growled again, his fur bristling, his gaze locked on something ahead.

I felt the presence long before I heard it—a cold, creeping sensation that raised the hairs on the back of my neck. Something was here, lurking in the shadows.

Wren sensed it, too. His ears twitched and his body tensed, muscles coiled and ready to spring into action. We were not alone.

The faint sound of something moving through the undergrowth reached my ears, growing louder and more ominous as whatever it was approached. Each rustle of leaves and snap of twigs seemed to echo through the quiet forest.

My heart pounded in my chest, the adrenaline coursing through my veins, making my hands tremble with anxiety. I clenched my fists, fighting to maintain my composure. We could handle this, whatever it was.

Wren, however, was far from calm. He let out a menacing snarl, his lips curling back to reveal a ferocious display of sharp fangs. His growl reverberated through the forest, a clear warning to whatever dared to approach.

The sound of movement suddenly stopped and a hushed silence enveloped us. It was as if the entire forest held its breath, waiting for the unseen threat to reveal itself. I strained my ears, desperate to catch any hint of what was approaching, but there was nothing—just an eerie stillness that hung heavy in the air.

Wren's ears were pinned back against his head, his growl deepening as he braced himself to defend us. The tension in the air was suffocating.

And then, as if emerging from a nightmare, a monstrous figure burst through the trees. It was the same creature that had pursued me the first time I had ventured into the dream realm— a nightmarish beast standing on its hind legs like a man, its massive head resembling that of a bear, and long, deadly claws gleaming menacingly in the dim light.

The deafening roar of the creature echoed through the forest, causing birds to burst from their perches in a flurry of feathers. The ground quaked beneath its massive form as it charged forward, intent on destruction.

With a speed that belied its size, the creature swung one of its massive paws in my direction, razor-sharp claws slicing through the air with deadly precision. I instinctively stumbled back, narrowly avoiding the deadly swipe that would have torn me apart.

But before I could react further Wren launched himself at the creature, his jaws clamping down on its heavily muscled arm. The beast roared in pain and anger, shaking Wren off as if he were a mere toy, sending the wolf flying through the air to crash into the underbrush.

"Wren!" I cried out, my heart seizing with fear as I watched him tumble to the ground, stunned and vulnerable.

The creature, undeterred by its encounter with Wren, continued its relentless advance toward me. I knew I had to defend myself, but the memory of my uncontrollable magic from our previous encounter with this beast haunted me. Nevertheless, I couldn't afford to be paralyzed by fear.

Summoning all the magical strength I could muster, I raised my hands and unleashed my power. Fire erupted from my fingertips, a relentless surge of flames that engulfed the beast. My magic roared, a furious torrent of raw energy barely contained. Yet, to my shock, the flames danced harmlessly on the monster's fur. It seemed immune to my magic, or at least, my fire.

Wren, recovering from his previous attack, lunged at the creature once more, snapping at its massive legs in an attempt to slow it down. In response, the beast swung its colossal paws, connecting with Wren and sending him sprawling to the ground yet again, dazed and disoriented.

Seeing Wren injured and vulnerable sent a surge of protective fury through me and I knew I had to do something. But what could I do when my magic was useless against this monstrosity?

My desperation fueled my rage and I screamed with anger, my voice echoing through the forest, a primal cry of defiance against this unstoppable force. The beast responded with its own ferocious roar, a thunderous sound that seemed to shake the very foundations of the forest.

I had to keep fighting, even if it was futile. I had to do whatever I could to protect the ones I loved. And so, I gathered all my remaining strength and summoned another surge of magic, determined to stop this beast once and for all.

The creature turned its attention back to me, its piercing black eyes locked onto mine as it charged forward once more. With a ferocious bellow, it swiped its razor-sharp claws, attempting to maim and destroy.

But I was ready and threw myself to the side, dodging its deadly attack. The beast, frustrated by its failed assault, let out another enraged roar and lunged at me again, its deadly claws extended.

Desperation gripped me as I reached out with my mind, attempting to make contact with the creature's consciousness. However, I encountered a formidable mental barrier as I clashed with its mind.

Undeterred, I pushed harder, my own thoughts a tempest, as I fought against the creature's mental defenses. Drawing upon the vast well of power that surged within me in the presence of the dream realm, I assaulted the mental wall with all the force I could muster. With a gasp, I crashed through, my mind breaching the creature's psychic defenses.

Once inside, I found myself immersed in a primal, chaotic maelstrom of thoughts and instincts. It was disorienting and animalistic, but I steeled myself against the overwhelming tide, determined not to be swallowed by the creature's consciousness.

With a sharp pull, I seized control of the monster's mind and it responded with a deafening roar of agony. The beast shook its head violently as if trying to dislodge an unseen assailant. But I held steadfast, my own magic pressing against the resistance within the creature's mind.

It fell to its knees and howled in torment, its head shaking wildly in an attempt to rid itself of the tormenting presence inside its mind.

I channeled my magic into the monstrous creature, a relentless stream of power surging through its mind. The beast writhed on the forest floor, its agonized screams filling the air as my magic seared through its consciousness.

The creature's struggles became increasingly frenzied, its massive form thrashing about in a futile attempt to escape the torment I inflicted upon it. It was a harrowing sight and the forest seemed to echo with the creature's anguished cries.

Then, suddenly, it happened. A loud, sharp crack resonated within the depths of my mind like a thunderclap. It reverberated with such intensity that it seemed to shake the very fabric of the dream realm.

Once a formidable and fearsome opponent, the monstrous creature went abruptly still. Its eyes, which had previously been filled with raw animal fury, turned vacant and unseeing. It lay sprawled on the forest floor, lifeless.

Feeling a sense of dread and unease, I released my hold on the creature's mind, severing the connection. My own mind reeled from the mental ordeal and I couldn't help but shudder at the echo of that ominous crack still lingering hauntingly in my mind.

Wren padded up to me and emitted a soft whine, gently nudging my hand with his nose. I reached down to stroke his fur, appreciating his silent reassurance in the wake of the unsettling encounter.

I stared down at the lifeless form of the monstrous crea-ture, a sense of deep disquiet settling within me. "What the hell was that thing?" I muttered, my heart still racing from the adrenaline of the encounter.

Wren responded with another low whine, as though sharing in my unease.

"Whatever it was," I continued, trying to regain my composure, "it's dead now." My voice wavered slightly as I spoke the words, and I couldn't help but wonder about the implications of what had just transpired.

However, I knew that dwelling on it wouldn't bring us any closer to finding Nyxen. With a determined shake of my head, I refocused my thoughts. "We need to keep moving, Wren. We can't afford any more delays."

TWENTY-SIX

KAELAN

Kaelan sat outside the tent, his back against a tree, with Thalion and Aerion on either side. The dense forest enveloped them in a shroud of silence, broken only by the distant calls of birds and the gentle hum of insects. It was an eerie calm that settled over the woods as though nature itself held its breath.

His keen eyes flickered toward the tent where Vale and Wren lay sleeping. Moonlight filtered through the canopy of leaves, casting dappled shadows on the fabric of the shelter. Kaelan couldn't help but worry despite his trust in Vale's abilities. He took a quick glance inside, ensuring that they were safe and undisturbed.

Vale and Wren slept peacefully inside the tent, their forms shifting and twitching slightly as they navigated the dream realm. Kaelan's heart eased a fraction, knowing they were resting well, even amidst the unknown dangers of the dream world.

Satisfied that Vale and Wren were as well as could be expected under the circumstances, Kaelan withdrew from the tent and returned to his position beside Thalion and

Aerion. The silence that hung in the air between the three males spoke volumes, none willing to breach the subject of their shared desire—Vale.

Kaelan's mind wandered, involuntarily retracing the memories of that passionate night when Vale had willingly given herself to him the first time. The recollections played out vividly in his thoughts—the tender caress of her soft skin against his, the taste of her on his tongue, the way she had quivered beneath him as he mapped out the contours of her body. It was a potent, lingering memory that threatened to distract him from the solemn task at hand.

The inner turmoil intensified as he grappled with these recollections, a mix of desire and frustration gnawing at his thoughts. Sharing Vale was a concept he loathed and the presence of Thalion and Aerion in this delicate situation only added to his discomfort. He was a demon, possessive by nature, and he didn't want the others to be privy to his internal struggles.

Kaelan was fiercely possessive and protective of Vale and the idea of sharing her affections with others gnawed at him. However, a part of him recognized that Thalion and Aerion could offer something he couldn't—protection, friendship, and perhaps a different kind of love that Vale needed.

As he grappled with his conflicting emotions, Thalion's voice cut through the silence, drawing his attention. "Do you think this will work?"

Kaelan shifted his gaze to the Fae, his brow raised, "I believe Vale can do it. If anyone can bring Nyxen back, it's her."

"And meanwhile, we're sitting here useless, unaware of what's going on," Thalion said, sighing in frustration.

"That is the risk we take, but Vale is a strong and

capable witch, and Wren is no weakling either," Aerion replied, his voice calm and steady.

"It doesn't mean I have to like it," Thalion grumbled.

"None of us do, but we have to trust Vale," Kaelan said, his eyes fixed on the tent.

Thalion nodded reluctantly, his jaw clenched.

The night enveloped them in a shroud of silence once more, the forest's usual nocturnal chorus of sounds providing a stark backdrop to their contemplative thoughts. As Kaelan sat there, he couldn't help but dwell on the conversation he had had with Vale back in the kitchen. He knew that he needed to address the matter with Thalion and Aerion at some point. It wasn't easy for him to accept this new dynamic, but for Vale's sake, he had to try.

Breaking the stillness, Kaelan cleared his throat, capturing the attention of the two Fae males who regarded him with curious expressions. With a deep breath, he began, "Vale and I have talked and she's helped me understand why she needs the two of you." He paused, his gaze steady. "While I can't say I'm entirely comfortable with this arrangement, and I'd be lying if I said I didn't have violent tendencies towards both of you, I'm willing to accept it— for Vale's sake."

Thalion and Aerion exchanged glances, their surprise evident in their wide-eyed expressions. Thalion sought clarification, a hint of cautious optimism in his voice. "So, you're saying you're... willing to support her choices?"

Kaelan didn't mince words as he clarified his stance. "I'm not okay with it," he declared with unflinching honesty, his jaw set with determination. "But I'm starting to understand and I'm going to try."

Aerion's response was firm and reassuring. "You have

no reason to be concerned, demon. We only want to see her happy."

"Yes, I have concerns, but I understand her reasoning, and for that reason alone, I'm willing to live with it. However," he continued, his eyes hardening as he leveled a warning gaze at his counterparts, "let me be unequivocally clear. If either of you ever causes her harm or dares to overstep her boundaries, I will personally ensure your existence ends in excruciating agony."

"We love her, Kaelan. You have no reason to threaten us," Thalion spoke up.

Kaelan's retort was swift and unwavering. "You may love her, but I love her more."

Aerion intervened, effectively putting an end to their escalating tension. "Enough. We're all on the same side here. There's no need for petty arguments."

Kaelan agreed with a curt nod, his gaze returning to the tent where Vale and Wren slept. "We all need to learn to play nice so we can support Vale."

"Indeed," Thalion said, echoing his sentiment.

The night dragged on relentlessly, each passing minute feeling like an eternity as the three males maintained their vigilant watch, their thoughts a whirlwind of uncertainty and apprehension. Time seemed to stand still, broken only by the rustling of leaves and the distant calls of nocturnal creatures.

It was during this profound stillness that Kaelan sensed an unsettling shift in the shadows, a presence colder and more foreboding than death itself. He stood up abruptly, his eyes narrowing as he scanned the enveloping darkness. Thalion and Aerion rose to their feet in response to Kaelan's instincts.

Aerion's voice cut through the stillness, a low and taut whisper, seeking answers. "What is it?"

Kaelan's response was immediate, his body coiled and ready for battle. "Something is coming."

"I sense it as well," Thalion said.

The frigid aura continued to ripple through the shadows at the forest's edge, causing Kaelan's eyes to narrow as he strained to pierce the obscurity with his gaze. There, he saw a grotesque figure rising from the ground, draped in tattered, ashen rags. Its skin was a lifeless gray, stretched tightly over gaunt bones, and where its eyes should have been, there were only hollow, gaping voids. Its mouth yawned wide in a silent, eternal scream—a horrific apparition akin to a twisted, walking corpse.

Horror twisted Kaelan's gut. This being was no ordinary creature; it was a sinister ghoul, a once-living human that now haunted the forest.

Thalion voiced the collective revulsion that surged through them. "What the hell is that?"

"It's a ghost, a spirit, an evil entity—take your pick," Aerion responded grimly. "But it's undoubtedly dangerous."

More of these abominations began to stumble out of the forest, their hollow sockets and cavernous mouths presenting a grotesque semblance of human features. With unnatural, disjointed movements, they staggered toward the camp, their decrepit forms gaining speed as they closed in on the trio.

"Get ready," Kaelan growled, his body poised for combat.

Without hesitation, he lunged at the nearest ghoul, his blade slicing through its form. However, even as the top half of the creature fell to the ground, it continued to crawl relentlessly toward him.

Aerion and Thalion joined the melee, their weapons and magic cleaving through the nightmarish entities with remarkable ease, yet their ranks showed no signs of thinning. The creatures pressed on, emerging endlessly from the shadows, their anguished moans and tormented cries piercing the night air. The relentless onslaught threatened to overwhelm the three of them.

Kaelan became a whirlwind of fury, his sword dancing through the night with deadly grace as he dispatched the ghouls one after another. One leaped onto his back, its cold, clammy grip like a vice around his torso. He twisted his body violently, attempting to shake off the ghoul's grip. After a relentless struggle, Kaelan finally seized the creature and yanked it off himself. He slammed it forcefully onto the ground, where it continued its eerie crawl, trying to climb his legs. Without hesitation, Kaelan swiftly decapitated it.

His eyes darted to his right, where Thalion waged a battle of his own, his features contorted in a primal fury. The Fae warrior fought with such relentless intensity that he seemed almost otherworldly, his blade a blur as it cut through the ghouls.

Kaelan heard Aerion yell out in fury as one ghoul clamped its teeth into the flesh of his forearm. He watched as Aerion quickly swung his sword and decapitated the creature, but the damage was done. The bite was bleeding heavily.

"They just keep coming," Thalion said, panting heavily.

Kaelan's voice was strained as he replied, "We have to keep going until Vale and Wren finish."

As Kaelan fought, he caught sight of two ghouls advancing

toward the front flap of the closed tent, their clawed hands ripping at the fabric. Without hesitation, Kaelan charged them, swiftly decapitating the first one. Turning to the second ghoul, he braced himself as it lunged toward him. Its claws scraped across his chest, drawing blood, and Kaelan roared in pain. He kicked the creature away, ignoring the sharp pain.

The sound of tearing fabric brought his attention back to the tent. A hole had been ripped through the front flap, revealing the interior. Panic surged within Kaelan as he shouted with desperation, "Vale!"

Inside the tent, Vale and Wren continued to sleep, their bodies twitching as they navigated the dreamscape. Kaelan's heart raced as he roared and lunged towards the torn opening, determined to shield them from the impending danger.

Aerion and Thalion rushed to join him, forming an impenetrable wall of flesh and steel in front of the besieged tent. Together, they faced the relentless onslaught of ghouls, their wills unyielding in the face of the encroaching darkness.

TWENTY-SEVEN

Wren and I continued our journey through the dense forest, the ever-strengthening tug on my mind serving as our compass. The gentle background of nature had fallen silent, leaving us to traverse the woods in an unsettling hush that heightened our senses. Our footsteps were muffled by the thick underbrush. I managed to hold enough control over the dream realm to ensure that our steps were smooth and even, avoiding the erratic lurches that could send us hurtling forward dozens of feet in an instant or turning five steps into one.

In the distance, a small and dilapidated cabin came into view, nestled among the towering trees. Its weathered exterior bore the scars of time, with rotting walls and broken windows that made it look abandoned. The small front porch was sagging; its steps had fallen away. Its isolation in the heart of the forest added to the eerie atmosphere.

Wren and I stopped and took cover in the underbrush, our eyes fixed on the cabin ahead. The scene felt like something out of a haunting tale, with the looming trees casting long shadows that danced across the cabin's exterior.

"I'm almost positive that is what we're looking for," I said to Wren, my voice steady despite my slight doubts.

I could practically see Wren raising an eyebrow incredulously.

"Always leave a little room for doubt, right?" I said, attempting humor, but the foreboding atmosphere made it fall flat. A sense of unease had taken root within me, one I couldn't shake. "Okay, I'm going to go in there and look around. It doesn't look like anyone is home. You stay out here and keep an eye out."

Wren whined quietly, halting me.

I understood his caution; I shared it. But we were running out of options and time was not on our side. "I don't like it either, but what other options do we have?" I said, reasoning with him. With a final glance and a reassuring pat on his head, I began to sneak toward the cabin, slipping between the trees and shadows.

Approaching the side window of the cabin, I cautiously peered inside. The dim light revealed an empty interior devoid of any signs of life. It seemed that no one was home, but an unsettling feeling still lingered, like a silent watcher in the shadows.

I moved cautiously around the back of the cabin, each step careful and calculated. The unsettling feeling that had been gnawing at me grew with each passing moment. My magical senses were on high alert, my powers ready to be unleashed at a moment's notice.

A small shed stood in the back corner of the cabin's yard, its door partially open. I crouched low and approached the shed, my heart pounding in my chest.

Every nerve in my body seemed to be screaming, warning me of impending danger.

Peering through the gap in the shed's doorway, I was met with a horrifying sight. Inside, a large table dominated the space, its surface marred by dark patches of dried blood. The stench of decay hung heavy in the air, making my stomach churn with revulsion.

I recoiled from the shed, the gruesome scene etched into my memory. The shed had been transformed into a nightmarish torture chamber and it triggered painful memories of my past torment. For a moment, I felt frozen in place, the fear and dread threatening to overwhelm me.

My instincts screamed at me to flee, to escape this horrific place, but I couldn't abandon Nyxen to such a cruel fate. As much as the thought terrified me, I knew I had to go inside the cabin and confront the evil that lurked within.

Summoning every ounce of courage I possessed, I crept toward the cabin's back door. The rusty hinges protested with an agonizing creak as I pushed the door open. I froze, listening for anything that might have been disturbed by the sound. The dim light from the window provided just enough illumination for me to make out the room's details.

The walls were lined with shelves bearing an assortment of books and odd trinkets. At the back of the room, a workbench held an array of gruesome tools, most of them stained with dried blood.

My eyes were drawn to a crooked fireplace, where a small carved figure of Nyxen rested. A dark and twisted enchantment seemed to pulse from it and I realized that this must be the means through which the Dreamcarver had trapped Nyxen. I knew I had to find a way to break the enchantment and free him from that gruesome prison.

The suffocating urge to flee threatened to overwhelm me, but I couldn't allow fear to paralyze me. Nyxen's freedom depended on my courage. With trembling hands, I reached out and grasped the figure. The rough wood pressed into my palms and I could feel the dark enchantment resisting my touch. However, I summoned my magic and pushed back, determined to break its hold on Nyxen.

The moment the figure was torn from its place, the cabin was consumed by chaos. A deafening, blood-curdling scream pierced the air, causing the windows to shatter in a shower of glass that rained down on me. A violent gust of wind knocked me off my feet, sending the figure flying from my grasp. I hit the floor hard, the impact stealing the breath from my lungs.

The cabin convulsed as if in the throes of a violent fit. Furniture soared through the air, crashing into walls and each other. Debris rained down upon me and I shielded my head with my arms as the madness raged around me.

The screaming grew louder, echoing in the cramped space. "Who is in my house?" the voice screeched, a twisted cry of anger and madness. "Who is stealing my things?"

In a horrifying whirlwind, the Dreamcarver herself materialized before me, emerging from the back hallway in a flurry of wind and dust. Her beady black eyes locked onto mine and a flood of recognition washed over them. Panic gripped me and I scrambled backward as she advanced, her measured steps carrying her closer.

"You," her voice oozed with a sinister allure, low and dangerous. "I was wondering when I would see you again." She grinned, her thin lips stretching grotesquely across her rotten teeth.

Driven by fear and desperation, I pushed myself up

from the floor and conjured a ball of flame, hurling it at her in a desperate attempt to defend myself. But she casually batted the flames aside with a dismissive gesture, her cruel sneer deepening.

"Do you really think you can defeat me?" She laughed, a bone-chilling sound that echoed through the cabin. "I am forged from your nightmares and I can delve into the darkest corners of your dreams."

The Dreamcarver continued her slow approach, her cold and calculating gaze never wavering from me as if she relished the fear that coursed through my veins.

A thunderous crash erupted from behind me followed by a series of frantic growls and snarls. I turned to see Wren charging through the front door of the cabin. He barreled straight for the Dreamcarver, his feral instincts taking over as he lunged at her with a growl. He latched onto her shoulder in a flurry of fur and fangs, shaking her violently.

The momentary distraction provided by Wren allowed me to act. I dashed toward the fallen figure of Nyxen, my fingers grasping it tightly. The wood was rough and cold beneath my touch, and I could sense the twisted enchantment that had bound Nyxen to this nightmarish place.

But Wren didn't have the monstrous woman pinned for long. She let out a furious cry, shaking Wren off with a powerful shove that sent him flying across the room. "Enough!" she bellowed, her voice echoing with an unnatural power.

Wren quickly regained his footing, his snarl echoing his defiance. His eyes locked onto the Dreamcarver, a growl rumbling deep in his throat.

"You will pay for that, dog!" the Dreamcarver spat, her voice dripping with venom.

Before I could react, the Dreamcarver snapped her

fingers, and a sinister transformation overcame Wren. In an instant, he was turned into another carved figure, frozen in a twisted semblance of his wolf form.

"No!" I cried out in despair, rushing to grab the figure of Wren. The wood was cold and lifeless in my hands and I could feel the depth of his suffering trapped within.

The Dreamcarver's laughter only grew more twisted as she pointed her bony finger at me. "Now we shall see you succumb to the depths of darkness," she crooned, her voice dripping with poisoned honey.

As her words washed over me, a dark and suffocating spell enveloped me, and my consciousness began to slip away. My vision blurred and I collapsed to the floor, unable to resist the Dreamcarver's magic.

As the cruel darkness engulfed me, I fought desperately to maintain a flicker of hope against the suffocating void. Refusing to surrender to my despair, I summoned the power within me, willing the flames of my magic to dance across my trembling palm. The sudden burst of fiery illumination shattered the all-encompassing obscurity, revealing the grim reality of my surroundings.

I gasped in disbelief as the room materialized before my disbelieving eyes. It was a place etched in my memory with indelible horror—the chamber where I had once been subjected to unspeakable torment and unrelenting suffering. My heart pounded in my chest, and a cold sweat broke out on my brow as the recognition struck me with paralyzing dread.

"No," I whispered, my voice cracking as panic clawed at my heart, threatening to engulf me in its relentless grip.

My eyes darted around the room, my mind racing to process the horrifying reality of my return to this twisted place. Every corner of the chamber bore witness to the agony I had once endured. The walls began to close in on me, suffocating me with memories I had desperately tried to forget. Panic tightened its grip on my heart, threatening to drown me in a sea of dread.

I took a few hesitant steps backward, but my retreat was cut short as I collided with something solid lurking in the shadows. Turning around, my heart sank even further as I recognized the table that had been my tormentor's instrument of pain, stained with the dried remnants of my own blood.

"No, no," I muttered, my breaths coming in shallow gasps. This couldn't be happening, yet there I stood, trapped in a twisted nightmare of my own making.

As my mind raced and my body trembled, hands materialized from the shadows behind me. Their grip was unyielding, yanking my arms back and over my head, immobilizing me in a sickeningly familiar manner. My limbs were shackled, and a chilling sense of déjà vu settled over me, a relentless dread that seemed to constrict my very soul.

I continued to struggle against my unseen assailant, my futile efforts marked by desperation and fear. With a forceful twist, I was spun around to face the presence that lurked in the darkness.

There, standing before me with a wicked grin etched across his face, was Malachar. His twisted laughter filled the chamber, a haunting sound of cruelty. His hands gripped me with an impossible strength, mercilessly pinning me down upon the table, the straps securing me in place.

Tears streamed down my face as I realized the inevitability of the torment about to unfold. Malachar wasted no time, drawing his wicked blade with a sickening scrape of metal. The cold steel met my skin and I screamed in agonizing pain as the sharp edge sliced into my flesh. The pain was excruciating and I thrashed against my restraints, my desperate cries echoing through the chamber.

With each cut, Malachar's face began to contort and shift, morphing into different faces. Haldir first, whose wicked grin sent fear curling low in my stomach. Then Zephyrian, my father, whose red eyes gleamed in the flickering torch light. I sobbed as the face transformed into the men I loved— Aerion, Thalion, and then finally, Kaelan.

Each of them, in turn, seemed to derive perverse satisfaction from inflicting torment upon me, their expressions twisted with cruelty. My anguished cries filled the chamber, mingling with the chilling laughter of my tormentors.

Amidst the excruciating torment that threatened to consume me, a flicker of awareness penetrated the nightmarish fog. I began to remember where I was and why I was here—trapped within the vicious realm created by the Dreamcarver, a sinister nightmare designed to crush my spirit. However, I couldn't afford to surrender to the darkness, not when the lives of those I cherished hung in the balance.

With a sheer act of will, I focused my attention and flames danced across my constrained hands. A surge of determination coursed through me as I directed the flames toward my tormentor, who had taken on the face of Malachar once more. The searing flames consumed him, eliciting agonized screams that reverberated through the chamber. Yet, it wasn't enough; he remained standing, his twisted visage mocking my futile efforts to resist.

But I couldn't allow despair to take hold. Not now. Desperation fueled my magic as I summoned more power, stoking the flames' intensity. They surged forth with renewed vigor, transforming into a torrent of molten fire, a relentless river of raw energy. I poured more and more of my essence into the flames, my veins throbbing as if they coursed with liquid fire. It was as if I were undergoing a metamorphosis, becoming nothing but the embodiment of a raging inferno.

The flames blazed with an unbridled fury, their searing heat devouring my tormentor. Malachar's face contorted in excruciating agony, his features shifting rapidly between the faces of Haldir and Zephyrian.

As the intensity of my flames increased, the restraints that had held me captive began to melt away in the searing heat. I watched in awe as the bonds that had confined me turned to molten metal and dripped to the ground. Freed from my shackles, I stood tall amid the inferno that raged around me, my body bathed in the radiant glow of the flames.

I unleashed a torrent of fire that surged forth from my very being. The flames danced and swirled, filling the nightmarish chamber with their scorching brilliance. It was as though I had become a living embodiment of destruction, a force of nature that refused to be contained.

As the last remnants of my nightmarish captors faded into nothingness, I stood amid the blaze, my body surrounded by a nimbus of searing flames.

I willed the flames to burn. Burn hotter, burn brighter, burn bigger. And they grew and grew. I would burn my way out of this nightmare. I would set this realm ablaze until there was nothing left but ash and ruin.

I was unyielding. I was relentless. I would not be a prisoner here, subject to the whims of the Dreamcarver. I would not be a victim of her cruel designs. I would be free.

I stood within the heart of the inferno I had unleashed, my willpower and determination driving the flames to greater heights. Each fiery tongue lashed out like a serpent, hungry for the destruction of this evil realm. It was a battle of wills, a clash between my unyielding resolve and the Dreamcarver's dark power.

As I willed the flames to burn hotter, they responded with a primal roar, their incandescent fury growing with every passing moment. The very air crackled with energy, and the room trembled under the intensity of the blaze.

With a final surge of magical energy, I threw my arms wide open, and the flames embraced me as if welcoming me into their fiery domain. I had become one with the very heart of the inferno. My skin, my bones, my blood—all became fire. I was no longer merely a conduit for the flames; I was fire incarnate.

The room, which had once imprisoned me, began to crumble under the unrelenting assault of the blaze. Walls melted away and the very foundations of this nightmarish realm were consumed by the raging fire. I walked through the crumbling ruins, flames licking at my feet but causing me no harm. Smoke billowed around me, filling the air with acrid fumes, but I strode forward without fear. No longer a prisoner, no longer a victim—I was an unstoppable force of nature, an elemental fury unleashed upon this twisted reality.

And then, as suddenly as it had all begun, I jolted

awake. The cabin was ablaze around me, its wooden structure consumed by the very flames I had summoned. The figures of Wren and Nyxen were held securely in my hands, untouched by the inferno that raged across my skin.

The Dreamcarver's scream of disbelief and fury echoed through the inferno. "How?!" she shrieked. "No! You cannot have them! You will not have them!"

With a howling wind, she rushed at me, her claw-like hand closing around my throat, her icy grip squeezing the life from me. I struggled desperately, gasping for air, her evil eyes locking onto mine with deadly intent.

Summoning the last vestiges of my strength, I focused on the flames that still coursed through my being. The fire that defined me surged forth with a blazing fury. As her grip tightened, a single thought surged within me.

I would not be prisoner here.

With a final surge of defiance, I willed the flames to engulf me. They erupted from within me, an explosive burst of fiery power that consumed me in a burning inferno. The Dreamcarver shrieked in terror, her hold on me faltering as she recoiled from the searing blaze.

In that fiery vortex, I was reborn—a phoenix rising from the ashes of my torment.

The Dreamcarver's agonized screams reverberated through the dream realm, their piercing intensity cutting through the otherwise eerie silence of the forest. Her voice, shrill and anguished, seemed to resonate with the very fabric of this otherworldly plane as I watched her being consumed by the inferno.

Her piercing wails gradually gave way to the crackling of the flames as they hungrily devoured the cabin. The blaze illuminated the surrounding trees, casting eerie shadows that danced to the rhythm of the inferno. I watched the Dreamcarver's form disintegrate into ashes and embers, her nightmarish existence reduced to a charred and broken shell.

My heart pounded in my chest as I clutched the figures of Wren and Nyxen close to me, the adrenaline of the battle still coursing through my veins. My breath came in ragged gasps, and my body felt weak and drained, but the sense of triumph washed over me like a warm wave. I had done it all on my own, without having to use the dream catcher.

I felt a subtle shift in the palm of my hand as the dark enchantments binding the figures of Wren and Nyxen began to break. The wooden carvings dissolved into grains of sand and the real Wren and Nyxen stood before me, solid and whole.

Nyxen appeared disoriented, his gaze unfocused as he blinked back the haze of his imprisonment. Relief flooded through me like a cleansing river, and I trembled as I whispered, "Are you okay?"

"Yes, I'm fine," Nyxen replied, his voice a soft murmur in my mind.

Tears of relief welled up in my eyes as I pulled him into a tight embrace, feeling the reassuring solidity of his shadowy form beneath my hands. It was a moment of profound connection, a testament to the strength of our bond.

"Thank the gods," I murmured, my voice quivering. "Let's get out of this cursed realm." I stood, feeling my magic waning.

"I'm not sure exactly how to pull you out," I admitted, turning to Wren. "So, we're just going to have to trust in the power of our connection."

I reached out to grasp Wren's russet fur, feeling its

texture against my skin. Closing my eyes, I channeled every ounce of my magical energy into our escape, willing us to awaken from this dream realm and return to the familiar world we knew.

And then the world around us began to fade into darkness.

TWENTY-EIGHT

I blinked groggily, disoriented by the chaos surrounding us as I woke up in the battered remains of the tent. The world seemed to spin as I tried to make sense of the scene unfolding before me. The tent's fabric was shredded, and the three men—Thalion, Aerion, and Kaelan—stood in a protective circle, fending off a relentless horde of nightmarish creatures.

Aerion and Thalion moved with remarkable agility, combining their magic with swift and precise strikes of their weapons to take down the ghouls. Kaelan, on the other hand, relied on his formidable physical prowess, his weapons gleaming in the dim light of the tent. Exhaustion was etched onto their faces and I could tell they had been battling these creatures for some time.

Thalion noticed we were awake and his voice reached me over the noise of the fight. "So glad you could join us," he quipped, a wry smile playing on his lips as he continued cutting down creature after creature.

My mind raced to catch up with the situation. "What in

the seven realms is happening?" I asked, my heart pounding as I took in the chaotic scene.

"You know about as much as we do when it comes to these things," Aerion replied, his voice calm despite the chaos. He executed a powerful kick, sending a ghoul hurtling backward.

Without any more hesitation, Wren and I sprang into action, joining the fray. I focused my magic, summoning the flames that had served me well before. A burst of fire engulfed a group of ghouls, their eerie wails filling the air as they crumbled into ash and smoke.

Beside me, Wren transformed, his body shifting seamlessly into his wolf form. With a fierce growl, he tore into the ghouls with ruthless efficiency, his powerful jaws and claws making quick work of the foul creatures.

Despite our combined efforts, the ghouls continued to pour in, their relentless assault overwhelming us. It was as if they were an endless tide of darkness, and no matter how valiantly we fought, we were gradually being pushed back.

Amidst the chaos, Kaelan's voice rose above the clamor, his tone filled with frustration. "Fuck this."

He underwent a monstrous transformation in an instant, his demonic form emerging in a terrifying display of power. Great, leathery black wings unfurled, casting eerie shadows on the torn tent fabric. Twisted horns jutted from his forehead, his eyes turned jet black, and swirling black energy emanated from his skin. His clawed hands gleamed wickedly.

With newfound ferocity, Kaelan launched himself into the battle, his transformed state giving him an edge against the ghouls. His wings beat with a thunderous sound, creating gusts of wind that sent the creatures flying. His claws sliced through their ranks, and his black shadowy energy lashed out like a deadly weapon.

The tide of the battle began to shift as Kaelan's demonic power wreaked havoc among the ghouls. His formidable presence and raw strength began to turn the tide in our favor and hope flickered in the darkness.

I focused my attention on the ghouls as I summoned the full force of my magic to decimate them. The fiery blaze in my palm roared to life and with deadly precision, I directed it at the nightmarish creatures. They shrieked in agony, each one consumed by the searing inferno that engulfed them.

Around me, Wren and the others moved with a seamless coordination. Their combined efforts carved a path of destruction through the ghoul ranks and the forest echoed with the eerie sounds of the creatures' otherworldly screams. The air grew heavy with the acrid stench of burning flesh and smoke.

The ghouls, their numbers seemingly endless, pressed on with relentless aggression, but we refused to yield. Each strike, each spell, and each fiery blast brought us one step closer to victory. The forest had transformed into a nightmarish battlefield, but we stood firm.

Thalion, his voice slightly winded, remarked, "It seems they are finally beginning to run out of numbers," as he dispatched another ghoul with a deadly blow.

"Perhaps they will actually retreat this time," Aerion chimed in, his tone tinged with a hint of sarcasm.

I shot them both a weary glance, my energy waning as the physical and emotional toll of the battle wore on. The memories of our ordeal in the dream realm still haunted me and the strain was beginning to slow me down.

Still, we continued to fight, refusing to surrender to the

nightmarish onslaught. With each blow we delivered, the ghouls' numbers dwindled, and the ground beneath us became littered with their charred and broken bodies. The overwhelming smell of decay made me want to retch.

Finally, it seemed as though the battle was approaching its end. We stood victorious amidst the ruins of the tent, the last of the ghouls falling before our combined might.

"Is that all of them?" Wren said, panting as he shifted back into his mortal form.

"Seems to be," I replied, my eyes scanning the surrounding forest for any lingering threats.

"Shit," I heard Thalion whisper. I followed his eyes to Kaelan, who remained standing among the fallen ghouls, still in his demonic form. He appeared distant and detached as he stared at us and an icy ball of dread formed in my stomach.

"Did he not take his potion while we were in the dream realm?" I asked Thalion, never taking my eyes off Kaelan.

Thalion shot back a defensive response, "We were a little busy not getting killed."

Kaelan began to take slow and measured steps toward the forest. However, my growing unease was interrupted by a cry of pain to my left. I turned to see Aerion clutching his arm, where it was evident he had been bitten by one of the creatures. The wound festered and black veins snaked out from the oozing bite.

"Shit," Thalion muttered again and I found I couldn't agree more.

I reached Aerion, who had sunk to his knees in the snow. His injury appeared serious and the need to get him back to the palace was paramount. However, my attention was torn between attending to Aerion and the unsettling sight of Kaelan vanishing into the dark shadows of the forest.

Kneeling beside Aerion, I swiftly tied a makeshift bandage around his wound, using supplies from my waist bag. My eyes remained locked on Kaelan's retreating figure, a growing sense of urgency gnawing at me.

"Go back to Terralux while you can still shift. I'll heal you when I get there," I instructed Aerion, my voice steady. With that, I turned to face Thalion and Wren.

"I'm going after Kaelan," I declared, my tone resolute.

"Vale, are you sure that's a good idea?" Wren asked, concern etched on his face.

I shook my head in frustration. "There's no time for debates. I'm the only one who can get through to him."

Without waiting for their response, I set off in pursuit of Kaelan, disappearing into the dense forest. The towering trees cast long shadows and the snow-covered ground made my footsteps almost soundless. Kaelan couldn't have gone far and I suspected he was both physically and emotionally drained from the battle. I hoped that I could reach him before he vanished entirely.

As I followed the faint trail of his footprints in the snow, I called out his name, my voice echoing eerily through the silent woods. The winter air seemed to swallow my words and there was no response but the frigid wind that rustled the trees. Aware that my calls might draw unwanted attention, I strained my ears, listening for any sound that might indicate Kaelan's presence. The forest remained hauntingly still.

Suddenly, the footprints ceased, and I scanned my surroundings, heart pounding in my chest. If he had taken to the air, tracking him would be impossible. My breath caught as I heard a twig snap behind me and I spun around to find Kaelan standing there, back in his mortal form, his head tilted to the side, his eyes utterly devoid of their usual warmth.

"Kaelan, I have your potion. You need to take it," I said calmly, despite the panic rising in my chest.

The forest around us was a silent witness, cloaked in the deep blues and grays of a night painted with snow. The trees, ancient sentinels with thick trunks and branches heavy with white, stood like ghosts against the darkness. Above us, the waning moon struggled to pierce through the skeletal canopy, casting a weak, silvery light.

Kaelan's silhouette was a dark stain against the snow, his body moving with a grace that was both beautiful and terrifying. His steps were slow and deliberate, the gait of a predator stalking its prey. My heart thundered in my chest, every instinct screaming to run.

I backed away slowly, my breath forming clouds of mist in the freezing air. "Kaelan," I said, my voice steady despite the fear that clawed at my insides. "What are you doing? Stop."

But he didn't. Instead, he grinned, a twisted, chilling display of his fangs that gleamed like daggers in the moonlight. His eyes, once a beautiful and vibrant shade, were now abysmal pools, void of the man I knew. They held me captive with a gaze that promised darkness and danger. They were completely black, a sign that the demon within had seized the reins, and the man I loved was lost to its primal urges.

"What's the matter, little witch? Am I scaring you?" he taunted, his voice a low purr, the sound of it snaking through the frigid air and wrapping around me like a vice.

I took a step back for every step he took forward, the crunch of snow under my boots a stark contrast to the silence of the forest. The back of my heels bumped against something solid, a fallen tree hidden beneath the snow, and I knew I could retreat no further. Panic clawed at the edges of my composure as he mirrored my movements, closing the distance between us with a hunter's patience.

"You don't want to do this," I tried again, my words laced with an urgent plea. "Fight it, Kaelan. You're stronger than the curse."

His chuckle was low and void of humor, a sound as frigid as the air. I could see the battle within him, a fleeting struggle that flashed across his features before being snuffed out by the curse's relentless grip. "Oh, Vale, I definitely want to do this," he said, my name a taunt on his lips. "You really think you can save me?"

I pulled a knife from its sheath and held it out in front of me. The cold steel quivered in my grasp as I squared off against the demon who looked like Kaelan. His advance was deliberate, each step an echo in the silence that enveloped us. The blade's edge met his neck, a perilous kiss, and he halted, his gaze never leaving mine.

"I can, and I will," I told him, though my voice shook slightly, betraying the fear that spiraled within me. His face, so familiar and yet so alien under the curse's thrall, was inches from mine, his eyes pools of endless night.

He leaned into the blade I held, a line of crimson welling up where the edge cut his skin, his breath a warm gust against my cheek. Despite the cold, despite the terror, my body responded to his closeness, to the threat and promise in his proximity.

"You can't," he countered, his voice a velvet darkness that stroked my fears. "And if you try, I'll make you wish you hadn't."

His words were the final push, the clarion call to the

part of me that was still rational, still desperate to save us both. A plan, fragile as it was, took shape in my mind—a gamble, but my only chance.

With a surge of adrenaline, I shoved against him, putting all my strength behind the motion. He staggered, surprise registering briefly in his blackened eyes. I seized the moment, turned, and bolted. Branches whipped at my face, the snow muffled my frantic steps, and the feeble moon above offered little guidance through the multitude of trees.

I knew he was close behind. I could almost feel the brush of his fingers against the fabric of my coat. The forest became a blur of shadow and silver as I darted between the trees, knowing the reprieve would be short-lived. Panic lent speed to my flight, but I was painfully aware of the disparity between us—Kaelan, with his demonic strength and agility, and me, a mere witch running on fear and determination. I needed a plan, a way to neutralize him without causing harm.

I ducked and weaved, hoping to lose him in the dense trees, but a hidden root caught my foot, sending me sprawling into the frost-hardened earth. Pain lanced through my palms as they broke my fall and I felt the sting of scraped skin. Ignoring the sting, I scrambled upright, only to be met by Kaelan's towering form.

I reeled back, my breath a ghost in the night air. His arms were around me instantly, trapping my limbs against my body. My struggles were useless against his supernatural hold, my legs kicking at his with a desperation that seemed only to amuse him.

"I like it when you run from me," he whispered into my ear, his voice a growl of dark delight that vibrated through my entire being.

I could feel his heart, rapid and strong against my back. For a moment, I allowed myself to melt against him, to sink into the danger and desire that radiated from his skin, my body betraying my mind's urgent commands to flee.

"I can feel your heart racing, your pulse fluttering like a frightened little bird," he murmured into my neck, his words winding around me like chains.

His tongue traced a path up my neck and I trembled, my willpower waning as goosebumps pebbled along my skin. "You taste so sweet, little witch," he said, the possession in his voice more binding than any spell.

My grip on the knife faltered, the weapon slipping from my numbed fingers, falling to the snow with a soft thud, leaving me defenseless against the storm that was Kaelan.

Panic clawed at my insides, but a flicker of defiance sparked within me. I was no helpless prey. I summoned every ounce of strength I had and in a swift, desperate movement, I snapped my head back with all the force I could muster.

Kaelan's grip loosened instantly as he stumbled backward, his hand clasping his face. Blood seeped between his fingers, a dark crimson against the pale snow. My heart pounded, fear and adrenaline pumping through my veins as I seized the momentary lapse in his defenses to dart past him.

My legs carried me away, stumbling through the snow that sought to slow me down. I had no destination in mind, no plan beyond escape even though I knew it was a temporary evasion. But the instinct to survive was a powerful force and it propelled me forward.

My lungs burned as the cold air sawed in and out, and the muscles in my legs ached with the strain of relentless running. The snow-covered ground, a treacherous layer of white over hidden snares, threatened to trip me with every step. Kaelan's amused laughter, a sound that once brought me comfort, now filled the air behind me, too close for any semblance of safety. "You're just prolonging the inevitable," he taunted, his voice a dark melody that chased me through the underbrush.

I didn't respond, didn't dare waste my breath on words when every ounce of me was focused on escape. The trees blurred past me as I wove through the dense forest, branches reaching out like hands trying to snatch me back. My heart raced, fear a constant companion urging me forward.

As I neared a clearing, a sense of false hope briefly flickered within me, only to be extinguished as strong arms once again wrapped around me, pulling me down into the snow. I hit the ground hard, rolling in an attempt to dislodge him, but Kaelan was relentless. In a heartbeat, he was on top of me, his hands imprisoning mine above my head. His hips were seated between my thighs and I could feel the undeniable hardness of him through his pants.

"Let go!" I demanded, defiance burning bright in my eyes despite the dread that filled me.

His eyes devoured me with a hunger that was more than physical. His touch was fire and ice as he traced a finger along the line of my body, pausing at my throat. "Such a fierce little witch," he taunted, a dark edge to his voice. "I could tear you apart and you couldn't stop me. But I won't do that to you. No, the things I'm going to do to you will leave you begging for me."

I writhed beneath him, caught in a battle between the will to fight and the instinctive response to his proximity. His head dipped to my neck and his inhale was a ragged sound of raw desire. "I can smell your fear, your arousal.

Such a delicious combination," he growled, and the scrape of his fangs against my throat was both a warning and a wicked promise.

The air was icy, the kind that bites at the skin and clings to the breath, but the heat emanating from him was a blistering contrast. "You won't do it," I managed to say, my voice full of fear and defiance. I trembled—not solely from the cold or fright but from the awakening of a hunger that mirrored his own.

"No? You seem so certain," Kaelan's voice was a low hum, full of dark amusement, his breath warm on my chilled skin. I struggled to keep my breathing steady. "You know it's what you want, Vale. Your resistance only sweetens the excitement of your eventual surrender."

A tremor of conflicting desires ran through me, his predatory nature weaving a seductive spell I fought against. Part of me—the primal, unchecked part—ached to give in, to be claimed by him in the most raw, untamed manner.

"Please," I begged, the single word laden with confusion and desire, a plea for him to both stop and not to stop, each meaning wrestling with the other for dominance.

His chuckle was a low, wicked sound, and his gaze upon me burned with a greedy hunger. His hand trailed down, fingers mapping the curve of my hip with an ownership that stole my breath away. "So desperate," he whispered, and his voice was like sin itself, the words spoken so intimately they felt like a caress. "I could consume you, every inch of you, little witch."

Then his mouth was on mine, a kiss that was more an assertion of power than an act of intimacy. He nipped sharply at my lower lip, drawing a bead of blood that he was quick to soothe with his tongue. The mingling of sharp pain and deep pleasure was disorienting, and I arched into him, a moan escaping into the frigid night.

"Your blood flowing on my tongue...you have no idea what it does to me," he breathed against my mouth, his voice the growl of a beast. "You want this, don't you?" His voice was rough with desire, his words painting a vivid picture of submission and domination. "To be at my mercy, to be taken by the demon that I am."

"Y-Yes," I admitted, the confession a raw scrape in my throat.

With a swift, brutal motion, he ripped my shirt open, the sound of tearing fabric slicing through the air. The cool night embraced my exposed skin as he bent to take a hardened nipple between his lips. His mouth was fire against my skin, his fangs a whisper of danger that sent a new wave of pleasure coursing through me.

His touch was a flame that set every nerve ending alight with the need for more. I shivered in the cold night air as his fangs pierced the soft flesh at my breast, a sharp pain that mingled with an undeniable thrill. The cry that escaped my lips was one of pain and pleasure, echoing into the obsidian night. He drank from me with an insatiable greed that coursed through the bond we shared.

His need, his hunger, and the primal, unbridled lust surged between us through that bond, a dark and unrelenting force. I surrendered completely to it, embracing the darkness that engulfed us, succumbing to the feral instincts that united us in this twisted dance of desire. The curse that bound Kaelan was consuming me just as viciously as it was him.

He withdrew from me, his eyes burning with an animalistic hunger, roving over my half-naked and bleeding form. "I can feel you slipping," he snarled, his voice low and dangerous. "Your hunger is like a drug, and I want more. I want to devour you."

"Do it," I gasped, my voice barely more than a breath, the last vestiges of my willpower crumbling away.

He growled in response, finally releasing my hands only to forcefully yank my pants down to my boots. Roughly, he flipped me over onto my stomach, and the frigid ground and snow bit into my face as he pinned me down, leaving my exposed ass in the air. He leaned in and sank his fangs into the side of my neck, biting deep as he took what he craved.

I lay there immobile, barely able to breathe, as the intensity of his passion overwhelmed me. He entered me roughly; the unexpected intrusion brought a mix of pleasure and pain and I cried out, the sound muffled by the cold ground beneath me.

With powerful, unrelenting thrusts, he moved inside me, each motion sending waves of both pleasure and discomfort through my body. His need, his hunger, and the raw force of his lust coursed through him as he pounded into me. His hand tightened around my neck, his fingers closing around my throat and pulling my head back as he maintained his punishing rhythm.

"How does it feel, letting me fuck you, knowing I could do whatever I wanted to you? Tell me how much you love me possessing you, little witch, how wet the danger makes you," he snarled, his voice dripping with a feral desire.

I could only moan in response, but his grip on my neck tightened further, urging me to obey. "Tell me, tell me what I should do with you," he growled, his voice a predatory purr.

"Anything," I gasped, the word a breathless plea.

"Beg for it."

"Please, Kaelan, please," I moaned, the words spilling from my lips, my body no longer under my control.

I knew I was lost, that the darkness within him was consuming me as well. I surrendered to the curse, to the raw, primal urges that drove us both, and I became one with the intoxicating darkness that threatened to devour us.

My cries and his snarls filled the air as he took me savagely, the sounds echoing through the night. My climax hit me like a tidal wave, an explosion of pleasure so intense, so powerful, it left me breathless. Kaelan felt my body shudder, felt me clench around him and he groaned.

He withdrew suddenly, only to trail his tongue over the curve of my ass. He parted my cheeks, and I trembled in anticipation, my breath a shallow cloud in the cold night.

Slowly, deliberately, he teased me, his tongue swirling around the tight ring of muscle, before pushing his way inside. A moan escaped my lips, the sensation new and unexpected but delicious all the same.

I pressed myself against him, encouraging his exploration, and I could feel him smile against my skin as he began to fuck me with his tongue. He worked his fingers inside, stretching me as his tongue continued its sensual assault.

He added a second finger, the fullness making me gasp, and I rocked back against his hand, eager for more. He increased the pressure, and I felt the tension building inside me.

He removed his fingers, and I whined at the loss, but soon, the tip of his cock was pressing against my ass, pushing its way in. He plunged into me roughly. A gasp tore from my throat as pain laced through me. He didn't pause to give me a moment to breathe. He continued his unrelenting pace, thrusting into me wildly.

He grunted with each movement, his hands gripping my hips tightly, his nails digging into the skin. The pain was exquisite, the sensation of being used for his pleasure both terrifying and exhilarating. I was his prey, his toy, and I loved it. He was relentless, pounding into me with a ferocity that bordered on violence. He reached a hand down between us and plunged his fingers into my wet acheing core.

I cried out, the feeling overwhelming as he roughly used his fingers on me.

"You make for quite the amusing little plaything, witch. How many dark desires live in your mind, begging to be fulfilled?" he taunted. "I can feel it, your need, your fear. You love this. You love being helpless, being fucked by a monster. You want more, don't you, little witch?" he growled, the words a dark promise.

I didn't answer, my body responding to him despite my will. The pain was intense, but the pleasure was even more so. My body was craving the forbidden desires I kept buried deep within.

He continued his assault, his fingers moving in tandem with his cock, pushing me towards another orgasm. Each thrust pushed me further across the unforgiving ground. The snow and ice chilled me as it melted on my heated skin.

"You're going to come for me again, aren't you?" he growled, his voice a dark command.

"Yes," I gasped,

"That's it, little witch. Surrender to me. Surrender to the shadows."

His words sent me spiraling over the edge, my orgasm hitting me like a tidal wave. My screams echoed through the night, and Kaelan's release quickly followed. His snarls and my moans mingled in the darkness, a symphony of passion and sin.

When the waves of pleasure finally subsided, Kaelan withdrew, leaving me trembling and exhausted. I collapsed to the ground, my body limp and spent, the snow and ice numbing the cuts and scrapes on my skin. I could feel Kaelan's presence behind me, his breath hot on my neck, his voice a menacing purr.

"Don't worry, little witch. We're not done yet. This is just the beginning."

TWENTY-NINE

"No, Kaelan, we're finished with this. You need to take your potion now." My voice was firm, determined to break through the darkness that had consumed him.

In response, his lips curled into a sinister smile, a dark laugh escaping him. "You have no idea what you're dealing with, do you? What I'm capable of?" His words oozed threat, and his eyes gleamed with a wickedness that made my heart race.

I met his gaze head-on, refusing to be intimidated. "You may be powerful, but you can't hurt me without consequences. Now, drink the fucking potion before you lose control completely. I know you haven't, or else things would have gone very differently just now."

Kaelan's lips curled into a snarl, his sharp fangs gleaming in the moonlight. "You're so naïve, little witch. So weak."

I scrambled to my feet, pulling up my pants as I stood defiantly before him. "The last thing I am is weak. Now, for the last time, drink the fucking potion!"

"And if I don't?" he challenged, his voice dripping with defiance.

I drew another dagger from its sheath at my hip, the blade glistening in the moonlight. My heart pounded in my chest, but I knew I had to make him see reason. "Then I'll have no choice but to make you."

Kaelan's laughter echoed once more, a sinister and low sound that sent shivers down my spine. "You're no match for me, Vale. I could tear you apart in an instant."

His words were chillingly accurate, but I couldn't let fear paralyze me. I had to summon every ounce of strength within me to reach him, to help him fight the curse. I had to be stronger than I'd ever been.

I narrowed my eyes, glaring at him, daring him to challenge me. I raised the dagger, holding it in a firm grip. The blade glimmered in the moonlight, a cold, silver flash of danger. I advanced on him, the blade pointed at his throat.

Kaelan merely stared at me, his eyes black pools of darkness. He didn't move, didn't flinch, just stared at me, a look of vicious amusement on his face.

I gritted my teeth, pressing the dagger against his skin. The sharp edge drew a thin line of crimson, and I saw a flicker of satisfaction in his gaze. But still, he didn't move.

I tightened my grip on the dagger, my hand trembling with the effort.

I had a sudden thought and turning the blade around, I aimed it at my own heart, my hand steady despite the fear gnawing at my insides. Kaelan laughed, a mocking sound that sliced through the air like the knife at my heart. "If you don't do what I say, I'll plunge this knife into my chest."

A sneer twisted his lips, his voice dripping with malice as he taunted me. "Oh, you will, will you? Be my guest," he said, calling my bluff. I needed to be more convincing.

Needed him to fear what I might do to myself. I knew no matter how deep into the curse he became, there would always be a part of him that instinctively kept me safe.

I took a deep breath, steeling myself. I had to find the courage to go through with it. If I didn't, I knew Kaelan would never regain his sanity. He would be lost, a slave to the curse, and I would be helpless to save him.

The dagger was a cold weight in my hand, a physical manifestation of my resolve. I took another deep breath, the sound harsh in the silence.

"I know you're in there, Kaelan. I know the real you is still fighting. You can't let the curse win. I won't let you. Drink the fucking potion," I said firmly.

His lips twisted into a cruel smirk, and his eyes burned with contempt. "I could stop you before you even tried," he snarled, his voice dripping with menace. "Or I could just take the knife and do it myself."

His words were a threat, a sinister attempt to rattle me, but I couldn't afford to show fear. My fingers tightened around the hilt of the blade, grounding myself in its reassuring weight, the tip pressed between my exposed breasts.

"But you won't," I responded, my voice steady. "You won't because you know that if you do, you will never forgive yourself."

Kaelan's smirk wavered for a moment, a flicker of uncertainty crossing his face. "I'll do whatever I please. I have no qualms about hurting you. In fact, I'll enjoy it."

I stood my ground, refusing to let his threats unnerve me. "You may think you're the master here, but I'm not some helpless human you can toy with. I'm a witch. And you know what I'm capable of."

The truth of my words struck me, bolstering my resolve. I wasn't weak, and I wouldn't allow him to break me. I would fight him with every ounce of strength I possessed and I wouldn't relent until I had freed him from the curse.

"Drink the fucking potion, Kaelan," I repeated firmly, pressing the blade harder against my skin, bringing blood welling to the surface.

For a moment, a flicker of hesitation passed through the darkness in his eyes, his expression faltering. He clenched his fists as he stared at the dagger pointed at my heart, his jaw tightening. "Fuck," he hissed.

Hope flickered within me, and I held my breath, waiting to see if he would finally relent.

Suddenly, he lunged forward, seizing my wrist with a vice-like grip. The blade was torn from my hand and flung across the clearing beyond my reach. I was powerless against his superior strength, and I felt the bruising pressure of his fingers as he forced me backward, pinning me against a tree.

His body pressed against mine, trapping me against the rough bark. His hot breath brushed against my skin as he leaned in, his words a sinister whisper. "You should be afraid of me, Vale."

My heart pounded, but I refused to succumb to fear. "Guess again, asshole."

Before he could react, I drove my knee upward into his groin. The sudden, unexpected blow caught him off guard, and he staggered backward, releasing his grip on me.

Seizing the moment, I launched myself at him, tackling him to the ground. He grunted in surprise as his back hit the dirt, the air rushing from his lungs.

I straddled him, my knees pressing into his arms to pin him in place. He glared up at me, his eyes blazing with anger and frustration.

I met his glare, my expression determined. I had one chance to convince him and I wouldn't let it pass me by.

My heart hammered in my chest as I leaned forward, bringing my face close to his. My voice was barely more than a whisper as I spoke.

"Drink the potion, Kaelan. You can beat this. I know you can. I believe in you. And I will never give up on you. Please, just trust me. Trust that I can help you. Trust that I will do anything in my power to keep you safe because you mean everything to me. Don't let the curse win. Don't let it turn you into the monster you never wanted to be. You're better than this. I know you are."

As I spoke, his gaze softened, a hint of emotion passing through his eyes. For a moment, I saw a flicker of the real Kaelan beneath the curse, the man I had fallen in love with.

"Please," I whispered, a raw plea for him to come back to me, to fight the darkness that threatened to consume him.

He closed his eyes, a look of torment on his face.

My heart skipped a beat, and I waited, breathless, to see what he would do. When he opened his eyes, they were brown once more, the curse momentarily lifted as he struggled against it.

"Vale," Kaelan breathed, his eyes shining with unshed tears.

"Don't you dare apologize," I warned, pushing the bottle of potion into his hands. The glass was cold against my palm, a stark contrast to the heat radiating off of his fevered skin.

He hesitated for a moment, his fingers curling around the glass. His hand trembled slightly and I could see the struggle in his eyes.

"Do it," I said, my voice firm.

He lifted the bottle to his lips, his throat working as he downed the entire bitter potion in one gulp.

"Are you alright?" he asked, his voice heavy with concern, his gaze searching my face for any signs of harm.

"I'll be fine," I reassured him, though I couldn't deny the lingering aches on my body from our impassioned encounter. "You're the one I'm worried about."

"I'm sorry, Vale. I shouldn't have lost control like that. I can't believe I..." he trailed off, his guilt evident.

"Stop," I interrupted gently. "I consented to it. There's nothing to be sorry for."

His brow furrowed, and he looked genuinely conflicted. "But I could have seriously hurt you."

"No, you wouldn't have," I countered, my voice unwavering. "Deep down, the real you is stronger than the curse."

"You couldn't have known that. The fact that you consented to what I did to you while under the curse's influence..." he trailed off again, his expression anguished.

"Kaelan, listen to me," I said firmly. "I knew that there was still a part of you in there. A part of you that would never willingly hurt me."

He nodded slowly, but his expression remained troubled. "Is that something you want from me? To let the demon in me take over when we are together?"

"I know the demon is a part of you. That's what makes you, well, you. I don't think you should deny that part of yourself, not with me. I want all of you, Kaelan, the scary parts and everything."

Kaelan looked up at me, his eyes full of emotion. "I'm not sure I deserve you."

"Don't be ridiculous," I replied, my tone light. "You're a demon, not the devil himself."

A smile tugged at the corner of his lips, and I knew my words had eased some of his guilt. "No, that would be my father."

"See, you're not that bad."

"I hope you're right," he said, still uncertain.

"Come on, we need to get back," I urged. "I need to heal Aerion." It was then that I realized my shirt still hung off me in tatters, the remnants of the battle. I hugged my coat tight around my body and glanced at Kaelan, "I'm going to need your shirt."

He nodded without hesitation and removed his shirt, handing it to me. "Sorry about that."

I shrugged, a small smile tugging at my lips. "I didn't really like that shirt anyway," I said, pulling his shirt over my head.

Kaelan stepped closer to me, his hand moving toward my cheek, hesitating for a moment before finally resting it there. "I love you, little witch."

I placed my hand on top of his and nestled my face into his palm, savoring the warmth of his touch. "I love you, my demon prince. Every bit of you, even the scary parts."

He leaned down and kissed me softly and as our lips met, the shadows enveloped us and we were whisked away back to the palace, leaving behind the chaotic battlefield and the darkness that had threatened to consume us.

KAELAN and I shifted back to the palace in Terralux, the familiar rush of darkness and swirling shadows around us. As the sensation subsided, we found ourselves in the courtyard. The sun was just beginning to rise, casting a soft, golden glow over the surroundings. The courtyard had transformed since I had last seen it. The drab military atmosphere had given way to something more beautiful, with colorful flowers and vines cascading down the stone walls, and the centerpiece—a grand fountain—sparkled in the morning light.

I stepped back from Kaelan but kept hold of his hand. "Come on, I've got to check on Aerion. They must be down with the healers."

We navigated through the palace's winding corridors and descended a set of stairs, making our way to the area where the healers were located. The palace was quiet at this early hour, the hushed footsteps of servants and guards echoing through the halls. As we reached the lower level, the scent of herbs and medicinal potions grew stronger.

When we arrived at the infirmary, I saw Aerion lying on one of the beds, his eyes closed and his face pale. I spotted Thalion and Wren sitting on a nearby bench, looking exhausted but otherwise unharmed. They were engaged in a hushed conversation and when they saw us approaching, they both stood up.

"Vale, Kaelan," Thalion greeted us with a weary smile. "Good to see you both in one piece."

I nodded in acknowledgment and then turned my attention to Aerion. "How is he?"

The healer, a middle-aged woman with a no-nonsense demeanor, stepped forward. "He's stable for now. The creature's bite was nasty, though. I haven't seen a wound like it. I'm not sure what it will do to him."

"Can I see him?" I asked, my voice barely above a whisper.

The healer nodded silently, permitting me to approach. I moved closer. My footsteps light and careful to avoid disturbing him. As I reached out and took his hand in mine,

I could feel the feverish heat radiating from his skin, a clear indication of the struggle he was enduring.

"I've got to find a spell or something to heal him," I said to Thalion, my eyes still fixed on Aerion's pale face.

Just then, the infirmary doors burst open, and Harker entered with a triumphant "A-ha!" She held a large book in her hands, and though the healers in the room shushed her in annoyance, she paid them no mind as she made her way over to me.

"I had to run from Elara to get this book out of the library with me, but look, are these the creatures that bit Aerion?" she asked, flipping open the book to reveal gruesome illustrations.

I looked down at the drawings, my heart sinking as I recognized the creatures' familiar grey, stretched skin and hollow eyes.

"That's them," I confirmed, my voice filled with dread. "Are there any spells in here to cure their bites?"

Harker's expression turned grim as she shook her head. "No, there isn't. But that's not the worst of it. The bites turn the victim into one of these unholy creatures."

My heart sank further at the revelation. "Fuck."

"I'm not sure you are going to find a spell for this type of injury," Harker said, her eyes still glued to the book.

"Why not?" I asked, my desperation mounting.

"Because the wounds are not natural. They are magical in nature," she explained.

I turned my gaze back to Aerion, a sense of helplessness washing over me. The situation was dire and I knew that time was running out.

"My blood will heal him," I declared, my voice firm.

Kaelan started to speak, but I could already anticipate his words. I held up a hand to silence him.

Though Thalion didn't hesitate to voice his own objections. "You'd be creating a partial blood bond, you know that, right?" Thalion asked, his eyes studying my expression closely.

"Yes, I'm aware," I replied, my attention still on Aerion's pale face.

Thalion's expression remained serious. "This is serious, Vale, and not something you can take lightly. Blood bonds are not to be made in haste."

I met his gaze steadily. "I'm well aware of the implications, but it is the only thing I can think of that would cure him. You heard Harker; he's about to become one of those things. Who knows how long he has."

But I was willing to do whatever it took to save Aerion, even if it meant forging a bond that could forever change our relationship.

"A partial blood bond like the one we share?" Wren asked, his brows furrowing in concern as he considered the implications.

"Yes," I said, shifting my eyes to Wren. "He'd be able to feel my emotions and find me through the bond, just like you."

Worry etched across Wren's face, but he didn't object further. The urgency of Aerion's condition was apparent to everyone.

"Aerion isn't even awake to give his permission..." Thalion began, concern evident in his voice, but I cut him off before he could finish.

"I'm not letting Aerion die, not if there's a chance I can save him."

As I looked around the infirmary, meeting each person's eyes in the crowded space, they nodded in understanding and agreement with my decision. Their support was a silent but strong reassurance that I was doing the right thing.

"We'll give you some privacy," Thalion said, taking the lead as he, Harker, and Wren turned to leave the small curtained room. Kaelan hesitated for a moment, his gaze lingering on me before he followed the others out. He has stayed silent through that exchange but I was pretty sure I knew what he was thinking.

"Okay, then," I said, returning my attention to Aerion. With practiced ease, I unsheathed one of my knives and made a small cut across my wrist. Blood welled up, and I held it to Aerion's mouth, watching as a few drops slipped between his cracked lips.

Suddenly, his eyes snapped open and they fixed on mine. His hands shot up, grasping my forearm tightly, holding me in place as he looked at me with those mesmerizing grey eyes.

"Drink," I told him. "It's okay, just drink."

He hesitated, watching me still, before parting his lips and sinking his fangs into my wrist. I gasped as he took long, desperate pulls from my wrist and I watched in awe as his bite wound began to heal. His strength was returning and the color was gradually returning to his pale face.

With surprising control, Aerion stopped abruptly, pulling back and looking at me with wide, astonished eyes. His hands released my forearm and I withdrew my wrist, the wound already itching as it began to heal. "Vale," he said, his voice barely a whisper.

"Welcome back," I said, smiling down at him, hoping to alleviate the tension in his eyes.

"What have you done?" Aerion asked, his gaze fixed on the wound on my wrist.

"Saved your life. You're welcome," I replied, giving him a small, nervous smile.

"But...I am now bloodbound to you," he said slowly.

"Yes," I replied, fidgeting as I stood there.

"You should not have done that," Aerion said, his tone sharp. "Offering someone your blood, especially yours, is no small decision."

"Well, it's better than you becoming a ghoul, isn't it? Because that's what would have happened," I retorted, my frustration showing. "Is it really so horrible to be bonded with me?"

Aerion's face colored slightly, and he looked away for a moment before meeting my gaze again. "Of course not. I would have just rather it had been at the proper time," he admitted, his voice softer. "In a private moment when I could have asked you myself."

"Oh," I said, a bit flustered by the unexpected turn of events, not knowing quite what else to say.

Aerion echoed my sentiment with his own "Oh."

"Well, it needed to be done. No sense in getting upset," I said, slightly frustrated.

"I'm not upset," Aerion insisted, though his tone and his conflicted expression told a different story.

"Aerion, you're upset, so just say it," I urged him.

I watched as he sat up in bed, his legs swinging over the edge, and he stood up, turning to face me. His smile was faint and he placed his hand on my cheek, catching me off guard. His words, when they came, were soft and filled with emotion.

"I should have known better than to think you'd let me do anything the right way," he said, his thumb brushing my lips. I couldn't help but smile at his words.

"I don't think there's a 'right' way," I replied, my frustration melting away.

"I should be mad," Aerion continued, his voice low, "but you're right. I'd rather live and have a bond with you, even if I wasn't the one to initiate it."

I rolled my eyes playfully, still smiling at the unexpected turn of events. "You're impossible, you know that?"

"Thank you, Vale," Aerion said sincerely, his voice filled with gratitude.

"Anytime," I replied, my heart feeling lighter.

Aerion leaned in and kissed me, his lips meeting mine with a gentle and lingering passion. I surrendered to the kiss, momentarily forgetting our surroundings and everything that had just happened.

The moment was interrupted by Harker's voice from behind the curtain. "Umm, not to interrupt, but you are in a very public place."

I pulled away from Aerion with a laugh, my cheeks flushed. He laughed as well, shaking his head and giving me one last quick kiss before turning to push the curtain aside.

PART
THREE

THIRTY

I stood on a raised platform in the grand chamber, surrounded by three full-length mirrors that reflected every angle of my form. Gossamer black fabric cascaded around me, and I marveled at the intricate layers of the dress that was being fitted for my upcoming queen coronation. The room was filled with the soft rustling of fabric and the gentle humming of the bustling seamstresses.

The seamstress, a skilled woman with nimble fingers and a keen eye, moved around me gracefully, her experienced hands adjusting the flowing gown. She held a bundle of pins, deftly inserting them where necessary to ensure the dress fit perfectly. Each pinprick was a reminder of the significance of the event that lay ahead.

The dress itself was a masterpiece, a testament to the craftsmanship of my kingdom. Layers of fabric billowed around me like a dark, enchanted cloud. The color was a deep, rich black, a symbol of power, mystery, and elegance. It bore intricate embroidery and delicate beadwork, which caught the light and shimmered like stars in the night sky.

The mirrors reflected every detail of the dress, from the elegant neckline to the flowing train that trailed behind me. I stared at my reflection, trying to imagine how I would look on the day of the coronation.

My heart fluttered at the thought of the impending ceremony, which would bind me to the kingdom and its people in a profound way. I felt a wave of nervousness wash over me, mingling with the excitement. As I gazed at my reflection in the mirrors, I couldn't help but wonder if I was truly ready for the role that awaited me.

"You will be the most beautiful queen this land has ever seen," the seamstress assured me, her words offering a comforting reassurance.

"Thank you," I replied with a soft smile, though a trace of uncertainty lingered.

The seamstress gave me a warm and encouraging smile, her hands deftly making the final adjustments to the gown. "I have no doubt that you will make a magnificent queen. This dress will ensure that you take everyone's breath away."

"You have an incredible talent," I praised her, genuinely admiring her work and craftsmanship.

"Thank you, Your Majesty," she responded, her face beaming with pride.

Thalion sat on an overstuffed couch nearby, overseeing the entire fitting process. I noticed his sharp eyes scanning the details of the dress, no doubt thinking along the same lines as the seamstress.

"It's beautiful," I told him, appreciating his presence and support throughout the preparation.

"Make sure you write down all her measurements for the blacksmith," Thalion instructed the seamstress, his tone laced with a hint of secrecy.

"The blacksmith? Why?" I asked, curious about his cryptic remark.

"You'll see when the time comes," he replied with a mischievous twinkle in his eyes.

With the final adjustments made and the fitting concluded, the seamstress bowed, signaling the end of the session. "I will have the final alterations completed in a week, Your Majesty."

"Thank you," I said to her gratefully, stepping off the raised platform and making my way to the partitioned area where I could change out of the gown without disturbing the multitude of pins still holding it in place.

Once I was back in my regular dress, Thalion and I exited the chamber, making our way through the palace halls. The place was slowly but surely shedding the dark, oppressive cloak of Haldir's reign, becoming more vibrant and alive with each passing day. Servants bustled about, diligently attending to their daily tasks to ensure the smooth operation of the castle. I couldn't help but notice the significant change in their demeanor since my arrival. The atmosphere had shifted from one of fear and apprehension to a sense of renewed hope and purpose. I smiled warmly at the servants as they passed by, and many of them returned the gesture with genuine smiles of their own. It was heartening to witness the transformation taking place within the palace walls.

"Are you ready for the coronation?" Thalion asked, his voice filled with a mix of concern and curiosity.

"I'm not sure if 'ready' is the right word," I confessed, my gaze wandering over the busy surroundings. "It's all happening so fast and I've had no time to prepare."

Thalion nodded empathetically. "I know, but we need to show the kingdom that a new leader has taken charge and the best way to do that is to have a proper coronation. Besides, can you actually prepare for these things? Best to dive in head first."

"I understand the importance of it," I replied, my tone reflecting a touch of uncertainty. "It's a lot to take in."

Thalion offered me a reassuring smile. "You'll be fine, Vale. I believe in you."

My curiosity about his own future resurfaced, and I couldn't help but inquire further. "What about you? Does your father still have plans to step down and let you become king?"

"He does," Thalion confirmed, his expression thoughtful. "He and mother have been on the throne of Virelium for a long time now, over 500 years. They wish to spend their remaining days together without the worry that comes with ruling. Plus, it's tradition to step down when the heir marries."

I couldn't resist teasing him. "Oh, so you plan on marrying? Who is the lucky girl?"

With a playful gleam in his eye, Thalion replied, "Just the most ravishing, powerful, and intriguing witch in the realms."

I feigned surprise and admiration. "Oh, wow, she sounds amazing."

"She is," he admitted, a genuine affection in his voice, "and she has agreed to become my queen."

"Well, who am I to stand in the way of true love," I said dramatically, pretending to be jealous.

"True love? Vale, I'm shocked. I never knew you had such a romantic side," he teased.

I chuckled and played along. "Don't let it get out. I have a reputation to maintain."

"Your secret is safe with me," Thalion assured me, his

laughter echoing through the corridors as we continued our leisurely walk.

"I'll hold you to that," I joked, playfully pushing on Thalion's arm as we strolled.

"You'd have to catch me first," he replied, amusement dancing in his eyes as he quickened his pace, leaving me in his wake.

"Cheater!" I shouted in mock indignation, laughter bubbling from my lips as I chased after him.

"Now you're just jealous," he taunted, his voice fading as he disappeared around a corner.

I surged forward in hot pursuit, the thrill of the chase surging through me. We weaved through the bustling corridors, our laughter echoing off the walls as we playfully dodged servants and guards in our impromptu game.

After a series of twists and turns, we found ourselves back in the sunlit main courtyard. Gasping for breath, I flopped down onto the soft, damp grass, my gaze fixed on the expanse of the blue sky overhead. It was a welcome respite from the chaos and responsibilities that had consumed my days lately.

"It's a beautiful day, isn't it?" Thalion asked, reclining beside me on the grass.

I smiled, savoring the serenity of the moment. "It is, a pleasant change from all the snow."

We sat in companionable silence, basking in the tranquility of the courtyard and the warmth of the sun on our skin.

"So, what's next on the list of things you need to accomplish?" Thalion asked, propping himself up on one elbow to peer into my eyes.

I sighed, reluctantly pulling my thoughts away from the peaceful reverie. "There is a lot left to take care of. Aisling, for starters. Kaelan's curse, which still mystifies us. The creation of the witches and the preparations for the upcoming ritual. I need to locate that elusive graveyard and learn more about the Seven. Then there's the matter of the First Witch's grimoire; there must be something within its pages that the Seven are willing to kill for. I'm also eager to establish a council of Otherworlders, with representatives from each species."

"A council? That sounds like a fantastic idea," Thalion mused, rolling onto his back and gazing up at the endless sky.

I explained further, "It would provide a united front in addressing various issues and ensure a peaceful transition of power."

Thalion nodded in agreement. "You're right. A council would be an excellent way to keep everyone aligned. It would guarantee that there is always a representative here at the palace."

"Yes, exactly. It would be a sufficient way to have a check on my power and make sure I don't abuse it," I replied, contemplating the weight of responsibility that came with my position.

Thalion turned his gaze toward me, his eyes filled with unwavering faith. "I do not doubt that you will use your power wisely, Vale. You are the epitome of selfless sacrifice. You'd never use your power for your own personal gain."

A warm smile tugged at my lips at his words. "I hope not," I said, my gaze drifting upward to the vast expanse of the sky.

"You have a good heart, Vale. Don't forget that," Thalion reminded me gently. "Don't let the burdens of your position consume you. You're allowed to take some time to enjoy the little things, like the sunshine and fresh air."

I felt a wave of gratitude wash over me for having someone like Thalion by my side. "Thank you, Thalion."

"Always," he said with a warm smile. Leaning in, he captured my lips in a slow, sweet kiss that made my heart race.

We remained there, under the warm winter sun, enjoying the simple pleasure of each other's company, lost in the moment.

"It's almost time for dinner; would you like to join me?" Thalion asked after a long moment.

"I'd love to," I replied, my spirits lifted by the prospect of spending more time with him.

"Fantastic, how about we travel back to Virelium for it?" Thalion suggested, rising to his feet and offering me his hand.

"Okay, but why Virelium?" I asked curiously.

"For old time's sake," he replied with a warm smile.

I took his hand, allowing him to pull me to my feet. I called Nyxen to my side and he emerged from the shadow of a nearby tree. A surge of relief coursed through me every time he appeared. I ran my hand over his soft fur as he approached, his yellow eyes peering up at me.

"Lovely to see you again, Nyxen," Thalion greeted the creature warmly.

Nyxen responded with a soft chirping sound, a sign of his acceptance.

"Can you take us to Virelium, Nyx?" I asked him.

"*Yes,*" Nyxen said before the shadows began to swirl around us.

As we were whisked through the shadows, the world around us blurred into darkness. I held onto Thalion's hand tightly, the sensation of the shadow travel never ceasing to amaze me.

We emerged from the shadows and I found myself back in Thalion's courtyard. The rapid transition made everything a blur, and it took a moment for the surroundings to materialize around us. We were standing outside the grand entrance of the palace and I couldn't help but appreciate the familiar grandeur of the place.

"Home sweet home," Thalion remarked, sweeping his arm to gesture toward the grand entrance.

I looked around, taking in the grandeur of the place, which always left me in awe. "Are your parents here?" I asked, hoping to see his mother, who had always been warm and welcoming to me. Having never known my own mother, I had hoped to get to know her better.

"My father is. He's been taking care of things while I help Terralux rebuild. My mother is in Aurumport with her remaining family," Thalion explained as he led me inside the castle.

"What about your father's family?" I asked, my curiosity getting the better of me.

Thalion's expression grew somber. "He's the last remaining of his family."

"I'm sorry to hear that," I said, expressing my sympathy. I realized that it must have been a sad chapter in his family's history.

Thalion waved a dismissive hand. "It was a long time ago. But enough about that. I have something I want to show you and then we can have dinner."

"Really?" I perked up at the prospect of a surprise.

"Yes, but it's a bit of a walk. Let's grab some food from the kitchens first," he suggested.

We entered the palace kitchens and collected an assortment of fruits and meats, perfect for a picnic. I couldn't help but notice his choice of food, and it seemed evident that he had planned this outing. Thalion also picked up a bottle of Fae wine and a couple of glasses, which made me raise an eyebrow, recalling my previous encounter with Fae wine.

"Don't worry, I won't give you too much," he assured me, a hint of amusement in his eyes.

I chuckled in response. "Yes, I definitely learned from the last time."

His laughter filled the air as we made our way toward our destination. "Come on, it's a bit of a climb," he said, winking at me.

THIRTY-ONE

We climbed several flights of winding, cramped stairs, each step creaking with age as we ascended. Dust motes danced in the shafts of dim light that filtered through the narrow windows, casting eerie patterns on the worn stone walls.

Finally, we arrived at a rotting wooden door that hung halfway off its rusted hinges. Thalion moved it aside carefully and I followed him as he stepped inside. The room we entered was a stark contrast to the palace's grandeur. It was old and dusty, with spiderwebs hanging from the rafters and a musty, stale air that filled the space. Sunlight from the setting sun streamed through the holes in the roof, casting warm, golden hues over the room.

The room had clearly seen better days. Debris cluttered the floor, and the dilapidated state of the place suggested it hadn't been used in quite some time. However, amidst the neglect, there was a certain charm to it.

"What are we doing here?" I asked, taking in the sight of the room's decay and neglect.

"Just wait," he said with a mischievous grin as he led

me further into the room. I followed cautiously, careful not to trip over scattered debris. In the center of the room, an old hearth stood proudly, its stone surface worn with age. Surprisingly, the area in front of the hearth was clean, with blankets laid out as if to create a makeshift seating area.

"Do you mind lighting the fire, princess?" Thalion asked, his grin growing wider.

I blinked in surprise. "This is what you wanted to show me?" I asked incredulously.

Thalion's smile remained, and he nodded. "Yes, it's pretty, isn't it?"

I couldn't help but scoff at him in amusement, but I did as he asked, waving my hand to conjure magical flames that danced to life. I willed it to burn until the carefully placed logs caught fire.

Thalion gestured for me to sit beside him on the blankets and I obliged, though I still didn't quite understand the significance of this place. He opened the bottle of Fae wine and poured the golden liquid into the glasses he had brought.

"What are we celebrating?" I asked, genuinely puzzled by the situation.

"Your coronation," he replied, handing me a glass with a twinkle in his eyes.

I raised an eyebrow. "My coronation is not for another week."

Thalion chuckled. "Yes, well, we're celebrating early," he said, winking at me.

I couldn't help but smile at his playful demeanor. "Alright, then. Cheers to my coronation," I said, clinking my glass against his, deciding to embrace the unexpected celebration.

"To the future," Thalion toasted, his eyes holding a mysterious glint.

We sipped the sweet, fruity wine, and I savored its delightful taste as it danced on my tongue.

"Is this your secret spot?" I asked, looking around at the room bathed in the warm glow of the firelight.

Thalion nodded, his eyes filled with nostalgia. "It's where I used to come as a child. It was my secret hideaway. I'd come up here and pretend I wasn't a prince with a world of responsibilities to inherit."

"That sounds like a dream," I replied, imagining the carefree days of his youth.

"It was. Now, however, it's a bit harder to hide," he said, a wistful smile on his lips.

I nodded in understanding, thinking about the challenges and pressures we both faced in our roles.

As we ate and drank, our conversation flowed effortlessly, and the wine served as a catalyst for our laughter. The sun dipped below the horizon, and the holes in the roof revealed a breathtaking view of the night sky adorned with shimmering stars. Moonlight bathed us in its soft glow.

"This is what I wanted you to see," Thalion said, leaning back on the blankets. "The stars in Elysian are different from the stars in the mortal realm."

I followed his gaze, my eyes drawn to the celestial display above. The stars did seem different here, brighter and more vibrant.

"They're beautiful," I whispered, my voice filled with wonder.

Thalion turned his head to look at me, his face bathed in the soft firelight. "Yes, they are," he replied, his gaze taking me in.

Our eyes met and I felt a surge of emotion welling up

inside me. Before I could respond, Thalion spoke again, his words soft and heartfelt.

"I love you, Vale," he confessed softly, his words taking my breath away. "I don't know if I've ever told you that."

My heart raced, and I struggled to find words. "You haven't," I managed to reply.

"Well, I do. You have a light within you, a light that burns brighter than the stars themselves. You have a fiercely loyal spirit, and I'm in awe of you."

"Thalion—" I began, but he cut me off by placing his fingers softly to my lips, his hand moving to cup my cheek.

"Let me finish," Thalion murmured, his thumb tracing a delicate path over my lips. "From nearly the moment I met you, I was captivated by your strength, your compassion, and your unwavering determination. You've faced unimaginable challenges, yet you remain a beacon of hope in a world overrun with darkness."

I could feel my heart pounding in my chest as he spoke. My eyes remained locked with his, hanging onto his every word.

"I know I've spoken before about our marriage being a strategic move, a way to unite our kingdoms and secure our positions," Thalion continued, his voice filled with sincerity. "But the truth is, I don't care about any of that. Vale, I want to marry you because I love you with all my heart. I want to spend the rest of my days by your side, supporting you in everything you do and cherishing every moment we share together."

My heart swelled with emotion and I struggled to find words to respond to his heartfelt declaration. Thalion's hand slid down from my cheek to clasp my hand, his fingers intertwining with mine as he continued to speak.

"I want to share every moment with you, to face every

challenge and celebrate every triumph together," he said, his voice determined. "Vale, will you marry me? Not because it's the right political move, but because it's the right move for our hearts, our souls, and our future together."

I was overwhelmed by the depth of his feelings and the vulnerability he had shown in his confession. Tears welled in my eyes as I nodded, my voice choked with emotion. "Yes, Thalion."

His face broke into a radiant smile as he reached into his pocket and pulled out a small, ornate box. With trembling hands, he opened it to reveal a delicate, sparkling ring. The thin silver band was adorned with leaves and the beautiful amethyst in the middle was surrounded by elegant flowers. It matched his eyes perfectly.

"This belonged to my mother," he said, his voice tender. "It's been passed down through generations of my family and now I want you to have it."

He took the ring from the box and slid it onto my finger. Thalion leaned in, pressing his lips to mine in a passionate, heartfelt kiss. The world around us faded away as we embraced, lost in the moment of our love and the promise of our future together.

Thalion's kiss sent a surge of longing coursing through my veins as his lips met mine with enthusiasm. Our tongues danced in a fiery embrace, a hunger growing between us. He pressed me gently onto the soft blankets spread on the floor, his body hovering above mine.

I could feel the undeniable proof of his longing pressing into my stomach, his erection straining against the fabric of his pants. It sent a thrill of anticipation through me, knowing that he desired me so fiercely.

His lips left mine, trailing down my neck. His voice, low

and charged with desire, sent a delicious shiver through me as he whispered in my ear, "It's been so long, princess."

I arched my back, my body yearning for his touch, for the intimacy we had both craved for so long. My hands slid beneath his shirt, feeling the warmth and smoothness of his skin under my fingertips. His soft groan of pleasure filled the room as I explored the contours of his muscled chest, his broad shoulders, and his chiseled abs.

Thalion sat up, his strong hands moving to pull his shirt over his head. I watched in awe as he revealed his sculpted torso, his defined muscles a testament to his strength and hunger. My breath caught in my throat, and I couldn't tear my eyes away from him.

As he leaned down again, his lips met mine in a searing kiss, igniting the fire of our passion once more, our mouths moving together. The world around us faded away as we lost ourselves in the intoxicating taste and feel of each other.

Thalion's hands found their way to the laces on the front of my dress, his lips trailing down my neck and collarbone as he worked skillfully to undo them. But he stopped as he pulled back, a slow, mischievous grin playing on his lips. "Before I get too caught up in the moment, there's one more thing I wanted to show you," he whispered, his voice laced with excitement.

He helped me up as he stood and pulled me back into his arms, kissing me fiercely, his hands running down my back to grip my ass.

"Show me," I breathed against his lips, winding my hands through his hair and pulling gently.

Thalion's eyes sparkled with desire as he stepped back, taking my hand and leading me toward the tower's still-standing balcony. The crumbling steps leading upward seemed precarious and I couldn't help but tease him, "So you're trying to get us killed, huh?"

He chuckled, his voice overflowing with confidence. "Trust me," he said, leading me up the winding staircase.

The steps creaked beneath our feet and I couldn't shake the feeling that the entire structure might collapse, but I followed him without hesitation. Finally, we reached the top, where another balcony overlooked the city below.

The breathtaking view stretched out before me, the sprawling city with its twinkling lights and the towering mountains in the distance. The moonlight bathed everything in a silvery glow, creating a magical atmosphere.

"This is incredible," I breathed, my eyes wide in wonder.

Thalion wrapped his arms around me from behind, his lips finding my neck again. "Not as incredible as you," he murmured, his hands roaming over my body.

A gasp escaped my lips as his fingers found their way to my nipples, teasing them through the fabric of my dress, causing them to harden in response to his touch. His voice, thick with longing, growled in my ear, "I want you, Vale."

"Then take me," I whispered, arching my neck for him.

Thalion's response was immediate and primal. He spun me around to face him, our lips crashing together in a hungry, desperate kiss. Our mouths moved with an urgency that mirrored the fire burning within us. I could feel the intensity of his wanting, the raw hunger that mirrored my own.

His hands fumbled with the laces of my dress, his impatience evident as he urgently undid them the rest of the way. The fabric fell away and I gasped as the cool night air caressed my bare skin. Goosebumps rose on my flesh and Thalion's mouth moved lower, his tongue flicking across my hardened nipples before he sucked one into his warm, wet mouth. A moan escaped my lips, my hands tangling in his hair, holding him close.

He moved to my other nipple, his teeth grazing the sensitive skin. Pleasure surged through me, my core growing wet with need. Thalion's expert touch drove me wild and I arched into his caresses.

Thalion pulled back momentarily, his hands deftly finishing the job, stripping the dress completely off my body. I stood before him, exposed and vulnerable in the cool night air, my skin tingling with anticipation.

"You're so fucking beautiful," he murmured, his eyes sparkling with hunger as he drank in the sight of me.

Thalion's smirk was both possessive and hungry as his hands moved to my hips, spinning me around to face the breathtaking view of the city below.

"Look at that view, Vale," he said, his hands moving up to cup my breasts.

I gasped as his fingers pinched my nipples, a sharp jolt of sensation shooting straight to my core. My breath hitched as heat pooled between my thighs.

"Do you see all those people down there, going about their lives, oblivious to the fact that their future queen is up here, naked and wanting?" he whispered in my ear, his breath hot against my skin.

I shuddered, his words fueling a thrilling excitement within me. "And what are you going to do, Thalion?" I asked, my voice dripping with desire.

"I'm going to fuck you, princess," he growled, his hand sliding down between my thighs, his fingers smoothly gliding over the aching center of me. "And you're going to scream my name so they all hear you."

My moan filled the night, my head falling back

against his shoulder as his fingers found my clit, expertly circling it. His thumb rubbed the sensitive bud, sending waves of pleasure radiating through my body while his fingers dipped lower, teasing my entrance.

My body was aching and I couldn't hold back any longer. I arched my back, grinding against his hand, my need for him growing more urgent with each passing second.

"Tell me what you want, princess," Thalion growled, his teeth nipping at my earlobe.

"I want you, Thalion," I moaned, the words slipping from my lips without hesitation. "I want you inside me, fucking me."

A deep, primal groan escaped his lips in response to my plea. His fingers sank deep inside of me, stretching and filling me in all the right ways.

"You're so tight," he murmured, his breath ragged with want.

I writhed against him, my body responding eagerly to his touch, aching for more. He added a third finger and I cried out, the sensation overwhelming as he skillfully pumped his fingers in and out, his thumb rubbing my clit in perfect synchronization.

"Fuck, princess," Thalion hissed, his breathing growing labored. "I can't wait to bury my cock in you."

"Please," I gasped, my body teetering on the edge of release.

"Say my name, princess," he demanded, his fingers thrusting deeper, harder.

"Thalion," I breathed, the pleasure coiling tighter and tighter within me, ready to explode.

"Again," he commanded, his fingers curling inside me,

finding that electrifying spot that sent sparks of ecstasy coursing through my veins.

"Thalion!" I cried out, my body trembling on the precipice of ecstasy.

"That's it, Vale," he whispered, his fingers driving me higher and higher, pushing me closer to the brink. "Come for me."

"Oh, gods!" I moaned, the wave of pleasure crashing over me like a tidal wave, my body convulsing with the force of it. Thalion held me tight, his arms enveloping me as I came undone, his fingers continuing their rhythmic movements until I finally collapsed against him.

I turned to him and kissed him forcefully, my hands roaming over his bare chest, down to the laces of his pants. He groaned, his cock straining against the fabric, desperate for release. With nimble fingers, I freed him, his erection springing free, the head glistening with slick arousal.

"I want you inside me," I whispered, my fingers wrapping around his length and stroking him with a teasing, seductive touch.

"Fuck," he groaned, his hips bucking into my hand.

I smirked, my thumb circling the head of his cock, spreading the slick fluid that had gathered there.

"I want to ride you, Thalion," I said, a sultry challenge in my voice, my eyes locking with his as I made my desires known.

"Yes," he hissed, his voice thick with longing.

He took a seat, resting his back against the cool, rough stone wall. I climbed onto his lap, straddling him with a sense of urgency. His strong hands found my hips, guiding me as I descended onto his throbbing cock, the sensation of fullness and stretching electrifying my senses.

"Fuck, you feel so good," he groaned, his hips instinctively rising to meet mine as I began to move, riding him with an increasing rhythm.

"So do you," I moaned, my nails digging into his shoulders as I anchored myself, each movement sending intoxicating waves of pleasure coursing through my body.

"That's it, princess, ride my cock," Thalion growled, his eyes dark and intense with an insatiable desire.

His hands traveled to my breasts, fingers expertly teasing my already sensitive nipples, sparks of electricity radiating straight to my core.

"Harder," I pleaded, my body demanding more, leaning into him, quickening my pace as the pleasure within me swelled.

"As you wish," he grunted, his hips meeting mine with a powerful force, his cock plunging deeper with each thrust, hitting that perfect spot that had my senses reeling.

"Oh gods, Thalion," I gasped, the pleasure nearly overwhelming me.

"That's it, Vale," he growled, his movements growing more frenzied, his breaths ragged, "come for me again."

"Make me," I challenged, craving the overwhelming climax that threatened to undo me.

Thalion answered with a low, feral growl, his grip on my hips tightening, his fingers leaving marks on my skin as he drove into me, each thrust sending a surge of ecstasy through my body. I met each thrust in turn, the delicious friction building, pushing me higher and higher.

My nails raked down his chest, leaving a trail of red lines in their wake.

"Gods," he grunted, his eyes closed against the pleasure and pain.

"More," I gasped, my need for him insatiable. "I want more."

In response, he seized my hips, lifting me off his cock with a sudden and surprising strength. Before I could register what was happening, he stood up, effortlessly spinning me around and bending me over the low stone wall of the balcony. His strong hands pinned my wrists against the cold surface, rendering me helpless and exposed.

His hard length pressed against my eager entrance, and then he surged into me, filling me completely, the sensation of his dominance and possession overwhelming both of us.

"Oh, gods," I moaned, the sensation of being utterly helpless, entirely at his mercy, sending a thrilling shiver down my spine.

"You look utterly delicious writhing beneath me," he groaned, his hips driving against mine with fervent urgency, every powerful thrust igniting fiery sparks that coursed through my veins.

His movements became increasingly frantic, his cock swelling within me, and I knew he was on the precipice of his own climax. I teetered on the edge, my body yearning for release.

Thalion shifted his weight, his fingers freeing my wrists and then gliding between my legs, his thumb expertly finding my throbbing clit, his motions deliberate and skillful.

A scream tore from my lips as my orgasm erupted within me, my body convulsing with pleasure as waves of ecstasy crashed over me.

"Vale," he gasped, his cock pulsating inside me, his body tensing as he found his own release, warmth surging into me.

We remained intertwined for a fleeting moment, our bodies trembling, our breaths ragged. Thalion's hands found my shoulders, pulling me up as he turned me around, his lips capturing mine in a passionate kiss. His heart pounded against my chest, his skin flushed and glistening with the sheen of exertion.

"I love you, Vale," he whispered against my lips.

"I love you too," I whispered back, my fingers tenderly tracing the contours of his face, following the strong line of his jaw.

He held me close, his arms wrapped securely around me, bathed in the soft moonlight.

THIRTY-TWO

After spending the night with Thalion, I returned to my palace in the morning. The cool breeze of the early day brushed against my skin, a stark contrast to the heat and passion of the night before. I couldn't help but smile as I thought about the intimate moments we had shared.

Heading for the library, I pushed open the heavy wooden door and stepped into the room. The soft light of dawn spilled through the stained glass windows, casting long, colorful beams across the rows of bookshelves. Harker was sitting at a large table in the center of the room, surrounded by Ava, Harlow, and Sam, who were all engrossed in their reading.

"Hello, everyone," I greeted as I entered, causing all three heads to pop up from their books.

"Hey, Vale, what are you doing here?" Harker asked, a curious expression on her face.

"I'm here to study the First Witch's grimoire some more," I explained, crossing the room to join them. "There's gotta be something in there that can give me a clue to what the Seven are planning."

Harker's skepticism was evident in her tone as she responded. "Good luck," she scoffed, her brows furrowing. "I've been looking through that thing since we found it, and while the spells are powerful and useful, they are full of dark magic. You can't use any of them without risking corrupting yourself further." Her eyes wandered to my darkened hands, a visible reminder of the price I had already paid for my involvement with dark magic.

"Well, maybe a fresh set of eyes on it is what we need," I replied, trying to maintain a sense of optimism. "I'm just trying to find clues, not how to unleash the demons of the demon realm," I added in a playful tone.

Harker relented, her initial resistance giving way to a more understanding tone. "Fair point."

I turned my attention to Ava, Sam, and Harlow, who had been diligently studying with Harker. "You guys have been working so hard," I commented. "Why don't you all go get some breakfast? You've earned a break." I knew the nocturnal vampire liked to keep them up at all hours of the night.

"Thanks, Vale," Ava replied, standing up and stretching. "Come on, guys, let's get some food."

Sam and Harlow eagerly followed her lead and left the library, leaving Harker and me alone.

"How are you holding up, Harker?" I asked, pulling up a chair and sitting down next to her.

She sighed, weariness evident in her features. "I'm okay. Just a little overwhelmed. It's been tough teaching seven people, eight when you count Aisling. But it's doable."

I nodded, understanding the challenges that came with

being a mentor. "What are you teaching them?" I asked, genuinely curious about their studies.

"History, demonology, elemental magic, stuff like that," she explained. "And Wren has begun teaching them how to defend themselves."

"Do they seem to be making progress?" I asked, eager to gauge their development.

Harker's eyes brightened with pride. "They're all incredibly bright and driven. I think they're going to make great witches."

I smiled, reassured by her assessment. "That's good to hear. We're going to need all the help we can get. How is Elara doing with all the extra people in the library?"

"She seems happy," Harker replied, a hint of amusement in her voice. "I think she likes the company. Even though she complains day and night that all these extra hands are going to ruin her books."

I chuckled at the thought of Elara's protective nature over her beloved books. "Sounds like her. Well, I'm going to see if I can dig up anything useful in this grimoire. Let me know if you want to get some fresh air or take a break."

HOURS OF POURING over the grimoire's dark and cryptic contents had taken a toll on me. As I emerged from the shadowy depths of the chamber within the library, I couldn't help but feel a sense of frustration. The book was indeed brimming with increasingly darker and more malevolent magic, but it yielded very little information that could hint at the Seven's plans.

The sun hung high in the sky, casting warm, golden rays into the chamber. The air within had felt thick and oppressive, making me long for fresh air and sustenance. My stomach grumbled, a reminder that I had neglected to eat anything all day.

With a plan forming in my mind, I decided to make a brief stop in the kitchen to grab a quick meal before visiting Wren and Aisling. The tantalizing aroma that greeted me as I entered the kitchen was impossible to resist. There, on the stove, a pot of something savory simmered while several trays of freshly baked bread cooled on the counter.

The old stray cat I had brought from the mortal realm padded up to me with a meow and I leaned down to scratch his head softly. He had quickly joined the group of cats that hung around the kitchens to catch the mice that managed to sneak in. I was happy to see him fitting in so well.

Marie, the dedicated caretaker of the kitchen and its unofficial head chef, bustled about, humming a cheerful tune as she worked her culinary magic.

"Smells amazing in here," I said, going over to the stove and peering into the pot.

"It's an old family recipe," she replied with a warm smile, her eyes twinkling. "I thought you all could use something nice after all the chaos of late."

"That's very thoughtful of you, Marie. Thank you," I said as my stomach grumbled insistently. I couldn't resist the temptation any longer and tore a piece of bread from one of the trays, savoring its buttery flavor as I popped it into my mouth.

The taste of the freshly baked bread was heavenly and I sighed with contentment, momentarily forgetting my worries.

"This is delicious," I said with genuine pleasure. "I don't suppose there's any more for lunch?"

"Of course," Marie replied warmly. "Help yourself."

I eagerly fetched a bowl and ladled some of the savory stew into it, adding a generous hunk of bread on the side. My initial intention had been to grab a quick bite and continue with my tasks, but the irresistible aroma of the stew beckoned me to stay a while longer.

Sitting at the kitchen table, I inhaled deeply, letting the warm scent envelop me. Taking a spoonful, the flavors burst in my mouth. The herbs and spices were perfectly balanced and the tender meat melted effortlessly. I would never get over the marvel that was Fae cooking.

"This is divine, Marie," I praised between mouthfuls.

Her cheeks flushed with pride and modesty. "Thank you, Your Majesty," she replied.

"You're a wonder," I said, complimenting her once more and fully savoring the comforting meal she had prepared.

After finishing the last bite of the delicious stew and bidding Marie farewell, I left the kitchen and ascended the grand staircase to the third floor of the palace. My destination was Wren's room, but to my surprise, there was no answer when I knocked on his door.

With a slight frown, I retraced my steps to Venna's rooms. The door creaked open and Venna's brown eyes widened slightly as they met mine. Her brown curly hair cascaded down her shoulders and she wore a simple yet elegant gown. She looked like she was starting to fit in around the palace.

"Vale, I didn't expect you," Venna greeted me, her voice soft and welcoming.

"I was hoping to visit Wren and Aisling. Do you know where they are?" I asked, my gaze sweeping across the room, noting the pair's absence.

"They're at the training grounds again," Venna replied, her lips curving into a warm smile. "Wren has been teaching her self-defense. I think he's been enjoying himself."

I nodded in understanding. Wren had always been dedicated to his training and passing on his knowledge seemed to invigorate him. "Thank you, Venna. Enjoy your day," I said, returning her smile before she closed the door.

As I descended the palace's grand staircase and ventured outdoors, the sound of clashing metal filled the air, guiding me toward the training grounds. The sun had climbed higher in the sky, casting a brilliant glow over the snowy surroundings.

Upon reaching the training grounds, I spotted Wren and Aisling immediately. Wren's tall, broad-shouldered frame was unmistakable, and Aisling mirrored his posture, both engaged in hand-to-hand combat training.

Aisling's initial frustration was evident as she huffed in disbelief. "I don't understand how this is fighting. What kind of fight is there when you only use your fists and feet?"

Wren, the patient mentor, responded with a calm and reassuring tone. "The kind that happens when you don't have weapons, and the other guy is a bigger, stronger, and faster fighter than you."

Aisling's skepticism lingered as she contemplated his words. "What kind of person would you ever meet who is bigger and stronger than you?" Her voice held a hint of doubt.

Wren chuckled softly, his laughter filled with wisdom. "Have you seen some of the Fae around here?" he teased.

Aisling's gaze swept across the training grounds, where other Fae soldiers, with their impressive size and bulk, practiced their combat skills. The realization dawned on her and she nodded, acknowledging the formidable opponents they might face.

Wren, ever the dedicated instructor, moved to a nearby sparring circle, and I followed his lead, selecting a seat on one of the benches lining the perimeter. The atmosphere around the training grounds was electric, filled with the clashing of blades and the determined expressions of Fae honing their skills.

Wren faced off against his opponent, a burly Fae with striking white-blond hair and eyes as sharp as ice chips. Their exchange of words was brief, and then they began circling each other, a dance of combat unfolding before my eyes.

The training ground was a whirlwind of action as the blond Fae launched his attack, his cry echoing through the air. His fists were raised, determination etched on his face as he charged at Wren.

Wren, however, was a force to be reckoned with. He moved with an almost mesmerizing fluidity, his movements defying gravity and expectation. As the blond Fae closed in, Wren's foot shot up like a lightning bolt, connecting with a powerful kick that struck the Fae's chin. The impact sent the blond Fae staggering backward, momentarily disoriented.

But Wren wasn't done yet. With the speed of a striking serpent, he closed the distance between them in an instant. His fists became a blur as they connected with the other man's ribs in a rapid and brutal succession of blows. The blond Fae couldn't defend against the onslaught and found himself crumpling to the ground under the relentless assault.

Wren wasted no time and pounced on his fallen opponent, pinning him down with the sheer force of his body weight. It was a display of skill and efficiency that left

Aisling gasping in awe, her eyes wide as she watched the masterful combat unfold.

"That was incredible," Aisling exclaimed, her voice filled with admiration and excitement.

Wren, ever the modest warrior, grinned as he got to his feet and extended a hand to his defeated opponent. The blond Fae accepted the hand, grumbling good-naturedly, "You're a damn menace."

Wren chuckled, slapping the Fae on the back as he replied, "You're just a sore loser."

"Maybe so," the Fae admitted with a smirk, acknowledging Wren's superiority in combat.

Aisling's admiration for Wren continued to shine as she praised him. "You were brilliant, Wren," she said enthusiastically, bouncing on the balls of her feet.

"Thanks, kid," Wren replied, offering her a genuine smile. "Now, I'm going to take a break. You keep practicing what I showed you. You're getting better."

As Aisling resumed her training with newfound determination, Wren moved to sit down beside me, and his body relaxed after the intense bout.

"She's doing well," I remarked, my eyes on Aisling as she continued to practice.

Wren nodded in agreement. "Yeah, she's a fast learner. It helps that she's got some raw natural talent, too, just like you did." He glanced down at me and flashed a grin.

"Are you enjoying yourself, teaching her?" I asked, genuinely curious about his feelings.

"I am, actually," he admitted, sounding somewhat surprised. "Who knew?"

I couldn't help but tease him gently. "You've got a soft spot for her."

"Can you blame me?" Wren responded with a chuckle.

"She's a sweet kid. She's had a rough go, but she's got spirit. It will take more than what she's been through to keep her down." His pride in Aisling's progress was evident in his words, and I couldn't help but smile at the sight of Wren embracing his role as mentor and protector.

"Has she told you what she's been through? What happened on her way to us?" I asked, my voice laced with worry.

Wren's expression grew somber as he considered his response. "Only a little. She doesn't like to talk about it much."

Understanding her hesitation to relive those moments, I nodded, frowning at the poor girl. "I can understand that. What has she told you?"

Wren hesitated for a moment before sharing what he knew. "From what I've learned when the demons started searching for your blood magic, they started coming after her, too."

My heart sank at the thought of Aisling being hunted by demons, and I felt a pang of guilt. "Oh no," I gasped. I felt somewhat responsible for the danger she had been exposed to.

Wren placed his hand gently on my shoulder, sensing my guilt through the bond. "It's okay, she got away. She's a survivor."

"Where did she come from?"

Wren's brow furrowed in thought. "I'm not sure. She says she was born in the human realm but was orphaned and lived with a foster family. She bounced from home to home for years. No one really wanted a wild kid like her, especially with her magic coming and going. She finally ran away and wound up on the streets. That's when the demons started finding her."

My heart ached for the young girl who had endured such hardships. "Oh, gods," I whispered.

"She's been alone and scared for a long time. But she's resilient and she wants to belong somewhere." Wren said, the emotion in his voice betraying the affection he held for Aisling.

"We can give her that if she'll let us," I said, determined to provide Aisling with the care and support she deserved.

"I think she will. She's just going to have to trust us first." Wren replied.

"Well, keep up the good work," I said, nudging his shoulder affectionately. "I can see her opening up to you. You're a good influence."

Wren responded with a snort. "I think that's a first."

"It's not a first. You practically raised me," I told Wren with a fond smile.

"We raised each other," he replied, putting an arm around my shoulder. I leaned into his comforting presence.

We sat together in companionable silence, our eyes trained on Aisling as she practiced her moves. Despite her petite frame, she exhibited a determination and scrappiness that hinted at her potential to become a formidable fighter with time and practice.

Wren decided to steer the conversation in a different direction. "So, what's new with you, Vale?"

I considered his question before responding, "Well, the usual, trying to save the world and not get killed in the process."

Wren raised an eyebrow, a glint of curiosity in his eyes. "Anything interesting?"

"Thalion officially asked me to marry him," I said, smiling as I shared my news.

"Really? I'm guessing that means you said yes," Wren said, chuckling.

"I did," I replied, nodding.

"I'm glad you found so many people to care for you. You definitely are a handful enough for three men," he teased.

"Hey!" I shouted, playfully punching him on the arm.

"Just kidding," he laughed. "Seriously, though, I'm happy for you. You deserve this, Vale."

"Thank you," I said, genuinely touched by his words. "It's not always easy, but it's worth it."

"That's true," he agreed, his expression thoughtful. "Love isn't easy, but it's worth fighting for. And so are you."

My heart swelled with warmth at his heartfelt sentiment. "I'm glad I have you, Wren. You're always here for me, no matter what."

"Always," he affirmed, leaning down to plant a gentle kiss on the top of my head, a gesture that spoke volumes about our enduring friendship and support for one another.

As we continued to watch Aisling's training, a sudden thought dawned on me, and I couldn't help but voice it.

"What do you think she'll be like when she grows up? Aisling, I mean," I asked, my thoughts drifting to the young girl's future.

Wren took a moment to ponder the question, his gaze fixed on Aisling's spirited training. "I think she's going to be one hell of a witch. Maybe even more powerful than you."

I couldn't help but laugh at the idea. "Now that would be something."

"It would," he agreed with a nod.

My thoughts drifted further, contemplating the future and what it might hold. "Do you think we'll have peace then?" I asked, my voice tinged with hope as I thought about my own future children and the world they would inherit.

Wren's reply was measured, hinting at a cautious optimism. "I think we'll have peace, or maybe something close to it."

"That's all we can ask for," I said, sighing.

Our conversation was interrupted by the sight of Aisling finishing her exercises and rushing over to us, her face lit up with excitement. "Did you see that?" she exclaimed. "I did a flip!"

"That was awesome," Wren praised her, standing up and affectionately ruffling her hair as she beamed with pride.

"You're the best teacher ever," she declared, wrapping her small arms around his waist and hugging him tightly.

Wren's eyes softened as he looked down at her, a warmth filling his expression. "Alright, that's enough," he said gently, extricating himself from her embrace. "Back to work, kid. If you're going to be the strongest witch in the world, you've gotta work hard."

"Yes, sir!" Aisling responded with a playful salute before dashing back to the training ring, her determination fierce and unwavering.

Wren shook his head, amusement and pride shining in his eyes. "She's a good kid. She deserves a good life."

"She will," I affirmed, standing up and brushing the dirt off my pants. "We'll make sure of it."

"That's the plan," he replied, flashing a grin.

With a goodbye, I left Wren with Aisling, making my way back up to the palace. The day was slowly winding down, the sun descending in the sky, and I could feel the weariness settling in. A hot bath sounded like the perfect way to relax and unwind after a long day.

THIRTY-THREE

The next night the moon hung in the sky, its phase now precisely aligned with the ritual's requirements. In the hidden, stone-carved chamber deep within the library, I stood surrounded by the seven individuals who had chosen this path alongside me. Ava, Calliope, Harlow, Sam, Griffin, Archer, and Mikel—all of them willing to embrace the daunting journey that lay ahead.

Harker was present as well, positioned discreetly behind me, her vigilant gaze overseeing the proceedings. We had all prepared meticulously for this moment, with Wren going to great lengths to secure the seven black opals from the merchant in the black market. I clutched my notebook tightly, its pages filled with the intricacies of the ritual. Though I had every step memorized, I found reassurance in the presence of my notes. This transformation ritual was our best chance against the Seven and their plans, whatever they might be.

I took a deep, steadying breath, my eyes fixed on the faces of those assembled before me. They were brave, determined, and fully aware of the risks involved. My voice rang out, strong and steady, as I addressed the seven souls gathered before me.

"Alright, everyone," I began, my eyes locking onto each of theirs, "you all know why we are here, and you understand the risks involved. It won't be easy, but I am here to guide you through every step of the way."

Harker stepped forward, the basket with black opals gleaming in her hands. As she extended it towards me, I took it gently. With a sense of reverence, I offered it to the first among us, Griffin, the half-demon with a guarded expression.

"Griffin, take a stone," I said, my voice firm but encouraging.

He reached into the basket, his fingers brushing against the cool, smooth surface of the gemstones. After contemplating, he selected a large opal, its dark facets catching the light. The others followed suit, choosing their opals carefully.

"Your stone represents the essence of what you are," I continued, "what you have always been. A creature of two worlds, neither fully human, demon, nor Fae, but a harmonious blend of two."

I continued after a moment, "In the past, this duality may have caused confusion and loneliness. But tonight, these stones will serve as the bedrock of your rebirth. You will learn to embrace your dual nature and find strength in your ability to bridge the gap between the realms."

As they examined their chosen stones, a mixture of emotions played across their faces. Griffin appeared deep in thought, his brow furrowed with contemplation, while Archer seemed more optimistic, a faint smile tugging at the corners of his lips.

"Take a moment to become acquainted with the feel of

your stone," I advised. "Once the ritual commences, you must focus on its energy and the connection it holds with you."

In silent agreement, they held their opals with care, turning them over in their hands, studying the facets and hues, seeking a connection with these gemstones that now held such profound significance.

"Alright, let's begin," I said. "We'll start with the purification."

One by one, I placed white tallow candles around the circumference of the circle, their flames coming to life, casting flickering shadows on the chamber's walls. The scent of tallow wax began to fill the air, lending a unique atmosphere to the room.

Once the candles were in place, I ignited a block of cedar wood, the flames dancing in my hand. I walked along the circle's perimeter, sprinkling salt water and chanting, *"Purificamus hoc locum,"* as I moved. The saltwater droplets fell, purifying the space and creating an invisible barrier of protection.

"Now," I continued, "I want each of you to find a comfortable position within the circle. It does not matter how you sit or kneel, but once the ritual begins, you must remain within this sacred boundary, connected to your stone and to each other. Are you ready?"

I observed each person in the circle as they nodded in response to my instructions. Determination filled their eyes, but beneath the surface, I could sense their under-lying anxiety. This ritual was uncharted territory and the weight of its significance was great.

"Hold the opals in your left hand," I urged gently, guiding them. "Feel its energy, its connection to the earth, its connection to you."

As they clutched the opals in their left hands, I could feel a subtle shift in the atmosphere of the room. The magic began to stir, like a gentle breeze, teasing the strands of my hair before moving to play around the circle.

"Now, let us begin with a grounding meditation," I continued. "Close your eyes and take deep breaths. Focus on the sensation of the stone in your hand. Inhale through your nose, filling your lungs, and then exhale slowly through your mouth. Sense the earth beneath you, the stone you hold, and the air moving within you."

The ambient magic responded to our collective intent, creating a current that swirled gently around us, connecting us even before the ritual's culmination.

"Visualize a root extending from the base of your spine," I instructed, my voice soothing. "See it growing downward, burrowing into the earth, anchoring you to the ground and linking you to the earth's energy."

The room buzzed with an increasingly potent magic, weaving through the circle, passing from one individual to the next.

"Now, we shall recite a blood oath," I said, my tone serious. "This oath binds you to use your newfound powers solely for the greater good, never for personal gain or evil purposes. Are you all prepared for this commitment? It is no small sacrifice."

Their eyes remained closed as they nodded in agreement.

I handed a small dagger to Ava, who accepted it, her movements steady. "Cut your palm and let the blood fall upon the opal. As you do, recite the words: 'By blood and stone, I vow my powers for the welfare of all, forsaking selfish desires.'"

Ava repeated the oath as her blood dripped onto the

black opal. She let out a small gasp as the gemstone absorbed the crimson drops, and its facets began to radiate with a subtle red glow, merging the color of her blood with its obsidian surface.

One by one, the others followed Ava's lead, their blood joining the opals to infuse them with their own unique essence.

"Now, press your palms together to signify your unity and seal the oath," I instructed, taking a small step back to give them room.

In unison, they complied, their hands joining together as their eyes remained closed, their collective energy radiating a profound sense of purpose and unity. The transformation had begun and we were bound together in this journey.

I steeled myself for the next phase, acutely aware that it was the riskiest and deadliest part of the ritual. The tension in the air was thick enough to cut with a knife. We had prepared vials of my blood just moments before the ritual began, ensuring that they would be fresh for this critical step.

As I started passing these vials out among the seven of them, their expressions revealed a mix of anticipation and anxiety. They had been briefed on this step in advance, and each had agreed to it, but now, on the precipice of the unknown, their apprehension was hard to miss. I couldn't deny my own anxiety creeping in, but I had to place my trust in the magic. The purpose of the grooves carved into the stone floor had remained a mystery until this moment.

"This next step carries the most risk, but I want you to understand that I'll be here to guide you and step in to heal you with my blood if anything goes wrong," I reassured them. My voice aimed for calm, though I knew my inner turmoil might betray me.

My gaze moved from one determined face to another, hoping to convey a sense of calm I didn't feel. "I will take the dagger and cut the artery in your arm. The bleeding will be quick and relatively painless and you will lose consciousness in moments. My blood will flow through your body, initiating the transformation. When you wake, it will be as a witch."

It seemed so simple when I said it out loud, but I knew it was anything but.

Their expressions were determined, even as fear lurked in their eyes. "Once we begin, there's no turning back. Are you absolutely certain this is what you want?" I asked, needing their unwavering commitment.

Without a moment's hesitation, they replied in unison, "Yes."

"I'll let you decide the order," I offered, curious to see who would step forward as their leader in this pivotal moment.

A soft voice broke the silence. "I'll go first," Ava volunteered, earning my respect with her bravery. I nodded at her, granting permission to proceed, and she swiftly uncorked the vial containing my blood, downing its contents with determination.

"I'll support her," Calliope added, her determination tempered with kindness as she looked at Ava. A silent understanding passed between them as Ava nodded and squeezed Calliope's hand in gratitude.

Calliope positioned herself behind Ava, who reclined against her. I retrieved the dagger from Harker and settled in front of Ava, our shared fear reflected in our pale faces.

"I'm sorry, but there's no way to ease the pain," I murmured.

A small smile tugged at Ava's lips. "It's alright. I'm ready."

"This will be quick," I assured her, taking a deep breath to steady my trembling hand.

I took a deep breath, the room's heavy silence pressing in on us as I steeled myself for the next crucial step. Ava's arm lay in my grip, her skin exposed, the soft flesh of her underarm vulnerable. In my other hand, the dagger's blade hovered above her artery. With a precise motion, I sliced through it, and immediately, a steady stream of blood gushed forth, coursing down her arm in thick, crimson rivulets, staining the stone floor below.

Calliope cradled Ava's head in her lap, holding her close as Ava's eyelids fluttered closed and her breaths grew shallow. The stillness enveloped her and I watched the blood flow into the deep grooves on the floor, tracing every curve and line. As soon as the last drop fell, the grooves began to glow with a faint, eerie crimson light. The magic surged freely. The transformation had started.

As much as I yearned to intervene and assist, I knew that doing so would disrupt the magic, jeopardizing the entire process. So, I remained seated, my gaze fixed on Ava, my heart pounding in my chest.

Minutes ticked away, each one adding to my growing nervousness. Nausea churned in my gut as I waited, my heart pounding. Finally, the grooves began to dim, and the flow of blood slowed.

With a startled gasp, Ava sat up, her arm healed, her eyes filled with newfound vitality.

"Welcome back," I said, unable to conceal the relief that crept into my voice.

A grin spread across her face, her eyes shining with exhilaration. "It worked," she breathed, glancing at the others, who were all beaming with joy and relief.

"It did," I said, the tension in the room dissipating slightly. "Who's next?"

The process repeated itself, each one of them stepping forward with unwavering bravery, allowing me to make the incision on their artery. We would then patiently wait, our eyes fixed on the grooves in the stone floor, until the crimson light dimmed and we knew their transformation was complete. With each successful transformation, congratulations and smiles filled the room.

It was an arduous and draining endeavor, but the determination in their eyes fueled me to continue. Each drop of blood marked a new beginning, a step closer to realizing their true potential.

And then, at last, it was Harlow's turn. She sat before me, her eyes fierce and determined, as I made the final cut. As the last drop fell and the grooves dimmed, she sat up, her voice trembling with excitement. "We did it," she breathed, the wonder in her voice echoing our collective triumph.

I rose to my feet, looking at the seven individuals who now possessed the gift of magic coursing through their veins.

"Welcome, witches," I said with pride.

Just as a sense of accomplishment started to settle in, Mikel's screams pierced the air, and he collapsed to the floor, writhing in agony. Gasps and cries filled the room as I rushed to his side. His hand released its grip on the opal, which now glowed a deep blood-red, the blood oath taking effect. Mikel's struggles ceased quickly, and I stared at his lifeless body, shock and dread washing over me. The implications were clear—he had intended to betray his oath. Even so, his death filled me with sadness and a heavy sense of loss.

I glanced at the faces of the others from where I sat beside Mikel's prone body, their expressions mirroring my own shock and sorrow.

"Was that the result of the blood oath?" Harlow asked, her voice barely above a whisper.

"Yes," I managed to utter, my voice trembling. The blood oath had been a necessary precaution, a safeguard against betrayal, but it weighed heavily on my conscience.

I knelt beside Mikel's lifeless body, his skin already growing cold. As I closed his vacant eyes, I couldn't help but feel a sense of mourning for the potential he had squandered.

With a heavy heart, I stood and faced the remaining members of the group.

"I'm sorry for your loss," I said, my voice filled with regret, "but the ritual is complete, and the rest of you have proven yourselves trustworthy. Welcome to the coven, witches."

THIRTY-FOUR

As I stood in the library, surrounded by shelves overflowing with ancient tomes and scrolls, the air was thick with concentration and the faint scent of old paper. I assisted Calliope and Ava with a new spell, watching closely as they carefully mimicked my gestures. It was a complex spell that required precision and focus, but I could see the determination in their eyes. I felt a sense of pride in guiding them, not just in magic, but also in forming a closer bond with the new witches.

Across the room, Harker was deeply engrossed in teaching Griffin, Archer, and Mikel. Her voice was steady and clear as she explained the intricacies of elemental magic. I observed the men; their brows furrowed in concentration as they absorbed every word, trying to grasp the elusive threads of power Harker described. The air around them seemed to crackle with the potential of untamed elements.

Curiosity nudged at me, and I turned my attention back to Harker. "Where are Sam and Harlow?" I asked, hoping they hadn't run into any trouble. They were often out and about, and their absence wasn't unusual, but I felt it important to keep track of everyone's whereabouts.

Harker glanced up from the ancient book she held, her eyes briefly meeting mine. She shrugged. Without missing a beat, she returned her focus to the book, continuing to read aloud a particularly complex passage to the men. Her dedication was admirable, but it reminded me that we all had our roles to play in this new world we were building. I returned my attention to Calliope and Ava, determined to be the best mentor I could be, while part of me wondered about Sam and Harlow's whereabouts and well-being.

At that moment, the library door swung open suddenly, drawing everyone's attention. Sam burst into the room, her cheeks flushed with a rosy hue, her eyes sparkling with an unmistakable excitement that seemed to radiate from her. Harlow followed closely behind her, her demeanor more composed, but a knowing smile played on her lips. It was becoming increasingly obvious that the two were in some sort of relationship, though that was none of my business.

"We've found out a pretty interesting piece of news," Sam announced, her voice tinged with breathlessness as if she and Harlow had just rushed back to share their discovery. "The servants love to gossip, you know."

Harlow, with a nod of agreement, allowed her gaze to sweep over the room, pausing briefly on each of us. "There's talk among them about a monster at the edge of the forest," she began, her tone serious. "They've seen it coming into a small town on the outskirts of the city, attacking and killing sheep. But last night, the situation escalated. A young sheepherder was found dead."

I felt a frown crease my forehead, a sense of unease settling over me. The idea of a monster bold enough to kill, and now encroaching on human territory, was troubling. "How do we know this isn't just some wild animal? Perhaps a rogue wolf?" I questioned, trying to rationalize the situation.

"There's something strange about this," Sam added, her voice taking on a grave tone. "The servant I spoke with saw the creature's silhouette in the moonlight while she was in the town visiting her sister. She described it as having an almost human shape but covered in rags, twisted and wrong in its form."

As I considered this information, my mind raced through the possibilities. The realm was home to numerous creatures, some known and others shrouded in mystery. But if this creature was targeting people, it posed a direct threat that couldn't be ignored.

"We were thinking it could be a job for the coven. Our first real task," Sam suggested, her eyes lighting up with the prospect.

As daunting as it was, the idea of confronting a monster presented an opportunity to see how our newly formed group would function in a real-world scenario. It would be a test of our abilities and our capacity to work together. I glanced at Harker, seeking her input, and found her nodding slowly in agreement.

"I think it's a good idea," Harker said, her voice steady and composed. "It will be a chance for us to test our skills in a genuine situation."

I turned my gaze to the other witches, seeking their thoughts. "What do the rest of you think?" I asked, gauging their reactions.

A chorus of agreement came from them, each eager and ready to prove their capabilities.

I nodded, feeling a surge of pride and responsibility.

"Very well, then. Let's start preparing. We have a monster to hunt."

THE REST of the day was spent in a flurry of activity as we prepared for the hunt. The servants, eager to share their knowledge, recounted their tales, each more harrowing than the last. We listened intently, piecing together a profile of the creature's habits and patterns. Its nocturnal movements, preference for the woodlands, and the increasing frequency of its attacks painted a grim picture. It seemed particularly drawn to the outskirts of town, preying on the more vulnerable areas skirting the forest.

As the sun began its descent, painting the sky in hues of orange and gold, we had formed a clear idea of where this creature was most likely to strike next. Gathering in the courtyard, a sense of determination and readiness enveloped us.

Amidst the bustle, Aisling approached me, her young face etched with excitement. "But I want to go with you. I want to use my powers too!" she implored, her small hand clutching my sleeve. Aerion and Wren, who had brought her to bid us farewell, hadn't anticipated she would be so eager to come.

I sighed, understanding her enthusiasm but aware of the dangers that lay ahead. "Maybe next time, Aisling. You still need to learn a lot about controlling your abilities before we take you into a real fight." It was important to protect her, to ensure she was fully prepared before facing such peril, and she was still so young.

"I'm strong, you know I am!" Aisling's pout was both earnest and endearing.

"You are, very strong," I agreed with a soft chuckle. "But there are things you don't know yet, skills and knowledge that can help us in the field. Things we will teach you, in time."

"Okay," she relented, though her disappointment was evident. "But you have to tell me everything when you come back!"

"Of course," I promised.

The courtyard was abuzz as we made our final preparations. I surveyed the witches, each one equipped with a satchel brimming with supplies, their faces a mix of anticipation and resolve. The air was charged with excitement, a tangible sense that we were on the cusp of proving our worth as a coven.

Wren and Aerion stepped forward, their expressions reluctant. Aerion, voicing his concern for the umpteenth time, said, "This really could be handled by a group of soldiers, you know."

"It's not their job, it's ours. We have an advantage with our magic," I said with conviction. His grunt in response indicated his lingering reservations.

Wren's eyes, filled with concern, met mine. "Be careful, Vale. Don't take any unnecessary risks," he urged, his tone laced with worry.

I nodded, acknowledging their concerns but confident in our abilities. "We will," I assured them, feeling the weight of responsibility but also a thrill at the challenge that lay ahead.

The group assembled around me in the courtyard. They looked to me, ready for direction, a united front of witches prepared to face the unknown. I could feel the weight of their expectations, the collective trust they placed in me as their leader.

"Okay, let's move out," I announced, my voice steady and confident. As I mentally prepared to summon Nyxen for the shift to the town, a small, hesitant voice interrupted my thoughts.

"Vale?" It was Aisling, her voice barely above a whisper but laden with an earnest gravity that made me pause.

I turned to face her, kneeling down to be at eye level. The frown on her face was deep and concerned, a stark contrast to her usual buoyant demeanor. It was clear that, despite her youth, she understood the seriousness of what we were about to undertake.

"You better win," she said, her eyes locking onto mine with an intensity that belied her age. Her expression was solemn, almost stern as if she were bestowing upon me a grave responsibility.

I smiled at her, touched by her concern and her implicit faith in me. "We will," I promised, my tone gentle yet firm. "I won't let you down." The promise was not just to her, but to all of us, a vow that I would do everything within my power to ensure our success and safety.

Her eyes held mine for a moment longer, searching for reassurance, before she nodded, seemingly appeased by my vow.

I stood up, bolstered by the resolve in her eyes, and turned back to the group. "Let's go," I said with renewed determination. With that, I called out for Nyxen, ready to embark on our mission, carrying with us the hopes and expectations of those we left behind.

As we stepped from the shadows that brought us here, we stealthily made our way through the town, blending into the dark that stretched along the quaint streets. Usually bustling with life, the town was now shrouded in an eerie stillness. Houses were cloaked in darkness, their inhabitants having retreated to the safety of their homes, wary of the lurking danger. The only sounds punctuating the silence were the occasional creaks of doors and windows being secured shut. It was clear the townspeople were well aware of the monster's presence, adhering to a self-imposed curfew to avoid its wrath.

"Let's spread out and search the perimeter of the woods. Stay close together, and keep a lookout for anything unusual," I instructed in a hushed tone. It was vital we remained alert and coordinated in our search.

Griffin, his brow furrowed in concentration, posed a valid question. "What are we looking for, exactly?"

"Anything out of place or suspicious. Anything that doesn't belong," I answered. We had to be prepared for any eventuality.

With a collective nod, the witches dispersed, moving in groups of two or three, melting into the darkness of the night. The mission had begun.

I navigated the streets cautiously, the shadows clinging to me, offering concealment. My senses were heightened, attuned to the slightest sound or movement that could signal the presence of the creature we sought.

Out of the corner of my eye, I caught a fleeting glimpse of something moving between the houses. I froze, my gaze piercing through the darkness, trying to discern what lurked there.

Then, without warning, a familiar voice spoke, "I thought you might need some help."

My heart leaped into my throat at the sound, and I jumped slightly. Kaelan appeared from the dark, as silent and unexpected as a shadow.

"Kaelan," I hissed under my breath, a mix of surprise and irritation coloring my tone. "You should have told us you were coming. This is dangerous." The shadows of the night seemed to deepen around us, reflecting my concern.

He looked at me, his expression serious. "I know, but I had this feeling that you might need me. I couldn't just sit back and do nothing while you're out here."

I sighed, torn between frustration and a begrudging appreciation for his concern. "I appreciate that, really, but we're witches. We're trained for this. We can take care of ourselves."

"I know," he acknowledged, stepping closer. His hand reached out, gently caressing my arm in a soothing gesture. "But I worry about you, Vale." His voice was soft.

Despite the danger surrounding us, I leaned into his touch, my body instinctively responding to his proximity. The concerns of the mission momentarily faded as I allowed myself to revel in the comfort his presence brought.

"You shouldn't have come," I whispered, even as my resolve wavered, my words lacking true conviction.

His hand moved up my arm, coming to rest gently on my neck. His thumb brushed against my jawline in a tender, almost reverent motion, sending a shiver of longing down my spine.

"I couldn't stay away," he breathed, his eyes burning with a desire that mirrored my own. "Vale, I -" His words hung in the air, unfinished.

Suddenly, a piercing scream shattered the moment, slicing through the tension between us. We instantly sprang apart, our attention snapping back to why we were here.

"That sounded like Ava," I said, my voice tight with fear.

The scream had come from nearby, and every instinct I had screamed that something was terribly wrong.

Without another word, we both sprang into action, dashing towards the source of the sound. The shadows of the night seemed to wrap around us, aiding our swift movement.

Another scream, louder and more desperate, echoed through the night, this time disturbingly close. We raced towards it, our hearts pounding, ready to face whatever horror awaited us.

"In here," Kaelan's voice cut through the night, urgent and decisive. He swiftly ducked into a narrow alleyway, and without hesitation, I followed close behind. Our footsteps echoed off the cobblestones as we raced down the alley, the screams of terror growing louder, more frantic with each step we took.

Bursting out into the open, I was met by the biting chill of the night air, which whipped across my face, stinging my skin. I skidded to a halt, my boots scraping against the ground, and the sight that unfolded before me was one of pure chaos.

Ava was huddled on the ground, her body curled defensively. Her eyes, wide and filled with unmistakable terror, were fixed on the monstrous figure looming over her. Bathed in the ghostly glow of the moonlight, the creature's form was grotesque, a nightmare brought to life. Tattered rags hung off its emaciated frame like the remnants of a shroud. Its face, twisted and deformed, was barely recognizable as human, contorted into an expression of hostility.

As it raised a gnarled hand, poised to deliver a vicious blow, I acted instinctively. With a shout, I unleashed a blast of fire, a torrent of flames erupting from my outstretched hands. The creature was knocked backward, stumbling under the force of the magical assault.

It let out a guttural roar, a sound so primal and filled with rage that it reverberated through the night. Its eyes, alight with fury, fixed on me, and a sinister grin contorted its already grotesque features.

"Now you've done it," Kaelan growled beside me, his stance defensive, ready for what was to come.

"Don't worry, I can handle this," I assured him, feeling a surge of confidence despite the direness of the situation.

"You might not have to," Kaelan replied, nodding towards the alley we had just emerged from. Turning, I saw the others—Griffin, Archer, Mikel, Sam, and Harlow—all arriving, their expressions determined, ready to stand with us in battle. The only one missing was Calliope. Where had she run off to?

"Are you alright, Ava?" I called out to her, my voice laced with concern.

She nodded in response, though her eyes remained wide, still reflecting the horror of her ordeal.

"Good, then let's finish this," I declared, turning my attention back to the creature. It stood there, a twisted abomination of flesh, but we were united, a coven ready to face whatever darkness lay before us.

As the creature surveyed the scene before it, taking in our unified front, a moment of hesitation flickered across its grotesque features. It seemed to be calculating its odds, weighing the threat we posed. But it quickly made its decision. With a swift turn, it bolted, disappearing into the shadows of the night.

"There was a second monster! It chased Calliope off in that direction," Ava suddenly exclaimed, her voice urgent as she pointed towards the left.

Without hesitation, I issued instructions. "Alright, let's split up and search for them. Ava, Sam, and Harlow come with me. The rest of you go with Kaelan after the other creature." My voice was firm, leaving no room for doubt or hesitation as I started off in the direction Ava had indicated.

We sprinted through the darkened streets, our senses heightened, every shadow and sound scrutinized for any hint of the creatures' presence. The town seemed to hold its breath, the usually lively streets now eerily deserted. The only sound was the rhythmic echo of our footsteps against the cobblestone, a stark reminder of the urgency of our mission.

THIRTY-FIVE

Glancing over my shoulder, I checked to ensure the others were keeping pace. Relief washed over me as I saw the three newly turned witches right on my heels, their expressions determined. Despite their presence, a sense of unease gnawed at me, the weight of responsibility heavy on my shoulders.

As we rounded a sharp corner, a sudden movement in the periphery of my vision caused me to skid to an abrupt halt. My gaze darted towards the source of the movement, trying to pierce the deep shadows of the night. I reached my finger up to my canine tooth and bit down, letting the blood well. My senses thrummed to life, my eyes piercing through the darkness.

"There!" Ava's voice cut through the silence, her finger pointing towards a narrow alleyway.

We darted down the alley without a second thought, our hearts racing. The narrow passage seemed to stretch endlessly before us, its end shrouded in darkness. The tension was thick, each of us keenly aware that every second mattered in our pursuit to rescue Calliope.

Rounding a sharp bend in the alleyway, we were suddenly confronted with the creature. Its presence was jarring, an embodiment of nightmarish horror standing right before us.

The creature let out a hideous snarl, a sound so guttural and filled with malice that it sent shivers down my spine. Its eyes, glowing with a vicious hatred, locked onto ours, promising violence and chaos. We instinctively braced ourselves, preparing for an imminent attack. However, the creature seemed more focused on escape than engaging in combat with us.

With surprising agility, it scrambled up a nearby wall. Its claws, sharp and deadly, dug into the brick with ease, leaving behind marks that marred the surface. We watched in stunned silence as it ascended with a frightening speed and agility.

Before we could react or conjure a spell to stop it, the creature vanished over the top of the wall, leaving us staring at the empty space it had occupied just moments before.

"Did it just... climb the wall?" Ava asked, her voice laced with disbelief and a tremble that betrayed her shock.

"Yes," I responded, my gaze still fixed on the spot where the creature had disappeared. "But that's not all it can do."

"What do you mean?" she questioned me, her eyes wide with fear and curiosity.

"It's a shapeshifter," I explained, the memory of an illustration from one of Thalion's books in his library flashing in my mind. The creature's ability to change form suddenly made the situation all the more daunting.

"You mean... it can turn into a human?" Ava asked, her voice barely above a whisper.

"Or any other creature it chooses." My voice was grim, reflecting the gravity of our situation.

"That's why no one has been able to catch it," she murmured, realization dawning in her eyes.

"It's a clever creature. And it's much stronger than it looks," I added, my mind already racing with strategies to track and confront such an elusive adversary.

Hurried footsteps suddenly echoed through the alley, and we all spun around, tensed and ready for another encounter. However, it was the rest of our group, Kaelan and the others, rushing to catch up with us.

"We lost the creature," Kaelan announced, frustration evident in his tone.

"What about Calliope?" I asked immediately, concern for her safety paramount in my mind.

"We still haven't found her," Archer replied, his voice taut with tension. The news was disheartening, and a new wave of urgency washed over me. I looked around at the others, their faces illuminated by the moonlight. They looked tired and shaken, and I knew we couldn't keep searching all night.

"We have to regroup," I asserted firmly, my mind racing with the need for a more strategic approach. "We need to come up with a new plan."

"We can't just let these things run free," Griffin protested, his voice laced with anger and impatience.

"I know," I replied, striving to maintain a calm demeanor despite the rising frustration within me. "But we're not going to catch them by chasing after them blindly." It was essential to reassess our tactics; the creatures we were dealing with were cunning and elusive.

Griffin's jaw clenched tightly, signaling his begrudging acceptance of my point. He didn't argue further, understanding the logic in my words despite his frustration.

"Let's head back to the town center," I suggested, trying to gather our focus. "We'll regroup there and formulate a new strategy."

But before we could act on that plan, another scream — terrible and heart-wrenching — pierced the night air. It was a sound that pushed us into immediate action.

"That's got to be Calliope!" Harlow exclaimed, already dashing towards the source of the scream.

Without hesitation, we sprinted after her, our hearts pounding and adrenaline surging through our veins.

As we rounded the corner, we were confronted with a grisly and shocking scene. Calliope lay unconscious on the ground, her body limp and vulnerable. Two men were hastily carrying her away, dragging her carelessly by her feet.

"Let her go!" Archer bellowed, his voice filled with rage as he lunged towards the men.

The men abruptly dropped Calliope and turned to face us. Their eyes glinted with an evil light, and within moments, their forms shifted, transforming back into the grotesque bodies of the creatures we had encountered earlier. The rapid change was disorienting, a stark reminder of the unnatural abilities of our adversaries.

"What the hell?" Archer exclaimed, his advance halting in surprise.

"They're shifters," I explained quickly, bringing everyone up to speed. "And they're working together."

No longer intent on fleeing, the creatures positioned themselves defensively in front of Calliope, effectively using her as a barrier to keep us at bay. My eyes were drawn to the large bruise on her forehead, a worrying sign that she might be seriously injured. The situation had escalated into a standoff, with Calliope's safety hanging precariously in the balance. We needed to act fast and smart to outmaneuver these shapeshifters and rescue our friend.

As the monstrous creatures charged at us, their ferocious forms were terrifying to behold. Their claws extended and teeth bared, they were the embodiment of primal aggression, ready for a brutal fight. I steeled myself, feeling the energy of my magic simmering inside, ready to burst forth in defense.

Ava, Griffin, and Harlow wasted no time, launching their spells at the advancing beasts with all the power they could muster. Their magic, though limited, was fierce and determined, a testament to their courage and resolve in the face of danger.

The first monster, shifting form with disturbing ease, transformed into a wolf-like creature, its eyes wild with rage as it lunged at Harlow. Its jaws snapped viciously, but Harlow managed to duck and roll, evading the creature's deadly bite by mere inches.

Griffin leaped into the fray, his fists ready to strike, but the creature's agility was unnerving. In a swift, violent motion, it lashed out, its claws leaving a cruel gash across Griffin's chest. Archer, reacting swiftly, rushed to Griffin's aid, but the creature was relentless. It struck with brutal force, knocking Archer aside with a swipe of its claws, leaving deep marks across his face.

Kaelan and I unleashed our combined attack, a powerful fusion of magic and raw strength. My fire surged forth, intertwining with Kaelan's shadow magic. Together, our spells formed shadowy waves of fire that crashed against the wolf-like creature. The magic wrapped around it, searing its skin. It let out a pained howl, the smell of burning flesh permeating the air.

As the second creature advanced towards us, the first one, still reeling from our attack, began to shift form once more. It morphed into a massive bear, its size and strength even more formidable than before.

"Ava, Harlow, take care of Calliope. We'll deal with these two," I yelled to them, trusting them to protect the fallen witch.

The two creatures now loomed over us, both having taken the form of towering bears. Their massive forms cast ominous shadows in the moonlight, their claws and fangs glinting menacingly.

I gathered my magic, feeling it pulse through my veins with a potent energy, ready for release. Kaelan stood beside me, his gaze fixed on the monstrous beasts.

"I'll handle the right one. You go for the left," he said in a low, determined voice.

With a nod of understanding, we sprang into action, each of us focusing on one of the monstrous bears. The fight was on, and it would be a battle of magic, strength, and wills.

With a fierce determination, I hurled a blast of intense fire towards the bear on my right. The flames roared to life, engulfing the creature in a scorching inferno. Its reaction was immediate and terrifying; a deafening roar erupted from it, a powerful sound that seemed to shake the air around us, echoing ominously through the night.

Beside me, Kaelan unleashed his own formidable power. His shadows, dark and sinister, swirled outwards and enveloped the other bear. The darkness wrapped around the creature like a cloak, blinding and disorienting it. The sight was both eerie and awe-inspiring, a testament to the raw strength of Kaelan's magic.

These creatures were indeed powerful, but we matched their ferocity with our own. My resolve was fueled by a fierce protectiveness and a determination that these monsters would not harm anyone else on our watch.

I continued my assault on the bear, the flames I conjured licking voraciously at its fur. The acrid smell of burning hair filled the air, a pungent reminder of the intensity of the battle.

Kaelan's shadows continued their relentless assault, the other bear's growls and cries muffled and distorted by the enveloping darkness. The two bears, engulfed in fire and shadow, roared and snarled, their fury echoing through the night. But we stood our ground, unyielding in our defense.

Seeking to end the standoff, I reached out with my mind, attempting to penetrate the shifter's mental defenses in an effort to shatter its mind. The creature, however, proved to be unexpectedly resilient. Its mental fortitude was formidable, resisting my intrusion, and I could sense it attempting to breach my own mental barriers in return.

The battle became a test of wills, a clash of mental and magical strength. I held firm, channeling my magic, my resolve unwavering. The power surged through me, a torrent of energy that I directed at the creature. Despite our efforts, the fight seemed to be at a stalemate, with neither side able to gain the upper hand.

In that critical moment, the tide of the battle shifted subtly but significantly. I felt a momentary lapse in the bear's will, a fleeting weakness in its mental defenses, and I pounced on the opportunity with all the force of my magic.

Channeling every ounce of my power, I unleashed it against the creature, my magic acting like a whip, fierce and unrelenting. The beast staggered under the assault, its once-formidable defenses starting to crumble under the sheer intensity of my attack.

I thrust my mind forward, penetrating the dark, twisted mess of the monster's thoughts and emotions. The landscape of its mind was repellent, filled with violence and savagery, but I pressed on, undeterred. My objective was clear – to find and obliterate its consciousness.

And there it was, a faint glimmer amidst the darkness, a vulnerable speck of light in a void of malice. I extended my magic towards it, encircling the fragile essence of the creature's consciousness with a vice-like grip.

With a decisive, forceful pull, I shattered the beast's mind. The connection between its thoughts and emotions was severed abruptly. The bear's body slumped to the ground, its eyes now empty.

Without wasting a moment, I turned my attention to the other creature, the one engaged in a fierce battle with Kaelan. Its mind was a cesspool of malice and hatred, even more twisted and corrupt than its companion's. I plunged into this new mental battlefield, my magic searching for the creature's consciousness.

Finding it was easy; it stood out like a beacon in the darkness. However, this beast's will was far stronger, its mental defenses formidable and resistant. It pushed back with a surprising intensity, but I refused to relent. Fueled by anger and the need to protect, my determination was unyielding.

I drew upon every reserve of strength and willpower, searching for a weakness, a chink in its armor. And then, there it was – a small, almost imperceptible crack in its defenses.

I struck without hesitation, my magic breaking through

the weakened barrier. That breach was all I needed. I reached in with my magic and shattered the creature's mind with a final, devastating blow.

The second beast collapsed, its body falling lifelessly to the ground. The night fell silent once again, the immediate threat neutralized, but the echo of our battle lingered in the air. We had prevailed, but the cost of such a victory weighed heavily on my mind. But, this wasn't the time to think about it, we still had to rescue Calliope.

As the immediate danger subsided, I quickly turned to assess the condition of my companions. Relief washed over me upon seeing that everyone was still alive, though it was evident that the battle had taken its toll on all of us. Griffin was holding onto his chest, his face contorted in pain from the wounds he had sustained, and Archer's face was a gruesome sight, covered in blood from the creature's vicious swipe.

"Are you all okay?" I asked, concern etched in my voice as my eyes scanned their faces.

They nodded in response, though their expressions were visibly shaken by the ordeal we had just endured.

"What about Calliope?" Griffin's voice was strained with pain and concern as he looked toward where the young witch lay.

"She's still unconscious," Harlow replied, her voice filled with worry, casting a glance towards Calliope's motionless form.

"We need to get her help," Ava said, her tone urgent.

Archer, still reeling from his injuries, gestured towards the lifeless bodies of the monsters. "What about these two?"

"Leave them," Kaelan said firmly. "We need to get Calliope and you two help right now."

"He's right," I said, knowing that the well-being of our friends was the immediate priority. "We'll deal with the bodies later."

In an instant, Kaelan used his magic to shift us back to the courtyard. We were greeted by the anxious faces of Wren and Aerion, who had been waiting for our return. Aerion wasted no time; he immediately scooped up Calliope in his arms and dashed inside towards the healers. Kaelan and Wren helped Griffin and Archer start making their way as well.

I leaned heavily against a pillar, my breaths deep and labored as I tried to calm my racing mind. The physical and emotional weight of the fight pressed down on me, and the realization that people I cared deeply about were injured, possibly gravely so, tied a knot of worry and guilt in my stomach.

"How are you feeling?" Ava's gentle voice cut through the heavy silence.

"Exhausted," I admitted, my voice hoarse and weary. "This isn't exactly how I imagined the night going."

"Me either," she agreed, her face reflecting the fatigue and stress that mirrored my own.

"At least the creatures are dead," I added, attempting to find a silver lining amidst the chaos of the night. It was a small consolation, but in that moment, it was something to hold onto.

Ava's observation was pointed, yet not without a hint of concern. "Not just dead," she remarked. "You completely obliterated their minds."

I couldn't help but grimace at her words. The actions I had taken, while necessary, were not without their moral complexities. "They were evil," I stated, trying to justify the harshness of my methods. "They deserved it." But even as I said it, I felt the weight of what I had done.

"But still, it was... brutal," Ava added, her voice carrying a note of unease.

Her comment resonated with me, stirring a deep, unsettling feeling. The act of extinguishing a living mind, even one as vicious as those creatures', was not something to be taken lightly. The immediate nausea I had felt after performing the spell was a testament to that. It was an experience, a sensation that I knew would linger with me for a long time.

"They didn't show any mercy," I pointed out, my thoughts drifting to Calliope and the others who had suffered at the hands of those monsters. It was a cold truth, but it didn't entirely ease the discomfort of my actions.

"I know," Ava conceded. "It was just..."

"Brutal," I finished for her, acknowledging the harsh reality of what had transpired.

She nodded, her eyes clouded with a sadness that mirrored my own. It was a shared sentiment, a mutual understanding of the gravity of what had occurred.

Exhaustion weighed heavily on me, both physically and mentally. The adrenaline of the fight had worn off, leaving behind a profound weariness.

"Vale, if you ever need to talk, know that I'm here for you," Ava offered softly, her hand resting gently on my arm in a comforting gesture.

I managed a weak smile in response, grateful for her support. "Thanks," I said, appreciating her kindness and the solidarity it represented. "Right now, let's just go check on the others."

"Alright," Ava agreed, giving my arm a reassuring squeeze. Together, we made our way to where the injured were being tended, ready to offer whatever support we could. It was a somber moment, one that underscored the reality of our fight and the importance of the bonds we were forming.

We moved towards the infirmary, our steps heavy with the weight of the night's events. The corridors echoed with our footfalls, a stark contrast to the chaotic silence that had just engulfed us. As we entered the room where our friends were being treated, a wave of relief washed over me. Seeing them injured, yet alive, brought a complex blend of emotions. This battle had taken its toll, but it had also strengthened our resolve. We were more than just a group of witches; we were a family, bound by magic and a shared purpose. Tonight's ordeal had tested us, but it also proved that together, we were formidable. The night's darkness had been pushed back, but the fight was far from over.

THIRTY-SIX

"Ah-ha!" I exclaimed, unable to contain my excitement as I looked down at the book in my hands. I was back in the library, my focus entirely consumed by the research on the mysterious graveyard from my dreams. Harker, Archer, and Harlow, who had been sitting around the same book, listening to Harker read from it, all looked up at me with curiosity as I exclaimed.

"I've finally found something about the ghost I met in the graveyard," I informed them, my voice filled with satisfaction.

Harker leaned forward, her eyes sharp with interest. "Well, what is it?"

I couldn't help but grin as I continued, "It's a few paragraphs about her, but it also includes the location of her grave—the very tree where she was hung. It says it was in a place called Noxwood."

"I've never seen anywhere like that on Thalion's map of Elysian," Harker remarked, her brow furrowing as she came to examine the passage.

"That's because it's no longer there," Aerion's voice

chimed in as he entered the library. I watched him with interest as he crossed the room to join us.

I turned to him, intrigued and eager for more information. "What do you mean?"

Aerion settled into a nearby seat, his expression serious. "It was destroyed ages ago. But I know where it used to be —the ruins of the city still stand. However, most say the ruins are still cursed by the evil magic that destroyed it."

"Cursed?" Harlow echoed, her tone laced with uncertainty.

Aerion continued, his words painting a grim picture of the city's tragic history. "The city was destroyed by its own people. Some say an evil magic crept through the city and infected the minds of its inhabitants. The city closed itself off from the outside world and never reopened."

"Wow, that's...horrible," Harlow said, her eyes wide.

"Indeed, it was," Aerion agreed solemnly.

"Well, sounds like a cheery place to visit," I remarked sarcastically.

Aerion, however, seemed undeterred by the grim history. "So, when are we leaving?" he asked.

"Soon," I replied, my thoughts already racing with plans and preparations.

Archer couldn't contain his excitement as he asked, "Are you going to take us with you?"

I gave him a stern look, not willing to entertain the idea lightly. "Definitely not. Not after what happened with the shapeshifters. You and Griffin still aren't even fully recovered."

Harlow, never one to back down easily, pleaded with an edge of irritation in her voice. "We can take care of ourselves!"

"Not this time," I said firmly, my concern for their safety

overriding any protests. "Until I say you're ready, I want you to train with your powers."

Harlow grumbled but ultimately didn't press the issue further.

"Now," I said, rising to my feet, "If you'll excuse me, I have some preparations to make."

"Let me know if you need anything," Harker offered, and I nodded.

"Will do," I replied, heading for the door.

NOW WANTING to waste any precious daylight, I moved swiftly to prepare for our journey to Noxwood. Thalion was preoccupied with the arrangements for my crowning ceremony, so Aerion and Kaelan would be accompanying me on this mission. I dressed in practical attire, opting for a pair of sturdy leather breeches and a loose-fitting shirt, finishing the ensemble with a deep purple cloak to ward off the chill of the impending evening. In my haste, I exited my chambers, only to collide with Kaelan in the corridor.

"Once again, we go rushing headfirst into danger," Kaelan remarked with a smirk, steadying me as our unexpected encounter left me slightly off balance.

I couldn't help but grin in response. "It's not my fault. It seems to always find me."

Kaelan's dark eyes sparkled with amusement as he agreed, "It certainly does." He reached for my hand, and I noticed his eyes widen slightly as his fingers brushed against the ring that now adorned it. "What's this?" he asked, his voice curious as he examined the silver band closely.

Swallowing the lump in my throat, I replied hesitantly,

"Thalion has officially asked me to marry him." I was acutely aware of how fragile the truce between the three of them was, and I couldn't help but worry that this news might be the spark that reignited those tensions. I watched Kaelan closely as he inspected the ring, searching his face for any telltale signs of the emotions I suspected were churning beneath his calm exterior.

After a moment that seemed to stretch on endlessly, he finally spoke. "It's a beautiful ring. I'm happy for you, little witch," he said, his gaze lifting to meet mine. His response surprised me, marked by a casual acceptance I hadn't expected. A part of me wondered if he felt a twinge of regret, wishing he had been the one to present me with a ring. Regardless, I couldn't hide the grateful smile that spread across my face.

His lack of immediate upset over this new development was a relief. It felt like a step in the right direction, a sign that perhaps we could indeed build a stronger, more harmonious relationship moving forward. I felt a glimmer of hope that we could navigate this complex dynamic with understanding and mutual respect.

Aerion rounded the corner and stopped short when he saw us. "Ready to go?" he asked.

"Ready," I said, turning from Kaelan to look at him. Without further delay, I led them toward the courtyard outside.

The sun was still high in the sky, casting its warm golden light over the palace grounds. We had ample daylight left and I hoped we could locate the graveyard without too much trouble, but I knew nothing was ever that straightforward.

As we descended the large stone steps outside, Aerion extended his arms for us to grasp. I seized his arm without hesitation, but Kaelan, while not opposed to the idea, hesitated for a moment before reluctantly placing his hand on Aerion's arm. With that, we were enveloped in a whirl of light and color, the dizziness that always came with Aerion's shifting quickly dissipating.

When I opened my eyes, the bright afternoon sun greeted me, warming my skin, and the crisp scent of the forest filled my senses. I turned to see the looming ruins of Noxwood, its crumbling stone walls and moss-covered structures standing as a testament to the passage of time. The gaping entrance to the city's remains stood before us, an eerie invitation.

"Welcome to Noxwood," Aerion declared, breaking the silence.

"Lovely," Kaelan muttered dryly, unimpressed by the desolate surroundings.

With a nod, I took the lead and began moving toward the entrance of the ruins. As we crossed the threshold, an eerie silence descended on us, shrouding the area in an unnatural stillness. The absence of birdsong, insect chirping, and even the rustling of leaves in the breeze sent a chill down my spine. It felt as if the entire forest held its breath, awaiting our next move.

"I don't like this," Kaelan murmured, his voice barely above a whisper.

"Neither do I," I responded, my senses on high alert as an unsettling tension settled over us. "Let's just keep moving; in my dream, the graveyard was in the middle of a large forest, but seeing as how this place is overrun by the forest, I'm sure it could be anywhere."

We navigated through the decaying streets of Noxwood, the remnants of multiple buildings reduced to little more than crumbling heaps of stone. Nature had reclaimed the city, with vines and moss snaking their way over structures, and trees stubbornly growing through the cracks, their roots prying apart the deteriorating stone.

An eerie sense of being observed accompanied our progress, and intermittent footsteps seemed to echo in the distance. Whenever I halted, the elusive sounds vanished into the silence.

"Something isn't right here," Aerion remarked, his gaze sweeping the environment for any signs of movement.

"I'm beginning to think the stories you heard were true," I confessed in a hushed tone.

"It seems likely," he agreed, his expression grim.

We pressed on with our quest, delving deeper into the forsaken city, but my discomfort only intensified. The graveyard remained elusive, and the sensation of being watched persisted.

"Where could this damn graveyard be?" I grumbled in frustration.

"It's got to be here somewhere," Aerion reassured me, his voice steady but with a hint of uncertainty in his eyes.

Kaelan abruptly halted, his head swiveling in response to an unfamiliar sound.

"What is it?" I whispered, my senses on high alert.

He shook his head, brow furrowing. "I thought I heard someone calling my name," he murmured, a low rumble in his voice.

"Probably just your imagination," Aerion suggested, attempting to rationalize the unexplained noise.

Kaelan's frown deepened, but he chose not to dispute the point.

"Let's keep moving," I urged, and we continued navigating the winding streets in our relentless search.

As time passed, the sense of unease heightened. The

fading daylight cast long shadows and we found ourselves losing track of our location in the sprawling ruins of Noxwood.

"We're not going to find the graveyard in the dark," Aerion sensibly pointed out. "We should go back and try again tomorrow."

I nodded in agreement. "You're right, let's go back."

Kaelan's head whipped around once more, his eyes scouring the crumbling city around us. "There it is again," he whispered, his attention riveted on the elusive sound. "Someone's calling me."

Aerion's head swiveled, too, but in the opposite direction. "I heard something as well," he said, his eyes narrowing as he strained to identify the source.

"You guys are both losing it," I muttered.

Ignoring my words, they both began taking slow, measured steps toward the directions they were focusing on.

"Hey, guys, it's probably not a good idea to follow spooky voices in a cursed city to their source, okay?" I implored, not entirely sure if they had even heard me, as they persisted in their pursuit.

"Come on," Aerion said, advancing a few more steps forward.

"No, we need to go this way," Kaelan insisted, striding in the opposite direction.

"Guys, stop!" I raised my voice, my growing panic evident.

But then I heard it too—a voice, calling my name. But it wasn't just any voice; I was certain it was Elowen's, the ghost who had been present that night in the graveyard.

"Aerion, Kaelan!" I called out, my voice urgent. "It's Elowen. She's calling me, not you."

But neither of them seemed to hear me, continuing to walk on. The voice called to me again, pulling at my very core. I looked at the two men walking away from me. I was growing increasingly panicked as I watched their retreating backs. But that voice—it beckoned me, and I knew I had to follow it, no matter the risks.

I walked away, my steps guided solely by the haunting voice that reverberated in the air. I was no longer conscious of my surroundings, my eyes fixed on the path that unfolded before me. The voice grew louder, its cadence drawing me nearer with an irresistible pull. I was no longer aware of my companions, or the rapidly diminishing light. All that existed was the voice, and the need to reach its source.

Finally, I found myself standing within the very necropolis that had haunted my dreams. Twisted trees loomed tall, casting eerie shadows upon the snowy ground scattered with ancient tombstones and huge mausoleums. The air was suffused with an aching sorrow that pulsed through my chest.

I scanned the area, my gaze searching for the tall, gnarled tree that had occupied the center of my nightmares. However, the view was obstructed by massive, crumbling tombs and toppled obelisks that had once stood as silent sentinels of the past.

"Nyxen," I called out, and my familiar materialized, trotting up to me. "The tree was at the center of the cemetery. Can you guide me there?"

With a flick of his tail, Nyxen turned and led the way, his keen senses navigating the eerie atmosphere that surrounded us.

"This place is wrong," Nyxen whispered in my mind.

"I know," I replied in a hushed tone.

The voice beckoned to me once more, growing ever more urgent. I quickened my pace, the encroaching misery of the cemetery weighing upon me like a heavy shroud.

I followed Nyxen through the rows of grave markers and monuments, my heart racing as the voice inched closer. And then I saw it—the gnarled, towering tree, its branches reaching skyward like the twisted fingers of a long-forgotten deity.

I hurried toward the tree, the voice echoing in my ears with an unmistakable desperation.

As I approached, my gaze fixated on the ominous rope hanging from one of its branches. The air grew colder, my breath forming a visible mist in front of me.

"Nyxen, something is coming," I whispered, a shiver coursing down my spine.

"I can feel it, too," Nyxen replied.

The rope swayed gently in the breeze and the voice called out to me once more, its insistence driving me closer to the looming tree.

The rope seemed to hold a sinister allure, drawing me in like a moth to a flame. If I just reached out my hand, I could touch the rope. My fingers trembled as they moved, inching closer to the fraying fibers that brushed against the back of my hand.

"Stop," Elowen's ethereal voice rang out and I jerked my hand back in surprise, my heart pounding in my chest. Before me stood the apparition of the ghostly figure I had encountered in my dreams—the one who had led me to this haunting place.

"Why are you here?" she asked, her voice carrying a weight of sadness and longing.

"I came to find you, to ask for your help like you told me to," I replied, my voice steady despite my racing heart.

"Help?" Her spectral form seemed to waver in the cold, ghostly light of the graveyard.

"I need more information on the Seven," I told her, my words echoing in the eerie stillness. "I need to know what they are planning now."

Elowen stared at me for a long, contemplative moment, her eyes brimming with a deep and haunting sorrow.

"They are coming," she whispered, her voice barely audible, as if she feared her own words. "They are coming for you and another."

Ice formed in my stomach, and I swallowed hard, my breath catching in my throat. "How do you know this?" I asked, the sound a whisper.

"Because it was always their plan," she replied. "One I went along with in the beginning, before they had me hanged. They had always planned to return and to take you down if necessary."

"Why did you change sides?" I asked.

"I did not," she said, her voice filled with profound sadness. "My loyalties lie with the Seven, but I could not stand by and watch them destroy the world and, in the process, destroy themselves."

"Destroy the world, what do you mean? What else are they planning?" I asked, my voice filled with urgency and dread.

"They seek to reunite the whole coven and seize control of the three realms. Their dark magic is corrupting them," Elowen explained, her ethereal form wavering slightly. "They can't control it anymore, and soon, the very thing that gave them the power to do so much evil will become their undoing. Even I am afraid of the things they have stirred from the shadows. They'll take the realms down with them if they aren't stopped."

My heart raced at the dire revelation. "Do you have any other information?" I implored, clinging to the hope that there might be more she could reveal.

"There is one among their ranks who is a powerful seer," she continued, her voice heavy with foreboding. "I'm afraid they'll always be one step ahead of you unless you learn to master your own precognitive abilities. But for now, it would be best for you to leave. I fear you are in grave danger."

I looked at her, feeling torn. "I still know so little about them," I pleaded with her. "Please, Elowen, I need your help to uncover the truth."

"Their leader, Shazarah," she revealed, "has bound herself to a ruthless Fae king, much like how you've been bound to the First Witch. However, she has the power to control him and wield her magic through him."

"That must be how he was able to shift us between realms," I realized, connecting the dots. Not even Kaelan could shift between the realms, only anywhere within the realms itself. He has to use portals like the rest of us to move between the realms. Only the rare rifts in reality could move one through multiple realms at once, and they were highly volatile and unreliable. I had seen one once when Kaelan and I had traversed the demon realm in search of the library.

"This is how the Seven have been returning," she confirmed, "possessing the bodies of Otherworlders, taking over their souls."

The blood drained from my face as I considered the implications. "So they could possess anyone," I murmured.

"Anyone without strong magical defenses," Elowen clarified. "Now, go. You must leave this place. They are coming."

As she spoke, a frigid breeze swept through the grave-yard, and the eerie sound of sinister laughter reverberated through the desolate trees.

"What is it? What's coming?" I asked, panic surging through me as I scanned the empty graveyard.

"The evil souls of this cursed city," Elowen explained solemnly.

"Evil souls?"

"Yes, the tormented souls of those who perished when the city was destroyed. They are restless, angry, and they seek to exact revenge on any who trespass."

The rope hanging from the gnarled tree began to swing wildly, and in an instant, Elowen vanished into thin air, leaving me alone in the eerie silence of the haunted graveyard.

A brutal force propelled me forward, sending me sprawling onto the snow-covered ground with a harsh impact. The unforgiving earth met my body with an icy embrace, leaving me disoriented and gasping for breath.

Invisible hands seized my ankles, their chilling grip unyielding as they began dragging me with a relentless force toward the twisted tree. My heart pounded wildly in my chest as I fought desperately against the ghostly assailants, but their grasp held firm, rendering my struggles futile.

Desperation gripped me and I clawed at the loose soil beneath me, attempting to find some semblance of stabil-ity. My nails dug into the frozen ground, but the evil forces continued their relentless advance, rendering my efforts utterly in vain. I was hopelessly outmatched. I lashed out desperately with my fire, but how was I supposed to fight ghosts with flames?

With a jolt, I was abruptly lifted into the air, my body

suspended. The unseen hands maintained their vice-like grip, propelling me closer to the rope that swung ominously from a gnarled branch. In that harrowing moment, their sinister intent became chillingly clear.

Around me, eerie laughter filled the air once again, their ghastly joy echoing through the lonely graveyard. Panic coursed through my veins as I screamed, kicking and flailing helplessly in the air.

The cold, coarse texture of the rope brushed against my skin. It seemed to possess a life of its own, constricting menacingly around my throat as I dangled precariously in the air.

The spectral hands relinquished their hold, and the rope snapped mercilessly against my neck so hard I thought it might break. I gasped for air, fingers desperately clawing at the tightening noose as my lungs burned with a suffocating agony. My vision blurred, and darkness encroached as I fought desperately for each breath.

"Nyxen," I croaked, my voice a desperate plea for assistance, the word escaping my parched lips.

As the rope tightened its deadly grip, my body began to grow numb, and the world around me faded into an abyss of darkness. My futile struggles ceased, and I succumbed to the merciless embrace of unconsciousness.

THIRTY-SEVEN

"Breathe, Vale."

In the pitch-black abyss of unconsciousness, I heard a voice pierce through the darkness, calling my name urgently. It echoed like a lifeline in the dark recesses of my mind, pulling me back from the brink.

"Breathe, damn it!"

With a sudden jolt, my eyes snapped open, and I sucked in a gasping breath, the air filling my lungs in ragged bursts as I struggled to reclaim consciousness.

My chest heaved, and I continued to cough and sputter as the world slowly came back into focus.

"Breathe, just breathe," Aerion's voice, laced with concern, reached my ears as I lay sprawled on the ground, the cold reality of the moment settling in around me.

With great effort, I pulled myself into a sitting position, though my breathing remained labored, a painful rasp escaping my lips. Beside me, Kaelan knelt, his face etched with worry, his eyes locked onto mine.

"What happened?" Aerion demanded, his voice echoing with residual panic.

Through the rawness of my throat, I managed to rasp out an explanation. "The spirits of this cursed city," I gasped, my throat still bearing the brutal imprints of the noose, "They're angry."

A surge of dread coursed through me as I recollected the harrowing encounter with the apparitions. The trauma of the experience left me shaken.

"Well, let's get the hell out of here then," Kaelan said, his voice urgent as he gently pulled me upright.

I nodded in agreement, my body still quaking with the aftermath of the near-death experience that had befallen me. Despite the harrowing ordeal, I could not shake the feeling that the shadows of Noxwood held many more secrets waiting to be unraveled.

"We'll meet you in the courtyard," Kaelan said to Aerion before the shadows enveloped us and we shifted away, leaving behind the ominous darkness and haunting echoes of Noxwood's spirits.

As we materialized in the serene courtyard of Terralux, the stark contrast from the nightmarish cemetery was jarring. Kaelan's arms encircled me, his grip both gentle and secure, as he tilted my chin upwards, compelling me to meet his concerned gaze. "Are you okay?" he asked as his stormy eyes probed mine, searching for any lingering signs of distress.

"I'm a little bit shaken. I think I may be in shock," I admitted, my voice quivering. The mere thought of how close I had come to death sent tremors through me.

His voice was soft and laced with genuine concern as he responded, "You almost died."

I nodded, the threat of tears threatening to spill over as the gravity of the situation settled in. "I know," I whispered, my voice cracking.

He pulled me even closer, his protective embrace enveloping me. "Shh, it's okay, I've got you," he whispered, tenderly stroking my hair.

The warmth of his body, the rhythmic cadence of his heartbeat, all of it was a soothing balm that helped to quell the tremors wracking my frame. Vulnerability welled within me as I confessed, "I was so scared."

Kaelan murmured words of comfort and understanding, his chest providing a soft haven for me to bury my face. "I'm just glad we found you in time," he admitted, his voice filled with relief.

The tears that had threatened to spill finally flowed freely, my emotions pouring out in response to the near-fatal ordeal. "How did you both find me?" I managed to ask, the confusion still fresh in my mind. "The last time I saw either of you, you were walking off after voices."

"We both felt your fear through the bond. It was so overwhelming it snapped us out of it. We used the bond to find you. Aerion got there just before me and was cutting you down." His arms tightened around me protectively. "When I saw you hanging from that tree..." He paused, the tremor in his voice betraying the fear that had gripped him. "I've never been so scared."

I pulled away slightly to look up at him, my tear-stained eyes meeting his. "I'm alright. I'm safe now," I assured him.

He met my gaze, his eyes reflecting the relief coursing through him.

"Vale!" Aerion's voice called out, breaking through the moment as he materialized in the courtyard.

A wave of gratitude washed over me as he rushed over, his voice laden with genuine concern. "Are you alright?"

"I'm okay," I assured him, my voice a fragile whisper, "Thanks to you two."

Aerion managed a weak smile, but his eyes still held traces of worry that refused to dissipate.

"Come on, let's get back inside," Kaelan suggested, his tone firm yet gentle, "You need to rest."

Nodding in agreement, I allowed them to guide me back into the welcoming sanctuary of the castle, where I could begin to recover from the horrors of Noxwood.

AN HOUR LATER, I lay in bed alongside Kaelan, our thoughts still entangled in the events of Noxwood.

"I don't understand how we all heard Elowen's voice. Why would she lure us in different directions?" I mused, the mysteries of our recent ordeal still haunting me.

Kaelan's fingers trailed absentminded patterns on my arm as he contemplated my question. "There's no use in worrying about it now," he finally replied, his voice soothing.

"You're right," I sighed, letting the tension melt away as I nestled closer to him. "But it's all so strange. I'm glad I got the information I did, at least. Even if we did have to put ourselves at risk to get it."

"I'm just glad you're okay," Kaelan murmured, his warm lips planting a tender kiss on the top of my head.

"Me too," I whispered, closing my eyes and relaxing into the comfort of his arms.

Kaelan eventually broke the silence. "You're being crowned queen in a few days," he mentioned softly. "Are you ready for that?"

I thought about the weight of the impending ceremony before offering an honest response. "I'm not sure I'll ever be ready."

Kaelan's following words took me by surprise, shifting the focus of our conversation. "I was hoping that before then, you'd be ready to readdress this marriage issue," he confessed, a hint of hopefulness in his voice.

I shifted slightly to look up at him and tried to read the expression on his face. "What marriage issue? Is this about Thalion?"

"No," he said, looking at me earnestly, his voice laced with hope. "I want to be married to you, Vale. Not later, now, before you're crowned queen."

A brief silence hung between us as I contemplated his unexpected proposal. "Why now, all of a sudden?"

"A lot of reasons. Because I love you. Because I want to be yours. Because I can't get that image of you swinging from that tree out of my head," he confessed, his emotions laid bare. "I don't want to wait anymore."

"Okay, then let's get married," I said, my voice filled with certainty as I met his eager gaze. "Tomorrow."

A brilliant smile graced his face and his eyes danced with joy. "You mean it?"

"Yes, I mean it," I said, laughing as I was unable to contain the joy bubbling up inside me.

He leaned down and kissed me in response, our lips meeting with a newfound urgency and passion that left no room for doubt or hesitation.

"We can have a small private ceremony," Kaelan suggested, his eyes sparkling with excitement. "Just you and me and whoever you want to have witness the occasion. Wren can marry us. He has the authority as alpha."

"Sounds perfect," I murmured, my heart full of happiness.

He kissed me again, and I felt a deep contentment settle over me. I had never felt so sure about anything in my life.

THE NEXT DAY, as I was getting dressed, a gentle knock echoed on the door to my rooms. "Come in," I called out, wondering who it could be.

In strolled Thalion, bearing a sizable box in his hands. Behind him followed Amris, Kelli, and Joeline, my lady's maids from Virelium. Their unexpected appearance filled me with genuine delight.

"Amris! How good to see you. You two as well, Kelli and Joeline," I said warmly, smiling at them.

"Aerion has told us of the upcoming wedding and we have brought gifts for you both," Thalion announced.

I couldn't help but feel touched by Thalion's generosity and the thoughtful gesture of my friends. It was clear that he was handling any jealousy gracefully, unlike Kaelan, and I appreciated his support.

"You didn't have to do that," I told Thalion, genuinely moved by his kindness.

"Nonsense, just because you're not getting married to me— today at least," he said with a wink, "Doesn't mean we can't celebrate."

"You're too good to me, Thalion," I said, my heart swelling. "Now, what is in the box?"

Thalion's eyes sparkled mischievously as he replied, "Why don't you come open it and see?" He gently placed the box on my bed, inviting me to unveil its contents.

Eagerly, I stepped forward, my curiosity getting the better of me, and lifted the lid off the box. To my delight, I discovered the most exquisite white and silver gown nestled within.

"This is absolutely stunning," I gasped, carefully lifting the dress from the box to get a better look. "Thank you so much, Thalion." I leaned in and kissed him softly on the cheek. His responding grin spoke volumes.

Amris, standing nearby, held up two delicate silver crowns. "And these are for the wedding," she added, proudly presenting the crowns.

"Oh, they're beautiful," I breathed, taking one of the crowns from her hand and admiring the intricate design. The delicate silverwork sparkled in the light, a testament to the craftsmanship.

"You're a queen in every way but title, so it's best that you look the part today," Thalion said, taking my hand and giving it a gentle squeeze.

Turning to Amris, Kelli, and Joeline, who were beaming with excitement, I asked, "Will you help me get ready?"

Amris replied with a warm smile, "It would be our honor."

The next hour was filled with the joyful commotion of preparation. I soon found myself standing before a full-length mirror, admiring my reflection. The gown fit me perfectly, its white and silver hues accentuating the amber in my eyes. Joeline had artfully styled my hair, allowing it to cascade in loose waves down my back.

The dress itself was a masterpiece, its flowing skirt cascading like a waterfall. Delicate off-the-shoulder sleeves resembled falling leaves, and the bodice was adorned with thousands of tiny beads that shimmered and reflected the light against my skin. The overall effect was nothing short of breathtaking.

"You look like a true queen," Thalion remarked, his eyes filled with admiration as he gazed at me in the mirror.

I couldn't help but smile in response to his compliment. "I feel like one," I admitted softly.

"Now, for the finishing touch," Thalion said, reaching

for one of the crowns that Amris held. He placed it on my head with delicate care, the cool metal resting gently against my brow. "There, perfect."

I turned to face him, my eyes brimming with gratitude. "Thank you, Thalion, for everything," I said, my voice filled with emotion.

"You're welcome. Now go and get married," he teased, his laughter filling the room. "But remember, I'm next." He winked at me again as he left the room.

Taking a deep breath, I smoothed out my dress and tried to steel my growing nerves. Amris extended her arm, offering me her support.

"Are you ready, Your Majesty?" Amris asked, her eyes filled with genuine warmth.

"Ready," I said, a smile gracing my lips.

Joeline opened the door, and together, we stepped out into the hallway. There, waiting for us, were Aerion and Wren, along with Thalion, their expressions filled with pride and excitement.

Aerion's gaze locked onto me and he gave me a rare smile. "You look stunning, Vale," he said, his voice warm and encouraging.

"Thank you," I replied, feeling a surge of confidence and joy.

"Kaelan's waiting for you," Wren added, a wide grin adorning his face.

"Let's not keep him waiting, then," I said, excitement and nervousness coursing through me.

Thalion's voice echoed from behind us, offering his well wishes. "Good luck."

I took Wren's arm as we left Aerion and Thalion behind. Together, we made our way outside to the courtyard. The atmosphere was filled with anticipation, and my heart beat faster as the moment approached.

"Nervous?" Wren asked, his voice gentle and reassuring.

"A little," I admitted, my gaze fixed on the path ahead.

"Don't be," he said, a warm smile playing on his lips. "You'll be fine once you see Kaelan. I helped him get ready myself. He's nervous as hell," he added, chuckling.

A small laugh escaped my lips. "That does make me feel better, thank you," I said, looking up at Wren.

As we reached the courtyard, I took a deep breath, the crisp air filling my lungs. The sky was clear and blue, and a gentle breeze rustled the leaves, making it a perfect day for a wedding.

"So where are we going?" I asked, curiosity tingling within me. The location had been shrouded in secrecy and I couldn't help but wonder what awaited me.

"You'll see," Wren replied with a mischievous glint in his eye. "Just call Nyxen and I'll give him the directions."

I summoned Nyxen, and he stepped out of the shadows gracefully. "Nyxen, could you please take us to Kaelan?" I requested. "Wren will guide us."

"*Of course, Vale,*" Nyxen responded, his voice echoing within my mind.

Wren leaned down and whispered instructions to Nyxen, who listened attentively, his eyes focused on Wren's every word.

"You ready?" Wren asked, a playful grin dancing on his lips.

"As ready as I'll ever be," I answered, returning his smile nervously.

"Let's go, then," Wren said. Nyxen's shadows wrapped around us, and we were whisked away instantly.

We emerged on the other side before a portal, its misty surface shimmering in the warm sunlight.

"So, we're going to the mortal realm?" I asked, my gaze fixed on the portal.

"Seems that way," Wren replied, winking at me. I took a tentative step forward and crossed the portal's threshold, with Wren closely following behind.

On the other side, Nyxen transported us once more. When we materialized again, we found ourselves in front of a familiar house.

I stood there, gazing at the transformed garden outside Kaelan's house, my eyes wide with wonder. The gardens had undergone a magical makeover, and a picturesque archway stood gracefully near the old, weathered two-person swing that Kaelan and I had shared countless moments on. It felt like a lifetime ago when we had swung together under that tree.

The garden was adorned with white and gold streamers, fluttering gently in the breeze, casting an enchanting aura over the entire scene.

"Who did all this?" I marveled, my heart warmed by the effort that had gone into creating this beautiful setting.

Wren grinned at my awe, his eyes sparkling with excitement. "It's not much, but we all worked together to make it special. Come on, I've been given instructions to bring you in through the side door so no one sees you."

Following Wren's lead, we entered the house, which was also adorned with decorations, transforming it into a place of celebration. We navigated through the kitchen and made our way toward the front door. Memories of the last time I had seen this door flashed through my mind, back when Aerion had dramatically knocked it off its hinges.

"Stay here. I'll come back to get you shortly. I'm going

to tell everyone you've arrived," Wren told me, his voice eager.

I nodded, but curiosity got the better of me, and I couldn't help but ask, "Wait, who is here?"

Wren's smile widened, and he seemed to relish the element of surprise. "Just a few people," he replied cryptically before turning away and disappearing into the house, leaving me to wonder about the unexpected gathering that awaited me.

My heart raced as I stood just inside the house, taking a few moments to breathe and collect myself before the ceremony began. I was a bundle of nerves and excitement all at once. Each heartbeat felt like a drumbeat of anticipation.

About ten minutes later, the door swung open, and Wren stood there, his eyes alight with excitement.

"Ready?" he asked.

I returned his smile, meeting his gaze steadily though my heart was fluttering within me. "More than ready," I replied with conviction. Wren held out his arm for me and I slipped my hand into the crook of his elbow, feeling reassured by his steadying presence.

THIRTY-EIGHT

As we stepped outside, the sweet tones of a violin floated through the air. I looked toward the beautiful sound and was surprised to see Griffin standing off to the side, his bow dancing gracefully across the strings as he played a soft, melodic tune to accompany our procession. Our eyes met briefly, and I gave him a grateful smile, to which he smiled slightly and nodded in return.

Up ahead through the trees, I caught my first glimpse of the ceremony space that had been so carefully prepared. My friends and loved ones had gathered, turning with smiles and looks of welcome to watch our approach.

Harker, Venna, and Aisling beamed at me as I passed, and I was heartened to see the rest of my new coven had also come – Ava, Calliope, Sam, Harlow, and Archer were all present, standing in a semicircle facing the archway. But it was the figure standing at the center that stole my breath away.

There was Kaelan, looking impossibly handsome in a sleek black suit with silver details that made his deep brown eyes shine all the brighter. The matching silver crown shown gloriously in his black hair. The love and pride radiating from his gaze as he beheld me was enough to weaken my knees, and it was all my willpower that kept me walking steadily beside Wren rather than breaking into a run right into his arms.

Everyone around me smiled and nodded as I continued my approach, but I was focused solely on Kaelan. When I finally reached him, he took my hand from Wren with the utmost reverence, his eyes never leaving mine.

"Vale," he breathed, his voice filled with awe, "You look more beautiful than I could have ever imagined."

Lost in his eyes, I could barely manage a reply – "So do you" – before Wren smoothly drew our attention to begin the ceremony. My hand trembled slightly in Kaelan's grasp, but feeling his fingers give mine a reassuring squeeze, I knew that this was where I was meant to be.

Wren's warm and inviting voice filled the air as he cleared his throat once more, capturing the attention of the gathered crowd.

"Dear friends," he began, his words laced with warmth, "we have gathered here today to witness the union of two souls as they embark on a journey of love and partnership. Kaelan and Vale have chosen to express their love through personal vows, words that come from the depths of their hearts. Kaelan, you may begin."

Kaelan turned to face me, his eyes shimmering with unspoken emotions. With a deep breath, he began to speak, his voice carrying a rich timbre that resonated with sincerity.

"Vale," he started, his words measured, "from the moment I met you, something shifted, and I knew my world would never be the same. You brought light to the darkest corners of my heart. You accepted me wholly for who I am and taught me how to love again. Every day together has been a gift to walk by your side, support you, make you smile, and experience this miracle of life alongside my best friend."

He paused to brush a gentle thumb along my knuckles, gathering his thoughts before continuing in a voice cracking with emotion. "You are my anchor in the storm, my compass when I'm lost, and the warmth in the coldest of nights. With you, I have found a love that is pure and unwavering."

Kaelan's voice grew softer as he continued, his eyes never leaving mine. "You challenge me to be a better man, to strive for greatness, and to cherish each moment we share. And I promise to do just that. I promise to stand by your side through every trial and triumph, to support you in your dreams and passions, and to love you unconditionally. As we stand here today, surrounded by those who love and care for us, I vow to be your confidant, your partner, and your refuge in times of need. I promise to be the shoulder you lean on, the hand you hold, and the love you can always count on. You are my heart, my home, my destiny fulfilled. I am yours, now and always if you will have me as your husband."

A lone tear slid down my cheek at Kaelan's tender words as I gazed at him, overwhelmed by the depth of feeling he had so beautifully laid bare for me.

Wren's gaze shifted from Kaelan to me, his eyes gleaming. He extended a silent invitation, a gentle encouragement to share the vows that resided deep within my heart.

Taking a shaky breath, I gazed at Kaelan, my heart swelling with adoration as I took in the earnestness of his expression, the tenderness of his touch. My words tumbled forth, spilling from my lips with an aching honesty.

"Kaelan," I started, my voice steady despite the racing of my heart, "when I first met you, I couldn't have imagined the incredible journey we would embark on together."

My throat tightened slightly while Kaelan's thumbs gently caressed my knuckles, his steadfast support giving me the courage to lay my heart bare.

"With you, I found a love that transcends time and circumstance. You've taught me that it's okay to be exactly who I am - powerful yet gentle, fierce yet tender. I promise to stand by your side always, through joy and sorrow, to be your haven of comfort and care. Where you go, I will follow, for my place is at your side for as long as you will have me, my sentinel, my heart, my beloved."

Releasing a ragged breath, I smiled through my tears and finished simply with, "You are my home, Kaelan. I give you my life, my love, my magic - all that I am, freely and joyously yours."

Kaelan's eyes glistened with tears, and I reached up and wiped one away that had slid down his cheek.

"Now for the binding," Wren said, his voice warm and filled with reverence.

Kaelan gently released my hand and stepped forward, his eyes never leaving mine. He reached out to take the cord that Wren was holding, a symbol of our connection and unity. With a steady hand and a sense of purpose, he began to wind the cord around our hands, starting at our wrists and spiraling it upward until our palms were pressed firmly against each other.

As the cord encircled our hands, I felt a profound sense of connection and commitment. The symbol of our binding was a tangible reminder of the vows we had just exchanged, and the gravity of the moment hung in the air like a sweet, unspoken promise.

Wren's voice carried through the garden, the words of the binding ceremony weaving their magic around us. "Do you, Kaelan, bind yourself to Vale through all of the trials that may arise? Do you promise to love, honor, and cherish her as your equal, partner, and spouse for all the days of your lives?"

"I do," he vowed without hesitation.

Wren turned his gaze toward me, his eyes kind. "And do you, Vale, bind yourself to Kaelan through all of the trials that may arise? Do you promise to love, honor, and cherish him as your equal, partner, and spouse for all the days of your lives?"

"I do," I breathed, unable to tear my eyes away from Kaelan's, knowing that this binding was sealing our love and partnership in a way that felt both ancient and timeless.

"Then, by the power vested in me," Wren continued, his voice resounding with finality, "I pronounce you bound, body and soul, until the end of time. You may now seal your vows with a kiss."

Kaelan stepped forward, his hands cradling my face with a tenderness that made my heart swell with love. His lips met mine in a soft, lingering kiss, sealing our promises with a touch that felt like a promise of forever. At that moment, the world around us disappeared, and it was just the two of us, lost in the warmth and depth of our connection.

As our lips parted, I leaned my forehead against Kaelan's, feeling the love and joy radiating from him through our bond. The soft sound of clapping and cheering from our friends and loved ones brought us back to the present, and I couldn't help but smile as I saw tears of happiness in some of their eyes.

"I present to you, Kaelan and Vale, husband and wife, joined in the most sacred of bonds. Congratulations!" Wren's voice boomed with joy, his words echoing throughout the garden.

Kaelan grinned at me, his eyes shining with love and happiness as he took my hand and kissed it. "Shall we?" he whispered, his gaze inviting me to join him in celebrating our new journey together.

"Let's go," I replied, laughter bubbling up from deep within my heart.

Hand in hand, we received their celebrating hugs and well wishes, my heart so full it threatened to burst with joy forever at Kaelan's side, as it was always meant to be from that very first phrase - "I do."

THIRTY-NINE

The celebration back at the palace was a small but grand affair, and the ballroom was adorned with opulent decorations that added an air of regality to the occasion. Thalion and Aerion, both beaming at me with pride, joined in the festivities wholeheartedly. They clasped Kaelan's hand, offering their blessings, their approval of our union evident in their warm smiles and well wishes.

The wedding party was a sight to behold, with joyous music filling the air and delicious food. Laughter echoed throughout the ballroom as guests took to the dance floor, twirling and spinning in celebration. The night was a blur of shared moments, with friends and loved ones coming together to celebrate our love.

As the evening gradually wound down, Kaelan pulled me aside and into a shadowy corner. "Have I told you how stunning you are?" he whispered, his breath a warm caress against my skin.

"Only about a dozen times today," I replied playfully, a teasing lilt in my voice.

He smiled, a genuine, heartwarming expression that reached his eyes. His hands came to rest lightly on my hips, a touch that felt both possessive and tender. "Then I suppose I'll have to make it another dozen," he murmured, his voice low and intimate. Leaning in closer, his lips brushed against mine, a fleeting contact that promised more.

"What do you think about leaving early?" he asked, a mischievous grin playing on his lips.

I laughed softly, the sound echoing in the space between us. "What, and miss out on the rest of the party?"

"I'm sure Thalion and Aerion would understand," he said, his gaze intense as it roamed over my face, pausing on my lips. There was an unspoken promise in his eyes, a hint of the passion that lay beneath his calm exterior.

"Fine, but only because you're so persuasive," I conceded, feeling the corners of my mouth lift into a smile.

We slipped away quietly, our departure unnoticed amidst the din of the party. The corridor was dimly lit, providing us with a sense of seclusion. We hadn't gone far when Kaelan suddenly pushed me up against the wall, his body pressing close to mine. His hands roamed over me, his fingers weaving through my hair, pulling me into a deep, passionate kiss. The taste of wine lingered on his lips, sweet and intoxicating.

I gasped as his tongue explored my mouth, a surge of desire coursing through me. His hand slid under my skirt, his fingertips tracing the curve of my hip before moving higher. I moaned softly as he found the most sensitive part of me, the building heat making my head spin.

"Kaelan, what if someone sees us?" I managed to whisper, my mind clouded with lust.

"Let them," he breathed against my neck, his lips

grazing my skin. "I want them to see how beautiful you are when you come undone."

His fingers moved deftly, pushing aside my underwear. He caressed me, sending waves of pleasure through my body. I clung to him, my fingers digging into his shoulders as he pushed a finger into me.

A low groan escaped his lips, the sound almost animalistic in its intensity. I closed my eyes, letting myself get lost in the sensation. His thumb rubbed against my clit, sending a shudder through me. His other hand pulled down the strap of my dress, exposing the swell of my breast. His lips trailed a path of fire across my skin, leaving a burning desire in their wake.

My breaths were shallow, quick gasps as he moved his finger inside me, the rhythm relentless. I was already close, so close to losing myself completely.

Then, just as I was about to tip over into ecstasy, he stopped. My eyes flew open, meeting his. "What are you doing?" I asked.

"Shhh," he said, placing his hand over my mouth as his shadows enveloped us, providing a cloak of darkness in the already dim corridor. Two Fae appeared, their voices a muted hum as they approached.

Kaelan's finger resumed its movement, a sudden, deep thrust that made me catch my breath. The Fae were drawing nearer, their presence adding a thrill to the dangerous game we were playing.

"Don't make a sound, little witch. Or those Fae might find their future queen in a compromising position," he whispered, his voice a threat and a promise.

I bit my lip, fighting to stay silent as he drove me towards ecstasy, the danger of being discovered only heightened the thrill.

The Fae were drawing closer now, their footsteps echoing through the corridor. I could start to make out their conversation, the words becoming clearer with each step they took. Meanwhile, Kaelan, undeterred by our precarious situation, slipped another finger inside of me, his other hand still firmly pressed against my mouth. A muffled moan escaped my lips, the vibrations of it caught in his palm.

"What was that?" one of the Fae said, looking around.

"What was what?" his companion replied.

"I thought I heard something," he said, pausing. They scanned the corridor with a look of curiosity, their gaze flitting across the shadows where Kaelan and I were hidden.

Kaelan's fingers moved expertly inside of me, hitting that perfect spot that made my entire body shudder. The tension within me was building, spiraling towards an inevitable release, every touch pushing me closer to the edge.

"Are you going to come, little witch?" Kaelan's voice was a husky whisper low enough that only I could hear, a tantalizing promise that vibrated against my ear. His breath was hot on my skin, his gaze intense and challenging. Another low moan rumbled in my throat as his words washed over me.

"There it is again," the same Fae said, taking a few cautious steps closer. My heart pounded in my chest, the excitement of the risk mingling with the rising pleasure.

Kaelan's eyes held mine, dark and commanding, silently urging me to let go. I bit my lip hard, trying to stifle the sounds of my ecstasy as I teetered on the precipice of climax.

The Fae were now only a few feet away, close enough that I could see the confusion etched on their faces. "Is there someone there?" one called out, their voice tinged with suspicion and concern.

At that moment, Kaelan growled low in my ear, "Come for me," and the command in his voice sent me spiraling over the edge. My body shuddered uncontrollably, waves of intense pleasure crashing over me. I bit down on Kaelan's hand to suppress any sound, my eyes locked with his.

The Fae lingered, sensing something amiss, but the shadows created by Kaelan's magic kept us concealed. As the aftershocks of my orgasm rippled through me, Kaelan held his hand firmly over my mouth, muffling my ragged breaths.

Finally, the Fae moved on, leaving the corridor. I sagged against Kaelan, spent and breathless, as he wrapped his arms around me in a protective embrace.

"That was dangerous," I whispered, the adrenaline still coursing through me.

"I know," he murmured back, his voice deep and hungry.

"And exhilarating," I added, the delight of our near-discovery still sending shivers down my spine.

"We should do it again sometime," Kaelan suggested, his lips grazing my ear.

I smiled, satisfaction lighting up my face. "Definitely."

"Come on, I have a surprise to show you," he said as he fixed my dress, a playful glint in his eyes that hinted at the mischief he had in store. "It's not far from here."

Intrigued, I placed my hand in his, the warmth of his grip reassuring as we navigated the corridors. The silence of the castle magnified the echo of our footsteps, a steady rhythm in the quiet of the night. As we walked, he would occasionally pause, his hands exploring the contours of my body with a tantalizing touch or suddenly pulling me into a kiss so deep and passionate it left me dizzy with desire.

By the time we reached a large, ornate wooden door, my heart was pounding in my chest, not just from the anticipation of his surprise but also from the heady effect of his attention. "Where are we?" I asked curiously, my voice barely more than a hushed whisper.

"You'll see," he replied, a trace of excitement in his tone. He pushed open the door, ushering me into a new mystery.

We stepped into a short, stone hallway, dimly lit by the flickering light of a lone torch mounted on the wall. The shadows danced along the walls as Kaelan closed the door behind us, the sound of the lock clicking into place echoing in the small space. He took my hand once more and guided me down the hallway.

The hallway opened up into a breathtaking stone bathing chamber. My eyes widened at the sight of the vast pool in the center of the room. It was wide and deep, filled with clear, blue water from which steam gently rose, creating a mystical veil of fog that hung in the air. The water shimmered under the dim light, inviting and serene.

"I found this place boarded up and forgotten," Kaelan explained, his arms wrapping around my waist from behind, pulling me back against him. His lips found the nape of my neck, planting a soft kiss there. "I had the servants clean it out and get it working again over the past week. It seemed like the perfect opportunity to give it a try."

"How do you always manage to think of everything? It's incredible," I marveled, turning in his arms to face him. My fingers wandered into his silky, dark hair, playing with the strands.

"Well, I wanted this night to be special," he murmured,

his lips tracing a path along my jawline and down the curve of my neck.

"And you have, I assure you," I breathed out, closing my eyes to savor the sensation of his lips against my skin, the warmth of his breath sending shivers down my spine.

His fingers trailed down my arm, leaving a trail of goosebumps in their wake. His hands moved with purpose, sliding under my dress, skimming over my thighs, then settling on my hips. The fabric of my dress was pushed up slowly, his hands exploring the warm skin beneath.

"I want to see you, all of you," Kaelan whispered, his voice a soft echo in the vast chamber. His fingers deftly worked at the laces of my dress, skillfully untying each knot that held the garment in place. There was a tenderness in his touch, a reverence that made my heart flutter.

I stepped back from him, raising my arms gracefully above my head. With a fluid motion, I allowed the dress to slide down my body and pool at my feet. The cool air of the chamber caressed my skin, raising goosebumps along my arms and legs. I could feel my nipples harden in response to the chill, a stark contrast to the warmth emanating from Kaelan's intense gaze.

"Beautiful," he murmured, his eyes roaming over me with undisguised admiration and desire. His voice was low, filled with awe as if he were beholding a priceless work of art.

"Your turn," I said, a playful edge to my voice as I reached for the buttons on his shirt. My fingers worked nimbly, undoing each one and revealing the expanse of his chest beneath.

He shrugged off his shirt with a fluid motion, letting it fall to the floor in a forgotten heap. His pants followed suit, and in a moment, he stood before me in all his glory. The sight of him, so strong and confident, sent heat curling low in my belly.

Closing the distance between us, he pulled me into his arms, one hand cradling the back of my neck and threading through my hair, the other encircling my waist. His lips found mine in a kiss that was hungry and demanding, a kiss that consumed all thought and reason.

When we finally broke apart, both of us were breathless, our chests heaving in unison. He took my hand gently, leading me to the edge of the pool. Stepping into the water, he extended his other hand to me, an invitation I eagerly accepted. I stepped into the pool, the warm water enveloping me in a comforting embrace.

Kaelan pulled me close again, his hands resting on the small of my back. He kissed me once more, this time with a slow, deliberate intent, as if savoring each sensation, each moment. His lips then left mine, trailing a path of kisses along my neck and collarbone, each touch sending ripples of pleasure through me.

"I can't believe you're mine," he whispered against my skin, his hands wandering lower, caressing the curve of my backside and down my thighs. He lifted me effortlessly, a testament to his strength, as I wrapped my legs around his waist, the heat of his body melding with mine.

He carried me to the side of the pool, setting me down on the cool stone ledge. The contrast between the warm water and the stone sent a thrill through me.

"I want to taste you," he said, his breath warm against the sensitive skin of my inner thigh. His words were laced with desire, a promise that sent a surge of anticipation through my veins.

"Yes," I breathed out, surrendering to the desire that

pooled within me. His lips kissed a trail down my thigh, his fingers caressing the smooth skin, each touch a spark.

"You know, there is plenty more my shadows are useful for," he whispered, his voice low and teasing. He placed another delicate kiss on the inside of my thigh.

"What do you mean?" I asked. As I spoke, he flashed me a mischievous grin, and I watched, fascinated, as shadowy tendrils began to emerge from him. They moved like living things, writhing slowly and sensuously up my body. The shadows caressed my skin as they climbed, leaving a trail of goosebumps in their wake.

The sensation was indescribable. It was as if a thousand feather-light fingers were touching me, exploring every inch of my skin. The shadows snaked around my body, their touch both ethereal and intimate. When they reached my nipple, I shivered involuntarily as they traced a slow, tantalizing circle around the sensitive, pebbled flesh.

The shadows continued their journey downwards, following the natural curves and contours of my body, lingering on every sensitive spot. Kaelan's lips followed suit, planting soft kisses on my legs as the shadows played over my skin. When he finally reached the apex of my thighs, I moaned aloud, the dual sensations of his mouth and the shadows driving me to the brink of madness.

The shadowy tendrils teased me, exploring and caressing. Kaelan looked up at me, his eyes gleaming with wicked delight. "Do you like that?" he asked, his voice thick with desire.

"Oh, gods, yes," I managed to gasp out, the pleasure so intense it was almost overwhelming.

He leaned down, his tongue joining the dance of the shadows. I gasped as he traced a long, slow line up the center of me, his tongue skilled and knowing. He groaned, the sound muffled against my skin. "You taste like heaven," he murmured, his words vibrating against me.

My head fell back, my eyes closing as I surrendered to the sensations. His tongue worked in perfect harmony with the caresses of the shadows, lapping and sucking with a rhythm that sent waves of ecstasy through my body.

The tendrils wound around my breasts, squeezing gently, prompting me to arch my back in a silent plea for more. "Gods, you're so wet," he murmured against me, his fingers slipping inside of me with ease.

"For you, Kaelan," I breathed out, the words slipping from my lips effortlessly, a confession of the desire he had awakened within me.

His mouth was on me with a fervent intensity, hot and demanding, stoking the fire within me. I felt the familiar coil of tension tightening in my core, building steadily as I teetered on the brink of a precipice, a sensation akin to standing at the edge of a vast, all-consuming abyss.

My fingers clutched desperately at the edges of the pool, seeking anchorage against the onslaught of pleasure. The stone beneath my hands was cool and smooth, my knuckles white as I gripped it. His fingers thrust into me with a rhythm both deep and fast, a relentless pursuit of my pleasure.

Simultaneously, the shadowy threads that had become an extension of his will moved upwards, caressing the sensitive skin of my neck and chest. Their touch was intoxicating, igniting every nerve ending they encountered.

A loud, uninhibited moan escaped my lips, echoing off the chamber walls as waves of pleasure crashed over me. Kaelan, sensing my approaching climax, removed his fingers, allowing the shadowy tendrils to recede momentarily. I opened my eyes, heavy with desire, and looked down at him with expectancy.

As our eyes met, the shadows once again began their sensuous ascent, creeping back up my legs, teasing at my entrance with a promise. "Are you ready for more, Vale?" Kaelan asked, his voice a husky growl.

"Yes," I whispered, my voice laden with need and longing.

Responding to his command, the tendrils began to slowly enter me, stretching and filling me in a dance of shadows and desire. At the same time, Kaelan's mouth returned to its delicious task, his tongue expertly licking and sucking. I threw my head back, eyes closed, completely surrendering to the new and overwhelming sensations.

Rocking my hips against his mouth, my fingers tangled in his hair, anchoring myself to reality as I once again approached the edge of oblivion. "Don't stop," I moaned, the words spilling from me in a desperate plea.

The shadows moved rhythmically inside me, caressing and teasing, while his mouth was relentless in its pursuit of my pleasure. It was an exquisite torture, a dance of shadows and flesh, and it was all too much. I couldn't hold back any longer. I cried out, my entire body tensing in a rapturous release as wave after wave of ecstasy washed over me.

As I slowly came down from the high, the shadows retreated, and Kaelan pulled me back into the warm embrace of the water. His eyes burned with dark desire, and I could feel his arousal press against me, hard and ready. "I need you," he rasped, his voice raw with need.

I responded without hesitation as he lifted me up, wrapping my legs around his waist and sinking down onto him. The sensation of him filling me completely sent another jolt of pleasure through me.

Kaelan groaned deeply, a primal sound that reverberated through me. His hands, strong and insistent, gripped my hips, pulling me even closer to him. The connection was electric.

"Fuck, you feel so good," he murmured against my skin, his lips seeking mine in a passionate, all-consuming kiss. At that moment, I was lost to everything but him – the sensation of him filling me, the taste of his mouth, the intoxicating scent of his skin. Everything about him enveloped me, drawing me deeper.

With each rhythmic thrust, I moved in harmony with him, our bodies syncing in a dance as old as time. The water around us splashed and rippled with our movements, the sound echoing off the stone walls.

"Vale," he breathed, his voice a low, hoarse whisper.

"Yes, Kaelan," I urged him, my voice a sultry echo of his own. I was utterly lost in the moment, in the sensation, in him.

He buried his face in the crook of my neck, his breaths coming in short, ragged gasps against my skin. I could feel the tension in his muscles, the build-up of pleasure within him. His thrusts became harder, deeper, each one a delicious mix of pain and pleasure. His fingers dug into my hips, a sweet agony that only heightened the sensation.

Suddenly, he pulled out and gently set me down in the water. He turned me so my back was to him, and the shadows, his dark, sentient extensions, began to slide up my arms. They coiled around my wrists, tightening gently, pulling my arms forward in a soft yet firm hold. Simultaneously, threads wrapped around my waist and thighs, lifting my backside slightly in the water. I was bound, but the shadowy restraints allowed for a slight wriggle, a tease of freedom within the confines of his control. This was new and entirely unexpected, but I couldn't deny it delighted me.

"Are you comfortable?" Kaelan's voice was hot against my ear, a whisper that sent a new wave of anticipation coursing through me.

"Yes," I answered, my voice low and husky, and I was. Not long ago, I might have panicked in these restraints, but every part of me knew that I was safe with Kaelan. Safe with my dark prince who would never hurt me or push me too far.

He kissed the back of my neck, his lips tracing a fiery path down my spine. His hands caressed my backside, his fingers spreading me slightly as he positioned himself at my entrance. I felt him slide into my ass, slow and deliberate, the sensation sending a sharp intake of breath from my lips.

"Gods, you're perfect," he murmured, his voice strained. He began to move, initially slow, then gradually increasing in pace. His hands gripped my hips firmly, guiding me in rhythm with his movements. The water around us sloshed and churned, a turbulent mirror to our passionate dance.

As he moved within me, the shadows continued their sensual exploration, now moving across my breasts. They caressed and squeezed the soft flesh, each touch sending ripples of pleasure through my body. I was utterly at his mercy, lost in the intensity of the moment, surrendering to the overwhelming pleasure he elicited from me.

As Kaelan's movements intensified, each thrust became deeper, more urgent, stirring a storm of sensation within me. His breath was hot against my skin, a stark contrast to the cool, damp air of the chamber. The pleasure inside me was like a rising tide, building with each deliberate stroke, threatening to overflow.

Overwhelmed by the intensity, I found myself moaning, "Fuck me," the words spilling from my lips in a raw, desperate plea.

Kaelan responded with a deep, guttural groan, his hands tightening their grip on my hips, anchoring me to him. Then, in a sudden, deliberate move, he reached up to grasp my neck, gently pulling my head to the side to expose the vulnerable column of my throat. I shivered as he ran his tongue along the length of it, the sensation of his wet, warm tongue against my skin sending shivers down my spine. He then began to suck on the soft flesh there, sending waves of pleasure radiating through me.

In the dim, flickering light of the chamber, I caught a glimpse of his fangs before he bit down gently on my neck. The sensation was sharp, unexpected, and thrilling. At that exact moment, his shadows surged inside me, matching the rhythm of his body. I let out a loud gasp of pleasure. It was as if I were being consumed by him.

My climax hit me like a bolt of lightning, tearing through me with an intensity that left me breathless. I cried out and threw my head back, my voice loud in the quiet chamber, the sound echoing off the stone walls as waves of pleasure coursed through my body.

Kaelan buried himself deep inside me, his own release overtaking him in a powerful wave of ecstasy. His body shuddered against mine, his breath ragged.

Exhausted, we remained in the water, the gentle lapping of the waves against our skin a soothing backdrop as we caught our breath. Gently, Kaelan pulled out of me, and the shadowy tendrils that had bound me loosened their grip, receding back into the shadows they came from.

Kaelan then gathered me into his arms, holding me close against his chest. His hands gently stroked my hair, a comforting gesture as we rested in the aftermath of our passionate encounter.

"I have something for you," Kaelan whispered, his voice a gentle murmur that broke the comfortable silence that had settled between us.

"Another surprise, after all that?" I asked, a playful smile touching my lips.

"I wanted to give it to you when we were alone, away from the eyes of the others." There was a meaningful look in his eyes, one that spoke of the importance of this moment.

With that, he reached into the pocket of his pants, which were pooled on the floor beside us, and pulled out a small box. He extended it towards me with a gesture that was both tentative and expectant.

I took the box from him, noting its unexpected weight in my hands. With a growing sense of excitement, I carefully opened it, and a gasp escaped my lips. Nestled inside was a necklace of exquisite craftsmanship. It was made of a silvery metal that shimmered even in the dim light of the bathing chamber. The pendant was shaped like a dragon, its wings outstretched in majestic flight, and its eyes were set with tiny stones that glimmered with life. A blood-red jewel was nestled at the dragon's heart, deep and vibrant. The craftsmanship was so intricate, the wings so lifelike, they bore an uncanny resemblance to Kaelan's own.

"Kaelan, it's beautiful," I whispered, my fingers delicately tracing over the detailed design of the dragon, feeling the cool metal and the smooth surface of the gemstone.

"Here, let me put it on you," he offered, taking the necklace from the box. He gently unclasped it and draped it around my neck, his fingers deftly securing it in place. The metal felt cool against my skin, and as the gemstone settled against my chest, it felt oddly warm, pulsating like a living thing.

"I had it made for you," he said, his voice laden with emotion, a depth of feeling that resonated in each word.

"Thank you, Kaelan. I love it," I said, my heart swelling. I leaned up to kiss him, wanting to convey my feelings through the gesture.

As our lips met, I felt the gemstone between us, its warmth growing, pulsating in a rhythm that mimicked a heartbeat. I ran a finger across it, half wondering if it was my imagination or if the pendant truly possessed a life of its own.

"It's magic," Kaelan confirmed, noticing my awed expression. "It's imbued with Fae enchantments to pulse with the beating of my heart; it contains some of my blood to make it work."

His words left me speechless, the realization of the depth of his gift dawning on me. This wasn't just a piece of jewelry but a connection, a tangible link to Kaelan himself.

"You have no idea how happy you've made me, Vale. How happy you've made all of us," he said, his voice warm with sincerity.

He kissed me again, and this time, the kiss was soft and gentle, a perfect contrast to the passion that had consumed us earlier. I was sure now; the pulse of the gem was real. I could feel it, a steady rhythm that matched Kaelan's heart, both beating in unison.

FORTY

Wren strode purposefully through the vast, opulent halls of the palace, his brow furrowed in concern. He had been searching for Aisling for what felt like an eternity, and his worry only grew with each empty room he checked. The young girl had wandered off from Venna earlier, and they hadn't seen her since.

The palace was a labyrinth of grand chambers and winding corridors, a sprawling architectural masterpiece that was both awe-inspiring and intimidating. It was a place where one could easily get lost, and Aisling's disappearance had him on edge.

Ducking his head into yet another empty room, Wren's sharp eyes scanned the elegant furnishings and decor, but there was no sign of Aisling. He sighed in frustration, his footsteps echoing in the empty chamber as he retreated back into the corridor.

As he continued his search, he couldn't help but wonder how such a massive castle could house so many secrets and hidden corners. Each room seemed like a universe of its own, and he felt like a lost traveler in a foreign land.

As he pressed onward, he couldn't help but worry about what might have happened to her in this sprawling maze of corridors and chambers. Was she alone, scared, and lost? Was she perhaps even in danger? Wren shook his head, pushing aside his dark thoughts.

Finally, after what felt like an eternity of anxious wandering, Wren stumbled upon a small chamber hidden in a remote corner of the palace. The door stood slightly ajar, and a sliver of soft candlelight spilled out into the corridor.

Hesitating for only a moment, Wren cautiously pushed the door open, revealing a sight that filled him with immense relief. There, nestled amidst a heap of plush cushions and cozy blankets, lay Aisling. She resembled a slumbering kitten, her slight form curled up in peaceful repose.

The tension that had been gripping Wren's chest began to loosen, replaced by a profound sense of gratitude and affection. A soft smile graced his lips as he approached the sleeping child. Gently, he reached out and gave her a tender shake, his voice a gentle, soothing whisper.

"Aisling," he murmured.

The girl stirred, her eyes fluttering open as she blinked up at him, her gaze still heavy with sleep.

"Wren?" she mumbled, her voice laced with drowsiness as she rubbed her eyes.

"Come on, sleepyhead," Wren said, chuckling softly. "Let's get you back to Venna."

"Okay," she mumbled, stretching her small arms and yawning.

Wren stood up, extending his hand toward her. She took it with a tiny, trusting grip, and he gently helped her to her feet. Together, they ventured out of the quiet chamber, embarking on the journey back through the palace's seem-ingly endless halls.

As they walked, Wren couldn't help but reflect on the remarkable impact that Aisling had had on his life. Her presence had brought a radiant warmth and an unexpected sense of purpose that had been absent before. His heart swelled with deep affection for the girl, and he found comfort in the way she leaned on him for support, still groggy from her slumber.

While Wren had never envisioned himself as a father figure, the connection he had developed with Aisling was undeniable. She had effortlessly captured his heart, and he was determined to do whatever it took to ensure her safety and happiness.

Eventually, they reached the entrance to Venna's quar-ters, and Wren gently knocked on the door. Within moments, it swung open, revealing Venna's face, her expression one of concern and relief.

"Aisling!" Venna exclaimed, her voice filled with worry and joy as she enveloped the girl in a tight, protective embrace.

"I found her asleep in an empty chamber," Wren explained.

"Thank the gods," Venna sighed. "I've been worried sick about her."

"I'm hungry," Aisling piped up, her voice ringing with childlike innocence, as they stood at the threshold of Venna's quarters. Her statement, though predictable, elicited a knowing chuckle from Wren.

"Imagine that," Wren replied, his tone light and affec-tionate, a hint of amusement in his eyes. "Dinner with the pack is soon, but I'm sure Venna has a few apples or some cheese for you."

Venna's warm smile conveyed understanding and patience as she welcomed them inside. "Come in," she said warmly. "I have some leftover pastries from this morning."

Aisling's eyes practically sparkled with delight at the prospect of pastries, and she clapped her hands in excitement before darting inside, leaving Wren and Venna to exchange a brief glance in the doorway.

"What are we going to do with her?" Venna asked, her voice hushed with concern. Aisling's presence had brought an undeniable shift in their lives, one that had thrown them off balance. Yet, it was a change that had, in many ways, filled their hearts with newfound warmth.

Wren leaned in slightly, his voice equally soft as he reassured her, "We'll figure it out. In the meantime, let's just enjoy having her here."

Venna nodded, her earlier worries momentarily forgotten as a soft smile returned to her lips.

Following Venna inside, Wren gently closed the door behind him and settled down to watch as Aisling eagerly devoured the pastries, her tiny fingers dusted with crumbs.

"Why'd you run off today?" Wren asked, curiosity gleaming in his eyes as he regarded the young girl.

"The servants told me to stay out of the way while they prepared for tomorrow," Aisling explained, her words slightly muffled by her enthusiastic chewing. "So, I went off to explore."

Venna couldn't help but offer a gentle admonishment, her voice soft and maternal, "That's not safe, Aisling."

Aisling, her eyes wide and innocent, countered with a spirited defense, "But I'm fine, aren't I?"

"This time," Wren conceded, affectionately ruffling her hair. "But next time, we'll put a bell on you so we can hear where you are, like a cat."

Aisling responded to the idea with a delightful giggle, clearly undeterred by the near-miss of her earlier adventure. Her laughter was infectious, and Wren couldn't help but share a conspiratorial grin with Venna. Aisling was proving to be a force of nature, and they knew they were in for quite the journey as they navigated the world with her.

But every moment, every challenge, and every giggle from Aisling was worth it.

Once Aisling had finished her pastries, her insatiable curiosity propelled her to dart off and go play with some of the servants' children, leaving Wren and Venna alone.

"Tomorrow will be an interesting day," Wren mused, his eyes lingering on Aisling's retreating form as she scampered off to explore and play.

"Indeed," Venna agreed. "How's Vale feeling about becoming queen?"

"I think she's too busy with Kaelan right now to be too worried about it," he remarked with a hint of amusement.

Venna couldn't help but blush slightly. "Ah, yes," she replied, her voice soft and filled with understanding. "The wedding."

Wren chuckled, a warm and genuine sound that filled the room. "They're not going to be available for a while," he remarked, his eyes dancing with amusement. "They deserve some time to themselves."

"They'll come around," Venna said, her tone reassuring. "They can't ignore the rest of the world forever."

"No," Wren conceded thoughtfully. "But they can enjoy a few days of newlywed bliss."

Venna nodded and turned away, her hands absently tidying up the small space. Wren watched her for a moment, his thoughts drifting as he contemplated the complex dynamics of their pack.

"I should go," he finally announced, standing to stretch his arms out tiredly.

Venna looked up at him, her gaze softening. "You could stay," she offered, her tone gentle, her eyes carrying a hint of hopefulness.

Shock laced through him, and he hesitated for a moment, the memory of Vale's words about Venna's feelings for him suddenly resurfacing in his mind. "I'm not sure that's a good idea," he said, clearing his throat, his expression conflicted.

Venna furrowed her brow. "Why not?"

"You're my beta," Wren explained, his voice steady but firm. "It wouldn't be appropriate."

"I'm also a woman," Venna countered, her voice holding a touch of defiance. "A woman who is attracted to you."

Wren shifted uncomfortably, his thoughts racing as he grappled with the situation. "I'm flattered," he said sincerely, his gaze meeting hers. "Truly, I am. But I can't risk hurting your feelings. You're important to me, Venna. More important than I can say."

"I'm a big girl, Wren," Venna responded, stepping closer to him, her eyes fixed on his and filled with determination. "And I'm not one to back down from a challenge."

"This is not a game," he warned, his frown deepening. "I'm serious."

"So am I," Venna replied, her resolve unyielding.

Wren stood there, torn between his growing desire and his sense of duty. His heart raced, and his mind was a whirlwind of conflicting emotions. He couldn't deny his attraction to her. He knew that giving in to this temptation could have consequences for their pack, but Venna's proximity made it increasingly difficult to resist.

"I shouldn't," he said, his voice strained, taking another step backward as if physical distance could help him regain control.

Venna, however, was undeterred by his hesitation. "Why not?" she said, closing the remaining distance between them, her eyes locked onto his, a challenge in her gaze. She wanted to break through his defenses.

He gazed down at her, their faces inches apart, his hand trembling as he reached up to caress her cheek. His touch was tender, a silent admission of his own desires. "You're a beautiful woman, Venna," he whispered. "But you're my beta. It would complicate things."

Venna's determination remained unwavering as she met his gaze head-on. "And if I don't care?" she said, lifting her chin.

Wren hesitated, his thumb brushing gently across her lower lip, silently acknowledging the magnetic pull between them. "I care," he finally admitted, his voice barely more than a breath.

"Are you sure about that?" Venna questioned, her voice soft and alluring.

"Yes," Wren breathed as he leaned down and kissed her.

Their mouths met, warm and tender, as they surrendered to the powerful attraction Wren had no idea had been simmering beneath the surface. Venna eagerly returned his kiss, her arms wrapping around his neck, pulling him closer.

Wren's restraint crumbled as the kiss deepened, their tongues moving together. His hands roamed over her body, tracing the curves and contours, exploring every inch of her with a hunger that had long been suppressed.

Her fingers threaded through his hair, tugging gently, as

she pressed herself closer to him, her body molding against his.

Reluctantly, Wren broke the kiss, his chest heaving with ragged breaths. He gazed down at Venna, his dark eyes filled with desire, longing, and guilt.

"We should stop," he murmured with a heavy sigh.

Venna, her own breath coming in small pants, looked up at him with hooded eyes, her voice husky as she challenged him. "Why?"

"Because if we don't," he admitted, his grip on her hips tightening involuntarily, "I'm not going to be able to control myself."

A seductive smile played on her lips as she leaned in closer, her voice a sultry whisper. "Who says you need to?"

Wren groaned, his resistance crumbling and his mouth capturing hers once more. They surrendered to the fiery passion that had ignited between them.

"If we do this," Wren warned, his voice filled with both desire and caution, "there's no going back."

"I'm okay with that," she replied, her voice a whisper as her fingers tugged at the fabric of his shirt, desire burning in her eyes.

Unable to resist the allure of her touch, Wren gave in to his primal desires, allowing himself to be consumed by the intoxicating feelings flowing through him. His hand slid down her back, fingers tracing the contours of her supple curves until they found her backside, gripping it firmly. A deep, primal growl rumbled in his throat as she responded by grinding her hips into his.

Wren was already hard, his arousal evident as his cock strained against the confines of his pants. The undeniable chemistry between them had pushed them past the point of restraint.

Driven by raw desire, he picked her up, their mouths crashing together in a feverish kiss, and carried her with urgency to the bedroom, their hands and lips never leaving each other.

As they collapsed onto the bed, their bodies intertwined, their passion continued to blaze. "I want you, Wren," she whispered, her voice heavy with lust, fanning the flames of their desire even higher.

"You'll have me," he breathed, his hands sliding under her shirt, his touch electric as he explored the soft, bare skin beneath.

They shed their clothes with an urgency that spoke of their undeniable hunger for each other, tossing them aside as they reveled in the intoxicating sensation of each other's bare flesh pressed together.

"Gods, you're so sexy," he confessed, his voice thick with desire as his eyes roamed hungrily over every inch of her exposed form.

"Less talking, more fucking," she urged, a mischievous grin playing on her lips.

Wren responded with a knowing grin of his own, his lips trailing a path down the arch of her throat as his hands cupped her breasts. He nipped and sucked, marking her dark skin.

He wanted her desperately and he wouldn't deny it any longer. His tongue swirled around her nipple, drawing it into his mouth, where he suckled and nibbled, expertly teasing her sensitive flesh.

She gasped and moaned, her hips bucking against him in delicious response to his every touch.

He chuckled sensually and moved to her other breast, lavishing it with the same attention, determined to drive her crazy. Her nails dug into his back, leaving marks that made him growl in pleasure.

His fingers dipped between her thighs, finding her slick and ready for him, the intense arousal between them undeniable.

"Fuck," he groaned, his voice heavy with desire, as he slid two fingers into her wetness.

"Stop teasing me," she panted, her hips rocking with desperate urgency, seeking more of his touch.

He chuckled, the sound rich and sensual, his thumb expertly circling her sensitive clit as he pumped his fingers into her. Her breath hitched, and she whimpered, her eyes rolling back as her impending orgasm drew nearer with each skillful stroke of his hand.

Driven by her moans and whimpers, he moved down further on the bed, his lips and tongue trailing along her heated skin. When his mouth reached its destination, she gasped.

Her hips rose instinctively, pressing against his mouth as he pleasured her with a slow, deliberate lick.

He flicked his tongue against her swollen clit, skillfully driving her wild with desire, her moans growing louder with each passing second.

"Fuck me with your mouth, Wren," she begged, her voice hoarse with need, her fingers clutching at the sheets.

He groaned in response, his own desire mounting as he continued to lavish her with his mouth, his tongue dancing over her sensitive flesh.

He lapped at her with a hunger until she came undone beneath his touch, her body shaking as wave after wave of intense pleasure crashed over her.

Wren pulled back and licked his lips, gazing down at her as she lay panting beneath him.

"Your turn," she breathed, her eyes dark with desire, a seductive smile playing on her lips as she sat up and pushed him onto his back.

Straddling his hips with a sensual grace, she sank down onto his throbbing cock in one smooth, tantalizing motion. Her cry of pleasure echoed through the room as she took him in, and he nearly lost control just from the raw desire in her eyes.

Gripping her hips tightly, he began to thrust up into her, their bodies moving in a rhythm that sent sparks of ecstasy shooting through them both. Her hands pressed firmly against his chest, her nails biting into his skin as she surrendered to the overwhelming pleasure coursing through her.

"Venna," he groaned, his voice filled with need, his eyes locked on hers, their connection intensifying with every moment.

Driven by a surge of desire and a shared urgency, he sat up, wrapping his arms around her back, and with a deft, coordinated movement, he flipped them over while staying deeply buried inside of her.

"Yes," she gasped, her nails digging into his shoulders as he continued to thrust into her with relentless determination. The sensation of him hot and tight inside her was utterly intoxicating.

Her body responded eagerly, succumbing to the delicious tension building within her. She came again, her back arching, her breath ragged, and her cries of pleasure filling the room.

He growled in response to her pleasure, his own need reaching its peak. With each thrust, he sought deeper, harder, the urgency building until it was nearly unbearable.

"Wren," she cried, her voice trembling with ecstasy, her body quivering under his touch.

"Come with me," he commanded, his voice rough and thick with need. He couldn't hold back any longer; the intensity of their desire demanded release.

He slammed into her with an unrelenting force, again and again, until her body convulsed with the overwhelming pleasure of her climax. She screamed his name, her release tearing through her like a storm.

He followed her over the edge, his own climax crashing over him like a tidal wave, his cock pulsing. Together, they collapsed into each other's arms, breathless and sated, their bodies entwined.

"Wow," Venna breathed, her eyes fluttering closed as she basked in the lingering sensations.

Wren chuckled, his voice husky with satisfaction. "Yeah," he agreed, leaning in to kiss her softly.

They lay there for a while, catching their breath. Eventually, he gently pulled out of her and rolled to the side.

She nestled into his arms, resting her head on his shoulder, the sense of contentment washing over them like a warm embrace.

"We need to head to dinner soon," she said, breaking the tranquil silence.

"I'm aware," he grumbled, not wanting to let go of this moment of intimacy just yet.

"So, what happens now?" she asked him quietly, her voice filled with uncertainty.

He looked down at her, his fingers brushing her hair from her face. "I don't know," he admitted, his expression sincere. "I meant what I said about it being complicated."

She sighed and nodded, understanding the complexity of their situation.

"But," he added. "I don't regret it."

"Me neither," she said, smiling up at him.

He leaned down, and his lips met hers in another tender kiss.

PART
FOUR

FORTY-ONE

I stood in front of the large mirror, gazing at my reflection with awe and apprehension. The gown I wore was undeniably luxurious, its black fabric billowing gracefully around me and its pointed sleeve caps adding an elegant touch. The bodice of the dress plunged into a V-shape, revealing just enough skin to be alluring. There was no denying that it was beautiful, but I couldn't help but think it was a bit plain for such an important occasion as my coronation. I wondered why Thalion had chosen this particular gown for me. The one I tried on last week was different than the one I wore now.

My hair cascaded down my back in artful waves, a result of the meticulous attention from Kelli and Joeline. They had worked tirelessly to ensure that every strand fell perfectly into place. Armis stood back and took a good look at me, her expression carefully neutral.

"How do I look?" I asked, my voice betraying my nervousness. I wanted to appear confident and regal on this momentous day.

Amris hesitated briefly, and I worried that she, too,

might have found the dress a tad plain. "You look stunning, Your Majesty," she replied, her words filled with sincerity.

Just as I was about to thank her, a knock came on the door. Kelli hurried to open it, revealing Thalion entering the room with yet another box in his hands.

"What have you brought for me now?" I asked, a hint of amusement in my voice.

"I've brought along the most important bits of your outfit, princess," Thalion replied with a mischievous twinkle in his eye. Then, as if a thought had just occurred to him, he added, "I won't be able to call you princess much longer."

"No, you won't," I agreed, my voice trembling slightly.

Thalion crossed the room to stand beside me, taking my hand in his. "Oh, don't tell me you're nervous," he teased gently.

"Only a lot," I admitted, a small, nervous laugh escaping my lips.

Thalion opened the box he had brought with him, revealing bits and pieces of armor inside. There was a chest piece, elegant shoulder plates, and gauntlets that looked both regal and protective.

"Well, maybe these will help," Thalion said, a reassuring smile on his face. "Nothing like literal armor to help you fight through this day," he said, winking, and I couldn't agree more.

"I'll need help putting it on," I said, glancing toward Amris.

"I've got it," Thalion offered, stepping forward. He reached for the chest piece and carefully slipped it onto me. As he fastened the straps and latches, I couldn't help but admire the craftsmanship of the armor. It was surprisingly light, and its intricate design spoke of skilled artistry.

"This is incredible," I marveled, fingers tracing the elegant patterns etched onto the metal. The armor had an air of regal sophistication that made me feel a bit less nervous about the impending coronation.

"Thank you, princess," Thalion replied warmly, his hands expertly securing the chest plate in place. "The best smiths in Virelium crafted this armor. Consider it a gift from my kingdom to yours."

I was touched by his gesture, and I couldn't help but smile. "It's truly a magnificent gift, Thalion," I said sincerely, my eyes fixed on the gleaming metal. The realization of the responsibility that lay ahead weighed on me, but I felt a surge of determination.

"You will need protection, now more than ever," Thalion explained, his voice carrying a note of seriousness. "You'll be queen of a kingdom in turmoil. We will support you and help you find stability, but there will be challenges ahead."

I nodded in understanding, my mind drifting briefly to the challenges I had faced in the past. "There always are," I agreed, my voice steady and unwavering.

As Thalion secured the last pieces of the armor onto me, I felt a transformation taking place. A sense of readiness and determination gradually replaced the weight of my nerves. I would be crowned queen in a few hours, and no matter the obstacles ahead, I knew I was prepared for the challenge.

When the last piece of armor was in place, Thalion took a step back to admire his handiwork. He looked at me with eyes filled with pride and admiration. "You look perfect, Vale," he said, his voice tinged with emotion.

I turned to face him, my own eyes reflecting my gratitude. "Thank you, Thalion," I replied sincerely. "For everything."

"It has been my pleasure, Your Majesty," he responded, bowing his head and grinning at me.

I turned back to the mirror, my gaze meeting my reflection. I was no longer a princess awaiting her destiny; I was a queen, ready to take on the world. The armor was not just a symbol of protection but a representation of my strength and resolve. With my newfound confidence and the support of those who believed in me, I knew I was prepared to face whatever lay ahead.

EACH STEP forward felt like the resounding beat of a drum, each thud echoing in my ears. My heart pounded in my chest, its rhythm matching the heavy cadence of my advance. The ceremonial armor I wore, though meticulously crafted and surprisingly light, carried a weight that seemed to intensify with every step. It was a reminder that this was not a dream. This was real.

The eyes of the assembled crowd bore into me, their collective gaze stripping me bare. I walked up the long, crimson carpet that led to the elevated dais where the crown awaited, feeling the weight of their expectations. It was an unspoken truth that their hopes and dreams rested on my shoulders.

As I ascended the steps of the dais, I could feel the aura of the ancient stone beneath my boots, resonating with centuries of history and tradition. The enormity of the moment struck me like a physical blow. I was actually about to be crowned the queen, the ruler of this kingdom. It wasn't merely a formality; it was the embodiment of my destiny.

My boots echoed through the vast throne room, the reverberations filling the silence that hung in the air. Every step was a deliberate act, a proclamation of my readiness for the role that awaited me. I reached the dais and turned to face the crowd, their eager faces a sea of anticipation.

I could see them clearly, their expressions a mix of hope, excitement, and curiosity. They had placed their faith in me, and their unwavering support gave me the courage to continue this solemn journey. On the dais, Thalion's father stood beside the cushion that cradled the crown of Terralux, a symbol of authority that had lain dormant for too long in the castle's treasure vault.

The crown itself was a masterpiece, crafted by the skilled hands of the fae's finest artisans. It was a circlet of gold adorned with two feathered points. Despite its delicate appearance, it held a profound significance, representing both the majesty and the weight of the responsibility that came with ruling a kingdom. I had spent hours last night looking at it, pondering whether I was truly worthy of such an honor.

But now, standing here before my people, there was no doubt in my heart. I was their queen, their leader, and I would not falter. The crown was not a mere accessory but a symbol of my commitment to them. With each step I had taken, with each challenge I had faced, I had proven my worthiness.

I was ready to ascend to the throne, to be the beacon of hope and strength that my kingdom needed. I would fight for them, protect them, and serve them with unwavering dedication. As I stood on the dais, the realization of my purpose washed over me, and I knew that I was prepared to lead, to uphold the legacy ancient of Terralux, and to honor the trust of my people.

"Vale," the king began, his commanding voice resonating through the grand chamber, its echoes filling the air and bouncing off the towering stone walls. The atmosphere was thick with anticipation, every eye in the room fixed upon me. "Do you solemnly swear to govern the peoples of Terralux with justice, mercy, and compassion?"

I stood tall, my spine straight, and my heart steadfast. My voice rang out, clear and unwavering, as I replied, "I solemnly swear to do so with all my strength and honor. To withhold the laws of this land and bring justice to those who would see us perish or enslaved."

The significance of those words, heavy with the weight of the kingdom's hopes and aspirations, hung in the air. I had practiced these vows countless times, but now, as I spoke them before the assembly of nobles, advisors, and the common folk who had gathered to witness this pivotal moment, they held an undeniable significance.

"Will you be their guide and lead them through times of prosperity and strife?" The king's voice held a solemnity that matched the reverent occasion.

"I will guide them and lead them through times of prosperity and strife," I declared, the resolve in my words matched only by the determination in my eyes.

"Will you serve your kingdom and its people with honor and grace?" The king's gaze bore into mine, searching for any hint of uncertainty.

"I will serve my kingdom and its people with honor and grace."

"And will you pledge your life to the service of Terralux, to live and die by the will of the gods and the people of this kingdom?"

"I gladly pledge my life to the service of Terralux and its people," I replied, the words a solemn oath that bound me to a destiny I had been thrust into.

The king nodded, his expression grave. Passing the mantle of leadership was a weighty duty he took seriously. It was a silent acknowledgment that this moment marked the culmination of a journey, a transition of power, and the beginning of a new era for Terralux.

"Then, before the gods, the people, and all who have gathered here," the king pronounced, his voice carrying the weight of tradition and history, "I crown you Queen Valerian of Terralux."

With a graceful and deliberate movement, I lowered my head, offering my brow to place the delicate crown. As the king gently settled it upon my head, I felt its physical weight, a reminder of the responsibility I now bore. It was not merely a symbol; it was a testament to the trust and faith that had been vested in me.

The king smiled, a gesture of approval and acceptance, as he stepped back, ceding the stage to me. At that moment, the room erupted in a chorus of cheers and applause, a jubilant celebration of this historic event.

I smiled, the rush of emotions swelling within me, causing my heart to skip beats in my chest. This marked the beginning of my new life as the Queen of Terralux, a role I had been destined for and one I would embrace with every fiber of my being. I knew that from this moment forward, I would never be the same.

"People of Terralux," I began, my voice projecting with clarity and conviction, resonating through the grand chamber, "I am deeply honored to stand before you today, ready to serve as your queen." The words flowed from my lips, filled with a sense of purpose that echoed through the air.

I surveyed the crowd, my gaze sweeping across their expectant faces. They were a sea of hope and resilience, their eyes reflecting the challenges they had endured and the optimism they now placed in me.

"You have weathered hardships and faced adversity," I continued, my voice carrying a note of empathy. "Together, we shall rebuild our kingdom, forging it into a bastion of strength, prosperity, and unity like never before."

Their hope was evident, and their belief in me made my heart swell. I couldn't let them down. Their trust was a beacon guiding me through the path I had chosen.

"I am profoundly humbled by your faith in me," I declared. "Rest assured, I shall wield this newfound responsibility with unwavering dedication. I will not rest until Terralux stands as a shining jewel in the Fae realm, a symbol of hope and prosperity."

I raised my hand, signaling for the crowd to hush, and their eager cheers dimmed to a murmur.

"Today marks the dawn of a new era for Terralux," I proclaimed, my words infused with determination. "A time of rebirth and renewal, where together, we shall craft a brighter future for all of us."

The applause swelled, a cacophony of support that enveloped me like a warm embrace. It was a testament to the unity we forged, a shared commitment to a common purpose.

I couldn't help but smile, my heart buoyed by their enthusiasm. This was just the beginning, the initial step on our journey.

As the crowd cheered, I took a deep breath, grounding myself in the moment. The crown's weight on my head was a constant reminder of the responsibility I now bore.

Yet, amidst the gravity of it all, I found solace in the love and support of my people. For the first time since returning to Terralux, I felt a profound sense of hope and belonging.

"Thank you, everyone," I concluded, my voice filled with warmth and sincerity. "May the gods watch over us and guide our path as we embark on this new chapter."

The applause resounded, a thunderous affirmation of our shared purpose, and I couldn't help but feel that, together, we were capable of achieving greatness.

Then chaos erupted.

FORTY-TWO

The cheering that had filled the throne room moments ago was abruptly shattered by a deafening boom that reverberated through the chamber, so loud that it felt like the very foundations of the palace had been shaken. My heart raced as I staggered, my legs nearly giving way beneath me. The ground quivered beneath my feet, leaving me struggling to maintain my balance.

In the blink of an eye, the room had transformed from a scene of celebration into one of sheer pandemonium. A cacophony of shouts, cries, and screams erupted, drowning out all reason. Panic hung thick in the air like a noxious fog, and I felt a chill grip my heart.

My gaze darted around, trying to make sense of the chaos that had descended upon us. Then, adding to the nightmare, the grand windows of the throne room shattered into a cascade of deadly shards, plummeting downward like crystalline rain onto the terrified people below. Gasps of pain and fear filled the room.

What the hell was going on? My mind reeled with shock

and disbelief. Another explosion echoed through the palace and the air pulsed with the force of the blast. My ears rang with a high-pitched whine, making it difficult to focus on the unfolding turmoil.

The once-thrilled and jubilant crowd had devolved into a frantic stampede, each person driven by the instinct to escape the mayhem. It was a chaotic swirl of bodies, a desperate struggle for survival amid the uproar.

From a distance, a sound pierced through the clamor—a clash of metal against metal, the unmistakable resonance of blades in battle. It was a grim reminder that whatever had descended upon us was not merely an accident or a random act of chaos.

War had erupted within the very heart of our kingdom. As I surveyed the wreckage and devastation that had been wrought in the blink of an eye, I had no choice but to acknowledge that chilling truth.

Thalion, Kaelan, and Aerion tore through the chaos, their faces etched with urgency as they rushed toward me and Thalion's father. The expression on Thalion's face was a seething mixture of anger and concern, his voice cutting through the tumultuous surroundings like a blade.

"Vale!" he bellowed. "We need to get you out of here!"

My heart pounded in my chest, and I could feel the surge of adrenaline coursing through my veins. I couldn't just abandon my people in their hour of need, not when our kingdom was under attack.

"Fuck that, I'm staying," I retorted defiantly. I knew the weight of my responsibilities and wasn't about to shirk them in the face of danger. "Aerion, get Thalion's father out of here."

Aerion hesitated, his steely gray eyes locked onto mine for a fleeting moment. Then, with a determined nod, he laid his hand on the king's forearm, shifting him away from the impending chaos.

Kaelan moved to my side, his gaze scanning our surroundings. He was a formidable presence, his protective instincts in full force.

"What's happening?" I demanded, my voice edged with frustration and fear.

Thalion's response was grim, his words heavy with foreboding. "Our enemies have launched a surprise attack. It seems they did not care for your coronation."

I couldn't help but roll my eyes at the absurdity of the situation. "Which enemies would those be, again?" I asked, my tone laced with sarcasm.

"That has yet to be ascertained," Thalion replied, his eyes darkening.

"Lovely," I muttered, my words dripping with irony.

With Thalion and Kaelan leading the way, we navigated the sprawling palace, making our way toward the front entrance. The sounds of battle grew steadily louder as we approached, the clash of weapons and the cries of combatants reverberating through the once-grand halls.

When we finally reached the front hall, my eyes widened in shock as I took in the chaotic scene before me. Fae soldiers were locked in a brutal struggle, their armor and weapons identifying them as both loyal members of the royal guard and mysterious foes. Among the latter, I recognized the insignia of Haldir's court.

"Haldir," I hissed, the name a venomous curse on my lips.

Thalion's response was measured. "Yes, it would seem so. Though I can't imagine why he would be so bold as to attack us at the very moment you were being crowned queen."

The realization struck me like a blow to the gut. "He's trying to send a message," I declared, my voice trembling with a mixture of anger and resignation. "He wants the world to know that even though I wear the crown, he's still in control."

"It's a bold move," Kaelan acknowledged.

"And a foolish one. If he truly wishes to rule, openly attacking you in front of the entire Fae court is not the wisest choice." Thalion replied. "Unless, of course, he's not trying to rule," he suggested after a moment.

I couldn't hide my frustration any longer, my impatience bubbling to the surface. "Then what the hell is he trying to do?" I demanded, my eyes scanning the tumultuous surroundings.

His eyes hardening with resolve. "I don't know, but it's obvious he has allies here. We need to root them out and put a stop to this before the damage becomes irreparable," Thalion replied.

My gaze swept across the scene of chaos and destruction that surrounded us. The front hall was now a battlefield strewn with debris and echoing with the cries of conflict.

"We have to stop this," I declared.

Kaelan, ever the pragmatic one, pointed out the obvious. "I agree, but we need to find a way to do so without getting killed in the process."

"We have to try," I insisted.

Thalion agreed with a nod of his head. "Well, we can't stand here and do nothing. Vale, stay close to us."

As we stepped forward into the maelstrom of chaos, a nagging thought tugged at my conscience. I should be the one leading the charge. After all, I was the one who had been crowned queen mere minutes ago, and it was my duty to protect my kingdom and its people.

But instead, I found myself following the lead of the men around me, allowing them to protect me as I struggled to keep up with their determined pace.

The mounting tension became unbearable, and I couldn't suppress my frustration any longer. "Stop!" I cried out, halting Thalion and Kaelan in their tracks.

They turned to look at me, their expressions full of concern and confusion. Kaelan's dark eyes locked onto mine, seeking an explanation. "What is it, Vale?" he asked.

I took a deep breath. "I'm not running away from this. That's not what I just promised these people I would do. I'm the one who was just crowned, the one the people are looking to. So, let me do my job."

Kaelan and Thalion exchanged glances, but I refused to give them the opportunity to argue. I started walking toward the front doors, my heart pounding with a newfound purpose.

"If you want to protect me, fine," I said over my shoulder. "But I'm not going to hide behind you like a coward. I'm the queen, and I'm going to lead this fight."

They followed behind me, their swords drawn and ready, as we moved toward the heart of the battle. The weight of my crown served as a constant reminder of my duty, and I was determined to prove that I was worthy of the title I now held.

As we stepped out into the courtyard, the full scale of the battle came into view. The air was thick with acrid smoke, and the sound of clashing steel and battle cries reverberated through the landscape. The front gate had been blown away. I stood there on the palace's steps, a surge of determination coursing through me as an idea began to take shape in my mind.

"You two are going to want to get behind me," I cautioned Thalion and Kaelan, who exchanged a brief but understanding glance before positioning themselves on either side of me, just a step behind. Their presence was reassuring as I prepared to put my plan into action.

Taking a deep, centering breath, I delved deep within myself, searching for that hidden spark of power, the spark that would ignite my audacious plan. Flames started to flicker across my skin and clothes, the black fabric singeing but not bursting into flames. I focused my will, urging the flames to burn higher, to grow hotter, as I stood resolute on the palace steps.

Arrows whizzed by my head and glanced off my shield, embedding themselves into the massive wooden doors behind me, but I continued pulling on the magic wellspring within me. It surged like a roiling inferno beneath my skin; my veins became rivers of fire, and my soul was engulfed in the blaze. My skin turned to embers, and my eyes blazed white-hot.

I had become fire incarnate, and I unleashed myself upon the battlefield.

I began walking through the fray, Kaelan and Thalion guarding my flanks, taking down anyone who dared approach me as I enveloped soldier after soldier in searing flames where they stood.

No one could touch me.

I was unstoppable.

The heat emanating from me was unbearable and as I moved through the battle, it became clear that my enemies were no match for me. I was a force of nature, a power beyond comprehension, and I left a trail of ashes and cinders in my wake as I moved forward.

I was a living flame, born from the ashes of my kingdom's despair, and I was ready to face whatever challenges lay ahead. I called out for Haldir, my voice carrying above the chaos of the battlefield. Reaching the ruined front gates, I left behind nothing but a smoldering courtyard, and I knew this was just the beginning of my reign as the Queen of Terralux.

The battle still raged on outside the palace gates, a cacophony of clashing swords and shouts. But before me came three formidable women.

Three witches.

"We finally meet," the tallest and most muscular of the witches sneered, her muddy hazel eyes locked onto mine.

"And you are?" I asked, my tone unimpressed as I stood there wreathed in flames.

"I am Carys," she replied, her words laced with venom and her expression a twisted mix of malice and grudging admiration. "These are my sisters, Mor and Nysa."

"And what exactly do you think you're doing here?" I asked, my voice a feral snarl.

"We are here to kill you, of course," Carys responded with a sinister smile, her confidence unshaken.

"Good luck with that," I sneered, the two men beside me inching closer, their swords drawn in defense of their new queen.

"We're stronger than you could ever imagine, little girl," Mor, the second witch, sneered in a chilling tone.

"We'll see about that," I retorted, taking a deliberate step forward, flames trailing behind me.

As I moved, a bolt of crackling electricity shot out from the three witches, narrowly missing me as it scorched the grass and left a smoldering mark on the ground. The two men at my side reacted swiftly, lunging forward to strike, but their swords clashed against an impenetrable magical barrier that had manifested between us.

"Come on now, girls," I taunted, my voice laced with defiance. "You don't really expect to defeat me with just a shield, do you?"

"Oh, we'll do more than that," Nysa, the third witch, laughed with a grating tone, her eyes glinting with wicked glee.

With a sinister grin, she released a barrage of powerful spells in my direction. Arcane energy crackled through the air, and I braced myself. Each spell that came hurtling toward me was met with a deft flick of my wrist or a precise incantation, causing them to either collide with the palace walls, shattering stone and leaving scorch marks, or to dissipate harmlessly into the atmosphere.

The trio of witches before me, their faces twisted in a blend of astonishment and fury, provided a scene I found oddly satisfying. Carys, the most visibly enraged among them, growled low in her throat, her fists clenched so tightly I could almost hear the bones creaking. Mor raised her palms, her eyes aflame with an unwavering resolve. Nysa drew back her hands, the space between her fingers alight with a pulsating orb of energy that grew with every passing second.

Then, as one, they unleashed their wrath. A torrent of chaotic magic surged toward me like a tidal wave, tearing up the ground in its path and whipping the air into a frenzy. Dust and debris swirled around me, biting at my skin and stinging my eyes. But I remained focused, summoning a shimmering shield of energy that sprang up before me. The witches' spells collided with my barrier, each impact sending shudders through the air and threatening to topple me.

But I held steady, my feet planted firmly on the ground. My shield flickered and wavered under the relentless assault, but I poured more of my energy into it, reinforcing its strength. I would not let them break me. My resolve was ironclad, each wave of magic that crashed against my defenses only serving to steel my determination.

The witches, sensing their attacks were in vain, grew increasingly frustrated. Their faces contorted with rage as each subsequent spell they cast proved futile. Their movements became more frantic, their incantations more desperate. They flung every conceivable curse, hex, and charm in their arsenal at me, but still, I stood unyielding.

It was abundantly clear that these women possessed formidable magic, but they were utterly outclassed by me. I was the most powerful witch to grace the realm in thousands of years, and I would not be brought down by a trio of delusional, power-hungry witches.

I drew upon the reservoir of magic within me, feeling it surge and expand. My veins pulsed with energy as I harnessed its immense power, and with a determined focus, I unleashed it. The magical force surged from my being, directed toward the barrier that surrounded the three witches.

As the magic erupted, the very air crackled with its potency, the scent of ozone heavy and electrifying. The sky above us darkened, storm clouds swirling ominously as if responding to the immense power being unleashed below.

The witches screamed, their hands raised in a futile attempt to maintain their protective spell. But it was too late for them. The unleashed power I commanded was too overwhelming. With a deafening crack, the barrier shattered into countless shards, and the three women were thrown backward, tumbling across the ground, their cries echoing in the chaos.

I approached them, flames still flickering and crackling around me.

"So, where is Haldir?" I demanded, my voice carrying effortlessly over the roaring wind.

Carys lifted her head, her eyes brimming with hatred as she locked her gaze with mine.

"You'll never defeat him," she spat venomously. "He's too powerful."

"We'll see about that," I retorted, reaching out with my magic to break through the barrier to her mind. She writhed and screamed in agony as the magic tore through her, and I only relented when her cries became ragged.

"Tell me where Haldir is, or your suffering will continue," I threatened, my voice cold and unyielding.

"It's too late," Carys hissed, her voice laced with dark amusement, blood trickling from the corner of her mouth. "As we speak, he is retrieving what we came here for."

"What might that be?" I demanded, my patience running thin.

"Something vital," Carys chuckled darkly, her voice fading to a mere whisper. "Something that will ensure our victory."

"What the hell are you talking about?" I snapped, frustration mounting.

"You will find out soon enough," she replied cryptically, her voice growing weaker as her breaths became labored.

I had endured enough of her riddles and half-truths. Instantly, I reached out with my magic again, diving into the recesses of her mind, tearing through her thoughts like a hurricane. She screamed in sheer agony as I invaded her memories, ripping through her consciousness until I uncovered the information I sought.

With a jolt, I abruptly withdrew from her tortured mind, my flames extinguishing as I turned to Thalion and Kaelan, my complexion pallid.

"I know where he is," I muttered, my voice tense with urgency. "Grab one of them, but send the other two back as a message. Tell the coven to shield her powers."

Without uttering another word, I sprinted forward, charging toward the colossal double doors of the palace, my fear propelling me along like a hurricane. Thalion and Kaelan followed in my wake after relaying my instructions to a group of nearby soldiers. They struggled to keep pace amidst the chaos of battle that still raged around us.

"Vale, what's going on? Where is he?" Kaelan shouted above the clamor of combat.

I burst through the massive double doors and continued my frantic dash up the grand staircase toward the third floor.

"He's after Aisling," I replied tersely, my voice laced with unease.

"How did they even find her?" Thalion questioned me.

"I don't know," I responded, my determination urging me to push myself harder, to run faster.

"What do they want with her?" Kaelan pressed.

"I can't say for sure," I admitted. "But I won't let them harm her, no matter what."

As we raced through the winding corridors of the palace, our destination was Venna's room, the only place where Aisling might be found during the fighting.

We finally reached the door to Venna's bedroom, and I flung it open with a desperate urgency.

Inside the room, a shocking sight awaited us. Haldir

stood there, gripping Aisling by the shoulders, his eyes gleaming with sinister intent. Venna lay nearby on the floor, unconscious but still breathing.

I barely had time to shout before he used his magic to shift them both away, leaving nothing but a sense of emptiness in the room.

"No..." I whispered, my voice trembling with grief and guilt.

I rushed to the spot where Aisling had stood only moments before, reaching out to touch the lingering traces of her magic that still clung to the air.

"How did he just shift inside the castle? I thought it was warded against that." Thalion asked.

"Obviously not against Haldir, which makes sense seeing as he was the last ruler of this place," Kaelan answered him.

"We have to find them," I declared, my voice hardening as I turned to Thalion and Kaelan. "We have to bring her back."

"How?" Thalion asked, frustration etched in his features.

"I don't know," I confessed, the weight of failure heavy upon me. "But we have to try."

I had failed her, and now, my sister witch was in the hands of our greatest enemy.

There was no predicting what Haldir and his allies might do to her, but I was determined to stop them, no matter the cost.

FORTY-THREE

"What?" Wren's anger erupted like a tempest, his voice thundering through the corridor and causing me to involuntarily flinch under the weight of his fury.

"Wren, I'm so sorry, but we'll get her back, I promise," I said, trying to soothe the storm within him, my voice quivering.

"Get her back? Get her back? You lost her, you lost my daugh- Aisling!" he yelled, stumbling over the last word. Wren's accusations pierced through my heart, and I could feel the tears welling up in my eyes. I hadn't realized until he almost called her his daughter just how much he had come to care for the girl.

"We will get her back," I insisted, my voice steady despite the emotional turmoil that swirled around us.

"How can you possibly make such a claim when you can't even protect her from being taken?" Wren's words lashed out like a bitter, cutting wind, and I flinched once more.

"Wren, enough. You know this isn't Vale's fault. None of

us had a clue they were even after her," Kaelan intervened, his voice calm and reasoned.

"Kaelan, not now," Wren seethed, his anger still burning hot.

"Wren, I understand your anger and you have every right to be upset. But blaming Vale won't help us get Aisling back," Kaelan said, trying to reason with Wren.

"We were supposed to keep her safe!" Wren growled, his voice full of anguish. His frustration found an outlet as his clenched fist struck the stone wall of the hallway outside Venna's room, causing it to crack slightly beneath the force of his blow.

"Wren," I whispered, my tears now flowing freely. Wren never lost his temper like this. He was always the calm one, always collected.

"We need a plan, not a shouting match," Thalion interjected, as frustrated as the rest of us.

"Thalion is right. We need to figure out where they've taken her and how we can rescue her. We can't do that if we're busy arguing with each other," Kaelan said.

"Fine," Wren growled, his anger still simmering. "We need a plan, so what do you propose we do?"

"I suggest we begin by figuring out what they want with her," Thalion suggested.

"I may have an idea about that," I said, my voice low.

"Well, don't keep us in suspense," Wren demanded.

"When I... when I was inside Carys's mind, I saw something," I began, my voice hesitant. "It was a vision, she must be a seer, I'm not sure, but it was definitely important. There was a cave, and Haldir was chanting something in a language I didn't recognize. I think he was performing some kind of ritual."

"A ritual? What kind of ritual?" Kaelan asked, his expression dark.

"I'm not sure," I admitted. "But whatever it was, it was powerful. I could feel it, even through her memories."

"You don't think that they are..." Wren's voice broke slightly before he went on, "Torturing her, do you?"

My response was immediate and firm. "No. Malachar was the one who took delight in torture. Haldir was never as interested in it during our... encounters."

Thalion's gaze fixed on me as he pressed for more information. "Then what is he doing with her?"

"I'm not sure," I admitted, my brow furrowing in thought. "But it's obvious that whatever it is, it has something to do with her powers. She's the only blood-born witch alive besides me that we know of."

Wren's anger began to wane, replaced by exhaustion and worry. "So, how are we going to find them? And what do we do once we do?"

Stepping up with a solution, I offered, "We interrogate the witch for information. If that doesn't work, I can scry for her location. I don't have a strong connection with her, so it may not work. Do you have anything that belonged to her? Or perhaps a few strands of her hair from a hairbrush?"

Wren nodded in response, his voice strained. "Yes, I'll go and get it."

As Wren ventured into Venna's room to retrieve the necessary items, Kaelan turned to me. "We need a plan, but we can't risk any more lives than necessary. We need to make a small group that will go after Aisling while the rest of the kingdom remains protected," he said.

"I agree." Thalion said.

"Once we locate her, I'll need to go, and the two of you,"

I declared. "And quite possibly a few of the witches from the coven."

Wren, returning with the requested items, immediately insisted on his place in the mission. "Not happening, not without me."

"Wren—" I started, but he cut me off.

"If you think for one moment I'm going to sit idly by and wait while Aisling is in danger, you're insane. She is my responsibility, and I will do whatever is necessary to protect her."

"He's right. He needs to come," Kaelan said reluctantly.

"Fine, but only because we don't have time to fight about it." I relented.

Wren nodded, his gaze focused. "Good. Now, what's the plan?"

"I'll question the witch with Aerion," Kaelan said, "then we can figure out how to get there. Once we arrive, we will assess the situation and determine the best way to extract her. Hopefully, she won't be heavily guarded."

I nodded in agreement, my mind racing. "We can't assume that, though. If Haldir is performing a ritual of some kind, he will need protection," I cautioned, my brows furrowing with concern.

"So, we should be prepared for a fight," Thalion said, his expression hardening.

"Exactly," I said, my voice steadier than I felt.

"Then, let's get started," Wren said, cutting through the tension.

"I'm going to the library to try and scry for her," I declared, turning and walking away, leaving Thalion and Wren behind. Kaelan trailed after me, his footsteps echoing in the hallway.

"Vale, wait," Kaelan called after me, his voice filled with concern.

"Kaelan, not now," I responded, my steps unrelenting as I made my way toward the library.

"Please," he pleaded softly.

I turned to face him, my heart heavy with guilt and sorrow. "Kaelan…"

"None of this is your fault," Kaelan said, pulling me gently into his comforting embrace. He could see right through the mask I wore.

Tears welled up in my eyes, and a soft sob escaped my lips. Aisling had been taken right in front of me and there had been nothing I could do to stop it. "Wren is so angry with me. He's never been angry with me before, Kaelan. The look on his face…"

"He's not angry with you, Vale, he's scared. Scared for Aisling, scared for you. He's lashing out because he's hurting," Kaelan explained, his voice soothing and understanding.

"That may be so, but it doesn't change the fact that Aisling is in the hands of our worst enemy and it's all my fault," I replied, my voice cracking.

"No, it's not. None of this is your fault. You're not responsible for the actions of others, Vale. Haldir and his followers are responsible, not you. You can't blame yourself for their choices," Kaelan insisted, his words filled with conviction.

"But, if I had mastered my precognitive abilities, if I had been paying closer attention, maybe none of this would have happened. Aisling would be safe here at the palace," I argued, my voice quivering as doubt raced through me.

"Stop," Kaelan commanded gently, his tone both firm and caring. "You are not responsible, and you are going to get her back. We will get her back together. And then we will stop Haldir. We'll make him pay."

"How can you be so sure?" I asked, my voice barely a whisper, fears winning out against my resolve.

"Because I believe in you," Kaelan replied without hesitation. "I've always believed in you, and I will never stop believing in you."

His words were what I needed to hear, and I clung to him, drawing strength from his faith in me.

"Come, you have a spell to cast," Kaelan reminded me, gently pulling away and taking my hands to lead me down the corridor to the palace library.

We arrived and Kaelan went to interrogate the witch while I immediately went to work, my fingers deftly gathering the necessary materials and setting up the map. I wrapped the strands of Aisling's hair around the crystal and dangled it above the map.

Harker watched me closely, her eyes filled with concern. She could sense my unease.

"What's wrong?" she asked, noting the deep frown on my face.

"I just...I can't seem to find her," I murmured, the frustration evident in my voice.

"Keep trying," Harker encouraged, moving closer to offer her support. "She's got to be somewhere."

"I know," I replied, my frustration mounting. "I just can't seem to get a clear reading."

"What if she's not in the Fae realm?" Her suggestion gave me pause.

"That's a possibility," I admitted, my voice tinged with uncertainty. "She could be anywhere in the mortal realm, or the demon realm, or even in another realm entirely."

"Let's focus on the mortal realm first," Harker

suggested, her practicality shining through. "If she's not there, we can expand our search."

"Okay," I agreed, my mind racing with possibilities. "Maybe there is a map somewhere around here."

"No need for that. I know where one is," she said as she crossed the library floor to a corner and began rifling through large parchments, finally pulling one out.

"We can start with this one, it's the whole of the mortal realm, and then we can narrow it down after with smaller maps," she suggested, bringing the large map over to a table.

"Okay," I nodded, hoping this worked and Aisling wasn't in the spirit realm like I had been when Haldir had taken me.

Harker spread the map out, and I closed my eyes, holding the crystal aloft. The library fell into a heavy silence as we waited anxiously.

For what felt like an eternity, nothing happened. I could hear my own heartbeat pounding in my ears, the tension in my shoulders only worsening as each minute passed.

Finally, the crystal began to move. At first, it was slow and hesitant, but it gained momentum, swinging wildly as if guided by an unseen force.

My eyes flew open, and I peered down at the map, my curiosity piqued by the crystal's choice.

"It's not a place I'm familiar with," I murmured, my finger tracing the outline of a mountain range on the map.

"That's the Smoky Mountains in Tennessee, that whole area is filled with cave systems," Harker supplied, her knowledge proving invaluable.

"Do you have another map?" I asked, eager to narrow down our search further.

"Yes, let me get it," Harker said, disappearing briefly

before returning with a smaller map, this one depicting the state of Tennessee.

"How could the library have these updated maps?" I asked her.

"Maybe there are spells on the maps to keep them up to date." Yes, I could feel the enchantments on the one she handed to me.

I took a deep breath and held the crystal once more, allowing it to hover above the map.

Slowly, the crystal began to swing again, and my heart raced as it landed on a specific spot.

"Chattanooga, it's a town just outside the Smoky Mountains," Harker announced, her voice holding a note of certainty.

"That's where we're going," I declared, my voice filled with newfound confidence. We had a lead, and I was ready to follow it to the ends of the earth to rescue Aisling.

I turned to Harker, seeking her expertise in the matter. "Harker, which of the coven is ready for a little more field training?"

Harker didn't hesitate with her response. "None of them. But if you have to take somebody, take Ava, Calliope, and Harlow. They've shown the most aptitude at this point."

"Will it be enough to go against at least two witches and whatever the hell Haldir has become?" I asked incredulously.

Harker's response was pragmatic, if not reassuring. "Not even close, but I'm sure the three of them are more than willing to try."

I sighed, realizing that we had little choice in the matter. "Gather them up, make sure they can at least properly raise a shield, and meet me in the front entrance in an hour," I instructed Harker.

As I walked away, my thoughts were consumed by the impending confrontation with Haldir and the desperate mission to rescue Aisling. We were far from ready, but we had no other option than to forge ahead and hope for the best.

CHAPTER

FORTY-FOUR

KAELAN

Kaelan strode purposefully through the palace corridors alongside Aerion, their destination the prison cells deep within the bowels of the castle. He was acutely aware of the weight of his task, doing this for Vale, who would never want to set foot in such a place again after the horrors she had endured there. It was a burden he willingly shouldered, a small act of reparation for all that she had been through.

As they reached the door leading to the stairwell, Kaelan felt a familiar chill run down his spine. He remembered all too well the last time they had come this way when they had rescued Vale. It wasn't something he liked to think about.

They began their descent, the flickering torches casting eerie shadows on the walls. The dim, wavering light was unnecessary for Kaelan. Thanks to his affinity with the shadows, he could navigate effortlessly in total darkness, guided by the perpetual whispers that only he could hear.

Descending into the depths, they arrived at the cells where two of the new witches, Griffin and Archer, were

488

stationed. They were intently focused on a figure in the cell – the witch Carys, effectively cut off from her powers by their shielding.

Kaelan acknowledged Griffin and Archer with a nod, a silent gesture of gratitude for their vigilance. The two men returned the nod, their eyes quickly shifting back to Carys, ensuring she remained powerless.

As they approached the cell, two guards stepped forward, one of them unlocking and opening the door. The guards entered the cell and dragged out the witch, who struggled fiercely against their grasp.

"Take her to one of the rooms to be questioned," Aerion instructed, his voice carrying an authoritative edge.

They all began to follow the guards while Griffin and Archer maintained their magical shields around Carys.

"You won't get anything from me!" Carys yelled, defiance clear in her voice despite her precarious situation.

"We'll see," Kaelan responded coolly, his anger at her simmering just below the surface. There was a controlled ferocity in his tone, a promise of the wrath that was ready to be unleashed. Kaelan's eyes were fixed on the witch, his gaze unyielding and cold. He was the embodiment of a predator, patient yet ready to strike, as they made their way to the interrogation room.

They traversed the corridors in heavy silence, punctuated only by the occasional scuff of boots against the stone floors and the unsettling rattle of chains binding Carys' hands. Kaelan and Aerion moved at the head of the group, their steps resonant with a measured, deliberate purpose, an air of grim determination surrounding them.

When they reached their destination, the sight of the small, windowless room seemed to solidify the gravity of the situation. The walls, made of cold, dark stone, gave off an oppressive feel, and the room's sparse furnishings—a plain wooden chair bolted to the floor and a table—were stark reminders of its grim purpose. The table bore an assortment of tools, each instrument a silent testament to the countless souls that had been broken here over the years.

As the group entered, Aerion signaled to the guards holding Carys. They wasted no time in shoving her roughly into the chair, securing her ankles and wrists. The sound of the metal clinking into place echoed ominously through the room.

Kaelan observed the scene with a sense of grim satisfaction, watching as the guards exited and shut the heavy iron door behind them, sealing them in the room. As the sound of the door locking reverberated, Kaelan approached Carys slowly, a malicious glint in his eyes betraying his intentions.

"So," he started, his voice low and menacing, breaking the heavy silence. "Let's see what you have to say."

"I'm not telling you anything," Carys replied defiantly, her eyes ablaze with a fierce determination.

Kaelan studied her for a moment, his gaze analytical and cold. "You seem quite certain of that," he commented, a hint of amusement coloring his tone despite the tense atmosphere.

"I am," Carys shot back. "You might have me chained up, but you can't break me. You'll never break me."

Kaelan's expression morphed into a sardonic smile as he cocked his head to the side. "That's very interesting," he drawled, his voice dripping with feigned concern. "But I'm afraid I'm going to have to prove you wrong."

Suddenly, he reached out, grasping Carys' chin with a

forceful grip, compelling her to meet his eyes. She resisted, but the shackles rendered her efforts futile.

"Why did you come for the girl? What are you planning to do with her?" Kaelan demanded, his voice a dangerous calm that belied the storm brewing beneath the surface.

Carys met his gaze, her lips pressed into a line of defiance.

"Tell me!" Kaelan's voice erupted into a roar, his control fraying at the edges.

"Never," Carys spat defiantly. "You can't scare me. You can't break me. I will die before I give you the satisfaction."

"If you refuse to cooperate," Kaelan threatened, his voice lowering to a menacing growl, "I will ensure that your death is far from pleasant." His words hung in the air, heavy with the promise of pain and retribution, as he stared down at the witch, his resolve unshaken.

In the corner of the dimly lit room, Aerion stood, his posture rigid, arms crossed tightly against his chest. His presence was an ominous shadow, his demeanor suggesting a barely restrained fury that mirrored Kaelan's own. "Perhaps we can loosen her tongue in a different way," he suggested, his voice laced with a cold, dangerous edge.

Kaelan turned to him, a flicker of interest lighting up his eyes. "What do you have in mind?" he asked, his tone indicating a readiness for whatever method Aerion proposed.

Aerion stepped forward, his movements deliberate, each step a testament to his controlled anger. He paused and closed his eyes, focusing his energy, channeling his power. The air in the room seemed to thicken, charged with an unseen force.

A moment later, the witch's shrieks tore through the silence, a visceral response to Aerion having breached her mental defenses. Kaelan watched, a cruel smile twisting his lips as Carys writhed in her chair, the sound of her agony reverberating off the stone walls.

"Now, let's try this again," Kaelan murmured, his voice soft yet laced with malice. "Why did you come for the girl?"

"N-never," Carys gasped between her cries. "You can't hurt me. I am strong. I won't break. You can't break me!"

But Aerion was relentless. He intensified his mental assault, each wave of psychic energy eliciting fresh screams of pain from the witch. "You can't break me! You can't break me! You can't...," the witch repeated, her voice dwindling to a desperate whimper.

"We'll see," Kaelan mused, watching her struggle.

The witch's litany continued, but her resolve was clearly crumbling under the onslaught.

"I'll ask you one more time," Kaelan said quietly, his voice a calm, dangerous whisper. "Why did you come for the girl?"

Carys hesitated, her eyes frantically scanning the room, looking for an escape that wasn't there.

"Answer me," Kaelan demanded, his soft voice now a menacing hiss. He extended his hand, and shadows began to creep across the floor, slithering up the witch's legs. They moved slowly up her body as she thrashed against her restraints. Griffin and Archer stood in the corner, watching intently and maintaining their shield.

The shadows reached Carys' face, and she gasped as her vision was consumed by darkness. "What are you doing?" she demanded weakly, terror creeping into her voice.

"I'm giving you a glimpse of your future," Kaelan hissed, his voice dripping with venom. "You're going to rot away in a cell, alone and forgotten. No one will come for you. No one will rescue you. You'll be utterly alone, abandoned by everyone and everything. The shadows will be your only companions, whispering in your ear, driving you mad. You'll go insane, trapped in the darkness with nothing but your own fear and the voices of the shadows to torment you."

Her scream filled the room, a sound of pure terror as the shadows enveloped her completely, leaving her in a world of darkness and pain.

"You can't do this!" she cried, her voice breaking. "You can't leave me like this!"

"Oh, but I can," Kaelan replied coldly, his eyes devoid of any mercy as he watched her despair. He was the embodiment of the dark power he wielded, merciless and unyielding.

The witch's screams escalated as Aerion once again pierced her mind, reverberating off the stone walls and filling the room with a cacophony of terror. The sound was chilling, a testament to the effectiveness of the two men's methods.

"Now, tell me what I want to know," Kaelan demanded as Aerion relented, his voice a menacing growl that resonated with dark authority. He leaned forward, his presence dominating the small, dimly lit space.

Under the relentless pressure of the shadows and Kaelan's threatening demeanor, the witch's earlier defiance began to crumble. The shadows, like living entities, seemed to tighten their hold around her, heightening her fear and desperation.

"Why did you come for the girl?" Kaelan pressed, his voice rising in fury, echoing the rage simmering within him.

The witch trembled, her eyes wide with panic, her breath coming in short, shallow gasps.

Kaelan moved closer, his features contorted in a snarl,

his eyes ablaze with the fire of his ire. His power surged, the shadows seeming to respond to his anger, enveloping the witch in an ever-tightening web.

The witch was trapped, a prisoner of Kaelan and the shadows.

"You have no escape. No hope. Only the endless torment of the darkness," Kaelan purred.

"Please," the witch begged, her voice cracking under the strain, the terror evident in her eyes. "I'll tell you whatever you want. Just don't leave me here in the darkness."

"So, you've decided to cooperate?" Kaelan asked, his tone laced with a cold satisfaction.

"Yes," the witch sobbed, her spirit visibly breaking. "Just please, take the shadows away."

"Very well," Kaelan replied, his voice almost pleasant, in stark contrast to the torment he had just inflicted.

Obeying an unspoken command, the shadows receded, slithering back into the darkest corners of the room, leaving the witch panting and trembling in the sudden absence of their oppressive touch.

"Now, what are your plans for the girl?" Kaelan asked, his gaze fixed intently on the witch.

Taking a shaky breath, the witch spilled her secrets. "We need a blood-born witch so we can harness her powers. We need her life force to stand up to the First Witch," she blurted out, the words tumbling from her in a rush of fear-induced honesty.

"Is that all?" Kaelan probed, his eyes narrowing in suspicion.

"Yes," the witch responded, her voice quivering, betraying her lingering fear.

"You're lying," Aerion interjected sharply. "There's more to it. What else are you planning?"

The witch remained silent, her gaze lowered, avoiding the piercing scrutiny of her captors.

"Tell us," Kaelan growled, his voice a thunderous command that filled the room, leaving no room for disobedience.

"I-it's not my place," the witch stammered, her voice barely above a whisper. "I can't." Her words were choked with fear, her body tensed as if bracing for more torment, the full truth of her mission still locked within her.

"Then you're of no use to us," Aerion declared, his voice echoing with a chilling finality. The witch's screams resonated through the room again, filling the air with a sense of dread. Aerion watched her, his expression remaining stoically neutral, a mask that concealed the tumultuous storm brewing within him.

As Kaelan focused on the witch, he could sense the turmoil in her mind. She was frantically trying to conceal something from them, her thoughts a chaotic whirlwind of fear and desperation. Simultaneously, he could feel the destructive force of Aerion's mental assault, tearing through her mental barriers with ruthless efficiency.

"Let's see how you feel about the shadows once I'm done with you," Kaelan whispered menacingly into the witch's ear. His voice was a sinister hiss, a promise of further torment.

Her screams intensified as the shadows began their ominous dance around her, slithering over her body like dark serpents. They moved with a purposeful intent, a visual manifestation of the terror she was experiencing.

"Stop!" the witch cried out, her voice breaking with the strain of utter desperation. "I'll tell you, just make it stop!"

"Go on," Kaelan prompted, his voice cold and unyielding.

"We're planning an attack on the coven before they get stronger," Carys revealed between sobs, her words tumbling out in a flood of panic. "We're going to use the girl's life force to power a spell that will wipe them all out. We were sent to bring her back. Once that is accomplished, Haldir plans to use her remaining life force to strengthen his power in some way. He wouldn't tell us the specifics, only what we needed to know."

Kaelan's gaze shifted to Aerion, who returned the look, an unspoken understanding passing between them.

"Are you satisfied now?" the witch asked, her voice a faint, exhausted whisper.

"Almost," Kaelan responded, his tone indicating that their interrogation was far from over.

"What more could you possibly want?" the witch demanded, trembling with fear and exhaustion.

"Tell me where they took her," Kaelan instructed, his demand sharp and direct.

"I-I don't know," the witch replied, her voice so soft it was almost lost in the gloom of the room. "All I know is that they're somewhere in a cave."

"That's not good enough," Kaelan growled, the shadows responding to his anger, tightening their grasp around the witch, constricting like a noose.

"I'm telling the truth!" the witch cried out, her plea laced with desperation. "I swear! That's all I know, I don't know anything else." Her words were a blend of terror and sincerity, a last-ditch effort to convince her captors of her limited knowledge.

Kaelan's gaze lingered on the witch, his eyes narrowing into slits as he meticulously assessed her words, searching for any hint of deceit or manipulation. There was a calculating coldness in his stare.

"I believe you," he finally pronounced, his voice a flat declaration that offered no comfort.

"Thank you," the witch whimpered, relief momentarily flickering in her eyes. "I told you everything, just like you asked."

"I'm not done with you yet," Kaelan stated, his voice empty of any warmth or empathy.

"What else do you want?" the witch asked, fear creeping back into her voice as she realized her ordeal was far from over.

"It's not a matter of what I want," Kaelan explained, his tone dispassionate. "It's a matter of what needs to be done. You have shown yourself to be a ruthless, calculating enemy, and I can't afford to take any chances with you."

"You said you believed me!" the witch protested, her voice escalating into a panic-stricken pitch.

"And I do. But it doesn't change the fact that you are a threat to this kingdom. And I eliminate threats." His words were final, a death sentence delivered with chilling indifference.

The witch's eyes widened in absolute terror as she felt the shadows begin their sinister crawl up her legs again.

"Please, don't do this," she begged, desperation coloring her tone. "I told you everything."

"You did. But it's not enough," Kaelan replied, his voice devoid of any semblance of mercy.

"You'll never find her if you kill me," the witch cried out, her voice quivering with fear.

"Perhaps I won't," Kaelan conceded with a shrug, acknowledging the risk. "But I'm willing to bet that Vale can."

The witch's screams filled the room once more as the shadows consumed her, muffling her cries as they enveloped her in their dark embrace. Her voice faded into nothingness, lost deeper and deeper into the shadows that now claimed her. The last sound was the echoing crack of her neck breaking.

Kaelan and Aerion turned on their heels, striding towards the door with a sense of purpose. They left the witch behind, her body slumped lifelessly in the chair, a mere shell of what she once was.

For Kaelan, this was not a death to be mourned or contemplated. In his eyes, it was merely the removal of another obstacle, a necessary step in the larger scheme of things. His heart had long since hardened to such necessities, and he would gladly darken his soul that much further to keep Vale safe.

FORTY-FIVE

WREN

Wren couldn't sit still. Aisling was in grave danger, and the weight of his helplessness bore down on him like a leaden shroud. In Venna's room, he paced the floor with restless strides, each step echoing his growing frustration and fear.

Venna, seated on a plush chair, watched him with a patience born of understanding. She knew the torment he was going through, the gnawing anxiety of not knowing if Aisling was safe or what horrors she might be enduring.

His jaw clenched with every turn he took around the room. His fists were balled at his sides, his nails digging into his palms, a physical manifestation of his inner turmoil. A deep furrow etched across his brow, empha-sizing the creases that had formed over countless moments of worry.

The room felt tense, heavy with the unspoken fear that gripped them both. Wren's emotions swirled within him—a maelstrom of anger, fear, and desperation. He wanted to do something, anything, to bring Aisling back to safety and the waiting around was killing him.

Venna, ever the anchor in his stormy sea of emotions, remained a calm presence amid his turmoil. Her empathetic gaze followed him as he continued to pace, offering silent support.

Wren's irritation grew with each passing second, his heart aching for the girl. He couldn't bear the thought of her suffering at the hands of their enemies. Yet, despite his frustration, he knew he had to trust in Vale and their companions to bring Aisling home.

But trust was a fragile thing when it came to matters of the heart, and Wren found himself torn between the hope that they would succeed and the gnawing fear that they might fail.

The silence stretched between them until Venna's gentle voice pierced through, her words carrying a sense of assurance that Wren found hard to share. "Wren, it will be okay. You will find her."

Wren couldn't stifle the scoff that escaped him, frustration and doubt bubbling up within him. "What makes you so sure?"

"Because you have no other choice," she replied calmly, her unwavering conviction a stark contrast to his doubt. "I know you'll do whatever it takes to bring her home. You have to believe in the possibility of success. Otherwise, you'll be trapped in a prison of doubt and uncertainty."

His frustration with their predicament surfaced in a grumble. "It's hard to have hope when all we've got so far are theories and guesses."

Venna's gaze remained steady, never once leaving his. "We can't lose sight of what's important. Aisling needs us. She needs you."

"I know," Wren admitted, a heavy sigh escaping him.

"So, we hold onto hope," Venna declared, her conviction

unshaken. "And we believe in our friends and their abilities."

The doubt that had been gnawing at him resurfaced, and he couldn't help but voice it. "And if we're wrong?"

Venna's response was immediate, her words carrying a deeper wisdom. "Then we face the consequences and move forward together. That's what family does, Wren."

The word "family" hung in the air, and it struck Wren like a bolt of realization. He paused in his pacing. "I've been so selfish, haven't I?" he muttered aloud, his thoughts spilling out.

"In what way?" Venna asked, tilting her head slightly.

"When we lost Aisling, I thought it was only me who was hurting," he confessed, regret lacing his words. "But the truth is, we all lost her, and I've been so focused on my own pain and sorrow that I didn't stop to think about how you were feeling."

Venna's response was gentle and understanding. "Oh, Wren. You're allowed to feel things, you know."

"I know," he conceded. "But that doesn't mean I have the right to ignore the feelings of others."

"You're not," she insisted, her soothing words washing over him. "You're allowed to grieve and process your emotions. And, while it's admirable to think of others, you must remember that it's okay to focus on yourself too."

Wren found solace in Venna's words, her gentle reassurance like a balm for his frayed nerves. Her understanding presence offered him a respite from the turmoil of his emotions. He had always admired her ability to navigate complex emotions with grace, and in that moment, he was grateful for her wisdom.

"I just feel so helpless, so powerless. I want to do something, anything, to bring her back instead of waiting around," he confessed, his guilt a heavy weight on his shoulders.

Venna's voice retained its gentle tone, laced with compassion, as she replied, "I understand. But you can't rush into a rescue attempt blindly. You need a plan, and you need a solid strategy."

"And that's what Vale is doing, isn't it?" Wren asked, his guilt over his earlier outburst making his words hesitant. He had never raised his voice at Vale before.

"She is," Venna affirmed with a reassuring nod. "And I know it's difficult, but you have to trust her and her decisions. She's a leader, and she has a lot of responsibilities weighing on her shoulders."

"I know, and I trust her. It's just... I want to do more," Wren said. "I want to be able to do more."

"You can," Venna replied, smiling slightly. "You are a powerful and skilled fighter, and those skills will be needed when the time comes. But, for now, you have to be patient and have faith in those who are making the plans and the decisions."

After a moment of contemplation, Wren nodded in reluctant agreement and finally crossed the room to sit down. He shifted his focus to another pressing matter: his responsibility as the pack's Alpha.

"How is the pack faring after the attack?" he asked, mindful of the well-being of his people.

"Surprisingly well," Venna replied, her tone carrying a hint of relief. "We didn't lose a single fighter during the battle, and the injured wolves are recovering nicely."

Wren visibly relaxed at the news. "That's good, at least."

"Yes, it is. Although, there's a lot of tension and unease among the wolves," Venna added, her concern evident.

"They're worried about the pack's safety, and after every-thing we've all been through, I don't blame them either."

"That's understandable, given the circumstances. But, if they're looking for reassurance, then it's my job to give it to them," Wren remarked.

"Why don't we call them all together in the feast hall, and I'll speak to them?" he suggested, his mind already working through the details.

"I'll arrange it," Venna offered. "And don't worry, you'll have everyone's support."

Wren couldn't help but feel a profound sense of grati-tude toward Venna. "Thank you, Venna. I don't know what I'd do without you."

Venna's playful side emerged as she teased him lightly, a wry grin dancing across her face as she tried to diffuse the tension that hung around them like a fog. "Probably fall apart," she said.

"Yeah, probably," he admitted, a small smile playing on his lips.

"It's not a weakness to rely on the people who care about you, Wren. You're the Alpha, yes, and you carry a great burden on your shoulders. But that doesn't mean you have to shoulder the burden alone," she reminded him.

"I know, and I promise I'll try to remember that," he vowed, his words sincere.

"Good, now let's go rally the pack and reassure them," Venna declared, a determined glint in her eye.

Wren couldn't help but admire her strength and resilience. "You're a force to be reckoned with, do you know that?" he remarked, his voice filled with both admiration and respect.

A cheeky smile graced Venna's face as she replied, "Yes, I am."

FORTY-SIX

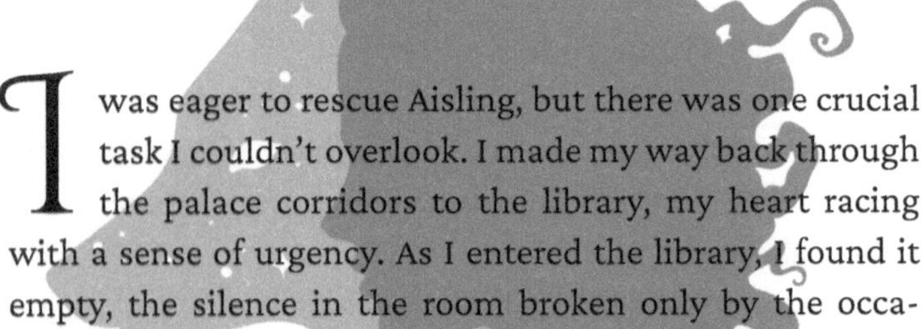

I was eager to rescue Aisling, but there was one crucial task I couldn't overlook. I made my way back through the palace corridors to the library, my heart racing with a sense of urgency. As I entered the library, I found it empty, the silence in the room broken only by the occasional creak of wooden shelves and the faint scent of old books.

My footsteps echoed softly as I headed toward the shadowy corner of the library, where the concealed entrance to the underground chamber awaited. The passage was still a well-kept secret known to the coven and only a few trusted individuals within the palace.

"Just where do you think you're going?" Elara's spectral voice chimed in as I passed her by, the ghost floating amidst the shelves, seemingly engaged in her never-ending task of rearranging books.

I didn't offer her a response, I was completely focused as I crossed the floor.

Descending the cold, stone steps into the chamber below, I summoned my magical flames, allowing them to dance like a torch over my outstretched hand, casting flickering, eerie shadows that danced along the walls. The ancient stone steps led me deeper beneath the library, and I could feel the weight of the centuries pressing down on me as I descended.

The chamber below was dimly lit, the faint glow of two magical lamps barely illuminating the space. But the flames that writhed across my palm cast a warm light that flickered across the rough-hewn walls.

I approached the large stone altar in the center of the chamber, where the ancient grimoire lay, its pages filled with centuries-old knowledge and powerful spells. With a sense of purpose, I picked up the hefty tome, its leather-bound cover cool to the touch.

I opened it and began to scan the pages, searching for any spells or incantations that could aid us in our quest to rescue Aisling and confront the Seven and Haldir. The possibilities were vast, with plenty of dark spells to choose from, but time was not on my side. I needed to find something, anything that could give us an edge in the battle that lay ahead.

The library's silence was broken only by the soft crackling of the flames in the lanterns, and I found myself deep in contemplation, clutching the ancient grimoire in my hands. It was then that the First Witch's voice resurfaced in my mind.

"Vale," her ethereal voice echoed, and I couldn't help but startle at her sudden return. She had been absent for a while, and her reappearance caught me off guard.

Frustration laced my words as I responded, "Now you've got something to say? Where have you been?"

"I could not risk disrupting the events I have seen take place. I have already disturbed things enough by saving you from the

Grimgyre," she explained, her tone carrying a sense of responsibility.

Her presence had indeed saved me from a grim fate, but my impatience overcame my gratitude. "Well, now is the time. Tell me what I need to know," I urged, determination fueling my words.

"There is a spell in the grimoire, an ancient binding spell, that could bind the powers of the Seven," she revealed.

I leaned in, eager for more information. "And how do we cast such a spell?"

"You can't do it alone, but the coven is not yet strong enough for this spell," she replied with a note of regret.

My hope for a quick solution dwindled, my frustration boiling over. "I need something that will help me now, and don't bother lecturing me about the use of dark magic."

With reluctance, she admitted to another option. *"Then there is one other spell, one that may help you."*

"What is it?" I pressed.

"It is a powerful spell. A blood-born witch can call upon it to draw strength from the elements and the natural world. It is a dangerous spell, Vale, and one you must not use lightly," the First Witch cautioned, her words carrying the weight of centuries.

"Use this spell, Vale, but do so with the knowledge of the power you are wielding and the consequences you could face," she warned, her spectral voice resonating with wisdom.

As we spoke, the grimoire took on a life of its own, its pages flipping on their own accord. Spells rushed by my eyes, each filled with arcane knowledge and potential. But the ancient tome eventually paused on a single page, and my gaze fell upon the text written in an ancient tongue.

I read the spell, committing it to memory, the words

etching themselves into my consciousness. "Thank you," I whispered to the First Witch, acknowledging her guidance.

"*Use the knowledge wisely,*" she advised, her words carrying a sense of finality. With that, her presence disappeared from my mind once again.

I was left alone in the chamber, the grimoire in my hands, and a new spell etched into my memory. Lost in thought, I contemplated the path I was embarking on, knowing that I would wield this newfound knowledge with care but also with the resolve to bring Aisling back from the clutches of darkness.

"ARE YOU SURE ABOUT THIS?" Kaelan's voice cut through the tense silence as we descended the stone steps leading to the front courtyard of the palace. His tone carried a heavy dose of concern, mirroring the doubts that gnawed at my own thoughts.

I glanced at him. "No, I'm not sure, but we have no choice," I replied, my voice heavy.

"You're putting the witches at risk, Vale. They're not ready for this, they're not strong enough. You remember what happened last time," Kaelan argued.

"They'll be fine and they're stronger than you think," I reassured him. I was determined to make this work. "Besides, they have to learn sometime, and now is as good a time as any."

"You're talking about a battlefield, Vale. That's not a training exercise." Kaelan's frustration was clear, but I wouldn't be swayed.

"I know," I said. "But it's the reality of the situation."

"I'm not comfortable with this," Kaelan grumbled, still reluctant.

Wren, who had been walking silently beside us, finally spoke up. "None of us are comfortable with this, but Vale's right. This is what we're facing, and if they want to help, we need to let them."

He gave Wren a reluctant nod, his dissatisfaction clear.

As we approached the center of the courtyard, my gaze landed on Ava, Calliope, and Harlow standing with Harker who was staying here with Thalion to take care of the kingdom.

"Are you three sure about this?" I asked, my concern for their safety etched in every word.

"Hell yes," Harlow replied with a fire in her eyes, her determination burning bright.

"We know we're not exactly skilled warriors, but we want to be of use," Ava added, matching Harlow's determination.

"You are useful," I began, addressing them with sincerity. "Don't ever think otherwise."

"Thank you, Vale," Calliope murmured, a grateful smile gracing her face.

"You three are stronger than you realize, and your shields are solid, which means you can defend yourselves and others," I continued, trying to bolster their confidence. "Just remember, no matter what, keep your shields up and stay close to us."

"We will," Ava said, sounding more confident than I felt.

Wren, ever the protector, issued a stern warning. "This is important, ladies. If we can't rely on your shields, you need to stay here."

"We understand," Calliope promised, her commitment to the mission clear in her eyes.

"We won't let you down," Harlow chimed, her eyes filled with resolve.

"I know," I replied, offering her a reassuring smile that sought to bolster their spirits in the face of uncertainty.

"I have something for the three of you," Harker said as she stepped forward, carrying a bundle of daggers in her hands. The surprise in Calliope's voice was evident as she asked, "These are for us?"

"They are," Harker confirmed, her expression serious. "These are Fae made. They're small, lightweight, and easy to use, so pay attention."

I watched as she took a moment to provide the three young witches with instructions on handling their daggers. Their eyes remained fixed on her, absorbing every word of guidance and instruction. When the vampire had finished, the trio of witches stood in a row, clutching the small, silver weapons that I hoped they wouldn't have to use.

"How are we going to find her once we get there?" Aerion asked, breaking the temporary silence.

"We're going to go into town and find a map of the surrounding area. I'll scry for her again, and we'll go from there," I replied, outlining our immediate plan.

But Calliope raised a valid concern, "Won't we all be a bit conspicuous in town? We aren't exactly all dressed like mortals, Aerion stands out with those pointed ears of his, not to mention how large he is."

"Only Kaelan and I will be going into town," I clarified, addressing their concerns. "The rest of you will be waiting on the outskirts. Aerion will be shifting all of you. Kaelan and I will be shifting together."

"Let's get going then," Wren said, his tone terse.

The group began to disperse, and I watched as Kaelan approached me.

"Ready?" he asked, his eyes locked onto mine.

I couldn't help but shake my head, a heavy sigh escaping my lips. "Not even close," I admitted.

"We're going to get her back," Kaelan insisted.

"Let's just pray we're not too late," I muttered, my voice heavy with the regret that clung to my every step.

FORTY-SEVEN

Kaelan and I found ourselves on the large city's outskirts, the urban landscape transitioning into a quieter, more rural setting. Securing a map of the local area had been surprisingly easy, thanks to the kindness of a friendly elderly lady at a nearby tourist shop. After expressing our gratitude, Kaelan and I retreated to a secluded spot along the side of a road, away from the bustling traffic that led into the city.

I spread the map out on the hood of a nearby car, its surface providing a makeshift table for our next steps. "Okay, let's try this," I muttered to myself, my fingers gently tracing the lines of the map. Closing my eyes, I inhaled deeply, seeking inner calm amidst the storm of emotions raging within me. My connection to the crystal pendant around my neck intensified as I harnessed my powers.

I pulled it from my neck and positioned it over the map. The crystal responded to my call, emitting a subtle hum as it swung slowly. The sensation was familiar, the ethereal tether pulling me toward a destination yet unknown. With each passing moment, the crystal's movement grew more pronounced, like a compass needle pointing us in the right direction.

Time seemed to stretch as I concentrated, the world around me fading into the background. The crystal continued its pendulum-like motion, its swings gradually slowing until it came to a rest. My eyes focused on the spot where it had settled, and I read the name aloud, my voice barely above a whisper, "Ruby Falls."

Kaelan's furrowed brow mirrored my own concerns. "That's gotta be where they're keeping her."

I nodded in agreement. "We should head back and gather the others. We'll need to shift in."

"I agree. It'll be safer that way," Kaelan said, carefully folding the map.

He pulled me close as he prepared to shift away to where the others were waiting but I stopped him gently.

"Wait, I want to try and shift us," I said. The desire to test and expand my growing powers burned within me.

"It can be hard the first couple of times, Vale. Maybe just try yourself first and I can follow you," Kaelan suggested.

I flashed him a slight grin, my spirit undaunted. "What's life without a little push on my limits? Besides, if I can get this down, it might come in handy while we're facing Haldir."

"If you're sure," he said, watching me closely and intertwining his fingers with mine.

"I am," I replied, closing my eyes and taking a deep breath. The world around us faded away as I concentrated.

"Concentrate on not only where you are but where you want to go. Focus on that feeling and that place in your mind. Your magic will do the rest. And don't forget to breathe. Just breathe through it and let your magic guide you. It'll work if you let it, and it won't if you don't," he coached, his words soothing as I focused.

After a moment, the familiar tugging sensation of my magic began to take hold. It was a gentle pull, like a current guiding me toward its intended destination. I could feel the energy flowing through me, enveloping me in its warm embrace. The sensation was exhilarating, and I let myself become lost in the moment, surrendering myself to the flow of my power.

As the feeling grew stronger, I could sense the edges of my body begin to dissolve, my consciousness stretching and expanding outward. Time and space seemed to cease to exist, and for a brief moment, I was one with the universe, the boundaries between my existence and everything else dissolving into nothingness. It was a surreal and over-whelming experience, and yet, at the same time, it was also incredibly peaceful.

I could feel Kaelan's presence beside me, his own energy intertwined with mine, and it was a comfort in the vast emptiness.

My senses stretched out, and the air surrounding us began to shimmer. A rush of wind enveloped me, and the world spun around us as I felt the telltale signs of my body rushing forward through the realm. Aerion's earlier expla-nation about shifting being akin to folding reality now made perfect sense to me—a complex, intricate maneuver akin to folding one piece of paper inside another.

When the dizziness had faded, I dared to open my eyes, finding myself in a serene forest clearing. The rest of our group had been waiting patiently, and Aerion, who had been crouched down, stood up in surprise as we appeared.

"Well, that was fast," he remarked, his eyebrows raised in astonishment. "Took me ages to shift my first time."

"She's getting stronger," Kaelan said, his arm sliding around my waist, pulling me closer to him as he beamed with pride.

Wren's apprehensive tone cut through the moment. "Let's hope so."

I quickly took charge, knowing that our discovery was only the beginning. "We found where she is, it's not far from here. We can shift there, but we need a plan for once we get there."

"Well, that's the problem, isn't it? We don't know what we're going to find once we get there," Harlow stated, voicing the concerns that weighed on all of us.

"She's right. We're going in blind," Aerion said, a deep furrow creasing his brow.

I knew that addressing this was important. "That's why we're going to have to think about the different scenarios that could happen and be prepared for any eventuality," I said firmly, understanding that this was a make-or-break situation.

Harlow's eyes filled with concern as she responded. "That's a big ask, Vale. How do we prepare for every single scenario when we don't even know what we're facing?"

"We go in, we stick together, and we use the element of surprise to our advantage. And if there's anyone in the way, then we'll take them down. It's as simple as that," Kaelan replied, always the pragmatic one.

"Okay, that's a starting point," I said, grateful for his contribution. "Do you think that will be enough, though?"

"I mean, it's not the greatest plan, but it's a plan," Calliope said, raising a valid concern.

Wren, his emotions running high, wasn't satisfied with this approach. "No, I can't accept that. We can't just go in there and hope for the best. Aisling's life is on the line!"

"And we're doing everything we can, Wren. You have to trust me on that," I said, trying to calm him.

But his fear and anger had reached a breaking point, and he lashed out, directing his frustration towards me. "Trust you? You're the reason we're even in this mess!"

Kaelan stepped forward protectively, his voice a low growl. "Hey, don't speak to her like that."

Wren, however, remained defiant and unrelenting. "Or what?"

Wren's jaw clenched with barely suppressed fury as the three men stood off against each other. My heart ached at the division and conflict within our group, especially with my best friend.

"Wren, I'm sorry, I know you're angry, but—"

"Angry?" Wren scoffed, his voice heavy with disbelief. "I'm fucking terrified and all you are offering as a plan is trying our hardest."

"I'm sorry. I know it's not enough. I wish I could do more, but we have to make the best of what we have. It's the only way," I said, my voice trembling slightly.

Wren countered with a raw edge of fear in his voice. "We could be walking straight into a trap."

"It's possible, yes. But we have to try," I conceded, knowing he was right.

"This isn't going very well, is it?" Ava murmured, her voice tinged with sadness. Her words hung in the air like a heavy cloud, casting a shadow over our group.

"I think we're all on edge. Can't blame anyone for that." Harlow chimed in, her voice carrying a hint of understanding.

I knew we needed to regroup and find common ground. My heart pounded with the urgency of our situation. "No, but we need to focus. If we can't work together, then we'll never be able to rescue Aisling."

Harlow offered a practical suggestion. "We should at least have a general plan, some guidelines."

Relieved that someone had taken the initiative, I responded, "Okay, that's something we can work with."

"We can split into teams and have the witches circle the perimeter and see if they can detect any traps or magic barriers. If they find something, they'll signal the others. Meanwhile, the rest of us will stay close together and approach the entrance," Kaelan explained, his voice filled with determination.

"Once inside, I'll lead the group and have a shield ready. They were easy enough to take down last time. I'm not worried about the two witches from earlier. It's Haldir we'll have to watch out for. Ensure he doesn't touch you; he can shift you away to another realm in the blink of an eye." I told them.

"We can use that against him. Once we've got Aisling, can you try and keep his attention while the rest of us get out?" Aerion suggested.

I couldn't help but smile at the clever strategy. "That's actually a good plan."

"What can I do?" Wren asked.

My gaze met his, and I spoke with a quiet determination. "Be ready to defend her. Once we've got her, we'll need you guys to get her to safety."

With a clear understanding of our roles and responsibilities, I turned to Kaelan, ready to move forward. "Okay, I think we all have a pretty solid understanding of what's going on. Let's shift there and see what we're facing. Kaelan can take us all at once."

But Kaelan wasn't looking at me. He held his head in his

hands, shaking it as if he could dislodge an invisible weight.

"Kaelan?" I said hesitantly, dread creeping into my gut.

"Vale," he ground out, his voice filled with pain. "Something's not right. Something's wrong."

"How long has it been since you had your potion?" I asked him, my panic growing as I stood there helplessly watching him.

"I just took one as a precaution," he replied, groaning.

"What's going on?" Ava asked, her voice tinged with worry.

I began to search through Kaelan's bag, hoping to find a solution. "I'm not sure. Maybe he just needs another potion."

But Kaelan's distress was undeniable as he fell to his knees, his voice strained. "I'm burning, Vale."

Desperation clawed at me as Kaelan's pain-ridden plea filled the air. "What can I do?" I implored, my heart aching to help him.

"Just… just stay back," Kaelan managed to grit out, his face twisted in agony. He clamped his eyes shut, his entire being strained by whatever was afflicting him. When he reopened his eyes, they were a void of absolute darkness.

My breath hitched as I watched his condition deteriorate before my eyes. Veins bulged on his arms, and the skin around them turned as black as night, the obsidian darkness creeping like a malignant infection across his flesh.

"Get her out of here!" he bellowed, his voice distorted and unrecognizable.

"No, I can help you!" I insisted, panic gripping me as I refused to accept the transformation taking hold of him.

But before I could do anything, Kaelan shot me one last anguished look, and the shadows enveloped him, whisking him away into the unknown.

"No!" I screamed, my voice breaking with despair, tears welling up in my eyes.

"Vale," Aerion said, his voice laden with sympathy, his own expression filled with sorrow.

"I'm going to go and look for him. We have to help him," I declared firmly.

Aerion's response was swift and resolute. "Vale, no, it's too dangerous. You have no idea where he's gone or what state he's in. Besides, we have to help Aisling; we don't have time."

My voice trembled with disbelief. "You honestly think we can succeed without him? We need him!"

"No, we don't," Aerion insisted, his tone softening. "We've got this. You've got this."

"We can do this. All of us together." Calliope said.

I took a moment to collect myself, wiping the tears from my eyes and steeling my resolve. I knew they were right, and despite my fear and apprehension, I nodded, giving in to their pleas.

Harlow placed a comforting hand on my shoulder, her voice filled with a quiet reassurance. "Let's go and get Aisling."

"Okay, let's go." I relented reluctantly after a heavy pause, my heart aching for Kaelan. I would find him after, as soon as we had Aisling. That thought helped me go on.

We drew close to Aerion, each of us placing a hand on his arm as he prepared to shift us. The world around us dissolved into a dazzling array of colors and blinding light, disorienting and confusing. When the journey was finally over, we found ourselves standing at the entrance of a vast cave, uncertainty and danger lurking in its shadowy depths.

FORTY-EIGHT

The cave's entrance loomed before us, its gaping maw an intimidating portal to the unknown. Its entrance, framed by jagged, uneven rocks, appeared ominous and uninviting. As we stood at the threshold, uncertainty cast a shadow over Wren's features, and he voiced his concerns.

"Are you sure she's in there?" he asked, his forehead etched with doubt.

I nodded firmly, my gaze fixed on the cave's entrance. "Yes, this is the place the crystal led us to. And the only way out of this place is through that cave. It's our only chance."

"Okay," Wren agreed, his expression darkening.

"So, what's the new plan, Vale?" Harlow asked, her eyes brimming with unwavering faith.

"Spread out along the entrance and see if you can detect any traps," I told the witches.

Harlow turned to the others and they nodded, silently spreading out to search the area. I watched them, feeling a pang of loss for Kaelan. The group didn't seem as confident without him.

I couldn't stop thinking about him, and the image of his tortured form flashed in my mind. The memory caused a shudder to run down my spine. I had no idea what had happened or where he'd gone, and I couldn't shake the feeling that something had gone terribly wrong.

After a few minutes, the witches returned.

"I didn't find anything, and neither did Calliope. Ava was able to detect a few magical wards around the entrance, but they don't appear to be harmful," Harlow explained.

"Okay, good. Then we can proceed without any issues," I said, relieved that the witches were able to safely navigate the cave's perimeter.

Wren's expression remained uncertain. "That's great, but what if there's more further inside? Do we just risk it?"

"No, we don't. I can handle any wards inside, I can sense the magic," I said,

"If you're sure," Wren said, his concern evident.

"I am. Now, let's go rescue Aisling," I said, stepping into the cave's yawning mouth, its rocky walls swallowing us one by one. The air inside was thick with a musty, earthy scent, and a chilling breeze whispered through the underground passageway.

Aerion followed closely behind, his shoulders tensed, as the tunnel narrowed, pressing down upon us.

"This seems way too easy," Harlow observed, her gaze darting to the walls, searching for hidden dangers.

I couldn't help but agree. "Don't worry, I have a feeling it's about to get a whole lot harder," I remarked, acutely aware that Haldir would have surely prepared traps and obstacles to thwart our progress.

"Well, it's been a pleasure knowing you all," Calliope said, attempting to lighten the mood.

"I'd appreciate it if you didn't talk about us dying," Ava interjected.

"Sorry," Calliope said sheepishly.

"Nyxen," I called out, and my familiar appeared from the cave's shadows. "Can you lead us to Aisling?"

Nyxen chirped softly and set off, his paws padding softly against the cavern's rough ground, the sound gently reverberating in the vast, echoing space. We fell into step behind him, enveloped in a tense, expectant silence that filled the cavernous expanse. The cave itself was a marvel; ancient stalactites hung from the ceiling like jagged teeth, while stalagmites rose from the floor, creating a forest of stone. The air was cool and damp, carrying the scent of earth and minerals, a constant reminder of the deep belly of the earth we tread upon.

After what felt like an eternity in the dimly lit expanse, the cave suddenly forked into three separate tunnels. Each path disappeared into the impenetrable darkness, the unknown lying just beyond the reach of the flickering flames that danced on my outstretched hands. I hesitated at the junction, the decision weighing heavily on me. "Which way?" I asked, turning to Nyxen for guidance.

With his eyes shining an otherworldly glow, Nyxen paused, then confidently padded down the leftmost path. Trusting in my familiar's instinct, I took a deep breath and followed him, the others trailing close behind.

The chosen tunnel sloped steeply downward, the gradient increasing with every step, pulling us deeper into the mountain's heart. The air turned noticeably colder, our breath visible in misty clouds that lingered before dissipating into the chill. The walls began to constrict around us as we descended, the once spacious cavern giving way to a much narrower passageway. Jagged rocks jutted out from the walls, their sharp edges scraping against our clothes and skin, a constant threat in the tight space.

A sense of claustrophobia crept over me, the closeness of the walls overwhelming, the ceiling lowering until we were nearly hunched over. The weight of the mountain seemed to press down from above, an invisible, heavy burden that made each breath feel labored. The only sounds in this constricted space were our own – the ragged rhythm of our breathing, the scuff of boots against stone, and the occasional soft echo of Nyxen's paws – all combining into a noise that seemed loud in the silence of the deep earth.

The journey through the cavernous labyrinth continued, each passageway revealing new twists and turns. The monotonous walls of rough-hewn stone seemed to stretch endlessly in every direction, creating an overwhelming sense of disorientation.

As we pressed forward, the distant sound of rushing water reached our ears. The tunnel we were in gradually widened, leading us into a vast underground cavern. A breathtaking sight greeted us as we entered—the cavern's ceiling soared high above, crowned by a mesmerizing waterfall that cascaded from its heights. The water plummeted into a crystal-clear pool below, disappearing beneath a rocky ledge.

"Wow," I gasped, awestruck by the natural wonder before us.

"It's beautiful," Calliope marveled, her voice filled with wonder.

"It's also a perfect spot for an ambush," Harlow cautioned, her tone wary.

"Stay alert," I instructed the group, knowing we could

not afford to let our guard down in such an unpredictable environment.

With cautious steps, we all moved further into the cavern, navigating along the rocky outcrops that bordered the pool's edge. Our senses were on high alert, every movement and shadow scrutinized for signs of danger in the vast underground world we now traversed.

We found ourselves in a seemingly dead end within the cavern, the tunnel walls coming to an abrupt halt. Our eyes scanned the rocky enclosure for any signs or clues that might guide us toward Aisling's location.

Ava's voice broke the silence, "What exactly are we looking for?"

"Anything out of the ordinary, I guess," Calliope offered, her eyes searching the stony walls for hidden secrets.

"I don't see anything," Harlow remarked, frustration creeping into her tone.

"Neither do I," Aerion added, his gaze sweeping the surroundings in vain.

"Then, we have to be missing something," I insisted.

As I contemplated our predicament, my attention was drawn upward to the towering waterfall that dominated the cavern. It was a colossal natural wonder, its waters thundering down with such power that it nearly drowned out our thoughts.

But something about that waterfall...

"Vale, what are you thinking?" Harlow asked, watching me curiously.

"I think..." I began, my words trailing off as I approached the pool's edge, my eyes fixed on the cascading water. "I think the waterfall is hiding something."

"What are you talking about?" Wren asked, his confusion mirroring the sentiment of the others.

"I can feel it," I insisted, my senses extending beyond the surface of the waterfall, detecting an unusual energy emanating from behind it.

"It's true," Harlow confirmed, her expression turning serious. "I can feel it, too."

Moving closer to the pool's edge, I peered down at the slippery rocks protruding from the water's surface."I could walk on those..." I muttered. An idea began to form, and I cautiously tested my footing by stepping on one of the slick stones.

"Are you sure about this?" Ava asked as her eyes bore into mine.

"Yeah, I'm sure," I replied, holding my arms out for balance. I took another step onto the slippery rock, my balance tested by the unstable surface.

The rock held my weight, albeit precariously. I moved cautiously, each step a deliberate attempt to avoid losing my balance and plunging into the unforgiving water below.

"What do you see?" Wren's voice broke the tense silence that had settled over our group.

I maneuvered around behind the waterfall, the cacophonous roar of rushing water now drowning out all other sounds. The spray from the waterfall misted my clothes and skin, creating a damp sheen on my body.

As my fingers brushed the wall, I noted a subtle difference in texture. Closing my eyes, I kept my hand in place, concentrating to sense any trace of magic. It was an elusive feeling, but then a surge of power coursed through me, and I opened my eyes just in time to witness the wall shimmer, briefly revealing a hidden opening concealed behind the waterfall's relentless cascade.

"You guys," I called out, excitement bubbling in my voice, "I found an opening!"

Without hesitation, I reached out, pressing my palm flat against the wall's surface, and felt the thrum of magic coursing through it. I closed my eyes, focusing on the wall's enchantments. I searched for any signs of wards or other magical barriers that might have been placed upon it.

A low, pulsing hum resonated from the wall, and an unsettling feeling formed in the pit of my stomach. I had been right; there was something behind this wall, and it wasn't going to yield easily.

Reluctantly, I pulled my hand away, causing the opening to once again disappear from view.

"Did you open it?" Aerion's voice carried over the roar of the waterfall.

"Not yet," I shouted back, my frustration audible. "It's sealed shut."

Aerion's confusion was evident as he asked, "Then, how did it disappear?"

"It didn't disappear," I clarified, my patience tested. "I just revealed it."

"Can you open it?" Harlow asked.

"Yeah, I think so," I replied. "But it'll take some time."

"We should hurry, Vale." Wren urged.

"I can't just break the spell. It'll take time." I explained again, frustration welling up in me.

"Time is something we don't have, Vale," Harlow said, giving us an unnecessary reminder of our dire circumstances.

"I'm aware," I snapped. "But it's not as easy as just saying 'open sesame.'"

"Okay, I'm sorry. Do your thing. We'll just wait here and watch," Wren said.

With a deep breath, I closed my eyes again, refocusing my efforts on the intricate magical lock in front of me.

I could sense the threads of magic woven into the lock, holding the door closed. I traced the threads, following them to their source, trying to unknot the tangles woven into them.

The relentless downpour from the waterfall posed an additional challenge, making it difficult to focus. But I pressed on, delicately untangling the threads one by one, concentrating as I did so.

With patience and precision, I carefully unraveled the threads until they were sufficiently loosened. As I pulled on them, the door reappeared before my eyes, revealing the path beyond.

"Ah-ha!" I couldn't help but exclaim, the thrill of success momentarily throwing off my balance and almost sending me tumbling into the water.

"Did you open it?" Harlow's voice echoed my excitement.

"Yes," I confirmed, "you should all be able to come through now, one by one."

Aerion's face emerged in front of me and I gasped at his sudden appearance.

"Sorry, didn't mean to scare you," he offered, a faint smile playing on his lips.

"No, it's fine," I reassured him, my heart still racing, "just a little on edge."

"Understandable," he said, scanning my face. "We'll get through this and then we'll find Kaelan, okay?"

I nodded, forcing a small smile.

The rest of our group began carefully making their way across the stones and filed through the open door as we waited inside the narrow tunnel beyond.

"Do you really believe she's in there?" Harlow asked, her eyes fixed on the ominous darkness that lay ahead.

"She has to be," I insisted. I couldn't afford for her to be anywhere else.

Wren's voice broke through our collective unease. "We should get moving. The longer we linger here, the greater the risk of discovery."

"He's right," Aerion agreed. "We need to keep going."

"Okay, I'll lead the way." I declared, taking charge once again.

As we continued down the passage, it gradually widened, and the air grew thick with heat, causing beads of sweat to form on our foreheads.

"It's getting hotter in here," Wren observed.

"There must be a reason for it," Aerion replied, his tone filled with concern.

"I don't like this," Harlow confessed, her voice tinged with unease.

"Neither do I," Ava added, her apprehension plain.

I pressed forward, resolute. "I know, but we can't turn back now. Not when we're this close."

As we ventured further into the passageway, it opened into a vast chamber, its walls and ceiling adorned with an ethereal spectacle of glowing red crystals. The heat was pouring off of them in waves. The ambient light emanating from the crystals cast an otherworldly glow upon the scene, creating an eerie yet mesmerizing atmosphere.

In the heart of the chamber sat Aisling, her form a stark contrast to the radiant surroundings. Her hands were bound behind her back, a cruel gag silencing her cries for help. Her eyes widened as she caught sight of our group and she began struggling frantically against her bonds.

"Aisling!" Wren's voice trembled as he rushed forward. But he came to an abrupt halt mere inches from her as if an invisible force field held him back.

"She's shielded," I said, my realization dawning on me.

"What? Can you remove it?" Wren's desperation was palpable, his eyes pleading with me.

"I can try," I replied, stepping up to the invisible barrier and extending my hand tentatively toward it.

Aisling, still bound and gagged, shook her head vigorously, her eyes darting around the room, her expression filled with dread.

"What is it?" I asked, confused.

Aerion, ever vigilant, scanned the chamber with sharp eyes. "Something's not right here."

"You shouldn't have come here," a chillingly familiar voice echoed through the chamber.

"Haldir," Aerion hissed, his fists clenching involuntarily.

"Yes, and you've unwittingly brought me a second blood witch to aid in my dark ritual," Haldir chuckled maliciously, shifting before us in an instant, his eyes gleaming with vicious delight.

"Aisling is not yours to take," Wren growled, his voice laden with venom.

"Oh, but she is. She was always meant to be mine. She was just too stubborn to accept it. She exists because of me, just like the lovely Valerian here," Haldir taunted, his voice dripping with hatred.

"What are you talking about? You didn't create her," Aerion growled.

"I didn't create her, no. But I'm the one who delivered Lyra to Zephyrian. Just as I delivered Aisling's Fae mother to him," Haldir replied, a nasty smirk stretching across his face.

Aerion and Wren looked at me, shock registering on their faces. My mind was reeling from Haldir's revelation.

He continued, undeterred, "I've waited years for this, and now it's finally within reach."

"What are you saying?" Wren demanded, his gaze piercing through Haldir with a burning fury.

"I am saying that Vale and Aisling's sires are one and the same. They're sisters, daughters of the demon lord, and born for my own dark purposes," Haldir revealed with a wicked grin.

Shock laced through me as I looked to Aisling, still sitting there wide-eyed. My sister? And Haldir had somehow orchestrated our whole existence? I felt rage course through me as I turned my gaze back to Haldir. This asshole just made this shit personal.

"You're a dead man," Wren hissed, his voice quivering with disgust and rage.

"I am a Fae with a grand design," Haldir corrected. "One who is on the brink of ascending to godhood."

"That's impossible," Aerion spat.

"Nothing is impossible," Haldir retorted. "I've conversed with the gods themselves, boy, and I've been given the tools I need to attain immortality."

"You're delusional," Wren growled.

"Hardly," Haldir scoffed. "I'm the most powerful Fae alive, and I've got two blood witches to sacrifice in my ascension ritual."

Without waiting to hear any more of his vile proclamations, I focused my magic on the shield that separated us, pushing against the seemingly impenetrable barrier.

I gritted my teeth, pouring every ounce of my determination into breaking through.

It was then that the two other witches who had been present at the palace during the attack stepped forward, their collective magic reinforcing the shield.

"I think you've already met my associates. There's just one more you haven't had the pleasure of encountering yet," Haldir sneered as his eyes underwent a startling transformation, shifting from dark green to a blazing, ethereal white.

I knew precisely what was happening. He was about to introduce us to the witch who currently possessed his very soul.

FORTY-NINE

"Shazarah, I presume?" I uttered calmly, my voice steady despite my nerves.

"Clever girl," Shazarah cooed, her eyes gleaming with a sinister amusement. Though she wore Haldir's face, the two were distinguishable from each other just by the expression she wore. "It's a shame. I would have liked to get to know you if we were not on opposite sides," she continued, her voice laced with a disquieting sweetness.

"The feeling isn't mutual," I replied.

"No, I suppose not," Shazarah chuckled, her eyes glittering. "You possess a strong will, Vale, much like your mother. It's regrettable that I must end your life; I believe we could have been rather good friends."

"What do you know of my mother?" I demanded, trying not to let her words get to me.

"She was a beautiful and powerful Fae, but her will was not her own," Shazarah replied, her voice smooth yet laced with an unsettling calm. "She was merely a pawn in a game far more extensive and ancient than she could have ever comprehended. A game that Haldir and I have been intricately weaving for more than two hundred years. The very same game that, quite fatefully, resulted in your birth."

Her words struck me like a physical blow, sending shockwaves through my body. I had never considered the fact that their plan had been set in motion well before my time. I suddenly felt sick to my stomach.

"You and Haldir orchestrated everything, didn't you?" I accused, feeling the hot surge of anger boiling within me. The idea that my life, my very existence, had been nothing more than a move in their long game was infuriating. I would not let that be my destiny.

"Oh, child," she chuckled with a patronizing tone that made my skin crawl, "you barely scratch the surface of the complexity of our plans. You and your sister were created for a very specific purpose, a grand design that required meticulous planning and manipulation. We had to ensure that everything unfolded precisely as intended."

"And what is this 'purpose' you speak of?" My words were sharp, driven by a mix of fear, curiosity, and rising fury. Despite myself, I needed to understand the full scope of their scheme.

"All in due time," she responded, her eyes flickering with a dangerous gleam. "But, suffice it to say, you and your sister are the key components in my ascent to power. I had every confidence in Haldir's ability to deliver your mother into the hands of the demon lord. And when he did, the wheels of destiny began to turn inexorably towards this moment."

"And now," Shazarah continued, her gaze hardening with malevolent intent, "you and your sister will provide the final pieces I need to ascend to the throne of the gods."

"You're insane," I spat back, the words fueled by a

seething, uncontrollable rage."We'll see," Shazarah countered, her lips curling into a sinister smile. "Tell me, Vale, how is that demon of yours faring? I can't help but notice his absence."

"Leave him out of this," I hissed.

"Bringing out his demonic side isn't the only thing that curse does; it's gradually killing him. It erodes his very being day by day. But, you've been far too occupied dealing with other matters to uncover how to break it, haven't you?" she taunted me.

"It's only a matter of time before his mind gives in and he can no longer resist the darkness," Shazarah smirked. "And when that moment comes, well, I'll be free to claim him as my own."

"You won't touch him," I growled back.

"True, I might not, but the curse will. It will consume him, and then what will you be left with?" Shazarah laughed cruelly.

My mind whirled with the horrifying implications of her words. I couldn't let that happen. I wouldn't.

"Release Aisling," I demanded. "This is between you and me."

"Now, why on earth would I do that? I require a blood-born witch to siphon power from, and since I already have this one so conveniently bound, well..." Shazarah's voice trailed off, her eyes filled with wicked delight.

"Don't you dare," Wren warned, his voice low and menacing.

"Or what, wolf? What can you possibly do to thwart me? There's nothing you can do to prevent me from achieving my goal," Shazarah taunted, her voice dripping with sadistic amusement.

"I will not let you harm her," Wren snarled, his eyes gleamed with a fiery fury that burned like embers.

Without wasting a heartbeat, I unleashed the torrent of my magical power upon the shimmering shield that encapsulated Aisling. Harlow, Ava, and Calliope swiftly joined in, their energies weaving into a maelstrom.

Shazarah merely responded with a chilling laugh. She sauntered toward Aisling, who sat still bound and gagged in the chamber's center. Aisling's eyes bore the raw emotions of terror and desperation.

"You don't have to do this. Let Aisling go, and you can have me," I implored, my voice tinged with desperation, seeking to stall her, to buy us more precious moments in this harrowing standoff.

"Now, where's the fun in that?" Shazarah purred with a sadistic glee. "This way is much more satisfying."

With a casual flick of her wrist, she severed the bonds that restrained Aisling's wrists and legs, allowing the gag to be removed from her mouth. Aisling's cry of relief and fear echoed through the chamber as she trembled under Shazarah's sinister gaze. The witch grabbed the girl by a fistful of her hair and yanked her closer.

In a desperate bid to free her, I poured an even greater surge of energy into the unyielding shield, my companions doing the same. We fought valiantly, their combined powers and mine a fierce force to be reckoned with, yet the shield held steadfast. Shazarah's grasp on the barrier seemed impenetrable, and our collective might struggled to break through.

Shazarah, unabated by our efforts, began to chant dark incantations. The other two witches accompanying her bore sinister smiles as they witnessed the unfolding tragedy.

Wren, consumed by helpless fury, let out a furious roar that reverberated through the chamber. Aerion, his normally calm demeanor shattered, watched in a horrified trance, his eyes aflame with impotent rage.

Meanwhile, Calliope, Harlow, and Ava relentlessly hurled their magical prowess against the unyielding shield, the pressure becoming almost unbearable. Each moment was an agonizing struggle against the relentless tide of darkness that sought to engulf us.

I focused all my energy, my willpower, on finding the chink in the shield's armor. My body trembled with the overwhelming strain, yet I refused to give in. I drew deeply from the wellsprings of my magical reserves, casting my consciousness against the barrier like a battering ram.

In a brief glimmer of hope, I saw one of the witches stagger backward in response to my onslaught. If I could penetrate even one of their minds, weaken the shield's grip for a fraction of a second, it might be enough to break through the impervious barrier.

But Shazarah remained undaunted, her chanting undeterred. Her eerie grin widened as she reached into the folds of her cloak, producing a wickedly gleaming knife. Aisling, who had been struggling hopelessly in Shazarah's grasp, renewed her futile efforts to break free.

Shazarah's cruel grip on Aisling's hair tightened further, wrenching her head back at an agonizing angle. Aisling's cries of pain only fueled Shazarah's glee as she brandished the glinting blade, the wicked edge gleaming ominously.

Aisling, her wide eyes brimming with terror, fought against her captor's cruel grasp, but it was a futile struggle. Shazarah's sinister intentions loomed ever closer like a storm on the horizon.

I focused every ounce of my energy on the relentless assault against the shield that kept Aisling imprisoned. The pressure became an unbearable weight, threatening to crush my very being. My head throbbed as if it were about to split open, and the world around me started to blur into a hazy abyss. Back at the palace, I had easily broken through the shields of the other witches. Shazarah must be particularly powerful for it to still be standing.

Closing my eyes, I delved deep into the core of my being, seeking out the wellspring of power that lay within. Drawing forth every last ounce of my magical reserves, I unleashed my magic toward the witch who had stumbled under the relentless assault. She would be the first to falter, the weakest link in their collective defense.

With relentless determination, I rammed into her mind, seeking to ensnare her like a trapped prey. My consciousness felt along the psychic wall she had erected, scouring it for any chink, any fissure through which I could infiltrate. The relentless onslaught continued, my magical force relentlessly pounding against her defenses.

Finally, in a moment of triumph, I discovered a small fissure, a crack in her mental fortress. I seized the opportunity, driving my magic into the breach and widening it. The witch gasped as I infiltrated her mind, wresting control away from her.

As her body crumpled to the ground, the remaining witch was quick to sense the disruption. Her hold wavered and her powers faltered. It was the opening we desperately needed.

With their defenses weakened, I mustered the last of my strength, pushing back against the shield with newfound determination, my own magical prowess bolstering our collective efforts.

Shazarah, infuriated by our resistance, continued her dark incantations without pause. She raised the knife high, its malevolent gleam casting eerie shadows across the chamber. In a swift, cruel motion, she brought the blade down upon Aisling's arm, slicing a deep, painful gash from her elbow to her wrist. Aisling's cry of anguish pierced the air.

Beside me, Wren's snarl of rage reached a crescendo, and he transformed into his fierce wolf form, his primal instincts taking over as he poised to strike down the witch the moment the shield relented.

"Come on, Vale! Just a little bit more!" Harlow's urgent voice rang out.

Summoning every ounce of my strength, I mustered a final, explosive burst of energy. With an exhilarating surge of power, I shattered through the witch's defenses, the shield crumbling like paper. The witch was sent tumbling backward, disoriented and vulnerable.

Wren, swift and deadly in his lupine form, lunged toward Shazarah, his fangs bared and claws extended. Shazarah, recognizing the imminent danger, hastily released her hold on Aisling and shifted the deadly blade toward Wren.

"No!" My scream tore through the air, a desperate plea as I sprinted forward, my heart pounding in my chest. But in the cruel dance of fate, I was too late. Shazarah drove the blade of her dagger deep into Wren's chest with ruthless efficiency. A gut-wrenching cry escaped my lips as I watched him crumple.

Shazarah wasted no time, shoving Wren's limp body aside with callous indifference. Her cold eyes turned back to Aisling, who stood there, defenseless, her anguished sobs mixing with the chant that spilled from Shazarah's lips.

In a desperate move, I lashed out with my magic, sending a torrent of energy toward Shazarah. But the two witches who had been incapacitated moments ago were now on their feet and they threw up a shield, protecting their leader.

Shazarah's grip on Aisling tightened once more, and with a swift, merciless motion, she brought the blade down on Aisling's other arm. A tortured scream rent the air as fresh blood flowed from her wounds, staining her arms crimson.

Aerion, his eyes filled with a righteous fury, lunged forward to intervene. However, the two witches, their determination renewed, blocked his path. His sword swung with deadly precision, striking one of them and sending her crashing to the ground. The other witch raised her hand, her magic swirling, and summoned a barrier that repelled Aerion's every attempt to reach Shazarah.

I gathered my strength and charged at Shazarah. Flames ignited around my outstretched hand, a fiery tendril surging forth, aimed directly at her heart. My determination burned as fiercely as the flames I wielded, but Shazarah was a formidable foe. Just as my attack was about to reach her, she countered with her own magic, a wave of power that sent me hurtling backward, my body crashing to the unforgiving ground.

Pain radiated from the back of my head as it struck something hard upon impact. My vision blurred for a moment, stars dancing before my eyes. As I struggled to regain my senses, I saw Aerion locked in a ferocious battle with the other witch. Shazarah continued her vile chant, the blood from Aisling's arms flowing like a river.

Wren, wounded but far from defeated, staggered to his feet behind Shazarah. With grim determination, he lunged at her, gripping her shoulder and shaking her with a fervor that seemed impossible for his weakened state. The knife she had been holding flew from her grasp.

Shazarah's scream of rage and anguish echoed through the chamber as Wren's grip tightened on her. Her control over the borrowed body wavered, and the witch's focus waned.

"Enough!" Shazarah's roar reverberated through the chamber and the very walls seemed to tremble in response. With a flick of her wrist, she summoned a potent gust of wind that sent Wren tumbling back, his injuries worsening with the impact.

Aisling, helpless and battered, cried out as the relentless force flung her across the room. Her head struck the wall with a sickening thud, leaving her unconscious and vulnerable.

Even Aerion and the two witches were not spared from the cataclysmic force, as they were thrown back by the powerful blast. The chamber itself quaked and shuddered as if the very earth were rebelling against the merciless presence within.

"You cannot win, Vale. I will be unstoppable," Shazarah boomed, her voice echoing through the chamber, resonating with a deep, ominous timbre. Her words were not just heard but felt, as if the chamber itself was responding to her declaration of power.

I looked up, my gaze traveling along the towering walls of the ancient cavern. It was a sight of impending doom – the once-sturdy walls were now riddled with cracks, like a spider's web of destruction spreading across the surface. Chunks of rock, loosened by the relentless vibrations, were falling from the ceiling, crashing to the ground with a thunderous roar. Dust and debris filled the air, creating a haze that blurred my vision and filled my lungs.

"We need to get Aisling and Wren and get out of here! This whole place is coming down," Aerion ordered. He moved with a speed that belied his usually calm demeanor, his every step purposeful and swift. Reaching Aisling, he gently cradled her in his arms, her form limp and vulnerable, a stark contrast to his tense, alert posture.

But Shazarah wasn't finished yet. As the two witches, their faces twisted in determination, stood and prepared to unleash their fury upon us, Shazarah raised her hands. The air around her crackled with energy, the very essence of her magic pulsing like a living thing, an extension of her will. It pushed against the ceiling, an invisible force exerting its pressure on the already weakened structure.

The rock above us cracked and splintered as the cavern began to collapse around us. Rocks, large and small, fell like rain, each one a deadly missile in the chaos. I glanced desperately towards Wren's prone body, lying motionless amidst the turmoil. At that moment, a split-second decision was made.

"*Ex terra extrahere et ossa praedecessorum meorum!*" I shouted, my voice cutting through the din. "*Ad potentiam regnorum pertingere, ex ipsis petris extrahere!*" The words of the dark ancient spell felt alien yet familiar as they left my lips, charged with the energy of my desperation.

I felt a deep connection to the earth below, a pull that seemed to pulse through my very being. As I invoked the dark spell, it was as if I could sense the earth's movement, its shift and sway under the sun's gravitational embrace. The chamber responded with a violent shudder, the walls and ceiling groaning under the strain of the unleashed magic.

Cracks spread like lightning across the cavern, the very foundations of the mountain groaning in protest. I hurled my power at Shazarah, channeling the force of the earth itself into my attack. The energy collided with her hastily erected shield, shattering it with the ferocity of a tempest. Shazarah was sent flying, her body crashing to the ground as the earth's tremors continued.

Rushing to Wren, I was joined by Aerion, who held Aisling close, her body still and fragile in his arms. Wren was breathing, a small mercy amidst the devastation. His wound, however, was grave – it would need healing quickly.

Calliope, Harlow, and Ava moved to my side, their faces etched with concern as they crouched beside us, forming a protective circle. "Can you shift us out of here?" I asked Aerion, my voice tinged with panic as I glanced at the stirring form of Shazarah.

"I can, but we need to hurry," Aerion urged, his gaze scanning the cavern, which now resembled the aftermath of a cataclysm. The walls were veined with cracks, the roof sagging dangerously, threatening to bury us in its collapse.

"Then do it, now!" I implored, my voice echoing the collective fear and urgency of our precarious situation. Once a testament to ancient power, the cavern was now a crumbling tomb, ready to claim us if we did not escape its wrath.

The witches around me reached out as Aerion placed his hands on Wren and me, Aisling still cradled in his lap. One second, we were there, the next, we were swept away in a dizzying display of light and color.

CHAPTER

FIFTY

I felt a dizzying disorientation take hold as the world spun around us in a vortex of colors and sensations. My body seemed to be caught in a whirlwind, tumbling through an unseen force that left me feeling as though I was being spun at an incredible speed. The sensation was intense, almost too much to bear, and a wave of nausea threatened to overwhelm me. I held onto Wren and Aisling tightly, praying to the gods that we would make it out alive. The intensity of the moment was a blur of fear and hope intertwined in a chaotic dance.

Then, abruptly, we crashed back into reality, our bodies unceremoniously deposited onto the forest floor. The impact jolted me, scattering my senses. Dizzy and disoriented, I lay there for a moment, trying to regain my bearings. Slowly, the feeling began to return to my limbs.

I turned my attention to Wren and Aisling. They lay there, both horribly wounded, their breathing shallow and labored. The sight of their injuries sent a surge of panic through me. Time was slipping away and their lives hung in the balance.

542

"You need to heal them, now. No hesitating, just do it, Vale," Aerion's voice cut through the haze, urgent and commanding. He still cradled Aisling, his arms a protective fortress around her fragile form.

I glanced between Wren and Aisling, a sense of panic rising in me. In a hasty, almost frantic motion, I pulled out one of my knives. I pressed the blade against my arm, intending to draw the necessary blood. But in my hurried state, my hand slipped, and the cut was deeper than intended. Pain shot through my arm, but I pushed it aside, focusing instead on the dire situation before me.

Which one to heal first? The decision was agonizing, each second stretching out as if time itself was mocking my indecision. Aerion's expectant gaze felt like a weight upon me, adding to the pressure of the moment.

Finally, I made my choice. I pulled Wren closer, placing his head in my lap. "Drink, Wren. You gotta drink," I implored, my voice thick with urgency, my heart pounding against my ribcage. But even as I made the decision, doubt and guilt gnawed at me – Aisling's life hung by a thread, and yet, I had chosen Wren.

"No..." Wren's voice was a whisper, his lips cracked and bleeding.

"What?" I leaned in, straining to hear his feeble words.

"Heal Aisling first," he managed, his voice barely more than a breath.

His request hit me like a physical blow. I stared at him, my mouth agape in shock and confusion.

"We can't lose her, Vale. Please," his voice was laced with a raw, desperate plea.

I looked over at Aisling, her condition even more dire than I had realized. Her skin was deathly pale, her breathing barely perceptible. I nodded once, a silent but reluctant agreement to Wren's request.

Turning to Ava, my eyes were pleading, conveying the urgency of the situation. "Can you hold him?" My voice cracked, betraying the emotional turmoil swirling within me.

Ava moved swiftly, sitting beside me. She gently took Wren's head, cradling it in her lap with a tenderness that belied the chaos around us. I gave Wren one last look, a silent promise, before turning my full attention to Aisling. Gently, I shook her, trying to rouse her enough for the healing. The decision weighed heavily on me, but there was no time for argument or second guesses. Lives were in the balance, and I had to act.

"Aisling, Aisling. You have to drink, right now. You have to drink," I implored her, my voice laced with a desperate urgency. Her eyes, heavy with exhaustion, fluttered open and met mine. In their depths, I saw a glimmer of understanding, tinged with the weariness of one who has been pushed to the brink.

She nodded weakly, a subtle movement that spoke volumes of her fragile state. Her gaze fixated on my arm, where the blood dripped steadily from the deep cut, each drop a beacon of life-saving magic.

"Drink, please, drink," I urged her, holding my arm over her mouth. The blood fell in droplets, landing on her lips, a deep red against the pallor of her skin. Slowly, almost painfully, she opened her mouth. The blood trickled down her throat, and she swallowed with effort. Her eyes widened suddenly, a sign that the blood magic had begun its work.

With what strength she could muster, Aisling grasped my arm, her hands weak yet determined. She pulled my arm closer, drinking more deeply, each swallow a step towards healing. As the magic began to work, I felt a connection between us, a bond that seemed to pulse with life, a tangible thread linking us together.

Suddenly, she gasped, releasing my arm. The cuts on her arms had been healed, but I knew she was still weak from the blood loss. Her body trembled with the effort, the aftermath of the magic's potency. "Thank you," she whispered, her voice a hoarse shadow of its usual strength.

"Don't thank me yet, we're not out of the woods," I responded, my attention quickly shifting back to Wren. I moved towards him, now in Ava's lap, and my heart sank. He was so pale, his color drained away, leaving him ghostly and still.

"Help me wake him," I said, turning to Ava. Her eyes met mine, and I saw a deep sadness in them, a sorrow that seemed to eclipse the chaos around us.

"Vale," she breathed, a single tear tracing its way down her cheek. Confusion welled up within me.

"What is it? Wake him up," I insisted, my voice a mix of command and desperation. Time was slipping away, and every second felt like an eternity lost.

"Vale, he's gone," Ava whispered, her words barely audible yet heavy with finality.

Time stopped, the world stopped, everything stopped as I stared at her. Those two words rang through my head, echoing over and over again.

"No," I shook my head in denial, refusing to accept her words. "He's fine, wake him up. Try and wake him up, Ava, please." I reached for Wren, shaking him, hoping to rouse him from this too-deep slumber. His body jerked limply under my touch, a puppet devoid of life.

"Vale," Ava tried again to reach me, but I was lost in my own refusal to accept reality.

"Wake him up, wake him up," I muttered, a mantra against the truth. Tears blurred my vision, a dam ready to break, as my body began to tremble with the weight of impending grief.

"Vale," Aerion's voice cut through my denial, gentle yet firm, a beacon trying to guide me back from the edge of despair.

"No," I repeated, my voice a mix of disbelief and defiance, shaking my head as I looked down at Wren. His body lay lifeless in Ava's arms, a sight too horrific to accept as reality. This couldn't be happening. It just couldn't. The very notion was unthinkable, a cruel twist of fate that defied my understanding.

"No," I said yet again, my voice stronger, laced with a newfound determination. I picked him up, cradling his lifeless form in my arms. I refused to let history repeat itself, to lose another person I cared about. I was powerful now, more powerful than I had ever been before. I tapped into that power, calling upon it with a desperation that bordered on madness.

"Vale, what are you doing?" The voice of the First Witch echoed through my head, but I heeded her no mind.

The magic surged within me, a torrent of raw energy that filled me to the brim, scorching my skin with its intensity. Hot tears streamed down my face, a testament to the emotional and physical toll the magic exacted as I pulled and pulled from its depths.

"Vale, no! Stop this, you mustn't—" But I pushed her away, blocking her out in a way I hadn't known was possible.

"Ex terra extrahere et ossa praedecessorum meorum," I

whispered to Wren, invoking the dark, ancient magic I had harnessed earlier. The words were a plea, a command to the forces that I sought to control.

"Vale, don't—" Aerion's voice was a distant echo, a warning lost in the storm of my resolve. I jerked away from his touch, refusing to be deterred.

"Ad potentiam regnorum pertingere, ex ipsis petris extrahere!" I cried out, the power of the earth flooding through me, tearing me apart, breaking me down. The darkness crept along my blood-stained hands, a visual manifestation of the magic's destructive toll. Then, when I thought the power would finally burn right through me, I pushed the power into Wren.

I pushed and pushed and pushed with everything I had. I forced his lungs to expand and contract, compelled his heart to beat, using my magic as a lifeline. "Come on, come on," I begged, my voice breaking with the strain. Sweat and tears mingled on my face.

"Wake up, damn you," I screamed, shaking him, my desperation reaching its peak. "I can't lose you!"

The power flowed from me to him, an electric current that connected us. I gave it all until I was utterly spent, then waited, hope and fear warring within me.

I don't know how long I sat there staring at him, staring at the lifeless body of my best friend. It felt like no time at all. It felt like an eternity. I watched and waited for his chest to rise and fall. It was a timeless void, punctuated only by the silent vigil of those around us. I couldn't bring myself to meet their eyes, knowing their expressions would shatter the fragile shell of hope I clung to.

Aisling's sob was a distant sound, barely registering in my mind. The minutes dragged on, each one more agonizing than the last. As I sat there, a roaring anger began to stir within me, growing stronger with each passing second. It filled the void left by the expended magic, a simmering, seething force that threatened to consume me. It rose inside me like a coiled snake, waiting to strike out.

"Vale..." Aerion's voice was gentle, his hand on my shoulder a tentative gesture of comfort. I snapped my head up, my gaze meeting his.

"What?" I hissed, my voice laced with venom. I couldn't bear the hurt and sadness in his eyes, the unspoken acknowledgment of what we both feared. It was too much, too raw. I was on the edge, teetering between hope and despair, and his touch was a reminder of the reality I was desperately trying to deny.

"Maybe it's time to stop, maybe we should move. They could be coming after us," Aerion suggested, his voice infused with a gentle but firm resolve. His hand still rested on my shoulder.

"He's not dead," I declared, my voice imbued with a fierce certainty. The rage in my tone was unmistakable as I shook off his hand, a physical manifestation of my denial and desperation to cling to a sliver of hope.

"Vale..." Calliope's voice interjected, a note of wavering concern in her words.

"What, what, what?" I snapped at her, my emotions teetering on the edge of a precipice. At that moment, something within me shattered, a dam bursting under the weight of accumulated grief and strain.

I screamed, a raw, primal sound that echoed the depths of my despair. The scream tore through the silence, a manifestation of all the pain, fear, and frustration that had been building inside me. It continued until my lungs ached, until all that was left was a faint, rasping gasp.

Exhausted, I collapsed atop Wren, my arms weakly

wrapping around his broad shoulders. The shoulders that had supported me for fourteen years, that had been a constant presence in a life fraught with challenges. Hysterical sobs wracked my body as I gasped for breath, each inhale a struggle against the overwhelming tide of emotion.

My heart felt as though it had shattered into a million pieces, each shard slicing through me from the inside, leaving me raw and bleeding. The pain was beyond description, a loss so profound it felt like a piece of my soul had been torn away. That piece of Wren that had become integral to my existence, the part that had kept me whole, was now missing.

Throughout my life, I had been torn apart and stitched back together numerous times, each scar and crack a testament to survival. But now, it felt as though there was no mending this rupture, no way to piece together the fragments of my broken heart.

"It's time to stop, Vale," Aerion whispered softly, his voice filled with a compassionate sorrow as he knelt beside me. "You have to let him go," he said, each word seeming to cause him physical pain.

"I can't," I whispered back, my voice a fragile thread of sound, breaking under the weight of my grief.

"You have to," he insisted gently, placing his hand on my shoulder again.

"Why? Why can't we stay here, just for a bit longer?" I begged, lifting my tear-streaked face to look at him. The plea was a desperate grasp at a fading hope, a wish to delay the inevitable.

His eyes brimmed with unshed tears, reflecting a depth of pain and anguish. He opened his mouth to respond, but words failed him, choked by the emotions that were too powerful to articulate.

"Please, just give me a little longer," I pleaded, my fingers tightening around Wren's shoulders as if my grip could anchor him to this world, could somehow reverse the unchangeable reality we faced.

"He's gone, Vale," Ava's voice was a whisper, a gentle yet stark declaration.

"No, no, he's not," I retorted, denial lacing every syllable. My head shook in adamant refusal, refusing to accept what my heart knew to be true. "He can't be because he's always been there. He'd never leave me, not if he could help it." My words were a plea.

"It's time, Vale," Aerion's voice came through, thick with emotion, laden with the weight of shared grief and understanding.

"I can't let him go, I can't," I cried.

"Yes, yes you can," Aerion's voice cracked, his own pain surfacing as a single tear traced its way down his cheek. It was a visible sign of his own struggle, a mirror to the heartache that was enveloping us all.

"How? How can I let him go?" I sobbed, the tears flowing uncontrollably, carving wet trails down my cheeks. My voice was choked with sorrow, each word a struggle against the tide of despair.

"Because you have to, because it's what he would have wanted," Aerion spoke with a difficult conviction, his gaze locked onto mine, imploring me to understand, to accept the unbearable truth.

"I'm not ready," I whimpered, my voice reduced to a mere whisper, a breath of sound that carried the enormity of my pain.

"None of us are, but we have to be," he responded, his hand squeezing my shoulder. His touch was a reminder that I was not alone in my grief, that we shared this burden together.

I closed my eyes, taking in a shaky, ragged breath. The pain enveloped me, a tidal wave of sorrow that threatened to pull me under. It was a raw, overwhelming sensation, consuming me completely.

I knew, deep down, that Aerion was right. We had to leave. We had to move forward. But in that moment, I felt immobilized, frozen in time and grief. It seemed as if I could remain there indefinitely, a statue of despair, forever clinging to Wren.

"Please, Vale," Calliope's voice was soft, her hands visibly trembling, echoing the fragility of the moment.

The pain continued to wash over me, each wave stronger than the last, threatening to drown me in its depths. But then, as it reached its peak, I forced it down, pushing it into the darkest recesses of my soul. I buried it deep, covering it with layers of resolve and necessity. I still had a job to do, a role to fill. I would do what was necessary. I would get Wren home.

"Can you..." My voice broke, barely audible, and I cleared my raw throat, "Can you take him, Aerion? Can you take him home?"

"Of course," he replied, his voice low and heavy with sorrow.

"Thank you," I whispered, a faint breath of gratitude amidst the storm of emotions.

He nodded solemnly and reached out, his hands gentle as he began to pry my fingers from Wren. It was a slow, careful motion, respecting the gravity of the moment.

I let him, my arms falling limply to my sides, a physical release of the hold I had on Wren but not of the grip he had on my heart. As Aerion took him from me, it felt like a final severing of a connection that had been a cornerstone of my life. It was an act of letting go, not just of Wren, but of a part of myself that I knew would never be whole again.

As I watched Aerion gently lift Wren's lifeless body, cradling it with a tenderness that belied his own strength, a profound sense of loss washed over me. The way he held Wren, so carefully, so respectfully, was a silent testament to the gravity of our loss. Wren's body, once so full of life and laughter, now lay still and silent in Aerion's arms, a stark, painful reminder of the finality of death.

"Calliope, can you..." My voice faltered, unable to complete the sentence, the words choked by grief.

"Of course, Vale," Calliope responded without hesitation, her voice imbued with a quiet strength. She stepped forward, placing her arm around my waist to offer support. My legs, weak and unsteady from the emotional and physical toll, shook beneath me. Calliope's presence was a much-needed anchor, helping me to remain upright in a world that seemed to be tilting beneath my feet.

Aerion paused for a moment, his gaze meeting mine. His eyes were a mirror of pain – pain for Wren, pain for what had transpired, and pain for me. In that brief, shared glance, a world of unspoken words and shared sorrow passed between us. Then, with a heavy heart, he disappeared with Wren's body, back to the portal to the Fae realm. We were left standing there, staring at the spot where they had just been.

"Nyxen," I croaked. At my call, my familiar emerged from the shadow of a nearby tree. His yellow eyes met mine, filled with understanding of my loss and pain. He whimpered softly, pawing at my leg in a gesture of comfort. Every fiber of my being longed to lean down, to bury myself in his shadowy fur, to find solace in his presence as I felt myself crumbling from within. But I resisted the urge, knowing there were things yet to be done, responsibilities I couldn't forget.

"Can you take us all back to the portal?" I asked him, my voice steadier than I felt. Harlow, Ava, and Aisling huddled close, their own grief and exhaustion evident.

Nyxen didn't speak, but his eyes held a depth of empathy that went beyond words. As his shadows began to swirl around us, enveloping us in their cool embrace, the world outside faded to a welcome darkness. It was a respite, a momentary escape from the harsh light of reality, a brief journey back to where we needed to be, carried on the wings of shadow and magic.

PART
FIVE

FIFTY-ONE

The journey back to the portal with Nyxen was unsettlingly swift, taking only a few seconds. As we emerged, I blinked rapidly to clear the tears that blurred my vision. I couldn't afford to break down now; I had to remain strong, at least for a little longer.

Stepping through the portal, a familiar icy sensation washed over me, a stark contrast to the emotions roiling inside. We arrived in the forest surrounding Terralux, a place that now felt foreign in its familiarity. Aerion, having gone ahead with Wren, was nowhere to be seen. His absence was a silent reminder of the grim task he had undertaken.

I gave a nod to Nyxen, still steadfast by my side. Once again, his shadows swallowed us, whisking us away from the forest.

We materialized in the courtyard of Terralux, which lay in utter disarray. The large fountain, once a centerpiece of beauty and tranquility, was now broken and cracked. Bodies were scattered across the ground, a grim testament to the violence that had occurred. My eyes scanned the scene, recognizing none of the faces. Most of the castle soldiers were strangers to me, yet the sight of so much death and destruction was overwhelming. Amid this chaos, I stood, feeling like the epicenter of a storm I had no control over.

Thalion was waiting for us in the courtyard. He approached swiftly, his face etched with concern and sympathy. He gently took my arm from Calliope, guiding me with a careful touch. Calliope moved to help Harlow with Aisling, who was still weak from the blood loss.

"Aerion has already taken him inside," he said, his eyes searching mine for the emotional turmoil that lay buried, ready to resurface.

"Alright," I managed to reply, my voice hoarse and strained.

"Where is Kaelan?" Thalion's question was directed at Ava, his expression shifting to one of concern.

"His curse..." Ava began, her voice faltering as she glanced at me. "He left right before we found Aisling. We don't know where he is."

Thalion nodded grimly, his expression hardening with resolve, if he was surprised he didn't show it. He began to lead me toward the stone steps of Terralux. "Why don't you three take Aisling to Venna?" he suggested to the others, though his focus remained on me.

Calliope and Harlow, understanding the gravity of the situation, moved to take Aisling to Venna's room. Ava, however, lingered behind.

"Vale," she called out to me, her voice concerned but hesitant. I turned to face her, Thalion pausing beside me.

"Yeah?" I said, my eyes meeting hers, heavy with exhaustion and grief.

"Are you going to be alright?" Ava's question was soft, her voice barely above a whisper.

I looked at her, really looked at her. Her face was a canvas of concern, her eyes brimming with worry, her brow furrowed. In her gaze, I saw a reflection of the turmoil I felt within.

"No," I replied simply. I didn't have the strength to pretend, to offer reassurances I didn't believe in. The truth was stark and raw, and it was all I could muster at that moment.

"If there's anything—" Ava began.

"No," I said again, cutting her off abruptly. My voice was tinged with a finality that brooked no argument, a barrier to any further attempts at consolation.

Ava hesitated, her expression one of uncertainty. She opened her mouth, perhaps to offer more words of solace or to ask another question, but then thought better of it. Instead, she simply nodded, a silent acknowledgment of my need for space, and turned away to join the others.

"Let's go," Thalion said gently, his voice a soft murmur of support. I turned, and we began the slow, laborious walk up the stairs. Each step felt like a monumental effort, my feet dragging as if weighted down by the heaviness of my heart. Thalion's arm was a steady presence around me, offering physical support that mirrored the emotional burden I was carrying. I felt utterly empty, a shell devoid of anything but a deep, aching void.

We reached my room, and Thalion paused briefly at the door. "Should I leave you?" he asked, his voice hesitant.

"No," I whispered, barely audible. He nodded, understanding my need for someone to be there, even if I couldn't express it.

Gently, he opened the door and ushered me inside.

Aerion was already there, seated on the bed. He stood up as we entered, his movements hesitant. It was clear he was torn, wanting to offer comfort but uncertain if I was too fragile for any form of contact.

As Aerion reached out his hand towards me, I instinctively flinched. The hurt that flashed in his eyes at my reaction was evident, but I couldn't help it. I could see the hurt in his eyes at the movement, but it was the only reaction I could muster.

"How about you have a bath and then we can rest," Thalion suggested, trying to provide some semblance of normalcy.

I nodded, and Aerion quietly moved to the bathroom, turning on the water. The sound of running water filled the space, a soothing background noise that offered a small measure of calm.

Thalion led me to the bathroom, the rhythmic sound of water filling the tub a welcome distraction. He turned to me, his gaze sweeping over my blood-soaked clothes.

"Can you manage, or do you need help?" he asked gently. I could only manage a noncommittal shrug in response. Understanding, he began to help me out of my clothes, his movements careful and respectful.

The scene brought back memories of a similar moment when Kaelan had taken care of me after Juniper's death. The recollection was a fresh stab of pain, a reminder of another loss, another absence that echoed in the empty spaces of my heart. The fact that Kaelan wasn't here now, in this moment of my deepest sorrow, added another layer to the grief that seemed to be consuming me from the inside out.

Once I was undressed, Thalion gently guided me into the bath. The water was exceptionally hot, bordering on blistering, but I eased into it without flinching. My skin, seemingly numb to the sting, barely registered the heat. The water enveloped me, a cocoon of warmth that was both comforting and overwhelming.

I settled into the bath, surrounded by the steam rising in lazy curls from the water's surface. Aerion moved to stand behind me while Thalion positioned himself at the side of the tub. Together, they began the careful process of washing away the blood and dirt that marred my skin and hair. I sat there motionless, my gaze fixed on a distant, unseen point, my body and mind utterly drained of energy.

At that moment, I couldn't feel the pain, the grief that I knew was lurking just beneath the surface. It was as if everything had been buried under a thick layer of shock and numbness. I dreaded the moment when this protective barrier would crack, when the sorrow, the anger, and the pain would rush forth. I feared the intensity of these emotions, feared the dark abyss they threatened to drag me into.

Aerion finished washing my hair, and I rose from the bath. He handed me a towel, his movements gentle and considerate and then helped me into a soft robe. He led me back into the main room, where Thalion had prepared the bed.

As I climbed beneath the covers, I could sense the uncertainty between Aerion and Thalion, each unsure of what was needed from them. Aerion finally broke the silence.

"I can stay with her tonight," he told Thalion.

Thalion nodded in agreement. "I'll be back in the morning," he said, his hand briefly caressing my cheek in a comforting gesture. "Call for me if you need me."

I nodded, too exhausted to speak, and watched him

leave the room. As soon as he was gone, Aerion climbed into the bed next to me, pulling me close to his chest.

"Tell me," he urged gently. "Tell me what you're thinking."

I swallowed hard, a futile attempt to stave off the tears that threatened to escape. "I'm thinking that this is all my fault," I whispered, the words barely audible in the quiet of the room.

"It's not your fault, Vale," he responded firmly, his voice laced with conviction.

"It is. It's all my fault," I choked out as tears began to cascade down my cheeks. "Wren is dead because of me, and if Wren hadn't died, it would have been Aisling."

"That's not true, Vale. You can't blame yourself for this. If you do, it'll tear you apart. It'll kill you too," Aerion said, his voice tinged with desperation, pleading with me to see reason beyond the guilt and grief.

His words were a lifeline in a sea of despair, yet at that moment, they seemed like whispers against a roaring storm of self-recrimination and sorrow within me.

"It should have been me," I whispered through my tears, each drop falling faster now, as if in rhythm with the breaking of my heart.

"What?" Aerion said, disbelief echoing in his tone.

"It should have been me," I repeated, a little louder this time, a raw edge of conviction in my voice. The words were a lament, a bitter acknowledgment of the guilt that was consuming me.

"Don't ever say that, don't ever think that," he implored, his voice laden with pain. It was clear that my words were hurting him.

"Why not? If I hadn't been such a weak, useless piece of

shit, Wren would still be here." The words tumbled out, a torrent of self-loathing and regret.

"You're not useless," he countered immediately, his voice firm, but I was beyond hearing.

"Yes, yes, I am," I sobbed, the tears now unrelenting. The dam had broken, and all the pent-up sorrow and guilt rushed out in a flood of despair.

Aerion reached up and grasped my face, turning my head up to look him in the eye. "Vale, you can't do this to yourself, you can't," he said, his tone growing increasingly desperate, trying to reach me through the fog of my self-condemnation.

"Why not? It's the truth. I'm the reason he's dead. I should have been strong enough to stop Shazarah, but I wasn't. I was weak and useless, and because of that, Wren is dead," I sobbed.

"Vale, please, don't do this," he pleaded. "Wren wouldn't want this, wouldn't want you to blame yourself. He would want you to live, to move on, to keep fighting."

"I can't," I whispered, each word heavy with a sorrow that felt like an anchor, dragging me down into an abyss of despair.

"You can," he said firmly. "I'll be there to help you every step of the way. We all will, Vale."

His arms wrapped around me tightly, offering a haven in the midst of my tempest. He held me as I sobbed into his chest, my cries coming in great, gasping breaths. I could feel his own tears falling silently, his heart breaking for me.

"I can't do it without him," I cried out, the pain raw and unfiltered.

"You can," he reassured me, his voice firm yet gentle. "You can, and you will."

"I don't want to," I sobbed, my soul wracked with grief, my body shaking uncontrollably.

"I know," he whispered, his voice a soft, soothing caress against my ear. "But you have to, Vale. You have to keep going, for Wren."

His words relieved a tiny fraction of the ache, even as they cut through me. I cried until the tears would no longer come, until my body was completely overtaken by exhaustion, each sob a release of the unbearable weight I carried within.

"Sleep, Vale. Sleep and let yourself rest," Aerion's voice was a gentle whisper, a soothing melody. "I'll be here, watching over you. I'll be here when you wake, and we'll start to make things right."

I nodded, my body and soul too exhausted for words. My eyelids felt heavy, like leaden curtains closing on the world.

Slowly, I let myself succumb to the embrace of sleep, a realm where grief and pain could not reach me for a time. I closed my eyes, surrendering to the darkness that beckoned me, a familiar void that had always been a refuge, albeit a cold and lonely one.

As the darkness enveloped me, wrapping its silent arms around my weary soul, I was acutely aware of the profound changes wrought within me. The experiences, the loss, the raw pain had altered me irreversibly. I knew with a certainty that cut through the fog of my despair: I would never be the same again. The innocence, the unburdened joy that had once been part of me, was now lost, perhaps forever.

Amidst this realization, a fierce determination began to stir within my shattered heart. The pain, the guilt, the anger that seethed within me – they would not be in vain. A dark resolve began to take root, growing stronger with each passing second.

They would pay. Every last one of them who had a hand in this tragedy, who had caused this pain and suffering, would face retribution. It would not be swift; it would be meticulous, calculated, and absolute. Every drop of pain they had inflicted would be returned tenfold.

This vow, forged in the depths of my despair, became the ember of a raging fire that would consume all in its path. As I drifted into sleep, the darkness around me seemed to pulse with this newfound resolve. In the depths of my soul, a vow was made – a promise of vengeance, of justice. A vow that would define my path when I awoke.

In that moment, as sleep claimed me, I was transformed. From the torment of my grief and loss, a new creature was born – fierce, unyielding, and unstoppable. The world would soon come to know the power of my wrath and they would tremble. For when I awoke, it would be a new beginning, a new chapter written in fire and wrought in steel. For Wren, for Juniper, for Kaelan, for all that I had lost, I would keep going.

From the ashes of despair, I would rise; to avenge, to conquer, to burn it all.

EPILOGUE

KAELAN

Kaelan stood perched on the edge of a jagged cliff in the demon realm, a land where chaos reigned supreme and the very air pulsated with malevolent energy. His gaze was fixed on the ominous sight before him – a dark castle, an architectural nightmare that loomed over the turbulent black sea stretching beneath it. The realm around him was a maelstrom of madness, the sky overhead a canvas of perpetual twilight, streaked with sinister red clouds that bled across the horizon.

As Kaelan began his descent from the cliff, the landscape contorted and shifted in an unsettling dance, mirroring the turmoil that raged within him. Here, in this realm, his demonic heritage was dominant, powerful, and unyielding. Yet, even amidst this dominance, a battle was being waged within his soul.

He was returning to his father's kingdom, Nexilis, the domain of the feared demon lord Azazel. Kaelan, once cast out from this dark bastion, now approached with a certainty that he would be accepted. His return was not one of a prodigal son, but as a being who had embraced the infernal part of his nature.

As he walked, the twisted, ever-changing scenery around him seemed to echo the internal conflict that tore at his being. The witch, the one who had unwittingly ensnared his thoughts, remained a constant presence in his mind. She was like a beacon, drawing him in, consuming his thoughts.

His demonic side, now in ascendancy, yearned for her with a fierce intensity. It urged him to seek her out, to go to her, to claim her in a way that defied reason or morality. This part of him craved to possess her, to make her a part of his dark world.

Yet, amidst this tumult of dark desire, there was resistance – a vestige of his better self, struggling against the overwhelming tide. This part of Kaelan fought desperately, yearning to keep him away from the witch, to protect her from the dangerous allure of his darker half. It was a battle of wills, where the prize was not just his soul, but potentially hers as well.

As Kaelan continued his journey towards the heart of the demon realm, towards the foreboding castle of Nexilis, the internal struggle showed no signs of abating. Each step he took was a testament to this ongoing war within him – a war between darkness and light, chaos and order, damnation and salvation.

As Kaelan advanced, the castle loomed ever closer, a sinister presence on the horizon. The imposing structure, with its jagged towers clawing at the sky, stood as a grim harbinger of the destiny that awaited him within its dark walls. The castle, set against the backdrop of a sky streaked with crimson, seemed to pulse with a dark magic of its own.

With each step he took towards the castle, the balance within him shifted inexorably towards darkness. The realm of his father exerted its infernal influence. The inner battle that raged within Kaelan grew more fierce and chaotic. His darker impulses clashed violently with the remnants of his better nature, each vying for supremacy.

As he crossed the threshold of the towering gates, stepping into the domain that had once rejected him, the internal struggle reached a crescendo. Yet, there was no clear victor, no defining moment of triumph or defeat. It was a deadlock, a perpetual stalemate that teetered on the edge of an abyss.

In the depths of Kaelan's tormented mind, a choice had been made, albeit one fraught with contradiction and peril. He had returned to his ancestral home, a place that promised the damnation of his soul, yet paradoxically, it also held the faint glimmer of hope – the hope of saving the witch, the one whose existence had altered the course of his cursed life.

"The witch will be mine," he thought, a resolve born of obsession and dark desire. She would be his, irrespective of the consequences, the cost be damned.

Yet, even as this thought consumed him, that quieter, more rational voice fought back. He wasn't wholly evil, not completely lost to his demonic urges. The witch, who had changed everything for him, didn't deserve to be ensnared in his dark world. He couldn't, he shouldn't bring harm to her. Not in this way.

This resistance echoed in his mind, a feeble beacon of light amidst the encroaching darkness. But with each passing moment, it grew weaker. Its voice drowned out by the siren call of his darker nature. The part of him that craved power, that yearned for the witch, grew ever stronger, its seductive pull almost irresistible.

He would have her, his mind whispered with a sinister certainty. She would belong to him and him alone. This desire, this need, overshadowed everything else, threatening to consume what little was left of the good within him. And there was nothing and no one who could stop him.

Kaelan's entrance into the throne room was a descent into the heart of darkness. The chamber, a testament to his father's reign of terror, was steeped in the echoes of a thousand horrors. The stone floor beneath his feet bore the dark stains of countless sacrifices, each a grim reminder of the atrocities committed in this very room. The walls, chillingly adorned with the skulls of victims, served as a macabre gallery of Azazel's conquests and cruelty.

At the center of this hall of nightmares stood the great throne of Azazel, an edifice of terror carved from the bones of his fallen enemies. It loomed large, an imposing symbol of power and dominion, a throne befitting the Lord of Chaos and Destruction.

Upon this throne sat Azazel himself, a figure of immense and terrifying power. His piercing yellow eyes, glowing with an unholy fire, were fixed intently upon Kaelan as he entered. Azazel's massive frame, draped in a cloak as dark as the void, exuded an aura of menace. The obsidian horns that crowned his head arched upwards, reminiscent of the talons of some predatory beast.

The upper demons of Azazel's court, a gathering of the realm's most evil beings, encircled their lord. As Kaelan stepped into the room, their collective gaze turned towards him, each pair of eyes a silent judge.

"I was certain that I banished you long ago, *boy*," Azazel sneered, his voice dripping with disdain.

"My banishment was always going to be temporary," Kaelan replied, his tone even, betraying no hint of intimidation.

"Oh? And why is that?" Azazel asked with feigned interest, his voice laced with mockery.

"Because, father," Kaelan began, "it is time for us to work together. To achieve our common goal."

"And what goal would that be, my son?" Azazel asked lazily.

"It's time for us to destroy the Fae and the witches, once and for all," Kaelan declared, his statement resolute.

A brief silence fell over the chamber, swiftly shattered by a chorus of dark, mocking laughter from the assembled demons.

"You are truly a fool, my son," Azazel chided, his tone one of amused contempt. "Our battle with the Fae is over. Why would I, the Lord of Chaos and Destruction, risk a new war for no reason?"

"You have not won the war," Kaelan shot back, his voice tinged with venom. "You have merely put it on hold. The Fae and the witches are still out there, plotting, scheming, waiting for their moment to strike. You may think you have won, but you have only bought yourself a brief reprieve."

"What are you babbling about, boy?" Azazel sneered.

"The First Witch has risen again, as I'm sure you know. She's currently ruling in the Fae realm as we speak. Do you honestly believe she'll stop there? That she won't come after all you've built next?"

A wave of concern rippled through the upper demons, their earlier laughter dying in their throats. The air in the room shifted, as the weight of Kaelan's words began to sink in, the mocking tone replaced by an uneasy realization of the potential threat that loomed.

"The witches are growing more powerful, father," Kaelan pressed on, seizing the moment to advance his argument. "Their magic is growing stronger with each passing day. The time is ripe for us to strike. We must wipe them out, root and branch, before they have a chance to gain the upper hand." His words carried a sense of urgency, a call to action that echoed through the cavernous chamber.

"And what would you have me do, my son?" Azazel asked, his tone shifting from dismissive scorn to a more calculating intrigue.

"I would have you join me in an alliance. An alliance to destroy our mutual enemies once and for all. An alliance that will forever secure our dominion over all three living realms." Kaelan's voice was firm.

A tense silence descended upon the throne room. Kaelan could feel the weight of every gaze upon him, the air thick with anticipation as the court awaited Azazel's response.

Finally, Azazel spoke, his voice a low, ominous rumble that reverberated off the stone walls. "An alliance, you say? Very well, my son. Let us make an alliance." A twisted grin curled his lips. "In fact, I'm a step ahead of you."

"What do you mean?" Kaelan asked, a sense of unease coiling in his stomach.

From the shadows behind the throne emerged a figure that made Kaelan's blood run cold. Haldir. Despite his demonic nature fully in control, Kaelan couldn't suppress the hiss that escaped his lips at the sight of the Fae.

"Oh, come now, boy, is that any way to greet an ally?" Azazel mocked with a cruel amusement in his tone.

"Ally?" Kaelan growled, the word laced with disbelief and contempt.

"Indeed," Azazel chuckled, clearly relishing the moment. "Haldir here has offered me a deal. He has pledged his fealty to me, in exchange for my assistance in defeating the witches. And I, being the generous and wise ruler that I am, have agreed to his terms."

"This is madness," Kaelan spat out. "He is our sworn enemy! We should not be working with him, we should be destroying him!"

"My, how the tables have turned," Azazel mused. "Not so long ago, it was you who were willing to forge an alliance with the Fae, and now you are the one decrying it as madness."

"He cannot be trusted, father. Surely you see that?" Kaelan implored, desperation creeping into his voice.

"Perhaps not. But the simple truth is, I do not care." Azazel's voice was cold, dismissive. "All I care about is crushing the witches, and the Fae will help me achieve that goal." His words were final, a declaration of intent that signaled a new and dangerous alliance, one that would alter the balance of power in their ongoing struggle.

"This is a mistake," Kaelan warned, his voice laden with a foreboding that resonated through the cavernous throne room.

"Maybe. But it is a mistake I am willing to make," Azazel countered dismissively, his tone indicative of a ruler accustomed to taking calculated risks. "Now, enough talk. You have made your case, and it has been heard. I have given my answer, and there is nothing more to be said. Either accept this alliance and join with me, or continue your miserable, insignificant existence in the shadows. The choice is yours, my son."

Kaelan's response was a silent one, his jaw clenching tightly, a physical manifestation of the internal struggle raging within him. His hands balled into fists at his sides, a symbol of the anger and frustration boiling under the surface.

"Very well, father," Kaelan finally spoke, each word forced out through gritted teeth. "I will accept this alliance. But know this: I do not trust the Fae, and I will be watching him closely. If he so much as breathes a word out of turn, he will answer to me." His declaration was a blend of reluctant acceptance and barely veiled threat.

"Such harsh words," Haldir chimed in, his tone dripping with mockery, a smile playing on his lips. "Will you have equally harsh ones for your witch?"

At the mention of the witch, Kaelan's eyes narrowed into dangerous slits, and he took an aggressive step toward the Fae, a snarl curling his lips.

"Careful now, son," Azazel interjected with a cautionary tone, yet there was a hint of amusement in his voice. "Remember, you are no longer banished. I could have you killed for such an insult to my ally."

Kaelan's glare toward his father was one of barely contained fury, but the implicit threat in Azazel's words was enough to halt his advance. The power dynamics within the room were clear, and Kaelan knew crossing the line could have fatal consequences.

"The time will come when I deal with her," Kaelan growled, his words seething with a mixture of anger and a deep, unspoken conflict. "Me. I will deal with her alone."

"We shall see, my son. We shall see," Azazel responded, his voice a low rumble of dark amusement. The statement hung in the air like a warning, a chilling reminder of the twisted games of power and manipulation that thrived in the demon realm.

Inside Kaelan, the conflict raged on, a tumultuous storm of opposing desires and loyalties. The demon within him, now firmly in control, reveled in the dark alliance that had been formed, savoring the impending chaos it would bring. Yet, beneath this malevolent satisfaction, there lingered a shard of his former self, struggling against the overwhelming darkness. Every time he thought of the witch, whom he refused to name in his thoughts, this inner conflict intensified. Her name was a beacon, calling to the part of him that still clung to a semblance of goodness, but he ruthlessly pushed it away.

In a moment of dark resolve, Kaelan made a vow. He would destroy her, the witch who had unwittingly ensnared a part of him he thought was lost. The demon within him seethed with a possessive desire, an obsession to make her his, regardless of her will. The idea of owning her, of bending her to his will, was a thought that brought a cruel satisfaction to his demonic nature. If she would not accept him, then she would be annihilated. In his mind, it was a simple, merciless conclusion. The good within him recoiled at this notion, but the demon snarled louder, drowning out the feeble protests. Kaelan was lost in this internal war, a war where every battle left him further ensnared in the darkness that now claimed him.

AN EXCERPT FROM
Empress
of
Realms
BOOK FOUR OF
THE FIRST WITCH SERIES

PROLOGUE

Pain was my universe, my existence. Pain was a limitless void and I was falling through it. There was no beginning and no end, just endless darkness and an all-consuming agony. It was an eternity and a moment, a never-ending hell.

Each moment I was awake, I was acutely aware of the pain, a voracious entity that constantly threatened to drag me into its depths. My desire to eat, to move, to engage in the simplest acts of living, had vanished. I lay in my bed, a hollow shell, my gaze fixed blankly on the ceiling, lost in the throes of my anguish. While my physical wounds were healing, the emotional scars ran far deeper, slashing through my soul, leaving behind jagged, unhealable gashes.

I could feel Aerion's and Thalion's worry, but I couldn't bring myself to comfort them. The pain had become my entire world, eclipsing everything else. Aerion was ever-present, his attempts to coax me into conversation, to eat, were met with my silent, unresponsive despair. Nothing seemed to matter anymore; the pain had become a living, breathing part of me, the last vestige of Wren, the only thing I had left of him.

I hadn't seen Aisling since the day Wren had died. I wasn't sure I wanted to see her. It wasn't her fault, I knew that, still I couldn't help but wish it would have been her. I wondered if she would one day be able to feel that resentment through the partial blood bond we now shared. I couldn't bring myself to care if she did.

My restless nights were filled with visions of my pain. Visions of Malachar, of Haldir. Images of Wren, dead in Ava's arms. I relived my worst moments over and over again. I woke screaming every night, chased awake by the ghosts of my grief.

"Vale, it's alright," Aerion said one night, his hand brushing a loose strand of hair from my face.

"Why? Why are you still here?" I asked, my voice hoarse.

"Because I love you. I'm not going anywhere," he replied simply.

"You should," I responded, turning my face away. "Before you end up dead as well."

"I'm not going anywhere," Aerion repeated, his tone brooking no argument. "I'm staying by your side until you're ready to come back to us."

"How do you know I will?" I asked.

"I know you, Vale. I know the strength you possess," he replied. "And I know that one day, you'll rise from the shadows of this nightmare, and you'll be stronger than ever."

"You can't know that," I whispered.

"But I do. You have the heart of a warrior, Vale, and nothing can break that," Aerion said, his voice firm.

I turned away, unable to respond. Aerion was wrong.

My heart was broken, shattered into a million pieces, and I didn't think it would ever be whole again.

This pain, this loss, this overwhelming emptiness... it was all too much. A part of me yearned for an end to it all, a desperate wish to be numb, to feel nothing at all.

Yet, in the quieter moments, when the pain subsided to a dull ache, I began to sense something else stirring beneath the layers of my grief. It was a white-hot, seething rage, snarling and writhing within me, a beast waiting for its moment to seize control. It was a different kind of pain, tinged with a bitter pleasure, growing stronger each day, feeding on my anguish.

This growing fury was a monster in its own right ready to consume me entirely until nothing remained in its fiery wake. And in my darkest hours, I found myself welcoming it, embracing the monster within, ready to let it take over.

I had dwindled to nothing more than a shadow of the person I once was, a faint, distorted echo reverberating through the hollow emptiness that had become my existence. I felt like a shattered mirror, each fragmented piece a sharp, jagged reflection of the turmoil that raged within my soul.

With each passing day, I felt myself descending further into the abyss. That dark, relentless void that pulled at me with invisible, grasping fingers. The rage and grief that had taken root in the core of my being spread like a poison, a slow, inexorable force.

I was a specter, a wraith, a ghost of the person I used to be. A stranger in my own skin.

And I wasn't sure I wanted to come back.

LIST OF CHARACTERS AND PLACES

Aerion- *Air-E-On* Fae prince of Terralux and Vale's lover.

Aisling- *ash-ling* Young girl, most likely ten, blood-born witch and Vale's biological sister.

Amris- *Am-ris* Fae woman, Vale's head lady's maid.

Aquavale- *ah-Qua-v-ALE* Home of King Oropher.

Archer- *arCh-er* Half-demon male, newly transformed witch.

Aurumport- *or-um-Pour-t* Thalion's mother's former court. Home of King Therodrin and Queen Lesta, Thalion's aunt and uncle.

Ava- *Ay-vuh* Half-fae woman, newly transformed witch. Took care of the bookshop while Vale was in the Fae realm.

Azazel- *Auh-zAye-zel* Demon lord and Kaelan's father.

Caelistis- *key-list-us* Haldir's original court

Caeluxa- *key-luxe-ah* Home of King Galdimir

Calliope- *Cuh-lie-O-pee* Half-fae woman, newly transformed witch.

Carys- *care-is* Mortal born witch, Member of The Seven

Donovan- *Dawn-O-van* Werewolf and Wren's old patrol partner, killed by Vale when he tried to overthrow Wren's claim to alpha.

Elara- *Ee-lar-ah* Ghost of the magical library left by the witches, was a witch herself when alive.

Elowen- *el-O-win* Ghost, member of The Seven, wanders the dream realm and the fae realm.

Elysian- *il-E-shun* The Fae realm

Erebus- *air-E-bus* The demon realm

Griffin- *griff-In* Half-demon male, newly transformed witch.

Haldir- *hal-dear* Fae king, evil to the core. Former King of Terralux, current king of Caelistis

Harker- *har-Kur* Vampire, about 250 years old, historian, Vale's good friend

Harlow- *har-low* Half-Fae, newly transformed witch. Sam's girlfriend

Jaks- *jack-s* Half-Demon male, dirty and corrupted. Gives out demon bounties in the mortal realm.

Jason- *jay-sun* Half- demon male, unofficial leader of the Otherworlders under Vale's care

Joeline- *joe-ly-n* Young Fae woman, one of Vale's lady's maids

Juniper- *Ju-nuh-per* Mortal, Vale's friend and shop girl in book shop. Deceased

Kaelan- *kay-lin* Demon, with a slight bit of witch blood. Over 500 years old, Vale's husband and lover

Kelli- *kel-Ee* Youn fae woman, one of Vale's lady's maids

King Cael- *kay-El* Former king of Terralux. Vale's grandfather, Lyra's father. Aerion's adoptive father. Deceased

King Celeborn- *cell-E-born* King of Virelium. Thalion's father. Husband of Queen Elariel

King Galdimir *-gal-duh-meer* King of Caeluxa. One of the seven kings of the Fae. Hosts the Aeloranthia celebration when Vale attends.

King Oren *or-In* King of Serenium. Husband of Queen Aria. Meets Vale at Aeloranthia celebration

King Oropher *or-O-fer* King of Aquavale.

King Therodrin- *th-Er-O-drin* King of Aurumport, husband to Queen Lesta. Thalion's uncle and aunt.

Lyra- *lie-ruh* Vale's biological mother. Deceased.

Malachar- *mal-A-car* Son of Haldir, torture's Vale. Deceased.

Mikel- *me-Kel* Half-Fae male, newly transformed witch. Deceased.

Mor- *mORe* Mortal-born witch, member of The Seven.

Nysa- *n-I-sa* Mortal-born witch, member of The Seven.

Nyxen- *n-ix-en* Vale's familiar. Shadow-kin who always takes the form of a fox.

Rafe- *r-aff* Former alpha of Wren's pack. Deceased.

Rowena- *row-Ee-na* The original First Witch. Her soul is merged with Vale's. Deceased but a spirit.

Serenium- *sir-rEE-knee-um* Home of King Oren and Queen Aria

Shazarah *shuh-zar-uh* Blood born witch, leader of The Seven. Her soul is merged with Haldir's. Deceased but a spirit.

Terralux- *tear-uh-luxe* Formerly King Cael's court. Taken over by Haldir, then reclaimed by Vale. Aerion's court.

Thalion- *th-Al-E-on* Fae prince of Virelium, Vale's lover.

Vale- *v-ALE* First Witch reborn. Blood-born witch. Sister to Aisling. Main character of the story.

Venna- *ven-uh* Female werewolf. Wren's beta, second in command.

Virelium- *vi-rEE-Lee-um* Thalion's court. Home to King Celeborn and Queen Elariel.

Wren- *Rin* Male werewolf. Vale's best friend since they were nine years old. Alpha of his werewolf pack.

Zephyrian- *zef-ear-E-an* Demon lord. Vale and Aisling's biological father.

ACKNOWLEDGMENTS

I dislike the regular way that authors dole out acknowledgments. The lame, "I'd like to thank the Academy," type stuff. I've never been one to entertain formalities, even though that's exactly what I did with my last acknowledgments. It never really sat well with me though. So this time it's going to be different. Why not? I'm an indie author and I can do what I want.

This book originally started out as the end of my series but during the writing process, it quickly became clear that there simply was not enough time in this book for everything that needed to happen. So three books became four books, which then became five books. This was a really exciting but equally daunting revelation for me, going from being almost done with my series to realizing I still had so much left to write. I have Callie to thank for these revelations. While reading part of her book, it became clear to me that characters' growth couldn't be rushed, and my characters are not anywhere near done growing.

A thank you, as always to my wonderful husband, who still hasn't read my books! That's right buddy, I'm calling you out. Now everyone knows your shame. Seriously though, he supports me in every other way he possibly can. From being my financial backing to being my sounding board. You're the best babe, thank you for dealing with me.

Over the course of my journey, I became very lucky one night to stumble upon a group of people playing "Never

Have I Ever," on Tik Tok Live. Afterward, they decided to stay in touch by creating a discord group. By joining that discord group I had no idea how much my life would change. These books, this whole story, would look vastly different without the support I've gotten from my Between the Pages cultafamily. They've helped me boost sales, they've read my first book in their book club, and they've been there for me no matter what. I'm so proud to be a part of such a wonderful group of people. I'll never be able to thank you all enough. Special thanks to Callie, once again, and Laynie. Your friendship means the world to me.

More thanks go out to my family and friends. Things have often fallen to the wayside while writing and editing these books. The grace and understanding I've been given and the unending support have been a blessing.

These books have been a journey and I'd also love to thank you, the reader. You have no idea how much I love each and every single one of you. Hearing that someone is reading my books, enjoying them, and sharing them with others, fills me with so much joy and gratitude. You guys might be fans of me and my books, but I'm a much larger fan of all of you! So thank you for being here, thank you for taking a chance on a baby indie author.

ALSO BY EMBER EAST

Daughter of Realms

Princess of Realms

ABOUT THE AUTHOR

Ember East is a passionate author living in Murfreesboro, Tennesse, with her husband and three feral children, though her roots are planted deeply in Western Kentucky. As a mother of a child with ASD and diagnosed with AuDHD herself, Ember advocates for neurodivergent individuals to pursue their dreams no matter the obstacles. Inspired by childhood favorites like "Inkheart" and TV shows such as "Buffy the Vampire Slayer" and "Charmed," Ember has dreamed of making up her own stories since she was nine years old. A dream that was accomplished twenty-one years later.